Third Monday in May

THIRD MONDAY IN MAY
A NOVEL CONCERNING THE REMARKABLE EVENTS OF THE FIRST KENTUCKY DERBY
BY

ROSS R. MOORE

Broadstone Books

Library of Congress Control No. 2017934162

ISBN 978-1-937968-34-2

Cover and Design by Larry W. Moore,
who thanks Chris Goodlett of the Kentucky Derby Museum
& Amy Purcell of the Ekstrom Library, University of Louisville,
for their assistance in obtaining the cover image of the original
Churchill Downs grandstand, from
"Louisville Illustrated" (1889)

Broadstone Books
An Imprint of
Broadstone Media LLC
418 Ann Street
Frankfort, KY 40601-1929
BroadstoneBooks.com

PROLOGUE

THE well-groomed man from New Orleans was in particularly good spirits on this unusually warm mid-May evening in Louisville, Kentucky. Smartly-dressed as always, light linen suit and bold red tie, he sat in silent thought as he stared out across the busy lobby of the Galt House Hotel. Business was good, primarily due to the upcoming opening of the new racetrack and the Derby on Monday. It was now the preceding Friday and the city was already abuzz, especially since the arrival of its most important guest just an hour or so earlier. No one could remember a more exciting time around the city, certainly since well before the War. Colonel Clark had guaranteed as much, and now he was to be congratulated.

This particular visitor was assuredly an ardent fan of this finest of sports, thoroughbred racing, especially back home at the Fair Grounds. It was his favorite place in the entire world and it had taken something extraordinary to bring him this far. But unlike the other horsemen and gamblers who had traveled to the River City, he had greater ambition than merely to attend the opening day races. If fact, he could not have cared less about this new track or its *Kentucky Derby*. His excitement lay in his certainty that this particular derby and all of the surrounding hoopla would provide the perfect opportunity for this handicapper to take the largest gamble of his life – one far greater than on any horse race. What is more, he was completely convinced that he would assuredly cash in.

He sat watching across the lobby, looking at no one in particular, his face covered in light perspiration from the warm, stuffy air hanging low around him. There was a stir over to his front, all the way across the large room, at the entry doors. In walked a tall man escorting a much smaller, somewhat rounded woman, obviously his wife. As the pair crossed the lobby to ascend the stairs, policemen following closely behind, the man in the red tie smiled as he stared at the face so familiar to millions of people around the world. He murmured aloud, softly to himself, "Sleep well, sir, sleep in peace," then added silently, with great confidence, *Enjoy this weekend, for it shall be your last.* It was Friday, May 14, 1875.

CHAPTER ONE

HE awoke suddenly, drenched in cold sweat, for a moment back in another time, another place. It was the same dream, the same nightmare that had haunted him so many times over the past decade, seemingly almost a nightly occurrence this particular time of year. The back of his head felt as if it were on fire. Reaching back he rubbed the rough, scarred skin, his mind flashing back to that terrible April night exactly ten years previous. The soft glow of light peeking in behind the thick blue curtains told him the sun was up, which meant his wife would already be in the kitchen, or perhaps sitting out in back of the house. It was a beautiful spring morning, the kind of morning that made one glad to be alive, glad to be in central Illinois.

He slowly raised his long, lanky body up from the feather mattress, old bones stiffly cracking, and sitting on the edge of the bed he collected himself. As his mind cleared, the burning at the back of his head passed. He pulled on an old pair of worn brown trousers and a pale cotton shirt, pausing to look at his reflection in the mirror. The last few years had done him wonders. In many ways he almost looked like his old self again. Grey hair and beard forced him to acknowledge, *perhaps a few years older.*

All was quiet in the house, except for the creaking of the back stairs under the weight of his six-foot four-inch frame, still unbent in his sixty-seventh year but now carrying close to two-hundred sixty pounds. Too many fancy dinners; too many fine hotels. It had been a busier winter than he would have liked, and he was glad to be back in his home, to have time for himself and his family. The photographs staring back at him on the wall of the stairway quickly reminded him that of course all the boys were now gone. Robert was – *what, thirty-two now?* – married and living in Chicago with a third child on the way. As for the others..., well, best not to dwell on that. Even their old dog was gone from his favorite horsehair sofa. Yes, just the two of them now, and all-in-all he had no complaints. He relished the peace and solitude of this familiar old house that they had done so much to make their own, when he could manage to get back to it. More time to read, more time to write. He so loved to write, with so much to write about.

He descended into the kitchen and, finding it empty, poured a cup of coffee from the pot sitting on the cast-iron stove. He looked out through the simple white lace curtains that hung in the window to confirm that his wife was indeed sitting in the back yard, slowly rocking back and forth. One of the cats she still allowed him as his "hobby" was stretched out in the sun at her feet. There was a vase of freshly cut white and yellow daffodils sitting next to her on a small wooden table, no doubt thanks to her sister Jane who tried to make up for the fact that neither he nor his wife was much of a gardener – as the bare yard attested. To the other side of the table another chair, much larger, sat waiting for him to join her.

She must have sensed him in the kitchen, for just then she turned and glanced back in his direction. He immediately noticed tears in her soft blue eyes, glistening in the bright morning sunlight as they slowly ran down her cheeks. He was not at all taken aback, but shook his head ever so slightly, even momentarily smiled. *Yes*, he thought, *she still had her problems.* But the last few weeks had done her wonders as well, perhaps even more so than they had him. No, she still was not *well*, and never would be. But lately she was more like that girl from Kentucky with whom he had fallen in love so many years before. He noticed that the sun brought out a hint of the natural reddish brown in her hair, now admittedly mostly grey. He opened the door onto the back porch and stepped out into the warming April sun.

"Good morning, my dear," he said gently as he walked up behind her. She slowly turned her head again and looked up into that long, kind face covered with those familiar whiskers. She sobbed softly, turning quickly away, staring blankly out towards the stables at the back of the yard.

"It's like it all just happened, all over again," she said, as if to no one in particular.

"Yes, I know," he sighed. "This is always a hard day for you – a hard day for the both of us." He placed his hand on her back reassuringly as his gaze joined hers, drawn in passing to the rear of the neighbor's house on across the way. Noticing a small patch of peeling paint on the upstairs trim, he thought, *Carrigan will need to do some painting this spring.* He sat down, pausing to bask in the solitude of this place, a place where they found escape from the world, escape from the past, from all of the horror and misery of life, escape from the *what might have been.* Ten years, gone so quickly, like a flash.

ABRAHAM Lincoln had heard it in the instant before he felt it: the sound that continued to haunt so many of his dreams. He was sitting there next to Mary in the theatre, truly enjoying himself for the first time in what seemed like his entire life. After years of so much death: two of his boys, the sons of thousands of others, so many brave and confused men. Yes, confused. He had seen it on their faces. Lying there, whether dead or alive, looking up at him with an expression that shouted, *Why? Why did you ask this of us?* The vision of those faces would never go away. And now that it was over, he felt that he still had no answers for them. But at least now *it was over.* Maybe now he could get on with the work that still must be done: how to stitch back the cloth that had been so utterly ripped apart?

Don't know the manners of good society, eh? Well, I guess I know enough to turn you inside out, old gal—you sockdologizing old man-trap. The audience erupted into laughter. Even his wife, seated next to him, could not contain herself. When had he last seen *her* laugh, seen *her* relax...just enjoy herself? He slowly reached over to take her hand.

Before he could complete that simple act of love and kindness, there was the sound – that deafening explosion – and then the heat of a fire that felt as if it would engulf his entire head. As he instinctively reached for the back of his head, he turned slightly and stared into the eyes of the man who now appeared before him. For a moment he felt as though he knew these eyes. At first they seemed blind with shock, filling then with rage, these dark piercing eyes. And then, with that strange trick of the mind that seizes on the mundane in the midst of chaos, he noticed the man's mustache. *Needs a good trim*, Lincoln had thought, before the pain at the back of his head so completely consumed him that he never even realized that the man had struck him across his face with something jagged, opening a small wound beneath his left eye. Blood trickled out of the gash and ran down his check onto his pressed white shirt.

The next few hours were a complete blur, consciousness ebbing and flowing. He was later told that after the shot failed the would-be assassin had tried to stab him with a bowie knife. If not for the efforts of Major Henry Rathbone, who had been sitting on the other side of Mary in the Presidential Box, the deed might still have been done. The major had managed to lunge between Lincoln and his attacker, blocking the knife thrust while sustaining serious injuries himself. But he had not been as successful in stopping the blow to Lincoln's face, which was accomplished with the remnants of the assailant's first choice of weapon, now practically fused into his hand. Still, Rathbone was being credited by the press and the public with having saved the president's life, and rightly so.

The coward had then jumped, or perhaps tumbled down onto the stage of the theatre, in the process catching his boot in the bunting draping the box so that he landed roughly. Even so he had staggered to his feet, limping badly and waving a mangled hand but still pausing a moment to shout what some in the audience heard as "Sic Semper Tyrannis" – though perhaps it was only a shriek. With that he had exited out the back through the stage door to a waiting horse, successfully escaping into the darkness of Washington, undoubtedly south towards Virginia.

As soon as the audience in the theatre fully comprehended the scene they had just witnessed, finally realizing it was not part of the production, complete pandemonium broke out and hysteria overcame them. The president was quickly carried down the steps and out through the front lobby across the street to a small rooming house. The blood pouring from the wound under his eye at first caused great concern that he had indeed been shot, but the doctor who had been summoned quickly confirmed that it was nothing quite so serious. But it was bad enough. There were severe burns on the back of Lincoln's head, as the flash had ignited hair and clothing. His cheekbone had been broken and he had lost a fair amount of blood. He would be scarred for life and in considerable pain for several months, but Abraham Lincoln would survive this attempted assassination.

After this initial treatment, the President was slowly carried by an ambulance back to the White House. Mary was of course at first uncontrollable, but with the help of medication and the constant attention of Mary Jane Welles, her best friend in Washington, she had managed to calm herself. Mrs. Welles, the wife of the Secretary of the Navy, came immediately to the White House upon hearing the news, even though she was herself suffering from a terrible cold. Having lost six children, no stranger to tragedy, she was fully aware of the First Lady's unpredictable mental state in the best of times, and knew how much Mrs. Lincoln would now need her, how important it was for her to be by her friend's side. For the next few weeks, while the president slowly recovered, Mrs. Welles was an almost constant presence at the While House.

Tad Lincoln, who had just turned twelve years old, had also attended the theater that evening, though fortunately a different one than his parents. He had been watching a performance of *Aladdin* at Grover's Theatre when news of the shooting reached his party. Tad was quickly taken directly back to the White House, arriving a few minutes before the ambulance that carried his father and mother. His older brother Robert, who had been serving on General Grant's staff in the last months of the war, was in his room at the White House when the news first arrived. He met his younger brother at the door and sent the boy directly to his room, accompanied by the White House doorman, Tom Pendel. Pendel often kept watch over the younger boy and the two had become close. After arranging for the care of his brother, Robert waited outside for his parents.

Upon arrival the president was taken directly to his bedroom, accompanied by two doctors and a nurse. Intense pain continued to cloud his vision but he maintained a sense of what was happening around him. Then, after Mrs. Welles had arrived to tend to Mary, Taddie was allowed a brief visit with his father, with Robert at his side. The wounded president managed a brief smile which seemed to reassure his younger son. Robert stayed mostly grim-faced but calm, showing no outward expression of the rage that grew within him. Finally, about two o'clock in the morning, confident that everything possible had been done, Robert retired to his room, finding sleep difficult.

For several days the president's bedroom was kept dark to help ease his suffering as much as possible. By the second afternoon his mind had cleared sufficiently that his staff could begin to consult with him for short periods. Much of this duty fell to John Nicolay, the man that Lincoln had made his private secretary as his first act upon assuming office. Nicolay had served his president well, had spent countless days and late evenings listening to Lincoln spin his yarns, complain bitterly about the inexcusable actions of his generals, and worry about his critics. This man had seen more clearly than anyone the burden and guilt the president bore. Now it was his job to tell his boss exactly what had happened that past Friday evening.

Nicolay began with the obvious, providing details of the failed assassination attempt. Lincoln's attacker had planned to shoot him in the head with a derringer, but whether by Divine Providence or carelessness in loading, the gun had misfired with a short start, practically exploding in the assailant's hand. Even though no bullet was fired, the gun had been so close to Lincoln's head that he could not have avoided serious injury. Fortunately, the shooter had held the gun with his right hand, which shielded Mary and the others in the box from injury from the blast. Authorities had identified the intended assassin as John Wilkes Booth, an actor but more importantly, a Southerner. It was just as many of the President's friends and confidants had been warning. Even though the war was over, there continued to be great danger all around them.

As he lay silently listening to his trusted aid, Lincoln began to realize that he *had* seen that face before. Less than two years earlier, in that very same theatre, in the *very same seat!* It was the face of that actor who had looked at him so menacingly that some thought the man might actually be intending to threaten the president. Dismissing it as merely a case of overacting, he had light-heartedly told a companion, "He does look pretty sharp at me, doesn't he?"

Lincoln momentarily became lost in this memory, but cleared his head again in time to hear that Booth had managed to escape Washington, or so they believed, under the cover of darkness. It would of course be only a matter of time before this criminal would be captured, if not killed. "He must not be killed," the president hoarsely whispered. "They must take him alive, John. He will only become a martyr to the Southerners if he is killed without trial."

Nicolay still had far worse news to report. It had been a much, much larger conspiracy. Both Vice President Johnson and Secretary Seward were dead. The president was told that at almost the exact moment as the attack on him, the vice president, who had retired early that night, had been shot in his bed at the Kirkwood House. A man named George Atzerodt, climbing unnoticed up the outside of the hotel and into the second floor window, had slipped into the bedroom and shot Johnson as he slept. Escaping back out through the same window, the attacker *was* noticed on his descent. A policeman was still questioning him when alarm of the shooting spread through the hotel and out onto the street. After a short scuffle Atzerodt had been captured without further incident.

Again at almost that same ominous moment, an at-first unknown man had entered Secretary Seward's home in Lafayette Park across from the White House, gaining entrance by claiming to have needed medicine for the secretary. It had been well reported throughout Washington that Seward was quite ill as a result of a serious carriage accident days earlier. Armed with a revolver as well as a bowie knife, this assassin first pistol-whipped the secretary's son and then entered the third floor bedroom. He proceeded to stab Seward several times whereupon in short order his victim bled to death. Cruelly attacking three others as he made his escape, the man had disappeared into the night. Under intense questioning Atzerodt had named Lewis Powell as this co-conspirator. It was not yet known if Powell had managed to meet up with Booth and escape, or if he was somewhere in hiding on his own, perhaps still in Washington.

Even in his weakened condition the president was now visibly shaken. Tears welled up in his eyes, and he found himself unable to utter any words. After a few moments he simply turned his head away, closing his eyes, trying to escape what was all too real, wanting to hear no more.

The public had been told only that the president had been slightly injured, but would fully recover and was firmly at the helm of state. With no vice president even to temporarily assume responsibility, it was more important than ever that the citizens of the recently reunited country believe that all was well with their president and their government. His advisors could only imagine what "those Southern bastards" might do next, given the opportunity.

Of course all was far from well, and lying there in his bed contemplating all that had happened and all that still lay ahead, Lincoln was completely aware of this fact. The country had now moved away from one crisis into a new and perhaps even more serious one. Was it now even possible to bring the two sides back together after what had happened that April night, an assassination conspiracy the likes of which no one could have imagined? Was the hatred so deep, so rooted that fear and revenge would trump all else? But as he lay there in the White House, the back of his head aching so, Lincoln thought, *Still I must find a way – we must find the way.* The war had been just the beginning; a much harder job now lay ahead. But for the time being he could not focus on these matters. There was only the pain—the mental perhaps worse than the physical.

It turned out to be even more difficult than he could have ever imagined. Lincoln had eventually recovered, but the country had not, and perhaps never would. The conspirators had been caught, Powell having suffered the bad luck to have shown up at a fellow conspirator's house just as the police arrived there. He had been hanged a few weeks later along with Atzerodt and all of the others who were involved in Booth's plot. Despite public outcry, the president had not attended. He wanted nothing to do with it. "A necessary but unwanted event with which the northern part of the country at least has taken great delight, I am afraid," he told son Robert. The young man found it hard to share in his father's sentiments, but out of respect, he too avoided the whole affair.

Despite all orders, including the president's own explicit instructions, after eleven days at large and on the run Booth had been killed after being cornered in a barn outside Port Royal, Virginia. The structure had been set ablaze in an effort to drive the fugitive out, but when he still refused a Sergeant Corbett had shot the would-be assassin claiming that he feared harm for his fellow soldiers. Only as Booth lay dying did his captors discover that his ruined right hand had been amputated at some point during his attempted escape, leaving him not much of a threat. Even so, many in the North considered Corbett a hero; but just as the president had feared, for too many in the South, Booth was but a martyr.

Then the political realities set in. The president had not been all that popular to begin with in many parts of the country. He had not even been able to carry his birth state of Kentucky in either election. Even though Lincoln had won the war and "saved" the Union, there was much second-guessing that had begun even before his wounds were healed. Sometimes, on his darkest days, he felt that perhaps more would have been accomplished if Booth's gun had not misfired. There was deep-seated hatred and the need on the part of the North for revenge. It had been such a bloody war, and most of the families who had lost sons wished the same on their former adversaries. In the South, with such tremendous damage and despair, there was nothing but mistrust and even calls from some quarters for the conflict to be reengaged.

Politically Lincoln had found he could accomplish nothing. Congress cared little for his plans for Reconstruction. He had believed that his new vice president, Andrew Johnson of Tennessee, would greatly help with efforts to get the Congress to pass what the president saw as the right and proper Reconstruction legislation. But of course poor Andrew was gone now, as were many of the president's closest friends and advisors. Days before the attempted assassination, Lincoln had appointed Nicolay to a diplomatic post in France and would not hear of any changes or delays. His trusted private secretary was now the United States Consul in Paris.

Another of his confidants, his assistant private secretary John Hay, was in Paris as well, having begun serving as the Secretary of Legation there shortly after the end of the war. In many ways Hay had been Lincoln's closest and most trusted aid and ally in Washington. The two had first met back in Springfield where Hay was clerking in the law practice of his uncle, Milton Hay, whose office was right next door to the future president's. When Nicolay had suggested naming Hay as assistant private secretary, Lincoln did not hesitate for a moment. Even though Hay was a relatively young man at only twenty-two years old, the president sensed there was something special about him, and he had not been disappointed. Hay and Nicolay, who had been schoolmates at Pittsfield Academy, shared a room on the northeast corner of the second floor of the White House, and as a result spent more time with Lincoln than anyone else, including Mary.

Hay had also been a good friend and social companion to Robert Lincoln when the president's son was in Washington, and in many ways it was these social activities that the elder Lincoln missed the most. Because Hay so often dined in the neighboring hotels with other Washington politicians and local figures, and was a constant presence at social affairs in their homes, he was in a unique position to become a key source of information for the president.

People liked this young, charismatic Brown University graduate as much as the Lincolns did, and the politicians and citizens of the Capital often confided in him, particularly after enjoying a few libations.

Sometimes Hay would stop by the president's bedroom late at night, or perhaps Lincoln would come to the second floor to visit with his assistant secretary, especially when he couldn't sleep, which occurred all too often. They could spend hours swapping the latest news, or good stories they had heard. Some said Lincoln was like a father-figure to his young aid, but it was far more than that. The president had great respect and regard for Hay, and Hay had complete confidence in the president. But now this young man had moved on, and especially as time went by, Lincoln missed him more than any other.

Lincoln also greatly felt the loss of his secretary of state. Like most of the men in his cabinet, William Seward had had second thoughts about serving this new president. Many had considered Seward the clear favorite for the Republican nomination in 1860, and his defeat at the hands of this folksy western lawyer had been a bitter pill to swallow. But in time Seward grew to be a good friend and trusted advisor to the president. As someone who had been very outspoken on the issue of slavery, often stating that in this matter there was "a higher law than the Constitution," Seward had constantly enflamed and outraged Southern politicians. But there could be no doubt that he would have been a particularly passionate and strong voice on the subject of Reconstruction. Seward had lived very close-by to the White House, and Lincoln had spent many evenings visiting in Seward's home receiving greatly appreciated advice.

Now Seward too was gone, and still another void was left for the president. Certainly there were those in Washington who strongly supported Lincoln's plans for Reconstruction, including Secretary Welles and Secretary Stanton. But even though Welles was a strong administrator, having received almost universal praise for modernizing the navy, and was highly regarded by Mary as well, people such as Gideon were simply not the strong political voices that the president now so badly needed.

As for Stanton, while Lincoln greatly respected and publicly praised his secretary of war, the president often found himself at odds with the man. More than once he had overturned Stanton's decisions, including the secretary's desire to have a man named George Vaughn executed for spying after the end of the war. Lincoln had pardoned Vaughn just one hour before heading to Ford's Theatre on that ominous night. Only a few weeks earlier, Stanton had tried to resign his post citing fragile health, but Lincoln had rejected this notion completely. The president had summoned the secretary to the White House and sat with him for an hour, explaining why he was needed now more than ever, and in the end Stanton had acquiesced. But especially after the Vaughn incident, he seemed to become more distant. While certainly a strong supporter of Reconstruction, he too, for whatever reasons, was not to be the political voice Lincoln sought. As a result, as the weeks went by the president could not achieve consensus, and the whole debate soon became beyond his control.

Slowly, Lincoln became more and more withdrawn. His closest friends and allies gone, he spent more time at the Soldier's Home than at the White House, away from Mary, away from the serious problems that he seemed unable to address in any meaningful way, away from the past. He would write, and read, and think, waiting for the end of his ordeal, too often consumed by guilt.

It was natural, then, that in those final months the one man upon whom he now came to rely the most was James Speed, his Attorney General, who had joined the cabinet shortly before the end of the War. James was the brother of Joshua Speed, Lincoln's closest personal friend before coming to Washington. Having a Speed nearby had provided at least some comfort. While Joshua had rushed to the capital in the days after the assassination attempt, he ultimately had felt out-of-place in the White House and his visit had been all too brief.

By the last year of Lincoln's administration, time – and the opportunity for great profits – meant that things did begin to improve, at least for many white men. As for Lincoln himself, he was tired of it all, worn down by the war and then by all of the constant bickering and debate, by what he felt were his failures, by his guilt. He felt that he could no longer accomplish anything for the country, that it was time for new leadership. For all of his self-perceived failings, talk of an unprecedented third term abounded in some quarters, a sign of the near reverence with which he was still viewed by his most ardent supporters. But Lincoln showed little interest in it and eventually made this clear to those closest to him within the party. He would not run. He and Mary were going home to Springfield – something they both desperately needed.

When he learned of Grant's plans to run to succeed him, the president felt that perhaps he was indeed the man to finish the work that still remained. Lincoln fully realized that he probably would never have been re-elected if not for Grant's military successes, so if for no other reason he owed much to the man. He offered the general his full support. By the election of 1868 and Grant's victory, Abraham Lincoln was ready to head back to Springfield and the peace and quiet that he hoped awaited him – and more than ready to leave politics behind.

AS the former president looked out over that sunny April morning of 1875, he could only chuckle softly as he remembered that thought. Peace and quiet? Far from it! Even though he had more than his share of critics, Lincoln was in constant demand to speak and make public appearances. But except for one trip to New Orleans, never in the South. There he was still too often vilified. Some Southerners realized the importance and necessity of what Lincoln had done, but there were far, far too many that claimed they would "never forget." Mary, along with many other of his closest friends and advisors, insisted that it was far too dangerous to travel among these people.

Lincoln's writings were in constant demand as well, both at home and in Europe. He had published two books and countless articles in less than two years after having left Washington. This had proved to be a special delight for him, since books had been so precious in his youth. The popularity of his writing led directly to their trip overseas. How glorious it had been, seeing so many new and different places, meeting heads-of-state. For someone who had never traveled out of the country, and had never even imagined that he ever would, it had been like a dream – like one of the adventures Lincoln used to imagine himself on back in the woods of Kentucky as a small boy.

The trip had been so very good for them all, especially Mary and the boys. Everywhere they went they were treated as celebrities, but with none of the negative political undertones that were to be expected when traveling back home. While in Europe Mary began to hear of various new techniques not yet available in America that might benefit their youngest son and his special problem. Tad had always struggled with stuttering, and his education had suffered greatly as a result of this condition. While nowhere near *wealthy*, book royalties and fees from the many speaking engagements made it financially possible for the Lincolns to take advantage of these opportunities. The decision was made that Mary and Tad would remain in Europe to seek help while Abe took his oldest son back to America so that Robert could begin to build a law practice in Chicago.

First in Germany, and then later in England, Tad received specialized help that was yielding promising results. Mary had written to her husband in March of 1870 that *Taddie is doubtless greatly improving in his studies*. The father had been so proud, hardly able to wait for their return home so he could witness his son's improvements first hand. With Robert's growing success in the bar, who knew what now might await his youngest son. The family was perhaps the happiest they had ever been.

Then a short time later Mary had written to Abe of her illness, but how she was now recovering. While concerned about Tad, who seemed even sicklier than she had been, Mary was sure that it was nothing too serious. The mother and son returned to America by early summer but decided to first spend a few weeks in Chicago visiting with Robert before heading downstate and home. Though Tad had continued to weaken, everyone thought that being back in America would revive him. His mother assured her husband and everyone else that there simply was nothing to worry about. And Tad indeed showed signs of recovery. Then, in early July he took a sudden turn for the worse. Before his father could manage to complete the two hundred odd mile trip north to Chicago, Tad Lincoln died on July 15th, only eighteen years of age.

The next morning the *Chicago Tribune* published an account of the boy's death:

> *At 7:30 on yesterday (Saturday) morning Tad*
> *Lincoln died at the Clifton House on Wabash*
> *Avenue, where he had been staying since his*
> *return from Europe. The cause of his death*
> *was dropsy of the chest. The first symptoms*
> *showed themselves while he was abroad, but*
> *it was not until his return...that his condition*
> *became alarming...He was convalescent at*
> *one time, but he got up one night slightly clad*
> *and swooned. This was followed by a relapse,*
> *after which he grew steadily worse.*

First they had lost little Edward, then young Willie, and now Tad, all gone from them. It was almost too much to bear. While he was devastated, he knew all too well what this would do to his poor wife. Mary instantly fell into an emotional and mental decline that lasted for two years. Through constant care and attention, and by having a secluded and well-ordered life at the house in Springfield, she slowly recovered, not completely but at least to the point where the couple were more able to enjoy themselves and their life at home. Lincoln had tried to limit his travels as much as possible, and over the last year had vowed to focus more on his writing and less on any speaking appearances.

Which is why this invitation from the man in Kentucky was at once so tempting and so bothersome. Should he go? Should he take Mary out of this secluded enclave, this bastion of peace and serenity? Was she ready? They could visit her family in Lexington, return to her favorite places and memories, back to a time and place before all of the death and suffering. Being back in Kentucky might do her some good. Or would it? Would the stress be too much and only cause a relapse? He would so love to visit Louisville again, especially to see his dear old friend Joshua Speed. It had been years since he had last seen Joshua, far too many. And just as he had when he was a young man, Abe needed Joshua, to receive his counsel, his comfort, his friendship, in some ways now more than ever. It was time to mend some old fences; see how the beautiful river city had changed in – what was it? – almost thirty-five years! This man Clark, with whom he had at least a nodding acquaintance, sounded so sincere and inviting. And a new horse race – what could be more exciting? Just a pleasurable trip, no politics, no public speaking, no appearances, a chance for Mary and him to enjoy themselves, and to have a nice visit with the home-folks. And really, it was barely across the Ohio River, not the Deep South. As Abe sat there by Mary's side in the warm April morning sun, his mind spinning with all of these questions, he asked himself again and again, *What should I do?* Something deep inside answered him back: *Yes, this is the time, this is the place.*

CHAPTER TWO

MERIWETHER Lewis Clark, Jr. – grandson of that greatest of great American adventurers, William Clark, and named like his father for the most famous of partners, Meriwether Lewis – was a troubled man. As he stood gazing over his uncles' farmland on which he had played as a boy, he hardly took time to notice what a fine April morning it was. Here, out beyond the outskirts of his hometown of Louisville, Kentucky, he was building a racetrack. This was not a new idea for his city or his country. There had been racetracks for champion thoroughbred horses a hundred years before. A half-dozen had already come and gone here in Louisville alone. But this was *his* track, *his* idea. He was putting everything he had into it, and as usual, he could not help but worry. It was his nature.

Clark was only twenty-nine years old, but in many ways so very much older than his years. Taller than average but by no means tall, he was thin, with brownish wispy hair, and what most would consider a plain face, with large sad eyes. Following the custom of his day he had married young, to Mary Martin Anderson, a fine woman, and they were now the parents of a son and two daughters. He was prosperous, but that had much more to do with his wife's large inheritance than any abilities he might possess. And he was living in what many would call a prosperous city, due in large part to its location on the mighty Ohio River.

Louisville had done all right for itself for most of the nineteenth century. But in these last few years, since the end of the War, there were growing questions and concerns among more than a few of its citizens. Many could not understand why after the War the city had seemed to turn itself to the south. Cities to its north and west – Indianapolis, Cincinnati, St. Louis – had all fared much better in the last decade. There was a kind of restlessness and uneasiness present in his city, just as there was in Clark.

If he had lived a hundred years later perhaps there would have been sound medical and mental diagnosis and treatment for his condition; but in the spring of 1875, he was left to wonder and worry excessively. How would they possibly finish everything in time? Opening day was only a month away and there was still so much to be done. True, the track itself and much of the facility had been all but finished for several months. The last group of the glistening new barns were nearly completed. Trainers had been most anxious to take advantage of the new facility and stalls were being occupied just as soon as they were readied. Soon all one-hundred-fifty stalls would be finished and filled. But the grandstand, second in size only to the fine structure at Saratoga, still was not nearly completed. In Clark's view there was still so very much left to do, and yet no sense of urgency on the part of the workers, especially the foremen. What was wrong with them? They assured Clark that everything would be completed, not to worry. But of course he would worry. It was his job to worry, his...*nature*.

He decided to clear his head by taking a short walk down to the old spring located just a short distance beyond the southern edge of the property. He had so loved this place as a boy, his games of exploration, pretending to be his famous grandfather somewhere on the Expedition out west. Or perhaps he would be fighting in the Revolutionary War, pretending to be his equally famous great uncle, George Rogers Clark. With his back soon turned to the cause of his consternation, this younger Clark quickly found himself not up North or far out West, but back in England. Back where the idea for all of this...this *madness*, had first started to so completely possess his every waking hour.

IT really had all begun at a dinner in the city back in the late spring of 1872.

Several prominent horsemen had been present among the company, all voicing the same dire consequences. *Kentucky means horses, and Kentucky has always meant horses, from our first day as a Commonwealth. Everyone knows that. But I tell you if somebody doesn't do something, it will all soon be lost. That damned War has ruined everything and everybody!*

To be fair, there were more than just emotions at play in their laments. Before the War, Kentucky had set the standard for the thoroughbred industry, almost from the moment the first thoroughbred arrived from England in Virginia, to which Kentucky then belonged, a century ago. What pioneer breeders like R.A. Alexander and those who joined him had accomplished since then – the application of science, careful study and planning, proven business principles – these ideas transformed the sport of horse racing and the breeding industry, transformed the rolling hills of Central Kentucky as well, creating the *Bluegrass*.

But then it had all been caught up in the middle of the War Between the States. As a border state passions had run high for both sides in Kentucky, as had desire for her thoroughbreds. The Union and the Confederate armies alike recognized the value of the stamina and endurance of this strong breed, and they had stopped at nothing to acquire them. Alexander and other successful breeders attempted to protect their stock, but in the end far too many great horses had been taken and forever lost. And with their loss, and the loss of their bloodlines, Kentucky had suffered a near fatal blow, far more damaging than anything any battle had ever inflicted upon the Commonwealth. What had begun almost one hundred years earlier appeared to be on the verge of quietly and dramatically coming to an end.

Even here in Louisville the ominous signs were unavoidable. A few weeks earlier the beautiful Woodlawn Track, which had shown such promise when it had opened back before the War, had closed for good and was being subdivided and sold. The Greenland Race Course, opened out on the National Turnpike right after the War, had fared no better. It seemed the main problem now was that most people simply did not show much interest in racing.

Nevertheless horsemen, politicians and businessmen alike were interested in seeing the market for Kentucky horses expand. So on that late April night the assembled company was united in their cause for concern, and in their dire predictions, but there was no consensus for any solution. As they dined on their roast pheasant and sweet potatoes and fresh spring asparagus, and drank their fine Kentucky bourbon, the closest they came was in that most universal of human sentiments: *We need someone to save us!*

Clark was among the company at the dinner, though he had had no particularly strong interest in horses or in racing them before that night. It was true that his wife Mary had been raised by her aunt, Pattie Anderson Ten Broeck, out at the Hurstbourne Estate on the Shelbyville Road. Aunt Pattie was the wife of Richard Ten Broeck, the most celebrated horseman in America prior to the War. Clark's father had owned horses as well. As a result the young man had spent more than his share of time hearing about racing and visiting racetracks, but he never considered himself a true horseman. He simply could not take it seriously. As a descendant of great explorers and of great leaders, he felt destined for greater things. He aspired to do more, to be more, perhaps all a product of his heritage.

Clark was a native of Louisville by right of his birth there in 1846, though his family shortly thereafter moved back to his father's home town of St. Louis. There the senior Clark was an architect and local politician who would go on to serve as an officer in the Confederacy. A business assignment had taken him to Louisville, where he met and married Abigail Prather Churchill, a daughter of one of the first families in the Commonwealth. After Abigail died in 1852, the younger Meriwether – or "Lutie" as he was called by the family – was sent back to Louisville to be raised by his uncles, John and Henry Churchill. Since 1787 the Churchill family had owned three hundred acres of land in the rural area south of the city, and Clark had fallen in love with this beautiful expanse of land - where his new track was rising – as soon as he returned to Kentucky.

As he sat alone in his parlor late in the evening of that fateful dinner, sipping his glass of bourbon and pondering the horsemen's dilemma, an idea had begun to take shape in Clark's mind. Perhaps *he* could be that *someone to save them*. As usual he was feeling restless and had been searching continually for a way to make his mark, to become his own man. He constantly felt the weight of his family's name on his back and on his mind, not to mention his wife's wealth. But how? He really knew little of racing, or of running such an enterprise. Yet somehow he could not shake the feeling that this was his calling, his mission. Like those Clarks who had come before him, he could be *the hero of this day*.

By the next morning he had formulated a clear vision. The best way to learn was to go back to where it had all started. He would take his wife on a voyage across the Atlantic, back to where the breed had begun and the first races had been run! Without disclosing the complete nature of the trip or his plans, he easily convinced his Mary to agree to tour the Continent, even though they had made a previous trip less than two years earlier. As Clark thought about it now, he realized that their earlier trip had in a way helped set the stage for his designs.

THE Clarks had first toured Europe for a month in early 1870. It was quite by chance that on their second night after arriving in Liverpool they received an invitation to attend a dinner given by the new American envoy to England in honor of former President Lincoln's last night in the country before his return with his oldest son to America. Clark was at first uncertain whether to accept. While he had not himself served in the War, he was the son of a Confederate officer and followed his father's lead in having no great regard for Lincoln. Both his and his wife's families had been slaveholders – his grandfather had even taken his slave York along on the Great Expedition – and even after this number of years he retained a bit of their resentment over the cost of the War and emancipation on their fortunes. In the end, though, he realized that he could ill afford to seem ungracious to his hosts.

The Lincolns, having no idea of Clark's political predilections, were delighted to learn that fellow Kentuckians were in attendance at their dinner, and Mrs. Lincoln insisted that they be seated together, no matter the disruptions to protocol and planning. Entirely in character and prompted by the meeting of this couple from Louisville, Lincoln regaled everyone at the table with stories of his visit to Louisville back in 1841, and in particular his fascination with Jim Porter, known then as the world's tallest man. After dinner he leaned back in his chair and slowly began to recount one of his favorite tales.

My good friend Joshua Speed asked me one day if I had ever heard of a local gentleman by the name of Jim Porter, who some claimed was the tallest man in the world. Now understand, great height was always a topic of particular interest for me, I guess you could say for obvious reasons. I told him that I was not at all familiar with the gentleman, so after lunch Joshua prepared his carriage and off we went headed up the pike towards Louisville and the mighty river. When we had made our way through town and were within smelling distance of the Ohio, with all of the people coming and going as they are prone to do on a busy afternoon, we turned to the west and headed downstream into the smaller community of Portland. I was particularly gladdened to be in the company of my good friend as I had never had the occasion to venture into this town and would certainly have made a fool of myself if left to my own devices, as seems to be my custom.

We came to a not too particularly pleasing looking structure just a block or so from the water's edge, and Joshua brought the horses to a halt. Above the door, which I had to state did seem to be a bit taller than the average, was a nicely painted sign simply stating, "Tavern", followed by "Jim Porter, Proprietor." In short order we entered the establishment, which was darkened due to the lack of outside light, which was in turn due to the smallish and limited nature of the windows.

Now I don't want to infer that I had never before entered such a place, for indeed even back then I had had more than a few opportunities in the course of my lifetime to do so. But I have to say that this particular establishment was one that I would not normally have sought out, or for that matter have gone particularly out of my way to avoid. Which is to say that it was decidedly average – decidedly average in every way for a tavern, with the assorted tables and chairs and longish counter and glasses and bottles and people who seemed to have no better or more important place in which to be at that particular moment.

Yes, decidedly average in most every single way, except for the gentleman standing behind that counter. Or perhaps I should say standing above it. For I had never in my life witnessed the height that this man exhibited. As I am within shouting distance of six and a half feet myself, I could only wonder observing him in that limited light, just what distance into the altitude he had managed to obtain for himself. Seven feet? No sir, surely more than that. Seven and a half? At a minimum. Perhaps even eight feet? Within the very realm of possibility. To put it more plainly, ladies and gentlemen, I was greatly impressed.

We walked up to him and Joshua proceeded to introduce me formally, whereupon I shook the largest hand I had ever grasped before or since. And the man's great size was only surpassed by his hospitality and quick wittedness. He was perhaps the most engaging storyteller I had ever encountered. Of course, do understand that this was before I had ever been to Washington and observed the Congress in action first hand.

Lincoln joined in his audience's laughter and then waited for it to subside before continuing.

As we sat and sipped the finest of spirits he regaled us with stories of his travels and adventures. But I was most impressed with a story of his youth. It seems that as a boy of twelve, before commencing on his sudden rise into the upper reaches, he actually rode horses in the races. This giant of a man had in fact been a jockey! I'm sure you are just as incredulous as I found myself to be on that afternoon so many years ago. But there were other old-timers, indeed you could say "regulars" present in the tavern that day, who willingly added their own tales of Porter's exploits as a rider at the races out at a place called Shippingport Island in the middle of the Ohio River. For that is where the races were first held in Louisville if you can believe it. I am not sure that I have ever heard a grander tale before or since. I would surely have invited him to the White House but alas I learned that he had passed away in the years before I had the opportunity. But I will surely never forget that encounter in his tavern back in '41.

By the end of this tale Clark realized that like so many others before him, he was being won over by the Lincoln charm. In person he found it was quite impossible to hold old inherited scores against this man. After a few more tales, along with the necessary toasts, Lincoln and Clark shook hands as the former president assured Clark, "Someday soon I shall return to Louisville. I can think of nothing more pleasant than to spend a few days in your fair city, visiting my friends and reacquainting myself with the warm hospitality and grand experiences I had there previously. Perhaps this time I shall even be able to see your Kentucky thoroughbreds in action. That is something I have always wanted to witness." In response Clark warmly thanked Lincoln and, as he bid him goodbye quite spontaneously offered to place himself at the Lincolns' disposal when they made their visit. He pledged to make sure that they enjoyed all of the finest things Louisville had to offer, and hopefully that would include the finest in racing at the finest of tracks.

OF course at the time this conversation had had no particular meaning to Clark, but as he and his wife sat down to breakfast on the first morning of their return to England, he recalled Lincoln's remarks and his own response with a new significance. It now seemed to him that his pledge was a sign of his predestination to build that racetrack. These thoughts ran through his mind as he attempted to relax, looking over the morning's *Times* and sipping a cup of after-breakfast tea – a change from his usual morning coffee in deference to the local custom.

Seated across from him at the table, Mary was fervently enjoying Lewis Carroll's newest work, *Through the Looking Glass and What Alice Saw There*. She had always been a great reader, and was especially fond of children's literature. The original *Alice in Wonderland* was a particular favorite. This newest "Alice" book was not yet available in America, so she had ordered the carriage stopped at the sight of the first bookseller on the way to the hotel, where without hesitation she had purchased a copy.

After a period of silence punctuated only by his wife's occasional soft laughter, along with the rattling of dishes being cleared from a nearby table, Clark offhandedly mentioned, "Well that was a far superior trip over than we had last time. The *Oceanic* is certainly a fine vessel, and White Star is to be commended. I have never traveled in more comfort nor been treated better. I believe I shall send a note to Mr. Ismay with our thanks and my congratulations." Sensing no reaction he stated with slightly more conviction, "And I much preferred sailing from New York over Boston, didn't you?"

He glanced in Mary's direction. No response. Undeterred, and quickly coming more to the point he continued, "This has gotten me to thinking about our last trip to this fine city and this very hotel, and the wonderful evening we spent with the Lincolns. Do you remember what he said about visiting *our* city?" She did not bother even so much as to look up from her reading.

Pausing to take a sip of his now lukewarm tea, he casually went on. "It is truly a shame that Louisville no longer has a decent facility for racing thoroughbreds, indeed no real facility at all. It would be quite the dishonor if the Lincolns should visit, and have to travel to Lexington or elsewhere just to witness the excitement of our sport. I was talking with several prominent horsemen before we left about this very thing. It is high time someone in Louisville took the initiative to right this wrong. If we could acquire a first rate facility, then it would be no time before the breeders would begin to benefit. Before you know it things would get back to how they were before the War, how they should be."

With her eyes still fixed on her reading, Mary responded with a slight annoyance, "Our sport? Since when is it *our sport*? I've never known you to have any real interest whatsoever in horse racing, Lutie." Finally looking up at him she continued, "I agree it would be of benefit to the city, but what is it exactly that you are thinking?"

"Just that someone needs to do something, and there is no reason why we can't help. I told them back in Louisville that while we are visiting over here I could certainly look around a little and see if any ideas about what to do might come forward. As a Clark I feel a certain responsibility to do my part to help the city and our Commonwealth. I have no grand illusions that I can do anything of significance by myself, but I do think I may have a role to play. Surely you would agree with that?"

Mary now put her book down. "Well what do you expect me to say? Clearly this has been on your mind and has nothing to do with Mr. Lincoln. Perhaps there was more to this trip than you originally mentioned?" Pausing for just a moment, glancing out of the large windows across the room, she then continued, "But I suppose it will do no harm. I have always enjoyed the races, and it will certainly do *you* no harm to have something worthwhile with which to involve yourself. I am more than aware of your restlessness. Just promise me that you will be realistic about this. If we really can help the city in some fashion I would not be the one to stand in the way."

"Of course I'll be realistic. I am well aware of my limitations." He looked slightly hurt, but undeterred. "I think a visit to some of the great racetracks here will not only be informative, but highly enjoyable. It just so happens that, with the kind help of your Uncle Richard, I have already laid out a schedule that will allow us to see some of the top events of the year, and have made some arrangements."

"Yes, I'm sure it 'just so happened.' Tell me, what would you have done if I had refused you?"

"My dear, I have never known you to refuse any honorable request, and I was counting on the fact that you wouldn't begin to do so today. And please bear in mind, we are doing it for our friends the Lincolns!"

"Well, *my* dear," she replied quietly, returning to her book, "I doubt seriously that the Lincolns even remember who we are. And for my part I would have difficulty ever thinking of Lincoln as a friend, though I admit I found his wife quite pleasant and would not object to being in her company again. But leaving all that, I am perfectly happy to spend a part of our time here on *our* sport."

There was another small detail Clark had failed to share with Mary. Before departing Louisville, with the assistance of a personal referral from Richard

Ten Broeck, he had written to the great English sportsman Admiral Henry John Rous, who was a long-time steward of the Jockey Club, to ask for his advice and assistance in arranging to tour the English racing circuit. The Admiral's cordial reply was waiting for Clark when their ship arrived. Clark then had the good fortune to encounter fellow Kentuckian and former Vice President John C. Breckinridge, who happened also to be abroad, and Breckinridge proved most willing to introduce him to other members of the Jockey Club. Over the next few months, thanks to the Admiral's kind assistance and contacts made through Breckinridge, Lutie and Mary managed to visit many of the great racing facilities not only in England but throughout Europe as well.

THAT spring of 1873 also brought a visit from John Churchill, whose arrival laid to rest a great anxiety with which Clark had been struggling. Clark's enthusiasm almost had been lost before he even had begun to contemplate any serious arrangements for the trip. Only a few days after that fateful dinner where he had first become so excited, Clark had awoken to some disturbing news in his morning paper. As he sipped his first cup of coffee, he picked up the *Courier Journal* and began reading.

> It has been for years a subject of remark that we have had no representative race-course. Oakland went down, Woodlawn followed and it has been said that Louisville could not sustain a race-course. This is an error. We are glad to say another is about to come into existence as the proprietors of Villa Park have donated a hundred and odd acres for this purpose. It is, in a word, all that is wanted for the National Race-course of America. The proprietors are already laying out the track. They are too late for the stake races this fall, but they propose to offer such purses as will draw together the best horses in Kentucky and the South, and there is no question but what the Association will give the most exciting races that have occurred in the Western country.

"Damn!" Clark exclaimed out-loud to no one, spilling coffee onto the fine white linen tablecloth. Before he even could start on his adventure, his dream already was derailed by competitors! What was the use of it all now? Mary had left with the children early that morning to visit at Hurstbourne. As Clark sat alone in their comparatively modest house at 8 Broadway he immediately fell into depression and despair. He had planned to lunch with some associates that day to discuss further plans, but now he hardly could motivate himself even to dress. Finally, he left the house and slowly walked to the corner and then headed north on First Street towards the river, making his way down to Main Street, his depression deepening.

Fortunately for all involved his friends had mangaged to console him, encouraging Clark to proceed as planned. Who knew if this venture would really materialize, they told him. Certainly Louisville had a recent history of grandly announced plans for some new establishment, only to see them go unfulfilled. This situation could very well suffer the same fate. After all, one couldn't believe everything they read in the newspaper, especially anything in Henry Watterson's paper!

When John Churchill arrived in London that May of 1873, he brought with him the news for which Clark had been quietly hoping for many months. The "other" project had indeed fallen flat because of the economic panic which had caused many local concerns to either cut back operations or to go completely out of business. The Villa Park project was dead! Clark had not discussed any of this with Mary, and now she could only wonder why her husband suddenly seemed to be so jubilant. She didn't wonder long, though, as she was so accustomed to his many changing moods.

IT turned out that of greatest importance to Clark was their visit to Epsom Downs on the first weekend in June to witness the ninety-fourth running of the Derby, the event that had brought John Churchill to England. Having been held continuously since 1780, it was the centerpiece of the English racing season. Through his contacts with Admiral Rous, not to mention his kinship to Richard Ten Broeck, the Clarks managed an invitation to be the guests of none other than the 15th Earl of Derby himself!

During their first encounter the Clark's host had explained that it was an earlier Earl of Derby who had first begun a race called the Oaks, for three-year-old fillies. It was named after the family home outside of London where the very idea for the race had first been proposed. But Clark was absolutely delighted to learn that the great Derby itself, begun the following year, had been named by a tossed coin. The Earl of Derby had won the toss from his great friend and competitor, Sir Charles Bunbury. The loser did receive some measure of revenge, Clark was told, by owning the winning horse of that first Derby, Diomed.

Clark had commented to Mary, in a manner than ensured everyone present would hear, "I shall have to share this gem of a story with Mr. Lincoln upon their next visit with us. You know how the president enjoys a good story." She smiled in response, but he could see in her eyes that she was less than pleased with his remark, and perhaps with him as well.

What a weekend it had been! And what an event they had witnessed: the crowds, the excitement, the continuous celebrations. There were people of all sorts, from the wealthiest gathered up in the grandstand, dressed in fine silks and jewels; to the perhaps not so wealthy but still men of title gathered below, observing the expected rituals befitting of their positions; to the common working families spread out across the field as if on a holiday or picnic; even gypsies up on the hill who had gathered from all across Europe. Everywhere you looked were throngs of people, whatever their station in life, celebrating and enjoying themselves as if they had never had the opportunity to do so before and never again would.

First there were the fillies on Friday for the Oaks. Clark had never before experienced anything like the atmosphere of excitement generated by these incredibly beautiful horses that seemed to fly down the track, barely bothering to touch their hooves to the grass. And then, even though unimaginable, the following day surpassed what he had already seen and felt in every way possible. As they stood and watched the colt Doncaster take the Derby by what appeared to be no more than a nose, Clark could not imagine a more perfect place, or a more perfect moment.

But then, as he stood silently immersing himself in that moment, he did begin to imagine that perhaps there could be another, even more perfect sight. For just a moment he was no longer on the Sussex Plains of England, but back on a piece of land he loved so well. On that land stood a magnificent grandstand, with pennants waving in the cooling breeze, and crowds of excited people of all walks of life bathed in beautiful spring sunshine, as magnificent thoroughbreds tested themselves against the finest competitors. For just a moment he saw the future, and it was his.

It was by coincidence at that very moment that Lord Derby turned to Clark and questioned, "Why do you not start a jockey club at the metropolis of your state and have representative races? If your people appreciate them, others will do so. Give class races, and by your stakes compel the large establishments to breed for them." Clark smiled guiltily thinking that somehow the great Englishman knew exactly what was on the American's mind. Why not indeed!

"Sir, I have to admit to you that that is precisely what I was just thinking. I cannot imagine a finer, nor more important thing to do for my city, my state, even my country. I shall forever be indebted to you for sharing this experience." He turned to see his wife and her all too familiar expression of *What can you possibly be thinking now?*

But from that moment on he could think of nothing else. He would return to Louisville, convince his uncles to provide the land and whatever other support he could finagle from them, appeal to the good citizens of Louisville, and most importantly, gain the trust and support of the horsemen who had so much at stake. This must be the answer they all sought, this *was* the answer. He had never been more certain of anything in his life. And *he* was going to do it. It would all be because of him. Yet another Clark would be added to the rolls of history!

For the next few weeks, no matter where they were visiting or what they might be doing, his mind was focused on this one idea. Finally he could stand it no longer, and insisted to Mary that they end the trip prematurely and return to Louisville immediately. His haste to return home to start on the project meant that they had traded the luxurious experience of the private first-class cabins with the latest conveniences on the *Oceanic* for a return on an older, slower and much less comfortable steamship. Mary would hardly speak to him. She had already grown weary of his constant dreaming and planning and *talking!* He just went on and on and on about it.

She knew all too well how this would go and how it would all end. He would start to lay out his plans, involving everyone they knew and then some. Then, assuming he could get the project off the ground at all, he would be consumed with worries and dark thoughts. Ultimately nothing would meet with his satisfaction. He would grow more worried, more consumed, more depressed. Finally he would throw up his hands and walk away defeated. She had seen it happen before, too many times. And these previous matters paled in comparison, much less complicated and demanding. But something as big as this? She didn't even want to imagine. She knew all too well that the higher one soars the farther and harder the ultimate fall.

They spent only one night in Boston before a late morning departure on the train to New York, then Pittsburg, then Cincinnati and finally home to Louisville. Clark spent all of his time, nights included, drawing up plans and writing and rewriting the proposals that he could not wait to present. Taking no time to rest, upon his arrival home he immediately went to the Churchill home on Sixth Street to visit his uncles, John and Henry, to apply for their assistance, and more importantly, their land. They turned out to be a quick sale, for with the city ever expanding southward, in the direction opposite the natural watery barrier to the north, the brothers often had extended discussions between themselves concerning long-term possibilities for some of their property.

As Clark began to meet with various horsemen and businessmen, and with city officials, he was somewhat surprised to find a welcoming audience. The horsemen were of course practically desperate for some type of salvation, especially after the latest planned track had failed, and Clark's ideas seemed as good as any. The businessmen, as well as the politicians, were in favor of anything that might expand business opportunities and draw positive attention to the city. But Clark often felt that they were all missing the most important point. It was not about the racetrack itself, which seemed to be of the most interest and importance to them, it was about the *Derby*! There had been other racetracks that had come and gone, and if that was the extent of it, this one probably would too. But with the Derby, the event...the spectacle, now that was something they could create that would be like nothing else in America.

"Gentlemen," he continually would ask of his audiences, "do none of you remember the atmosphere surrounding that great event back in 1839 at my grandfather's track just down the road from where we are today? Some of you were present that day. All of you have heard the stories. That greatest of match races between Wagner and Grey Eagle? The excitement felt by our citizens, the numbers of visitors that filled our lodging houses and hotels and taverns and, I might add, our pockets? The talk it generated all across the Commonwealth, indeed across the entire country, always about the great event in *Louisville*? I know it was practically 35 years ago, but one still hears about it even today. And imagine now if you will, in this day of advanced travel and communication, what the effects would be of a similar event? And not just a single event, but each and every year!

"I tell you I have seen it, in Epsom. The Derby can be ours, and not only will it bring business to our city, it will give the long-suffering breeders of our Commonwealth an opportunity to revitalize their businesses as well. What man of means would not want to purchase a colt that could possibly bring him such honor as to win the Kentucky Derby? This is the answer we have all been seeking. Help me build a new race track, by all means – indeed, it will be the finest this city has every seen – but more than that, help me start this *Derby*. I tell you within just a few years it will be the greatest sporting event known to America!"

How many times had he made that speech? Night after night, throughout the community, he endlessly promoted his cause and solicited support, both moral and financial. He knew of course that it would take money; but more than that, he needed the entire community behind his venture, not just the successful and the wealthy, but everyday working people, the kind of people he had seen scattered all around Epsom. If this Derby was going to become the thing of his dreams, it would take the support of everyone.

So not only did he meet with the businessmen and horsemen and the government *men*, he made sure to appear in front of every gathering of ladies that he possibly could as well. He was no fool, and knew that there would be those who would oppose him on moral grounds. Particularly when addressing the ladies, he presented an image filled with beauty and honor and grace, not to mention some innocent, clean fun. Of course no real lady would be seen anywhere near the gambling part of a racetrack. To ensure this, Clark told them of his plans to create a special section of the grandstand where ladies could gather, even bring their children. He would paint the picture for his audiences, weaving his magic.

"Ladies, if you could have seen the grandstand at Epsom, filled with the finest ladies wearing the most beautiful and timely of fashions, basking in the pure, warm sunshine, breathing the cool, clean country air. It was practically paradise, and I promise you today that is exactly what I am creating for you out on my uncles' beautiful, pristine land. Paradise! There will be no place finer for you to escape the heat, the grime, the daily toils and troubles of modern city life. And there you will have the opportunity to see these incredible creatures that God has given to us – yes, particularly to us here in our Commonwealth. What citizen, male or female, young or old, could possibly say that they are not completely enraptured with what is perhaps God's most beautiful and perfect creation, the thoroughbred? Come and join me, and I promise you will never have a troubled moment, a dishonorable encounter or anything less than an experience of pleasant perfection. I will bring you the glory of the 'Sport of Kings' just as I witnessed it in the company of the lords and ladies of Old England herself!"

Then, like any good pitchman, he added a new twist when seeking the support of the fairer sex. "Ladies, I know that when you join us on the opening day for the running of the first Kentucky Derby, you will want to look your finest. And trust me, we men will all desire this of you as well. Now I know that some may be concerned about how you will be able to maintain your pristine appearance as you travel the dusty roads out to our new facility. I pledge to you today, that in addition to the regularly scheduled watering that the road will receive from the pipes that have been laid with great effort, I will personally pay to provide additional watering on the day before, and if necessary, the very morning of Opening Day. Not one speck of dust will light anywhere on your adornments. I want the most beautiful of Kentucky ladies to be present to cheer on the most beautiful and fastest of Kentucky thoroughbreds. Come and join me for a day you will not soon forget!"

Mary did her part as well, for indeed horse racing was strong in her blood, as was the desire for her husband to succeed. She had never seen him so taken with any other endeavor during their years together. In recent weeks, as opening day drew closer, she and her friends would ride around town in brightly decorated carriages trying to create attention and interest in what was promised to be the coming spectacle. And the more she did, the more she became an integral part of the process. She wanted to have just as much to do with getting people interested in the Derby as her husband.

AS Clark slowly made his way back to his office in the new clubhouse, feeling more refreshed after his walk, he heard a now familiar whistle. He stopped for a moment and watched as the train passed by just to the east of the property. It reminded him that this very access to the railroad would be one of the most significant contributing factors to their hoped-for ultimate success. Of all of the previous racing ventures in the city, none had been in such a favorable geographical position to be able to take full advantage of this most modern means of transportation. With the junction a scant two hundred yards from the grounds, horses could be shipped from Lexington, New Orleans, Nashville, Mobile, New York, St. Louis, or any other point without even a change of cars. Of course, paying spectators could avail themselves of the comforts and convenience of rail travel as well, some in their private cars. Clark took great satisfaction in the fact that this was an advantage not possessed by any other track anywhere in the country. As he headed in to his office, Clark felt that this lonely whistle was one of his best friends.

Even though he now felt better Clark still could not clear his mind of the dark thoughts that were ever-present. He had created the Association and sold almost all of the subscriptions, 25,000 in $100 shares, raising the necessary capital, and at the same time thwarting his competitors. Indeed, upon his return from Europe Clark had discovered that yet another group was making plans to build a new track in Louisville, but he quicky had gained the upper hand. He had received the support of everyone he needed and respected, convincing most of the local politicians and civic leaders to support him in this enterprise. In short, he had done everything he had set out to do and then some. But Clark still had to get it all finished, and that was now his biggest worry.

He walked into his small office and picked up a copy of *The Daily Louisville Commercial* that was lying on his desk. Now a few days old, he liked to keep it handy so that he could read again and again the editorial inside that he had worked so hard to get published.

The inaugural meeting of the Louisville Jockey Club, commencing Monday, May 17, will mark an important event in the history of Louisville. As the metropolis of the State which has produced the finest and fastest horses that have ever stepped upon the turf, Louisville ought to take the lead of other cities in racing matter. The "Kentucky Derby", to be run on the opening day, is destined to become the great race of this country, and it has been suggested that "Derby Day" be observed as a holiday. It is just the thing. For one day let us lay aside business cares, get away from the counting-room, and spend an afternoon in the cool, fresh air of the country. It will make us feel better and happier. St. Louis has her fair days, New Orleans and Memphis have Mardigras. Let Louisville have her "Derby Day". Inaugurate such a custom, and that day will see thousands of strangers in the city. In England "Derby Day" is the greatest of all days, and it can be made the same here if everybody will just say so.

Clark walked back outside and made his way to the edge of the new racing oval. Looking up at the grandstand, he saw dozens of workers laboring away. So much on his mind, everywhere he looked there was something to trouble him. But deep down, in the darkest corners of his mind, his real concern was, *Would they come?* He had pulled it off, done what needed to be done; he was going to have his track and his Derby. But would anyone care? And at the heart of this worry was the one supreme underlying thought: *Will the Great Man come?* Why had he not yet heard from Lincoln? It had been weeks since Clark had written to him, and then written again. *If he will just come,* Clark told himself, the others will follow. The whole country will be watching. He must come! Still, another day had come and gone with no word from Illinois. And the days were beginning to run out.

CHAPTER THREE

ANSEL Williamson knew horses, knew everything about them. And he knew just about everything there was to know about training thoroughbreds. He would never say that he knew it all, for there was always more to learn. But he knew as much as anyone in the game, white or colored. You could rightly say that he was born into it.

He had drawn his first breath right in the middle of Virginia horse country, and his first breath of freedom right in the middle of the Bluegrass. As best as anyone could tell him he had been born about 1815, which meant he was now sixty years old. He didn't remember much about his mother or father, or to be more precise, he really had no idea who his father was – hell, he might even be white. His mother had been sold away from him when he only around six or seven. She had gone off to be a house slave in Charleston, and he had never seen her again. But all these years later he did still remember her warm smile, the smell of her skin, and her clear voice, softly singing as she went about her work in the master's house.

Ansel was never a house boy. He had always been around the barns, around the horses. The one man he did remember, the man who had in reality rais-ed him and taught him how to survive in life, how to survive as a slave, was James T. Only the white people called him James T. To his fellow slaves, and to Ansel, he was simply Jimmy.

Ansel's earliest memory was carrying buckets of water to bathe the horses, and then later hauling muck. This was while his mother was still around, so he must have been only four or five. When she was no longer there for Ansel,

Jimmy for all practical purposes became his father, or the closest thing he ever had to one.

While Ansel could remember only vaguely his mother's stories of their ancestors in Africa, passed down through the decades, his favorite tales were the ones about the horses, and the great races that Jimmy had seen, the ones in which he had ridden. All different kinds of people came to watch the horses race, white, black, red; Englishmen, American, Indian, free, slave; anybody and everybody crowding around parallel lines to witness a match between two powerful horses, short contests, usually for a quarter-mile or so. And so often, the riders were slaves, just like Jimmy. Then a different kind of horse began appearing, the thoroughbred, brought from England. This new breed was stronger, faster, able to run forever, or so it seemed. So they began racing them for longer distances, three, sometimes four miles. Tales of some of these slave riders began to spread all across Virginia, and Carolina, and on to other places where the speed of a horse was valued. Some became heroes, especially to their fellow bondsmen.

Ansel had loved particularly to hear again and again the tale of the Great Match Race of 1773, and the rider know as Austin Curtis. Some called him Austin Jones, after his owner Willie Jones, as was often the practice back then, but Jimmy would never do that. Jimmy would gather the boys around in the evening, after the horses had been fed and were in their stalls, the darkness punctuated by one small lantern illuminating his dark skin. *It was in the springtime, just as the dogwoods was startin' to bust out,* he would always begin,

> *and the smell of things new was all around. The challenge had gone out: five thousand pounds of the finest Virginia tobacco was on the line. I can't even tell you how much that was worth, but it was more than them horses and me and Austin and everything we had between us or ever would have, that's for sure. I could never understand why a white man that had so much would so easily just throw it all away on something he had no control over, but if I was to tell you all the times I seen it happen we'd still be here after the horses come back from their exercise tomorrow morning!*

His voice would slowly become louder, peaking on that last sentence, just to ensure that everyone listening was ready to hear the story, no matter how many times they may have heard it before.

Yes, there was plenty at stake, and me and Austin was right there in the middle of it all. Just down the road from here, not too far at all, down a few miles into North Carolina. People had started comin' in the day before. And I mean everybody. The white folks had filled up every rooming house in every little town for miles around, and the taverns was all bustin'. The plantation men from close by started arriving about mid-morning, and most of them brought their house slaves along. Others from further out keep pourin' in all day long. I always felt kinda sorry for them field hands what got left behind. They had to make do with hearin' tell of it all later that night from those who had been lucky enough to seen it all happen.

The free folks gathered in a small field just to the north near the river. Some of them had made camp, and it was about the biggest gatherin' anybody around there had ever seen. Early afternoon them Indians started to arrive, canoein' down the river from their camps. By race time there was more folks than anybody anywhere in any of these here Colonies had ever seen. Some say maybe fifty thousand people, maybe more. Who could tell? All come just to watch these two horses run.

Of course me and Austin had both been told what was gonna happen to us if we lost. But that didn't bother us none, we'd both heard all that before. Don't know why the white man always thinks they had to scare us to get us to ride hard. Once you're up on that horse, you can't help but ride it as hard as you can. It just gets in your blood. Anyway, while we was getting' ready, before it was time to mount up, me and Austin didn't say a word to each other. There really wasn't nuthin' to say. We both wanted to win, wanted it bad, both just as sure that we was a goin' to. He just smiled at me, and I gave a little wave back, and then we were up on them horses' backs and out to the startin' place.

When that crowd saw us come out, I mean to tell you ain't nobody never heard nuthin' like it before or since. That cry was enough to wake the dead and buried. It took everything we had just to keep them horses settled. I have to be honest here and tell you all that I don't really remember who said what and all the rest. All I know is that the next thing I did know we was circlin' our horses, waitin' to hear that startin' shot, when suddenly...there it was! And I didn't hear anything else for the next few minutes. All them people was a shoutin' and carryin' on so loud that I couldn't even hear my own horse's hooves hittin' on that ground below. All I know is I was in the lead, and my horse felt like he wasn't even runnin' yet. For the first part of that race things couldn't a gone no better. I'd steal a quick look back and there was daylight between us and them! I'd look again, and there was a little more!

Then he would always pause for a moment in the story, look around at all his listeners, dark faces staring back in the night, and then slowly start to chuckle.

But, boys, you know how horse racin' is. Just when I thought that the day was mine, just when I thought I couldn't be beat, well that's when I felt 'em comin'. Yes sir, I didn't see 'em, I felt 'em. Then I looked back, and all of a sudden Austin was a little bit closer. Then I looked again and he was closer still. I said, "Come on horse, we're almost there. I know you still got plenty left." But wouldn't you know it, Austin's horse did too! The next time I turned to look, I didn't even have to. He was right beside me. And then just like that, he was by. Boys, there wasn't nuthin' I could do but sit there and enjoy that view as Austin took his horse clear out in front of me, and that's how it was when we hit that finish.

Could I have done somethin' different? Nobody will never make me think so. Austin was just the better man that day. And in horse racin' that's just how it goes. Sometimes it's your day and sometimes it ain't. Nuthin' you can do about it, neither. Just get back up and go out and ride again tomorrow and wait for your turn. I don't have to tell you I heard some mean and ornery words yelled at me that day from that crowd after the race, but I didn't care. I was having too much fun.

After the race, after my master and them owners and all had settled for more yellin' at me instead o' the beatin' I'd been promised if I was to lose, me and Austin found a quiet little corner and shook hands. He didn't need to tell me "good try," and I didn't need to tell him "congratulations." We both knew we'd done our best, and we'd do battle again one day. He was the finest rider and the finest man I ever rode against, and he deserved all of the good things that he ever got in this world. And a few years later he got what he really deserved when old Mr. Jones set him free.

Jimmy always carried a small faded and yellowed newspaper clipping with him in his shirt pocket. It was Austin's obituary from the state capital newspaper. After telling the story he would take out the precious little folded piece of newspaper, slowly opening it with great care, and explain, "Austin was such a great rider, such a great man, that when he died they wrote about him in the newspaper in the *state capital*. You boys just don't realize what a special thing that is for a colored man. I want you to listen to what they said about my friend."

> *Died on the 10th, at Halifax, Austin Jones, a colored man, aged about fifty years; well known for many years past as a keeper of race horses, in the management of which useful animals he particularly excelled. His character was unblemished, his disposition mild and obliging...he possessed the esteem of many; the respect and confidence of all who knew him.*

And then Jimmy would fold up the paper and carefully place it back in his pocket, slowly shaking his head as if he didn't really believe what he had just read.

Jimmy had taught Ansel everything the older man knew about horses, about how to get them to run their best. He first taught the boy how to ride when Ansel was around ten, and within a few short months he had ridden in a few races. But one morning Ansel had gotten thrown off and had broken his arm, and the boy never recovered the strength needed to be a successful rider. So instead Jimmy began to focus on teaching Ansel how to condition a racehorse: the right things to feed a horse, and just as important how much and when to feed it; and how to take care of injuries, especially the ones you have to discover for yourself. Ansel remembered the old man telling him, "You got to go over that horse every day, every time, 'specially the legs. That horse won't always tell you what's botherin' him. Sometimes you got to find it out for yourself, with your hands, being slow and careful and takin' your time. That's the only way to do it. Them white trainers, they're always in too big of a hurry. They got *important* things to go do. But colored folks like us, we got all the time in the world. You take that time to care for your horse, and he'll take care o' you."

Most importantly, Jimmy taught Ansel all of his tricks in training the horse. Race horses were fine-tuned athletes, and every morning, seven days a week, they need to go out for their exercise. For Jimmy it was about getting just a little something out of each and every morning. He loved to say, "You don't gotta do a lot any one day, but you gotta do a little somethin' every single day. A horse ain't never stayin' the same. He's either getting' a little better, or he's fallin' off a little. The trick is to keep him goin' in the right direction. Just a little bit better each and every day. If you go too fast, you get to the end before you want to. The trick is to get there at just the right time. Then you give him a little break for awhile, and then start all over again. That's really all there is to it."

Ansel began to make a name for himself as a trainer there in Virginia when he was just barely twenty years old, and no one was prouder of him than Jimmy. But as with all things success can sometimes bring unintended consequences. Soon Ansel's abilities were highly valued, and it was only a question of time until he was sold. One day he found himself heading to the deep south of Alabama. He had been bought by a man named Goldsby, who very badly wanted to be known as a champion horseman. The only problem was, he didn't know much about horses, or people for that matter, as Ansel would discover all too quickly. Ansel at least had received decent treatment in Virginia, and had been as happy as a slave could be. It was his home, and he knew how to survive and deal with his owner there. But now he would never see Jimmy or hear his well-worn tales again, the old man's comforting and encouraging words. Ansel was in a strange and alien environment, and he would have to learn to deal with an entirely different sort of person. And he suffered greatly for it.

But by now Ansel knew everything he needed to know to become one of the top trainers in the business, and ultimately nothing or nobody could stop him. He helped Goldsby build up the white man's stable of thoroughbreds, even though Ansel ultimately despised him. Ansel had decided that he was more concerned with developing his abilities and his reputation, and less

concerned with his personal treatment. Ansel conditioned many great horses, in the process becoming famous in southern racing circles.

Most thought that his greatest success was a horse named Brown Dick. A
young slave named Ed Brown had ridden several of the trainer's horses including Brown Dick, the young jockey making quite a name for himself
along the way. But this horse was something else again, and Ed soon took on
the horse's name for himself. Together, the horse Brown Dick, the jockey
Brown Dick and the trainer Ansel Williamson took the South by storm, winning at all the top tracks – Charleston, Atlanta, Mobile – and then of course,
New Orleans. Ansel and this young jockey would find themselves crossing
paths again and again over their long careers.

As was so common in the life of a slave, Ansel was sold again a few years
later, this time to a man named Richards. And then in 1864 Ansel and his
services were sold one final time. But this time he couldn't have been more
excited. When he heard that he had been sold to that most famous of horsemen, R. A. Alexander, owner of the renowned Woodburn Stud, he knew that
this was his greatest opportunity. He was going to Kentucky! And by that
point in time most everyone with any sense, including a slave such as Ansel,
knew how the War would end, and that it wouldn't be long in coming. Alexander took Ansel aside on the first morning after he arrived at Woodburn
and told him, "Ansel, I want to be very clear about something. I brought you
up here because I know you are the greatest trainer in America, white or
colored. This damned war will be over soon, and I want you to work for me
starting today and continue right on after it is all over with. Anything you
need, you just let me know. If anyone doesn't treat you right, you just let me
know. You are going to be my trainer, and I won't stand for any damned
nonsense from anyone for any reason, you understand?"

And Alexander was as good as his word. Some people thought that the
slaves that worked with race horses had it better than the other slaves. In
some ways that might have been true. They traveled with the horses, and
particularly for the jockeys, felt the freedom of riding for the brief time they

were out on the track. But Ansel had always been very aware that he was a slave, and had always been treated as one, although certainly sometimes worse than others. But now, for the first time, he felt like he was truly valued by a white man for what he could do. It was the closest to feeling like a free man that Ansel had ever come. And in just a few short months, he finally gained that status. But as is true for most any man, white or colored, he was still beholden to the man for whom he worked. Some things never change.

Ansel stayed with Alexander, training some of his greatest horses, until the great man died in 1871. By then Ansel was regarded as one of the best in the business. He next went to work for another Kentucky horseman, H. P. McGrath. It was one of McGrath's horses that Ansel was studying out on the track at the Association Course in Lexington, on that fine April morning in 1875. The horse's name was Chesapeake, the leading three-year-old colt in the barn. Ansel had carefully laid out his plans for racing the horse, hoping eventually to make their way up to New York for the Belmont Stakes in a couple of months. But Mr. McGrath had thrown things off kilter when the day before he had told Ansel about a new race the next month down in Louisville. A couple of McGraths's friends were talking about entering their best three-year-olds in this new race, and McGrath would like nothing better than to beat them. He firmly believed that Chesapeake was just the horse to do it. "Stop whatever else you are planning, and get him ready to run in this new Derby down in Louisville". McGrath didn't have a habit of leaving much room for discussion.

Now that Ansel knew what he had to do, agree with it or not, he focused on the task at hand. As he watched the horse gallop around the far turn in the early morning mist, he started to formulate his plan. The race was to be run at a mile and a half. Chesapeake would handle that distance just fine. It was now a matter of finding out more about the competition, and to figure out just how the race would shape up. Chesapeake was a closer, with a powerful finishing rush in the last eighth of a mile. It would be vital that there was early speed to run against, to set up his late closing move. *It is so different now with these shorter races,* he thought to himself, *so different than how it used to be.* He stood there remembering some of the great distance horses he had trained in his early days, when races were still often three miles or more, with several heats. After the War everything had changed. Now the crowds, and the gamblers, relished in the excitement of these shorter sprint races. So Ansel had adapted and was equally successful. Just let him know when, where and how far, and give him a decent horse, and Ansel would be ready. Now he knew where, he knew when, he knew the distance and he had the horse. It was time to get him to Louisville. It was time to learn every inch of the new track, rate its speed, and find its low points. Nothing would be left to chance. Ever. Ansel, as always, would be ready.

CHAPTER FOUR

EIGHT hundred miles to the south, standing by the rail at the Fair Grounds race course, a different sort of horseman was also watching thoroughbreds train. He stood just over six feet tall and was naturally slim. His friends often commented on how he could eat his fill of the rich New Orleans food yet never seem to gain an ounce. He had piercing blue eyes and thick, wavy light brown hair, and both of these features held great favor with the ladies. There was a small scar on his left cheek, from a knife fight when he was twelve, which had the effect of giving his pleasant face even more character. He was dressed as usual in a fine cream linen suit, his frock coat and fashionably matching waistcoat set off by a scarlet four-in-hand tie fixed with a diamond cravat pin. He favored linen and silk for his wardrobe, and not for the sake of the Louisiana climate. He believed the style set him apart – and he had worn enough cotton and linsey-woolsey in his youth.

His name was Alexander Delacroix. Everyone of course called him Alex, and had done so ever since he was a small boy growing up on the outskirts of New Orleans in the booming port town of Milneburg, on Lake Pontchartrain. Alex's father had worked as a front desk clerk at the then newly opened Washington Hotel, supplementing his income running card games for well-to-do visitors from the city. The boy's favorite activity, besides hanging around his father's games, was to watch the steam locomotives of the Pontchartrain Railroad pull their loads out onto the pier to meet the immense ocean-going ships that docked there. He was still quite little when the Racer's Storm brought a surge on the lake of eight feet of water above high tide, resulting in mass flooding, destroying miles of railroad as well as the old Bayou St. John lighthouse. Yet Alex claimed that he could remember the old structure, as well as riding the mule-drawn barges that had plied the New Basin Canal in those days.

His mother had died in the cholera epidemic of 1832, just months after Alex was born. The cholera had spread rapidly among the Irish laborers building the canal and from them to the general population, killing over 6000 people in twenty days. His father never forgave the Irish, and had a well-developed, deep-rooted hatred and bigotry that he instilled in his only son. This hatred was only intensified in the boy when his father was killed in a bar fight with two Irishmen when Alex was only ten years old.

Milneburg was either the best or worst kind of environment in which a boy could grow up, depending on what sort of person you wanted that boy to become. What with the rapidly expanding number of hotels and bath houses and resorts, and the naturally accompanying saloons and gambling halls and music houses and other ventures designed to meet the needs of the wealthy residents and curious tourists, one could find most anything one desired, especially in a place so close to New Orleans. For a boy like Alex Delacroix, there was never much doubt about his outcome.

With only his father to guide him, Alex was exposed early and often to the underbelly of New Orleans society and enterprise. During the thirty year period before he was born, New Orleans grew faster than any other American city. This brought all types of opportunity, legal and illegal, moral and immoral. By the time his father died, Alex was well acquainted with it all and was more than ready to take on life on his own terms. He had already acquired the skills necessary to survive in this seedy and dangerous environment, and wasted no time in trying to make his mark.

He had done it all. He was a hustler, a con man, a thief, a swindler, some would say a degenerate. He cut his teeth as a pickpocket and petty thief when still a boy. He became involved with the worst of the booming New Orleans slave auctions, knowingly selling stolen slaves in "side" markets, slaves that he had paid others to steal. He was a pimp, and rumor had it that he had even worked for a while as a prostitute in the Quarter.

But most of all, Alex was a gambler. He would gamble for money, for trust, for love, and just for the sport of it. Somehow, he did it all with a certain amount of class, in such a way that most people could not help but like him, at least until he disappeared with their money, and maybe even then. Inevitably he first made his way to the horse races at the old Union Race Course in the summer of 1856, and then later when it reopened as the Creole Race Course right before the War. A bookmaker for a while, he became more involved in the backside operation as he felt it gave him an advantage in his ever-expanding propensity to wager heavily. He didn't like to lose, and made sure by whatever means necessary that it rarely happened, never really feeling that he was gambling at all. Alex had befriended many trainers and riders, applying his winning charms and resources to his great financial advantage.

Alex had held no use for the coming War, except for how it might help to line his pockets. While he passionately believed in the Cause, he felt there were better things in store for him than getting shot at on a battlefield in some God-forsaken place in which he had no desire to be. He had spent the War mostly traveling and gambling, often under assumed names. He had toured the west for the first eighteen months, cheating and stealing his way to enough funds to secure passage to Europe. He then spent the next year swindling charmed ladies out of a small fortune, which he promptly lost without a care at the racetracks and gambling halls in the finest cities across the Continent. Finally he returned to fleece as much as he could from Northern sources, especially when it became obvious how Southern fortunes were turning. But make no mistake, Alex held nothing but hatred for the North and what it had done to his beloved South, and he felt that by personally acquiring as much of their money as possible that he was doing his own small part.

He had arrived back in New Orleans along with the Carpetbaggers and

Reconstructionists, just in time to invest some of his hard-earned capital in the rebuilding that lay ahead, not to mention helping to provide the amusements and vice that would go along with it. In doing so he had become a wealthy man. All-and-all the decade of the 1860s had been very kind to Alex, especially compared to almost all around him. It had also been a time spent magnifying his bigotry for the many different groups of people for which he had developed a deep hatred.

While he may have prospered from the War, Alex still believed the North must be held accountable for what they had done. He for one believed that John Wilkes Booth had been a hero and martyr despite his ultimate failure, and when given the opportunity Alex was less and less shy about sharing his feelings about the matter. Alex had even entertained thoughts of organizing an attack on Lincoln himself when the former president had shown the audacity to come to New Orleans. He had gone so far as to design a plan of attack, finding opportunity in the local newspaper accounts of Lincoln's anticipated itinerary, and was bold enough to share his designs with his most trusted associates who declared them feasible and urged him on to the deed. But in the end he had lacked the courage to carry out such a thing, and ran off to spend the evening getting more drunk than he had been in many years, in the company of his favorite prostitute. Thereafter, most of his enemies and more than a few of his friends felt that Alex was all talk. But Alex swore if he ever had the opportunity again....

Alex was deep in thought as he watched the horses that same bright, sunny April morning. He looked around the magnificent Fair Grounds, successor to the Union and Creole tracks that had operated on that site in his earlier years. Along with many of the younger horsemen he had followed the newly founded Louisiana Jockey Club in breaking away from the Metarie Course that had operated in the interim, and in the three years since the Fair Grounds had reopened he had grown truly to love the place. There was nowhere in New Orleans, or the wider world for that matter, where he would rather be. "The finest facility for racing horses anywhere on the face of this earth," he would proclaim to anyone who would listen.

He had made himself quite at home at the track, and he found his way there every opportunity he could manage. He particularly loved to come out in the early morning and visit the stables, and the people gathered there. It was there he made some of his best contacts, got some of his best information. Ultimately all it took was knowing the right people to get the right information about the right race on the right day, and you could do very well for yourself. And no one knew the right people better than Alex.

As a result he was not particularly well thought of by certain other people around the racetrack, and around the city. But Alex hardly cared. Even though he had acquired wealth he had never aspired to be one of *those* people. He could feel a small anger simmering inside him whenever he thought about it. "They can keep all their sprawling houses and fancy clothes and beautiful women," he would say softly to himself. "Give me a good, kind-hearted sporting lady any day and I'll be perfectly happy!"

Alex's thoughts were interrupted by the approach of two young men who were slowly walking down the track along the outside rail in his direction. Charles Appleton and his older brother Robert were fixtures at the Fair Grounds this time of year. The younger brother was known around the track as "Charlie Apple," while his senior brother's often dour disposition had earned him the inevitably nickname of "Crabby Apple" – though few dared to call him that to his face. First Charlie, and then Crabby, reached across the rail to shake hands with Alex.

"Mornin', Boss," Charlie said brightly showing his customary big smile as he shook hands, "Bea-u-ti-ful mornin', ain't it?"

"Yeah, g'morning, Mr.Delacroix," his older brother mumbled.

Charlie always called Alex "Boss," even though technically he and his brother worked for the General. That was General Abe Buford, owner of Bisque Bonita up in Woodford County, Kentucky, one of the finest thoroughbred breeding operations anywhere. Charlie was a workout rider in the mornings, having grown too big to ride in any legitimate race, and Crabby was mostly a groom and a self-imagined assistant trainer, though they both answered to the General's real trainer, known universally as Old Tom. They had also done their share of "jobs" for Alex over the last couple of years, unbeknownst to the General and Old Tom. As with most of Alex's enterprises, nobody else needed to know anything about his business except for those he required. And he had found the Appleton brothers to be very useful on a number of occasions.

Like Alex, Charlie had a certain charm about him. Even though he wore the many scars of his occupation, he still had striking good looks and blond curls that helped him keep a youthful appearance, in spite of his already receding hairline. At twenty-six, his brother was two years older, noticeably stockier and taller though still well short of six feet, with short black hair touched with premature gray. He wore a thick mustache, less for fashion than to draw attention away from his plain face and to make himself appear older. Neither of the brothers had advanced beyond the typical few years of schooling, but Robert was certainly the more naturally intelligent of the two, often prone to long periods of silence. But his mind never stopped working, taking in all that was going on around him. People often mistook this for his "crabbiness," but in reality he was simply very deliberate and thoughtful about what he said and did.

"Good morning, boys," Alex replied with a pleasant smile. "Yes, Charlie, as per usual I can't imagine a better place to be on such a fine morning." Crabby hated it when Alex said "as per usual" – when the hell wasn't everything pretty much usual around this place? "I saw you come around a little while ago on that filly," Alex continued, ignoring Crabby's as per usual sour disposition. "She's looking fit and ready. When's the General going to run her next?"

"Well, from what I'm a-hearin' I guess we're gonna be headin' up north with her," Charlie slowly replied, watching two bay colts coming towards them, across the track, along the inside rail. "The General's got it in his mind to run her up at that new track in Louisville. Takin' five or six others and me and Robert" – he always used his brother's real name, at least when he was around – "and Old Tom, and I guess we're packin' it all up and takin' the train in the next week or so." He watched as the horses ran by and on into the turn, and then continued his thought, "And I don't know that I particularly care to be a-goin' back up to Kentucky already, 'cause you know I like it just fine right here where we are now, but then again I don't guess nobody's askin' me whether I care or not." Charlie could always extend a sentence with the best of them.

Alex frowned. "Now why in the world does he want to go all the way back up there to Kentucky when he can make plenty of money running that filly right here?"

"Well, Boss, you know from what he's done told me this fella up there, I believe he said the name was Clark or something like that, well, the General knows this fella and all, and they're a buildin' this brand new race track up there and the man's gonna have this big race just for the fillies, you know, the three-year-olds, and it's gonna be this great big damn deal, cause he's calling it the same thing as this big race the man saw over in England or somewheres over there, the Oaks it's gonna be called, and well, anyway, the General's just got his mind set on winnin' this race, not for the money you understand cause it ain't even that much money if you ask me, not nearly enough to make it worth goin' all the way up there, but it's just so as he can say he was the first man to win it, cause you know the General fancies himself bein' a Kentuckian and all and you know how they are, actin' like that really means somethin' and all that nonsense." His brother just stood staring down the track, slowly shaking his head without saying a word. "And oh, yeah, there's also gonna be this other big race, called the Derby. Gonna take McCreary along to maybe run in that one, too, but I don't know if it'll be no use 'cause that horse just ain't been right, been sickly and all. But you know the General, he's just gotta be a part of it all."

"Well, is that a fact?" Alex responded after picking his way through Charlie's exposition. "The Oaks...yes, I have heard of the Oaks, and of course the Derby. I saw the Derby when I was in England during the War, back in '63. They're both big over there, biggest races of the year. This man – Clark was it? – he must think he's pretty damned important to be calling some two bit shit races in Kentucky after really important English races." Alex was heating up at the thought of it. "Sounds like something a goddamn Irishman would do. Clark doesn't sound like any Irish name I ever heard, but he's sure acting like he could be. Think they're more important than anybody else. Only thing worse than an Irishman is a goddamn Irishman from Kentucky!"

"That's true 'nough," Charlie agreed, smiling. "My daddy told me once that him and his buddies thought they'd taught 'em all a lesson back in '55 on Bloody Monday. Thought they'd burnt 'em out fer good. But I'll be damned if it don't seem like they've takin' over the whole place now. That's one reason I'd just a soon a stay down here with you and the boys. Don't care nothing 'bout Lou-e-ville now, even if I was born there."

Crabby grunted softly and said, "I gotta be getting back. Got that two-year-old chestnut coming off the track, be needing a bath and all."

Alex looked at Crabby for a minute and considered asking why he was always in such a foul mood, but thought better of it. He simply replied, "You boys take care of yourselves now. Don't get into any foolishness. I'll see you tomorrow morning. I might have something for you then."

Charlie smiled again and said, "Sounds good, Boss. You know you can always count on us." He started to turn to follow his brother, and then paused to add, "I'll see if I can find out more about exactly when we're gonna be headin' north. That way we can take care of anything you might be need-ing before we go."

"Yeah, you do that." Alex watched as the two brothers walked back up the track. "Going to Kentucky," he mumbled to himself. "Why would anyone want to leave this place if they didn't have to?" He certainly had no interest in going to Kentucky, although a new racetrack would probably be filled with people and opportunities that would be ripe for the picking. Perhaps he should consider it. "No," he said out loud to himself, "I've got plenty to keep me occupied right here for this season." He turned without thinking any more about it, and headed back through the barns. He had one more piece of business to take care of before he headed back to town. There was the matter of that small side wager that he still needed to collect from yesterday's race.

Old Tom was watching as Charlie and Crabby made their way through the shed row. "Well, dammit, it's about time. I thought I was gonna have to cool him off myself!" He stood holding the chestnut colt that had just come off the track. "There's plenty of fellows needing work if you don't have the time to do your job!"

Crabby didn't show any noticeable reaction, but thought to himself, *If you don't watch it, I'll have your job one of these days.* But he just calmly lied, "Sorry, Tom, we got held up by a horse that got loose for a minute over yonder. I'll take him now." Crabby took the lead shank and began to walk the horse around the shed row of the barn to cool him out before his bath. Tom looked after Crabby, spit out a thick stream of brown tobacco juice, then headed back out to the track to watch another of his charges work.

Charlie just laughed at the exchange and strolled on past the General's barn and over to the back section of the stables. He quickly found what he was looking for. Gathered around on the far side of the last barn there were four small colored men, all jockeys, engaged in a game of dice. These four were some of the finest riders Charlie had ever seen in action, and even though he despised them for the color of their skin, he couldn't help but to respect them for their abilities as professionals. After the war and the end of slavery, many colored riders had continued to work the tracks, both north and south. Of course down here racing had declined dramatically and even practically died out for a few years. It was really only now gaining a foothold again in many places where it had traditionally thrived. As with these four men, many former slaves, and now their children, they were becoming the stars of racing.

"Hello boys," Charlie said, good naturedly showing his customary grin as he walked up behind them. "How much money you all got to give me this morning?" One of the small men turned and looked up at him, and it appeared as though his eyes were about to pop out of his head. "Damn it t'hell, Bug Eye, I hate it when you do that!" Charlie had stopped dead in his tracks. "You are the most ornery-looking creature on the face of this earth!"

"Bug Eye" Jenkins was called Bug Eye for the most obvious of reasons. He had been born with an unusual ability. He could make his eyes bug out of his head further than any man alive, and it was particularly effective on young jockeys who were trying to pass him out on the track. Some young boy would be sure he was about to make it to the lead and go on to glory when Bug Eye would flash that look and it would scare the young jockey so badly that he might even lose the reigns. This technique had helped Bug Eye win more than his share of races.

Kneeling next to Bug Eye, about to roll the well-worn dice, was an up-and-coming young jockey named Oliver Lewis. Having just turned nineteen, he had come down from Kentucky to try his luck riding at the Fair Grounds for the first time, and had only been in town for a few days. Oliver had immediately taken a liking to Bug Eye, who had in turn taken the new arrival under his wing.

"Who's this?" Charlie asked, looking directly at Oliver. "Surely not another colored rider. There's too many of you boys ridin' already. Gettin' so a white man ain't even got a chance around here anymore."

"Now jus' you don't worry none 'bout that, Mr. Charlie Apple. You ain't gonna be ridin' in no races anytime soon no hows." Gus "Peanut" White looked at Charlie with a cold stare. He might have been as small as a peanut, but he was anything but white. He had by far the darkest skin of any of the colored riders – "Black as the blackest stallion" some of the horsemen would say, "and just as mean." He was called Peanut because he was from southern Georgia, and he had probably the foulest disposition of anyone at the track. Compared to Peanut, Crabby was a bucket of sunshine.

Bug Eye quickly spoke up, before anything further could be said between the two men. "This here is Ollie Lewis. He's a fine young rider, just come down from Kentucky. You better get to know him, 'cause he's gonna be winning more than his share of races. If you're smart you'll be puttin' your money on him."

Still looking directly at Peanut, no trace of a smile, Charlie answered, "I don't need no *colored* rider tellin' me what to do with my money. I don't need no colored son-of-a-bitch telling me nuthin'!" After staring hard for another moment, just for good effect, Charlie turned to Oliver, and with his smile returning said, "I hope you ain't listening to this bug-eyed fool 'bout nuthin'. Anybody that looks like that can't be nuthin' but bad luck."

"Well now, I don't know about that. Looking like I'm about to take all this here money, so that seems like pretty good luck to me." Oliver smiled back at the white man. "Why don't you join us and maybe I can take some of your money, too?"

"Much as I'd like to, the last thing I need is to be back here rollin' dice with you boys. You know if Mr. Jones catches you you'll all be run off his property for good, that is if he don't shoot you first just to make an example of you."

The fourth rider, who often would go for hours without uttering so much as a grunt, looked up at Charlie and slowly remarked, "If you think that old man scares me and Peanut, you are surely dumber than you look. I'll shoot dice anywhere I want, anytime. That sumbitch try and mess with me and he'll be the one that gets run off for good."

Charlie started to say something, and then thinking better of it, just slowly shook his head and walked on back around the barn. To tell the truth he was scared to death of this man. He might have not even been five feet tall, but there was something about his presence that just made your blood run a little colder. His name was Calvin. No nickname, no last name that anyone knew, just Calvin. He was strong as an ox, which was less than apparent from his sleek build. It was rumored that he had killed more than one man who had crossed him, and probably wouldn't hesitate to do it again in the right (or wrong, depending on which side of the fence you were standing) situation. He and Peanut made quite a pair.

It was true that both men could ride, but they were known as much for their less-than-honorable tactics as for their pure ability. They had bounced around the South moving from track to track, riding at one place until trouble caught up with them, which was always just a matter of time, and then moving on to the next. More than one rider had regretted getting caught between the two out on the track, and most learned to avoid that situation, even if it meant losing the race. Which of course made them exactly the kind of riders to which Alex Delacroix was naturally attracted. It had not taken very long at all after hearing about this pair before he had befriended these two colored jockeys, at least as much as any white man could.

Oliver and Bug Eye had a healthy respect for them as well, at least as far as their own health was concerned. Bug Eye had laid out the realities about riding against them, and made sure that his new friend Oliver did not cross them in any way. "Just keep out of their way and you'll be all right," he had told Oliver on his second morning at the track. "They're mean and you can't trust 'em, but if you show 'em a little respect and don't cause 'em no concern, they won't really bother you none." Oliver had only needed to watch the pair ride together in one race to take his new friend's advice to heart. He didn't want any trouble. He just wanted to ride horses.

CHAPTER FIVE

AFTER his usual morning rituals and breakfast, Abraham Lincoln prepared to walk over to the small office in the Capitol building a few blocks away. Upon his return to Springfield in the late winter of 1869 he had had no real interest in actively practicing law and concluded therefore he would have no need for an office. But public demand and the advice of friends eventually led him to accept the offer of Governor John Palmer to take a small space in the Illinois Capitol. Much like Lincoln, the governor was a native Kentuckian who had grown up poor and somehow found his way to politics. Though he was an early associate and supporter of Stephen Douglas, Palmer had become a good friend of Lincoln's and was a Republican presidential elector at the 1860 convention in Chicago. Many believed he played a significant role in his friend successfully becoming the nominee. After the election the new president had appointed Palmer as a delegate to the unsuccessful Washington Peace Convention, but while this failed to turn the tide of secession and war, Lincoln had always greatly admired and valued his friend's efforts. Lincoln had actively supported Palmer's bid for governor, not that he had needed it – Palmer won in a landslide.

When the now former president arrived home, one of the first people to call on him in Springfield was the governor, who insisted that he establish an office in the statehouse. Lincoln initially resisted the idea, though he appreciated that the old building had been the birthplace of his political career – some insisted that his "house divided" speech was still echoing within its walls. And then there was the fact that the Capitol was already overcrowded and obsolete, with its splendid replacement rising a few blocks to the west. In the end, though, with the ultimate realization of the new and often unwanted demands on his time, he had agreed.

And what demands there had been! Requests for speaking engagements and endorsements, offers of honorary degrees and business ventures, demands for his opinions and support on any and all issues and causes of the day – the list went on and on. Lincoln had decided before leaving office that he would not remain actively involved in the Republican Party. As a former president, especially in this time when the nation was still healing from a war – a war which so many still blamed on him – he felt strongly that he represented all of the people and that party politics should be of no concern. He would speak out only on issues that he felt were of concern to and had an impact on all citizens. Even though he had limited funds, he had no interest in pursuing any kind of business opportunities. Additionally he felt it was totally unbefitting his position to accept paid appearances that used his position to benefit others financially. He would write, and fortunately for Mary and himself, discovered that a substantial income could be had from this most honorable activity, supplemented by what he considered "appropriate" speaking engagements.

Lincoln had returned to the White House but once, in March of the previous year for the wedding of President Grant's daughter Nellie. It had been a fine affair, and he had enjoyed himself. It had been an opportunity to see many of his former political friends and foes alike. In many ways he missed politics, but after all the suffering he had endured because of it, he had found it easy to walk away. Besides, he lived in the state capital so he was still surrounded by it all, and there was always a good argument to be had when he wanted one.

Mary had not been up to that return trip to Washington, choosing to stay home in Springfield. She rarely ventured out of the house, even to see her friends and neighbors, or even her three sisters, all of whom also lived in Springfield. Her husband so wanted to help her, to help her find a way to more happiness, but he did not know how. It was beyond him. He often could not help but feel that it was his greatest personal failure.

As Lincoln headed out for the short walk to his office the question of the possible visit to Kentucky was still in the forefront of his mind. He decided that he would need no topcoat this morning, his decision quickly affirmed as he stepped out into the warm April sunshine. He wore nothing on his head, having given up his signature stovepipe years before – truth be told, he never really had liked wearing it in the first place, being quite tall enough without it, and had favored it mostly as a place to keep papers handy. Now that he had less need of this service, he sometimes wore a plain felt hat, but most of the time preferred to be bare-headed. He believed that with his long face he did not look quite right wearing one; and no hat would hide the scar on the back of his head in any case. He was blessed with a thick crop of hair, most of which he still had, so fashion be damned!

Standing on the front stoop he looked up and down Jackson Street, taking in the comfortable surroundings. After a few moments he set out, down the two front steps, through the gate and onto the sidewalk. He turned left and headed north as was his custom, his large leather shoes making a familiar clacking sound as they struck the wooden planks. He quickly spotted his neighbor James Morse coming in his direction, on his way back from town.

"Good morning, James," he brightly greeted his friend, extending his hand. He indeed considered all of his neighbors and associates as friends – even if not all of his neighbors, even here in Springfield, shared this sentiment. "It looks as if spring has definitely arrived, if this morning is any indication."

"Yes it surely does, and none too soon for me. How are you this fine morning, Abe, and how is Mrs. Lincoln?" There was no "Mr. President" or any other such foolishness. Lincoln would have none of it in Springfield. For most of his life he had resisted the shortened form of his name, thinking it undignified; but with the trappings of office behind him he had found it possible to relax a bit – like so much now, that no longer seemed important. He even found he thought of himself as *Abe* occasionally.

"She is quite well, thank you, and may I say greatly enjoyed your wife's visit of last week. Her great kindness and concern is so very much appreciated, as is your own." Changing the subject quickly, he inquired, "Any news from town this morning?"

"None that I can report. I believe this spring fever has possessed the businessmen and politicians alike, and has totally distracted them from their usual unending complaints and concerns."

"That is indeed great news in and of itself. To think that those who would rather find fault and conflict in everything than to take the time to notice any good around them would pause for even a moment to enjoyed what Nature has bestowed upon us is greatly refreshing. I must say that I cannot wait to witness this phenomenon for myself first hand. I shall proceed with all haste!" Abe smiled and nodded slightly to his neighbor and continued in his customary direction.

When he reached Adams Street, hearing the familiar sounds of the children at the Catholic school, he turned left and proceeded one block, passing by the First Baptist Church. Then with a few more steps he was in front of his first law office. His mind briefly wandered to consider what he might have been doing this morning if he had not entered politics, if he had never been elected. Maybe he would still be up in his office working on his latest case, or perhaps across the street in the Courthouse, at this very moment involved in a trial or seeking some key documents. When he reached the railroad tracks, it was now the Episcopal Church that was to his right. The top of the grand old statehouse came into view. He walked one final block and then turned left at Second Street to head for the Capitol.

His attention was immediately drawn to two gentlemen who were obviously involved in an intense discussion of some sort. He easily recognized the two and walked over to join them. "Surely Shelby, you and Charles have learned by now that trying to convince the one of the other's point of view is a waste of such a beautiful morning as this. Why not just agree to disagree and get on to a matter of much more importance, such as whether or not this is not the best place in the world to be in the month of April? But of course you would just find a way to disagree on that subject as well!" Lincoln laughed heartily as he watched the two men now so thoroughly interrupted react to his statement with a look of questioning and innocence on their faces.

Shelby Cullom, who was twenty years Lincoln's junior, was the long-time head of the local Republican Party and yet another fellow Kentuckian. Charles Arnold, much closer in age to Lincoln, was an ally and neighbor also involved in local politics. But as is so often true in local matters, two members of the same party can find much on which to disagree. These two in particular were often observed strongly voicing their differences to one another. On this April morning they were discussing national, not local issues, specifically the recently passed Civil Rights Act.

"Abraham, I'm glad you are here," Charles said with some frustration in his voice."Maybe you can explain this thing to Shelby with more clarity than I."

"Good morning, Abe, as always an honor to be with you," the other man responded. "But for the record there is nothing that requires your clarification as far as I am concerned. Apparently it is Charles here who cannot understand basic common sense."

"Gentlemen! The streets of Springfield are no place for two men such as yourselves to be disturbing your fellow citizens in this manner. Perhaps we should all head over to my office and you can enlighten me further about the topic of your disagreement. As always, while I'm sure I will accomplish very little, it should be a fine way to pass part of the morning. And serve to distract me from matters for which I am indeed in no hurry to attend myself."

The three men walked down the block and crossed over Second Street, passing through the ornate iron fence and onto the grounds of the Capitol. As they approached the Illinois statehouse, with its wide front steps, four tall stone columns, grand red dome high above, they passed several acquaintances, pausing for a brief but cordial conversation with each. There was no more popular or convivial man in Springfield than Abe Lincoln. He could go nowhere without having to greet everyone who might cross his path. The amazing thing was how he never seemed to tire of performing this task, no matter his schedule or time of day. He truly loved people and was generally concerned with how they were and their cares of the day.

As they entered the building, passing through the center of the three imposing front doors, they encountered a man well-known to all three of them. Thomas W. S. Kidd, the court crier for the federal court in Springfield for many years, now was serving in a similar capacity for the state senate. A small ruddy man with little hair, he always seemed to be in good spirits, and was one of Abe's favorite people.

"Well I do wonder what could bring the three of you into this austere house, each in the company of the others. There must be pressing issues of state to bring about such a meeting as this. Shall I announce your presence, or perhaps send word directly to Washington that something is afoot?" Kidd could hardly contain himself at his supposed cleverness.

"Nothing so important as that," Abe replied with a laugh, and an extension of his hand. "Thomas, how are you this fine morning? Everything running smoothly I assume?"

"Nothing that can't be taken care of. Just trying to avoid trouble for as long as I can. Around here it is just a matter of time before it catches up with you, but so far today I seem to be staying ahead of it. Though I understand that plans are already underway for our move to the new Capitol, and that will bring a new measure of mischief I'm sure. I think it will be next year at the rate things are proceeding."

"Yes," Lincoln responded, "I have heard that in no time now I shall be left alone to haunt this old edifice when all the real solons have moved on."

"Never so, Mr. President." Kidd insisted on using the title, and Abe abided it knowing it was part of Kidd's professional bearing. "We will carry you forward with us in honor when the time comes. But more immediately, is there anything I can do today for you gentlemen?"

"No, thank you, Tom. We're just heading up to the office for a little polite discussion. There seems to be some matter of disagreement between Charles and Shelby here, as usual. Thought I would take them upstairs and see if we could come to some sort of compromise. Some have said that I am a good compromiser."

"You are indeed that, Mr. President." Kidd turned to leave. "If you have any trouble with them two, you just give me a shout and I'll come a-running. You gentleman all have a good day."

They walked up the grand stairway, flanked by two white columns, to the second floor rotunda, the Senate chambers to their right, the Representative Hall to their left. Turning back toward the front windows, they continued down a small hallway to the right, entering through the last doorway on the left. It was a small office, completely out of the way, which suited Lincoln perfectly. There was a large window, which at the moment allowed the morning sunlight to come pouring in. There was a nice view of storefronts across Second Avenue, currently at the height of activity. Inside the rather small office, well-worn like the rest of the building, was a medium sized desk – mostly covered with stacks of papers and a few books – four non-matching chairs and a small table. The wall between the door and the opposing window, behind the desk, was filled with three large bookshelves crammed absolutely full. Old law books attested to Abe's former professions, though there were also a few newer volumes, including multiple copies of all of his own books which he often dispensed to visitors. On the opposite wall was a large framed map of Illinois. Over in the corner, to the side of the window, a pile of newspapers and periodicals approached four feet in height.

Abe settled down into the wooden chair behind the desk while indicating that his guests should occupy any of the remaining chairs they saw fit. Arnold proceeded to light a half-burnt cigar, as was his habit, which prompted Lincoln to go and open the window. He had never been much for smoking himself, and having spent so much of his life in the company of men that did incessantly he took advantage of fresh air when it was at hand.

"Now, Mr. Cullom, please tell me, what exactly is today's discussion all about?" Lincoln asked settling back into his chair.

Waving away the smoke that his friend had just somewhat ceremoniously blown in his direction, Cullom replied, "Well, sir, I was trying to explain to Charles here that this new Civil Rights Act would be a major step forward in helping fulfill the promises that we have made to our fellow citizens, and that it was certainly the correct and honorable thing to do, and ultimately would be good for the country. He seems to believe that, quite the opposite, it will do nothing but increase divisions between our peoples and should never have been enacted." He looked over at Arnold expecting an immediate reply, but instead found the man taking another long draw on his cigar, staring out the window as if he had no interest in the conversation. "Surely you agree with me, Abe, that we had no choice but to do this thing, and that it was indeed the correct course to take?"

"I suppose I do, if pressed on the matter. But as I have learned over my years in politics, just because we may believe that something is the right and – how did you put it...*honorable* – thing to do, that all others may not agree with our position. I'm sure Charles here has some very well thought-out ideas and arguments on the matter as I have found him to be a deep and serious thinker. But my limited powers of observation tell me that he appears to be focusing upon other matters at the moment, perhaps matters of more importance. He no longer seems engaged by the debate at hand. Am I not correct in this, Charles?"

Arnold continued to look out of the window for another moment, and then quietly and calmly responded, "This is no longer a matter for my immediate concern. What is done is done, and I believe we should invest our time more wisely in the discussion of topics of more pressing import bearing on our lives and those of our good people here in Springfield and indeed throughout all of Illinois."

"My word, what is he going on about now!" exclaimed Cullom. "He is at his most dangerous when he is so quiet and soft spoken. I fear we are in for a true verbal assault."

"I speak, my dear friend, of the threat of this Greenback Party and what it is going to do to all of us if they get their way. Mark my words, if we do not support the banks and stop these people it will be the ruination of us all!" He had started quietly, but by the end of his short oration, *of us all* could be heard thundering down the hallway.

"Now *there* is a subject on which I believe we indeed can all agree," Cullom began. "These farmers and labor rabble rousers want control of all of the wealth, they want to promote their classist notions which have spread to this country like a pox. I tell you they will ultimately destroy the very fabric of our Midwestern society!" He was now visibly agitated. Lincoln and Arnold just gave each other a quick smile. "The Republican Party must unite to fight this menace. We are the party of patriotism, of financial responsibility. We know the value of owning property and producing goods. We must keep the government out of our business. I tell you all of this free-flowing paper money is just, just...why it's plain immoral!"

"Now, Shelby," Abe responded in a calming tone, laughing softly, "please try to control yourself. The capitol guards will be knocking at my door concerned that a row is about to break out." He slowly stood. "I agree that the Party must be strong and stand up for what we have accomplished and for what we believe, but surely you must understand that there are many working people who have suffered during the Panic and they are only desirous of what they believe will be a better way to provide for themselves and their families."

"Perhaps that may be so. But it will not be at my expense!" Cullom harrumphed.

"Hear, hear," Arnold nodded in agreement. He took one last good draw on his dwindling cigar and snuffed it out in the glass ashtray on the table. He leaned forward in his chair. "As much as I enjoy the company here, I have just realized that I have completely lost track of the time. I have an engagement this morning for which I am currently tardy. Shelby has once again managed to distract me as only he can do."

Walking over to look out the window, Abe took advantage of the momentary silence to change the subject. "If you could spare just one more moment before you adjourn to your business of the day, there is a somewhat personal matter on which I would very much value both of your opinions." He stared out at the busy street below. "I have been invited by a gentleman in Kentucky with whom I am only somewhat acquainted to visit the city of Louisville next month, to attend the inaugural running of what he assures me will become a significant horse race. This is to be purely a pleasurable trip and will require no significant public appearances or efforts on my part. I am sure he believes my presence there will help promote his new enterprise, which is all well and good as far as I am concerned. While I do not ordinarily allow my name to be associated with money-making enterprises, in this case I feel that doing something to assist the revival of horse breeding lately decimated by the War would be a worthy exception.

"More personally, I believe that I would very much enjoy the trip as it would provide an opportunity to become reacquainted with Joshua Speed, a man I know that you are acquainted with, Charles, from his days here in Springfield when we were both much younger. Joshua and I were the best of friends in my youth, and while we have maintained some correspondence, I have not seen him in many years. We had a bit of a falling out over some political and moral issues and I would very much like the opportunity to personally resolve them and renew our friendship as it used to be.

"However, I do not wish to leave Mary at this time as she has by all appearances greatly benefited from my presence over these last several weeks. My quandary concerns whether or not she would benefit from making the trip as well. We could also visit her hometown of Lexington, which I believe she might find beneficial. But she has not traveled since we returned from Chicago, and I have not been inclined to ask her to do so. My heart tells me that we should attempt this thing, but my head will not settle the issue so easily. It is indeed weighing heavily on my mind." He slowly turned and faced his two friends, attempting a small smile that quickly receded.

Shelby spoke first. "Have you talked with Mrs. Lincoln about this matter? How does she feel about it?"

"No, to this point I have resisted raising the issue. As I am sure you are both aware, and have been so kind as to not mention, this is a particularly difficult day for her, and I suppose for me as well. I have thought it best to wait until this cloud passes before mentioning anything. I believe she was quite taken with this man in Louisville and his wife when we met a few years ago in England, and indeed might again enjoy their company. But I am full of such doubts as to what might be best for her." Silence overtook the room for the next half minute.

"I believe, Abraham, my dear friend, I may have a suggestion that might be of some help to you," Charles finally offered, standing. "I understand that, for obvious reasons, you and Mrs. Lincoln have not recently been an active part of the social circles here in Springfield. We all remember how the two of you, particularly your lovely wife, would bring such joy and laughter to any occasion. And as much as we all would love to entertain you both again, everyone is respectful of your necessary privacy. You are probably not even aware that the Edwards are planning a dinner party for this Saturday. Helen would of course have invited you if she had for one moment thought it proper. If I remember clearly, Mrs. Lincoln has greatly enjoyed herself at previous parties there and is especially fond of Benjamin and Helen, not to mention your own rousing oratory over the years at some of their picnics and rallies. It has been a place of joy and comfort to you both. It might be a good opportunity to see how your wife does, shall we say how she holds up at such a social gathering, especially among good friends. If all goes well, might not you then inquire with her about the trip to Kentucky?"

Lincoln seemed lost in thought for a moment, as if he were revisiting in his mind the scene of past successes at the Edwards, relatives of Mary's sister Elizabeth's husband. He felt sure that Elizabeth would be at the party, and quite possibly her other two sisters and their husbands as well. They had not been particularly close, the four Todd sisters, all living in Springfield and married to local men. Abe himself had had his differences with Elizabeth's husband over the years, though since returning to Springfield he had done his best to let these things go, as he had with so much else. But there still could be some magic when the four Todd sisters came together, all "refugees" from Lexington and from their father's second marriage, which seemed somehow to unite them in a special unspoken bond.

"I believe you may have charted the correct path, Charles. Indeed if Mary enjoys herself there and is in good spirits, then we could discuss the trip on Sunday, and I could get a note to Mr. Clark by the end of next week. And if after Saturday night she does not seem enthusiastic about the notion, then I shall certainly have my answer as well." He smiled warmly at the two men. "Yes, gentlemen, I believe that is exactly what I shall do."

"Then it is settled," Charles replied, now wearing a look of satisfaction. "I will stop by and see Benjamin in his office directly. I am sure Mrs. Lincoln will have Helen's invitation by the end of the day."

Abe extended his hand first to Charles, and then to Shelby. "Excuse me if I do not walk you down. I have a few notes which I would like to write while my mind is still fresh. As always, it has been a pleasure, and again, thank you for your concern and advice. Good friends are the most valuable currency of all." And just for good measure he couldn't help but add, "The Greenbacks will never be able to change that fact!"

Lincoln worked on in his office for the next two hours, finding it hard to concentrate on his writing. Like a school boy, he was too excited at the prospects of attending the Edward's party to focus on the tasks at hand. He did so love a good party, and never tired of the entertaining conversation and stories, especially when the opportunity to tell them fell upon him. It was truly a personal sacrifice when he, believing firmly that it was for the good of Mary, began to politely decline all invitations until finally the citizens of Springfield had understood that they should no longer offer them. Now Abe felt lighter than he had in some time, practically bouncing down the steps of the state house as he headed to lunch at the Capitol Tavern on Second Street.

Afterwards he headed home rather than bothering to return to his office to try to do any more work, and while strolling back he began to think seriously for the first time about the realities of visiting Louisville again. Abe had neglected for much too long his strained relationship with Joshua Speed. The War was over, the years had gone by, and it was time for them to get past any differences that they may have had. Joshua had been such a good friend. *Why without his counsel,* Abe remembered, *I would probably have never married. And certainly God knows I could never have chartered my way through this life without my Mary.*

He entered the house as quietly as possible. Mary would not be expecting him home at this hour of the day, and he knew she had a habit of resting in the early afternoon. He quietly made his way through the house, into the kitchen and then on out to the back porch. He decided that he would draft a response to Mr. Clark, just in case one would be needed. He had no secrets from himself. He had to admit that without question he greatly desired to make the trip. *If only it will suit her, that she will allow herself to try, I know it will be for the best. Life is for living, and it's time that we get on about that task.* But he would have to be patient. Only time would tell, and he had learned too many times that Mary could be so unpredictable. But he decided, at least for his own mental health, to be positive. He picked up his pen, and set it to paper.

Dear Colonel Clark,

On behalf of Mrs. Lincoln and myself, thank you for your exceedingly kind invitation to come to Louisville and be with you on the day of your great achievement. Ever since the all too brief visit we had with you and your charming wife in Liverpool it has been in my mind that nothing would bring more pleasure and fulfillment than to visit your fair city again. And I can think of no better occasion than to come and celebrate the opening of your new venture and to witness firsthand the spectacular sight of these magnificent thoroughbred horses in the heat of competition.

I must offer my apologies for my selfishly slow response to your kind invitation, and hope that you will not think less of me for it. I want to assure you that, if it still stands in offer, Mrs. Lincoln and I would be most honored and humbled to be with you on this coming May seventeenth.

A Lincoln

As it happened, his draft was not in vain, and Abe could hardly contain himself when five days later he sent his reply on its way south to Louisville.

CHAPTER SIX

MERIWETHER Lewis Clark, Jr. found himself in an even deeper despair than usual. It had been raining for three full days now. Everything was a wet, muddy mess in his uncles' field south of town, and the work around him had ground to a complete halt. It was now Friday, the twenty-third of April; just twenty-four days to go. The still-to-be-completed grandstand was empty of workers. But at the moment the focal point of his deepening concerns were the barns. He had guaranteed the horsemen that the track and barns would be available to them by the first of May, which was now just a week off. For the most part he had kept that promise. Horses had been arriving since February. But the last few of the one-hundred-fifty new stalls still awaited completion and those were promised to some very important owners. He could not be satisfied until all had arrived, secured their spaces and were content. As he looked out the window of his office, listening to the pouring rain, he did manage to remind himself that much of the work had indeed been finished.

First had been the tracks themselves, though it had taken longer than expected, mostly due to the fact that Clark had decided to change the location of the grandstand, and thus the finish, midway through its construction. He had suddenly realized that the little grove of trees would be by far the better location for the clubhouse, their shade providing what would be a much appreciated respite from the sun. So he had moved the location of the home stretch from the west side to the southeast side, making most of the work that had been done to that point worthless. Eli Leezer, the best man in the country at building a racing track, had pitched a fit, even sued them, but eventually it had all been settled to everyone's satisfaction. The main track was separated from the inner driving track by a paling fence. A finer picket fence ran in front of the grandstand marking the edge of the outer mile oval.

The Porter's Lodge, with its wide porches and ticket offices below, grand twenty-foot wide entryways to each side, was also finished. It included a small room where Clark had slept more nights than he cared to admit. Mary had just accepted this as part of the ordeal. All of the grounds around the stands and stables, as well as the inner circle, had been graded and sown in blue and orchard grasses, which were now starting to fill in nicely what with the rains and warm spring sunshine. And of course the Clubhouse where Clark now sat in his office, capped with a fine observatory for the ladies, providing a view not only of the course and surrounding grounds but all the way across the fields to the Ohio River in the distance, sat finished. It featured large porches as well, where members could sit and enjoy the shade from the hot weather. Inside, half of the structure was set aside for the ladies, with a lunching area as well as a dressing room and parlor, the remaining areas reserved for the men.

Clark's concerns that they were going to cut it exceedingly close as far as the readiness of the remaining barns and the grandstand were rooted entirely in reality, not his usual self-imagined calamity. As if in an attempt to descend even further into the realm of despair, the thought suddenly occurred to him, *What if we have rain such as this for the Derby?* He had decided simply to pack up his papers and correspondence and make the soggy trip back into town to go home to dry off and, hopefully, find some way to improve his spirits, when there was a soft knock at his office door. "What now," he curtly shouted at the closed door.

"It's just me, Colonel. I've got your mail, sir," a weak voice came from the other side.

"Oh it's you, Vernon. I'm afraid the weather has gotten to me. Please come in."

The door opened and a smallish, older man dressed in well-worn clothes limped into the office, dripping water onto the wooden floor. The most noticeable thing about him was the absence of his left arm, that all-too-common badge marking a veteran. His name was Vernon Preston. He was not as old as he appeared, having just turned forty-four. To have met him on the street one would have easily guessed him to be a decade or more older. Much of his worn appearance was due to a taxing addiction to morphine, the result of his injuries in the War, and his lack of any noticeable self-control or confidence.

Vernon had been born in the Mississippi River town of New Madrid, in the furthest southwardly reaches of Missouri. As a boy he had still seen signs of, and heard many stories of the Great Earthquake, all quite frightening to a small child. This had rooted in him a desire to leave his hometown as quickly as possible. Lying about his age at fifteen, he enlisted with the Missouri Volunteers just in time to wind up in an artillery battalion serving in the Mexican War. Nothing could have pleased him more. He would rather take his chances with someone shooting at him – much preferable to the ground shaking and opening up below!

Vernon found that he was an excellent soldier and thrived in the military way-of-life. He had the good fortune to come under the command of Major Meriwether Lewis Clark, who took an immediate liking to the young Southerner. After that war ended, Vernon returned with Clark to St. Louis where the latter became the federal surveyor general for Missouri and Illinois, giving his associate a job as an assistant.

Among many other things the two men shared a strong pro-secessionist viewpoint. When Clark accepted a commission as a major of artillery in the Confederate Army he immediately sent for Vernon, who had already volunteered, and made the young man part of his staff. When late in the war Clark was taken prisoner at the Battle of Sayler's Creek, Vernon was left despondent. He was sure that he would never see his friend and mentor again, causing an even deeper hatred for the North, and particularly for the man he like to call, "that bastard Lincoln." Two days later, a cannon misfired and Vernon was badly injured, resulting in the loss of his left arm, his pronounced limp, and the beginning of his long addiction to morphine.

In reality the war ended just a couple of weeks later, and Clark escaped the worst of it during his relatively short confinement. After his release he moved to Louisville and resumed an engineering career. When he married Julia Davidson on December 30, 1865, Vernon was in attendance. The two men, however, were never again close, particularly as Clark could not tolerate his former friend's habit, which Clark saw with no sympathy as only a great weakness. When the colonel went to Frankfort to oversee the design and construction of several state buildings, Vernon remained in Louisville, never to see Clark again.

He did, however, maintain at least a passing acquaintance with Clark's son. Over the next few years Vernon sank deeper into the ravages of his addiction, and became a somewhat well-known, if often despised or pitied figure around Louisville, mostly depending on one's political views. The younger Clark was certainly very aware of Vernon, and of his former relationship with Clark's father. As the son of a Confederate officer, regardless of his father's viewpoint, the younger Clark definitely fell into the "pity" category and as a result was open to helping Vernon in at least some way. When the man showed up early on during the project, asking if there was something he could do to help, Clark decided on the spot to employ him in the role of "personal assistant," which in reality meant running all the ted-ious errands that Clark despised, and of course listening to the boss's endless worries. Vernon was particularly good at the latter.

"You look a little wet, Vernon," Clark tried to joke, not remotely in any mood to be doing so. "Do you think it's going to end soon?"

"Now Colonel, don't be worried about this rain." He knew his boss well. "By tomorrow the sun will be shining, the workers will be back at it, and everything will be fine. There is nothing at all for you to be worrying about. You've got good people here, and they know what's at stake. Not just about you or the horses, but for the whole town. They all know, and they're gonna get it done. You'll see."

Clark tried to smile, at least as best he could. This was one of the reasons he liked having Vernon around. For all of the man's problems – and you certainly couldn't help but notice them – he could build Clark back up better than just about anyone. Clark like to tell his closest friends when they asked about this sad, little man, "You know, if someone who's had it as bad as he has can get up in the morning and look at life and have something good to say, well there's something to be said about having that man around. Sometimes it's like he sees things that the rest of us don't see, and by God sometimes it helps that he is there to see them."

Clark also liked how Vernon called him "Colonel," as if he had inherited his father's rank in Vernon's eyes. The younger Clark had at first been taken aback somewhat and had asked Vernon not to use the title. But Vernon had gone right on doing it just the same, and pretty soon others started using the colonel moniker as well. Now he was officially known around town as Colonel Clark, even if some smiled about it behind his back.

Unfortunately Clark's treatment of his assistant did not always measure up to these fine sentiments, and as the pressure of completing the track on time increased he was more apt than not to lash out for no reason. He felt himself growing impatient. "I believe you mentioned something about mail?" Clark reminded him.

"Oh, yes sir, Colonel. And not to be nosey, but there's a letter here for you and judging by all these marks I think it's gonna be of some interest. I can't say as how I am too happy about it, but after all it is your affair and not mine."

Clark looked at his assistant with some displeasure. He was well aware of Vernon's sentiments and prejudices, especially when it came to the former president. But immediately the fear of what the reply might contain took control of his emotions, and he forgot all about Vernon and his attitudes. Clark hesitated in accepting the letter being offered to him.

"Just lay it on the desk, Vernon. I'll attend to it shortly. Why don't you go and check with Jennings and see if he needs any help."

"Yes sir, Colonel. But don't think you can fool me for a minute." Vernon glanced down at the letter he had just deposited in the middle of Clark's desk. "I know you've been worrying about that letter for weeks now, so don't try to act like you don't care and all. As for me, I hope he don't ever come anywhere around here. But like I said, it's your affair and not mine. Just don't expect me to get all excited or nothing. I don't give a damn about that... man." He bit off what he had started to call Lincoln, remembering his place at the last moment.

The words stung Clark so that he started to reprimand his assistant then quickly realized that it was pointless. *If Lincoln does come,* Clark thought, *I've got to make sure they don't get anywhere close to each other.* But it was still to be determined if that would even be a concern.

As Vernon left the room this brief exchange caused Clark to consider for the first time that if Lincoln were to come, there would be citizens of Louisville who would not share his excitement over welcoming the president back to town. It was hard for Clark to imagine that everyone else would not see the great benefit of Lincoln's potential visit and support of the Derby, and to set their personal feelings aside. Even after having been charmed by Lincoln at their meeting in England, Clark still felt he was a Southerner, but damn it, this was business! By God, the War had been over for ten years now. It was time to get on with things. Louisville could no longer afford such short-sighted and backwards attitudes. But ultimately he knew his neighbors all too well, and what they were capable of.

Clark stared at the letter for a good five minutes, studying the simple but elegant writing on the envelope and the marks that charted the course the letter had taken from Springfield to Louisville. He could not help but dwell upon the possible negative repercussions as he was so prone to do – this trap from which he seemingly never could manage to escape. He slowly stood up and walked around to the front side of his desk. Then picking up the envelope, he paused one last time to read the writing on it:

Colonel Meriwether Lewis Clark, Jr.
The Louisville Jockey Club and
Driving Park Association
Louisville

He reached for the beautiful ivory and silver letter opener that Mary had given him last Christmas, then turning the envelope over, with a last heavy sigh he slid the dull blade into the seal and removed the letter. "Well, Mary," he softly said out-loud, "let's see what the man has to say."

Clark stood there for a few moments, refusing to believe what his eyes had just taken in. He read it a second time to reassure himself. *He was coming! The Great Man was coming!* He carefully folded the letter and placed it back into the envelope, his hands shaking a bit. Still trying fully to comprehend this incredible news, thoughts were coming in a flurry. *What now must be done?* He had never truly allowed himself to believe that this moment would come. As his mind raced, he walked over and opened the office door and stepped out into the main hall of the clubhouse. At that very moment, as if by some Divine Intervention, looking through the large window Clark noticed a ray of sunlight breaking through the dark clouds and shining down onto the racetrack. It had the effect of a cold splash of water to the face, and immediately brought him back to matters at hand.

"Why I must let everyone know right away," he said to no one in particular. "This is glorious news. Glorious! The mayor must know. I need to get a wire off to the governor. My officers must know. And the workers, yes the workers should definitely know who is coming. The newspapers! Of course the papers, right away. By tomorrow morning the entire city, everyone will know. Lincoln is coming!"

As Clark rushed to his carriage to head into the city, he passed by his assistant, taking no notice that the man was even standing there. Vernon just shook his head and muttered to no one but himself, "Shit, that *bastard* is coming. Damn him and damn me!"

CHAPTER SEVEN

THE following Tuesday morning, Alexander Delacroix was at his customary position on the rail at the Fair Grounds, attempting to enjoy yet another fine morning in the warm sunshine, vaguely aware of the activity on the track in front of him. He had benefited from a particularly profitable Saturday, thanks in large part to Messieurs Calvin and Peanut, who had ensured that one particular horse and rider would enjoy less than their expected success. The two made a formidable team when properly motivated. Of course as was often the case, his successful weekend led directly to his current aching of head and queasiness of stomach, the unavoidable result of a continuous thirty-six hour indulgence in the upper confines of a particular establishment he favored. No matter the heights of his success, certain habits would always remain. This in turn had meant his tardy arrival at the track. The sun had been up for a full hour before he had taken his place at the rail.

In an effort to improve his overall condition, he removed a small silver flask from his inside jacket pocket and quickly consumed half of its contents. A small amount of perspiration appeared on his forehead, and noticing the growing intensity of the late April New Orleans sun, he removed the jacket and carefully hung it over the rail. He immediately felt somewhat refreshed as the result of both actions. A grey colt slowly galloped into his field of vision, breaking his vacant stare at the empty grandstand across from where he stood.

"Mornin', Boss. I was beginnin' to think you weren't gonna make it out this mornin'." It was Charlie Apple. "Thought maybe the party was still a-goin' on."

Alex's only response was to give a short wave as the horse and rider passed him. Charlie called back to him, "Don't go nowheres. I got some news you maybe ain't heard."

Alex thought to himself, rubbing his head, *any news at all from the last two days would certainly be news to me.* He emptied the remaining contents of the flask. Five minutes passed before he saw Charlie making his way down the track, now on foot, alone. His brother undoubtedly was hot-walking the grey colt that Charlie had just galloped.

"Damn, Boss, you ain't lookin' so good this mornin'. I figured you'd done gone and had a big time, but I believe maybe you even outdone yourself." Charlie flashed his familiar grin "Keep an eye on that grey colt. Named Storm Cloud. He'll be runnin' Thursday, and let me tell you, he's ready to *ex-plode.* I could barely hold him back this morning.

"Who's up?"

"Bug Eye."

Alex thought for a moment, watching two horses pass. "The boys riding anything?"

"Well course they are, or I wouldn't be botherin' you 'bout it. This one sets up even better than the one Saturday did."

Alex removed a little nub of a pencil and a small piece of folded paper from his pocket and scribbled a few words. "I'll look into it." He stared at the paper, reviewing his notes. For a moment Charlie thought Alex had forgotten that he was still there. Then suddenly, without looking up, Alex grunted, "Was that your big news?"

"Damn, Boss. You'd better get outta this sun and go take a nap. You're down right an-ti-soshul this mornin'. Maybe I won't even tell you."

Alex looked up coldly. Charlie just kept grinning. "Well it looks like we're packin' it all up after Saturday's races and jumpin' on that train to Louisville, early Sunday morning right after the horses gallop. Old Tom said the General's got everthing arranged. He's bound and determined to win this Oaks race, so we're taking the filly and McCreary and them other horses and heading up there to try out this new track. Son-of-a-bitch has lost his mind if you ask me, but what can I do? When you work with horses you gotta go where they go. And we're goin' to Lou-ie-ville."

Alex clearly was not happy to hear this piece of news, as it would directly affect his potential earnings in the short run. He made a mental note to take an even more active interest in Storm Cloud on Thursday. "Well you boys just have yourselves a fine old time up there," he commented mockingly, looking down at the ground, his head still pounding. At the same time he thought to himself, *damn the General, damn him straight to hell! I had plans for that filly.* Looking at Charlie he continued out-loud, "This means I want something good on Saturday as well. I don't care what you have to do to set it up, you tell the boys they owe me. This is nothing but a major goddamn inconvenience."

"Well there's the second part of the story. Peanut and Calvin are figurin' on heading up there with us. They figure it'll be worth their while to get out of here and try something new, before they get run off for a change. Said they ain't never been up to Kentucky before, want to see what it's like. I told them it wasn't nuthin' any different than here, but you know them. And of course Bug Eye is goin', 'cause the General'll want him to ride the filly, and he's taking that new boy Lewis along as well. He's from them parts up there and knows his way around a little. He's hoping to maybe pick up somethin' in that other race, that new Derby."

"Well, goddamn 'em all!" Alex's face was turning noticeably redder. "That's practically my whole operation. What am I supposed to do, just take off the most profitable part of the season?" He turned suddenly and started walking towards the barn, as if he were going to go and try physically to convince the General to alter his plans. But after a few steps he stopped and turned back to Charlie. "What do you know about this new track? Who's running it?" But before Charlie could answer, Alex continued, as if in a debate with himself, "No, no sir, I'm not interested in going to Kentucky. To hell with all of you and the whole god-forsaken state of Kentucky!"

"Now, Boss, there is one more little part to the story that you still ain't heard, and I think you just might find it interestin'." Charlie now wore what could only be described as a sly grin, which agitated Alex further.

Alex stared at the man, both looking and feeling like his head might literally explode at any minute, depending on just what was said next. Charlie, sensing that he'd better not push things any further, simply said, "Guess who's gonna be the special guest on openin' day when they run that Derby?"

Again, Alex said nothing, continuing to stare hard at his companion. There was no smile now on Charlie's face as he said, "That Illinois *son-of-a-bitch*, that's who!"

All of the rage drained suddenly out of Alex's face and a completely different look took control. He looked almost puzzled. "Lincoln? Lincoln is going to be there?" Charlie just nodded and looked down at his dusty riding boots.

Instantly Alex's mind started processing several simultaneous thoughts. Lincoln was going to attend the races, at a new race track, on an opening day, where things would undoubtedly be completely unorganized and unpredictable. In a city were his stooges were from, where he was certain they would know the right kind of people in the right kind of places, a city that was sympathetic. It was clear after the last time that Lincoln would not come to him, so why not go to Lincoln? It was as perfect a set-up as he had ever arranged in any horse race.

Not to mention that in one singular act he could put a dagger into the heart of the Bluegrass as well. He did so despise them. They thought they were so superior. It might as well be the North. Especially if Lincoln thought for a moment that he would be safe there. Not to speak of the money he could make. *Yes!* He would go in and fleece the city and all of its *fine citizens*, destroy their superior notions of racing, and succeed in avenging the South (as well as his own previous shortcoming), all in one glorious moment. How could God be rewarding him so?

But Charlie sensed none of this. Alex gave no outward sign of his many thoughts. He simply paused for a moment, looked back at the barns, and said, "To hell with it all. Let Lincoln go and have a fine day at the races. Let the

General go and win his race. You boys all go and get drunk on Kentucky bourbon and I'll just continue to enjoy myself right here in the finest place God every created and spend some of the money I've been earning. By the end of the month you'll all come running back and we can get on with business."

"Whatever you say, Boss." Charlie was grinning again. "I'll see what's up for Saturday and let you know. Just do me a favor and don't forget payday before we leave." He turned and walked away allowing for no response from Alex. Forgetting all about any plans he may have already formulated, Alex grabbed his jacket off the rail and immediately left the racetrack, headed into the city. He had arrangements to make.

CHAPTER EIGHT

ABRAHAM and Mary Todd Lincoln stood in the bright morning sun, waving to the crowd of people gathered around the Indianapolis train station. Everyone present was enjoying the clear skies after several grey, rainy spring days. In the twenty-odd years since it had opened as one of the first union railroad stations in the world, this site had hosted many important visitors, but no one could remember seeing a larger crowd. Since the famous couple's arrival the previous afternoon, increasing numbers of people had turned out whenever and wherever the Lincolns could be seen in public. The rain had done little to dampen the locals' spirits.

When news of the visit had first reached Indianapolis, Governor Thomas Hendrick immediately wired a request that the former president speak at an event intended to raise funds to help provide relief to the many victims of that spring's devastating storms, which had been almost unprecedented in number and severity. Several twisters had caused wide-spread damage throughout central Indiana, and the governor's wife had quickly organized an effort to try to help with the recovery. Hendrick was the first Democratic governor to be elected in the north since the War and he was having a particularly hard time of it dealing with the strong Republican majority in the Indiana General Assembly. Lincoln could certainly sympathize with the Governor's predicament and was more than willing to help in this completely non-political effort. The governor sincerely appreciated the Lincolns' support, which he related personally to them both at a private dinner that Monday evening after the rally.

It was precisely the type of event that attracted Lincoln's attention and efforts, and which he truly enjoyed attending as well. He fully realized that there were still many people who held him in less than high regard. By focusing on these sorts of non-partisan, non-political events he had managed over the last five years to begin to win over many of his critics. While self-serving, his intentions were genuine. Abe felt that after so much death and destruction – which he clearly understood so many lay directly at his feet – he must try and do some good, accomplish something of value for the citizens. His reception varied greatly as he traveled around the country. In many places, like here in Indianapolis, still in the Midwest he called home, he was usually greeted warmly, almost always enthusiastically. But in New England and New York, he could count on a good number of critics in the crowd, often shouting out ugly remarks and demonstrating with hateful signs. He always understood and expected it, even sympathized. He was generally surprised and pleased when they were *not* present.

The warmth of the Indianapolis crowd reminded Abe of the enthusiastic and supportive crowds he had witnessed out west the previous fall, when he visited California – perhaps the greatest reception he had received since leaving the White House. That trip was something he had always dreamed of doing, and he had spent two months touring: first to Denver, then west to San Francisco, up to Seattle, and finally, that glorious return trip across the northern plain states. The most beautiful countryside he had ever seen. He so wished Mary could see it. While he had purchased photographs for her of some of the sights from the studios that were popping up everywhere now, they of course could not do justice to the majesty of what he had witnessed. He was already secretly hoping that if all went well with this trip to Kentucky, they might yet travel west together.

The crowd at the rally had been large as well, mostly in response to the former president's appearance, with a significant amount of money collected. Abe had worked the crowd into a true frenzy, telling them that American's generosity in a time of need was matched only by their undying spirit and patriotism. His gentle but firm oratory had built to such a crescendo that even he had been moved. Some told him it was his finest speech since leaving office, and after dinner that night, he retired to the soundest sleep he could remember in months.

The train slowly rolled out of the station the next morning passing through much of the downtown area on its easterly path towards Cincinnati. Mary soon entered their car but her husband, wearing a plain, long, somewhat worn dark suit – clothes that made him feel comfortable – continued to stand at the back railing. He waved patiently to the people who were gathered along the tracks waiting to see him pass by. Here most were white, but then pockets of colored faces appeared. Within a few minutes the train had left the city proper and Abe joined his wife inside.

As their sponsor for the journey, Clark had used his relationship with the president of the Louisville and Nashville Railroad to secure the services of one of the newest of elegant private Pullman Palace Cars, in which the Lincolns were presently traveling. It would be at their disposal for the entire trip. As Lincoln entered the car he thought of how it lived up the company name, as it was indeed palatial. The car was large and spacious, paneled in rich mahogany adorned with gold trim. Beautiful hand-woven carpets covered the wood floors, on which sat oversized chairs covered in fine brown leather. The oil lamps on the walls and the solid mahogany tables were fitted with red silk shades. The latest in hot water heating provided warmth on the still-cool evenings. Abe had never become entirely comfortable with such plush surroundings, even after living in the White House and spending time in the company of European royalty. But it occurred to him that the railroad barons for whom such cars were built were becoming the new American royalty, especially since the opening of the transcontinental routes.

Mary was seated, enjoying coffee. She had awoken that day in a glorious mood. In fact, ever since the Edward's dinner party a little over three weeks earlier, she had been consistently in excellent spirits, the best her husband had seen since the death of poor Taddie. The whole notion of the trip had given her something new and exciting on which to focus her energies and attention. As he studied his wife watching the passing Indiana countryside, smiling and softly humming an unknown tune, Abe thought back to the party.

WHEN their invitation had arrived late that Wednesday afternoon, Mary had sat in the parlor for quite a while, holding the small card, deep in thought. Abe was about to suggest that perhaps it would be too much for her, when she suddenly turned to him and said, "Abraham, I believe I would like very much to have dinner with Helen and Benjamin on Saturday night. I believe it would be a pleasant thing to see some of our old friends, to catch up with them. I'm sure Elizabeth and Fanny and Ann will be there. I have spent too long in this dusty old house. Would you be at all interested in taking me there?"

Abe softly chuckled to himself remembering how he had attempted to conceal his immediate excitement and anticipation, not to mention relief. His instincts had been on target. He had sensed in those last few weeks that she was in need of some change, was ready for a change, but he still had depended upon her to show him that mentally *she* was ready. The next two days were a flurry of activity as Mary prepared for her first social gathering in years, indeed since her return from Europe.

The party itself had been a great success for the both of them. Their friends had truly missed them and genuinely worried about them, especially Mary but Abe as well. They could only imagine what he had endured in trying to bring Mary back, alone in that house. When she arrived at the party, dressed so elegantly, but more importantly much her old self, laughing and enjoying everyone and everything, it was as though a collective relief and celebration fell over not just the party but the entire town. It certainly had been the only subject of conversation in many a downtown church the next morning, especially with all four of the Todd sisters together again. And Abe could hardly contain himself. He had shared favorite stories, told often but not recently, laughed heartily and re-established himself as the wise but wily lawyer they had all known so well.

The next afternoon Abe and Mary sat out back enjoying another fine spring day. Mary had picked up a long-ignored handkerchief which she was needle-pointing. Abe carefully broached the subject of the trip. "Mary, do you remember Mr. Clark from Louisville, with whom we shared dinner on my last night in England?"

She paused for just a moment. "Why yes, of course, he and his lovely wife Mary. It was so enjoyable to run into fellow Kentuckians so far away from home. I do believe he particularly enjoyed your ramblings that evening." She laughed softly. "And Mary was such a lovely woman. They did seem so very happy together." She returned to her work. Abe could not help but to re-member the several sharp looks that Clark had received from his wife that evening, but knew better than to mention anything about that now.

"A while back I received an invitation from Mr. Clark in regards to a new enterprise he is establishing in Louisville. It seems that while in Europe he attended several important horse races, and returned home with the idea to build a new racing facility. Apparently he has been quite successful in his efforts, and indeed it will be opening the middle of next month. They are going to run what he reports will be a very important race, to be called the Kentucky Derby, patterned after the top race in England. Perhaps more importantly, they seem to think that this will be a critical event in re-establishing the Kentucky thoroughbred industry that was so damaged during the War. He has invited us to come to Louisville and be a part of the festivities. He assures me that it will be purely a social occasion – no politics, no speeches, just for us to enjoy and offer our support." He paused, drawing a short breath and holding it.

Mary again put down her work and stared out over the greening yard. After a few moments she smiled and replied, "I believe that was a speech you just delivered, husband, since there was an air of preparation in it." But before Abe could react she added, strongly, "Well of course we will go. It sounds as if they need us. It sounds as if it will be important for the Commonwealth. We may have not lived there for some long time now, but after all we are still Kentuckians."

Abe now smiled in return and in a caring voice asked, "Are you sure that you are up to such a thing, Puss?" It had been some while since he had last used that pet name, but she seemed so much her old self. "It was a somewhat easier matter to be among such old and dear friends as we were last night, but perhaps a much different one altogether to attempt a trip such as this. We must consider your health."

"Nonsense, I will be fine. Sometimes you just worry too much, my dear." She paused for a moment in thought, then asked "I wonder, could we possibly visit Lexington while we are at it? I believe I would very much like to see the city and the old home-place again after all of these years – why, it must be nearly thirty years now since we were last there together. I suspect I shall hardly recognize it."

He could only smile again. "This was the very matter I was next going to bring up. I suspected that you might feel that way. I think we could go down to Lexington from Cincinnati and spend a few days, and then head over to Louisville in time for Mr. Clark's celebration."

"Oh, I suspect a day or two will be plenty. It's not as if we can be in the old house, now that father is gone, that it has been sold. I think a pleasant afternoon touring the town will be more than enough."

"Fine then. It is settled. I'll begin making the arrangements in the morning. I believe we shall both benefit greatly from this trip."

"Yes, and I'll believe that there will be no speeches when I see it," she laughed merrily.

Abe had received Clark's enthusiastic reply within a few days of his letter accepting the invitation, along with assurances that their host would take care of all the arrangements. The next days had been a whirlwind of activity, with much shopping and preparations to be made. Mary had spent too much money, but what was unusual about that? She had always had a taste for fine things, which had more than once gotten them both into trouble, especially back in Washington. Abe could not get too upset, though, for she had spent so little for so long. If she was happy, he was satisfied. And for the first time in a long time, she did seem truly happy. But would it last?

ABE settled into the plush chair next to his wife, the train now rolling along at full speed, joining her observations of the beautiful Indiana countryside. A wetter than usual spring had brought on pronounced and vivid greens of all shades, offset by the fields of tilled brown earth, farmers busily preparing for the coming planting. It was as if a giant patch-work quilt had been draped across the hills.

The first night in Indianapolis had been a great success, and now they were headed to Cincinnati for a night before their return to the Bluegrass. They were to make only one public appearance, that afternoon at a base ball game of all things, which excited Lincoln greatly. He had become fascinated with this new American sport, along with the whole idea of professional players. He had first seen the game played by Union troops in Washington during the War. Nine-year-old Tad had been with him that day, and the soldiers had let the boy toss the ball with them and take a few swings with their crude, carved wooden bats. For the next few weeks all the boy had talked about was base ball. Abe mused as he sat on the train half-dozing, listening to the clacking of the wheels, that perhaps Tad might have become a professional ball player if he had just been given the chance.

Whether it was the soothing sound of the continuous rhythmic clacking, or the enormous amount of energy expended during the previous night's rally, or perhaps the larger than usual breakfast that he had enjoyed, Abe was dozing soundly when they passed from Indiana into Ohio. He dreamt of when he was a small boy on the Knob Creek Farm.

He was fishing in his favorite stream, the water running so cool and clear that he had removed his shoes so that he could feel it on his feet. Hearing a noise in the brush on the other side of the stream, without thinking he threw one of his shoes in the direction of a rustling bush. "Now, I will have to go and find it," he said to himself. But after climbing out of the stream and searching for a few moments, he could not find the missing shoe anywhere. Then the noise grew louder. Could it be a rabbit, or a fox? What if it were a cougar, or even a bear? He would have to run home without his shoe, knowing his mother would be very angry with him. He was too scared to look further for the shoe, but even more scared to face his mother without it. Just then he heard his father's voice calling, "Abe, where is that water you were supposed to get? How can your mother cook without the clean water she asked you to fetch?" Water, what water? He didn't remember that he was on any errand. Why, he was fishing, and now he had lost his shoe, and would now have to face his mother without shoe or water. He again heard the mysterious, unknown noise that had captured his attention in the first place, somewhere there behind him. And to his front, the sound of his approaching father. He was stuck good, with no way out. All he could figure to do was to jump in the stream and disappear! He fell forward, ready to make his escape....

Just then he awoke, momentarily disoriented.

"You'll sleep right through our arrival if you're not careful." It was the voice of his wife, not his mother or father. "There were already some people gathered at the last crossing, I suppose they wanted to see you."

As Abe recovered his bearings he realized they were just reaching the outer edges of Cincinnati. Coming fully to his senses, he responded, "Now Mary, you know people delight in seeing you as well. These are good people here in the Midwest, just like our neighbors at home. We must make the effort."

He stood up, the bones in his long frame resignedly popping. He had never shared with her the ugliness that the crowds could exude, always only the love and support. He was afraid she would see that side all too soon, and it concerned him greatly. But ultimately it was a fact of life with which she would have to deal if they were going to extend her world beyond the boundaries of their friends and neighbors in Springfield. At least the people of Indiana had been kind, and hopefully it would be the same in Ohio.

"I suppose we shall be arriving soon, from the looks of it." He walked over to the pitcher of water and basin placed on one of the tables, carefully wet his hands and rubbed his face, removing any last traces of his nap. "Time to greet the good people of Cincinnati."

CHAPTER NINE

THE train began to slow noticeably. It was now mid-day on a Tuesday, a business day, yet groups of people had still gathered along the tracks, and were increasing in numbers as the train made its way into the center of the city. As Abe prepared to step out onto the rear platform, he motioned to Mary. "Come and join me. It is the least we can do for these folks who have been kind enough to take time out of their busy day to come and welcome us, especially since you are practically a neighbor."

The pair stood in full view as the train pulled into the Plum Street Depot. A roar slowly swept through the gathered crowd, building to a climax as the train came to a complete halt. The porter who had been with them for the morning's journey came around from the front of the car to help the Lincolns step onto the raised platform that had been erected by the tracks for the occasion. Mary quickly recognized a cousin and her husband who were there waiting to great them, standing next to two other gentlemen dressed in fine dark suits Cordoning off the platform, and stationed throughout the area were the obligatory policemen who were present at any gathering the former president attended. The Lincolns first embraced Mary's relatives and then turned to the elegantly dressed men.

"Mr. President, Mrs. Lincoln, I am police superintendent Thomas Snelbaker. It is my great pleasure to welcome you to Cincinnati. Allow me to present to you the honorable mayor of our city, George W. C. Johnston." The superintendent stepped to the side, allowing the mayor to move forward. He immediately reached for Lincoln's hand.

"President Lincoln, what a great honor this truly is. And Mrs. Lincoln, so lovely and gracious. On behalf of all of the people of our city, we welcome you warmly and invite you to say just a few words to our citizens who have gathered here to greet you today."

With that, Abe turned to face the assemblage and an even louder cheer arose. As he scanned the crowd he realized that perhaps not all present there were so thrilled to see him. While there was no visibly organized demonstration, there were clearly folks who were waiting to see what this former president had to say. They were really not at all sure what they thought of him, and not a few had come predisposed to not like him, whether because of personal opinions or the influence of family histories. It was several minutes before the crowd settled enough for Abe to be heard. He would motion for quiet, but the crowd would respond with more acclaim. Finally, with Mary's urging as well, their audience became mostly silent and waited to hear what he had to say.

"Citizens of Cincinnati, on behalf of Mrs. Lincoln and myself, let me first say how much we appreciate your warm and, I must say, enthusiastic welcome, and how pleased and honored we are to be with you here today in your fine city." The crowd erupted again, and Lincoln smiled broadly. He patiently waited for quiet.

"Today I report to you that while this may be my first opportunity to arrive at this fine depot – which surely lives up to its renown as one of the finest in the land – it is not my first visit to Cincinnati. Indeed as some may know, this marks my fourth visit among you, and I am indeed pleased to return again; although in all honesty there are some who might tell you that my feelings on this subject may have been expressed in somewhat different terms upon the completion of my first visit. Some of you may not be aware of the story of my first adventure here back in 1855, and I believe that it is worth recounting so as to at least clear up any misleading or misunderstood statements that I have may have had the misfortune to have made back then." He paused for just a moment, for dramatic effect, sipping some water.

"When I first came to your city I was but a poor and struggling lawyer from Springfield, Illinois. The man who would one day become my secretary of war aptly, if not kindly, described me at the time as 'a gawky, long-armed ape'." Abe smiled broadly as laughter circulated through the crowd. "I was here to take part in an important case, at least important to me as I needed to make some money in the worst way! But yes, important to others as well. Especially I suppose to the conflicting parties, the Cyrus McCormick Company of Chicago to the north, and the Manny Company of Rockford, Illinois to the west. Now I am not going to bore you here and now with the details of this case, but let me just say there were many folks who had much riding on the outcome, especially several well-known lawyers, far better known than myself at the time. They were all staying over at the Burnet House, where I am happy to report Mary and I are greatly looking forward to enjoying ourselves this evening. But back then it was of course much too rich for my blood, so I spent the week as a guest of Mr. and Mrs. William Dickson, these fine people here with us again today, a good lawyer in his own right, and gracious enough to put up with me, mostly as Mrs. Dickson is a cousin of Mary's." Abe turned and nodded to his wife and extended family. The crowd politely applauded as Mr. Dickson doffed his hat.

"Again, without boring you with too many details, it seems that the other lawyers did not share my interest in the case, which is to say that they did not have any interest in *my* being involved. Which is why that it was almost by accident that I even discovered that the trial had been moved from Chicago here to Cincinnati. I decided I had better get on over here to find out what was going on. As I alluded earlier, Mr. Stanton and his associates were none too glad to see me, as you can tell from his colorful description of myself. I will tell you that I did remind the secretary of this fact more than once during cabinet meetings!"

Once more, he paused for the laughter to subside. "I was informed, that not only would I not be speaking in any proceedings, that further I was not even welcome to sit in the courtroom with my fellow lawyers. Understand this was not the opposition but the gentlemen who shared my side! All of the work and preparation I had done was for naught. Well, friends, as I found myself completely excluded from the proceedings, I proceeded to use my time to wander your fair city. I moved about, quite unknown to anyone, but must confess I was mostly in a state of depression and melancholy over the entire affair, and would not have been good company for anyone in any case. I did, however, have the great opportunity to explore extensively, and one afternoon even entered the gates of Belmont, exchanging a few words with the honorable resident of that grand estate, Mr. Nicholas Longworth. I must report that when I asked him on that occasion, 'Might a stranger be permitted to walk through your grounds and conservatories?', I believed him to be the gardener, not the occupant!" This brought on the loudest laughter of the day.

"Well, at the end of my week I told my hosts, 'You have made my stay here most agreeable, and I am a thousand times obliged to you. But in reply to your request for me to come again I must say to you, I never expect to be in Cincinnati again. I have nothing against the city, but things have so happened here as to make it undesirable for me ever to return.' But fine people, he quickly added before the crowd could react, there is much more to the story. I am happy to report that I indeed did return, and spent a very enjoyable three days in September of 1859, and on that occasion I did have the good fortune to occupy a fine room at the Burnet House. And I can tell you after my travels abroad that it is truly one of the finest hotels anywhere in the world. I remember clearly that I had the extreme pleasure of addressing a gathering similar to this one over at the Fifth Street Market. Any unpleasant previous experiences were completely purged and forgotten.

"And then again, on my fifty-second birthday, as I was traveling with our beloved Tad to Washington, an even larger crowd of your citizens came out to welcome us and to help celebrate. I recall fondly that at a reception – again at the Burnet House – so many came to greet me and shake my hand that we were up until an hour I do not care to report. When I departed the next morning, I recalled what I had said after my first visit, and I exclaimed to Tad, 'I cannot wait until I am so fortunate to return again to Porkopolis!'" The crowd erupted into a frenzy, from which they could not be quieted. It appeared that he had won them over, or at least the greatest part.

Abe turned and motioned for Mary to step forward, along with the mayor, and the three of them stood waving to the crowd for several minutes more. There were a number of photographers present to record the event, just as there had been in Indianapolis. With several thousand professional photographers scattered across the county they were now a common presence. As he posed for the cameras he thought back to what a novelty photography had been when he first entered the White House. Now, as he was such a distinctive and popular subject, Abraham Lincoln had become the most photographed person in the world.

After final handshakes with all on those on the platform, the honored guests made their way down to a carriage waiting on the other side of the train car. With the Dicksons joining them, they Lincolns quickly departed for the short trip to the Burnet House, while people gathered all along the way. A small contingent of police walked alongside the slowly moving carriage, keeping a watchful eye on the crowds. After the four of them enjoyed a private lunch at the hotel, Abe and Mary remounted the carriage for the journey to the ball field.

They were accompanied by Superintendent Snelbaker, whose job it was to provide personal security for the Lincolns, and their driver, an older colored man named Douglas. They were preceded by a wagon full of police officers. Behind was a second carriage carrying the Dicksons, along with the mayor and his wife, and finally two more wagons of officers. Abe could not help but notice the increased police presence compared to what he had observed during their time in Indianapolis. Kentucky was but a few miles away, and whatever its official allegiance during the War it was a former slave state and thus thought of by many both within and without the state as part of the South. Lincoln had not requested such a large and obvious escort – indeed, he would never have suggested the journey to Mary had he thought such measures necessary – but he felt sure that the mayor had insisted. No politician, at least in the North, would want to take any chances of anything marring a visit by the former president. Abe's only concern was any reaction or worry on Mary's part; but so far, at least, she seemed much too occupied and entertained to notice this detail.

As they made their way to the ball field located just to the north of the city proper, Abe chatted with the two other men in the carriage, frequently pausing to acknowledge the people gathered along the way to see them. "So, tell me, Superintendent Snelbaker, just what should we expect to see today? I recall watching the soldiers playing base ball around Washington during the war, but I must confess I am lacking in much real knowledge of the game."

"Well, Mr. President, if you want to learn about base ball, you have come to the right place. As I am sure you are aware, we had the first professional team right here in Cincinnati back in '69. But I must honestly confess that I am not the one you want advising you on this subject. That would be Douglas here. I have come to be very aware after often riding in his carriage over the last couple of years that he is much more of an expert than I."

"Is that so? Well it is indeed our good fortune then, isn't it, Mary?" His wife smiled politely, slightly adjusting the red hat that she had specifically selected for this afternoon's game. "Douglas, what would you share with us in preparation of this coming event? I place myself in your hands."

If the driver had felt any awe regarding his passengers, it was quickly overcome as he warmed to his subject. "Well, Mr. President, meaning no disrespect and all, but it's hard for me to get excited about any of this today. Understand, there is nobody alive who enjoys a good ball game more than me, especially on a fine spring day right here in Cincinnati. No sir. But this bunch that's playing today, especially that Mr. Harry Wright, well that don't give me no prospect of pleasure at all."

Abe could not help but be amused. "And please tell me, Douglas why that should be?"

"Well, sir, you may not a known but back in '69, Mr. Wright started the

Cincinnati Red Stockings, and just like the superintendent here said they was the first professional base ball team of any kind, anywhere. And there was nobody that could beat 'em. They traveled all over the country, playing anybody and everybody, fifty-seven games, and never lost a one of 'em. I was *there*, right where we are heading out to today, for their very first game."

"You certainly seem to be a true base ball man, Douglas. But again, why so much displeasure in regards to this particular occasion?"

"I'm just coming 'round to that now, sir. After that first season, it seemed like nobody around here wanted to play them no more just for the pleasure of losing, and it was getting too expensive to keep traveling all over the place to find teams they ain't beaten yet, so they just shut it all down. At least that's what some would have you believe. But then the next thing you know, ol' Harry and most of his boys show up in Boston, and the worst part was, they started calling their selves the *Boston Red Stockings*! I mean, can you believe that? At leas' they coulda come up with some other name. *That's* what really sticks in my craw. And guess who we're a going to see today? That's right, the Boston Red Stockings and old Mr. Harry Wright. Back here just to show off. I can't tell you how much that burns me up!"

Snelbaker quickly interrupted, "Now Douglas, I'm sure that there are others who might share your opinion, but in fact Mr. Wright has brought his team here to help raise interest in getting another team started. Now that professional base ball is starting to get organized there are several local leaders who believe that we should be a part of it. I'm sure that you would be in favor of another professional team here in Cincinnati. Whatever you do, don't let the mayor overhear such comments!"

Douglas did not hesitate, "It shouldn't be a matter of no new team. We shoulda had our team all along. There should be only one Red Stockings, and they should be right here in Cincinnati!"

Abe reflected, chuckling, "If your local team plays with the same passion that you exhibit, Douglas, I believe the Boston team will be in for a long afternoon. I must say that I am greatly looking forward to this contest. And

Douglas, I want you right by our side for the whole affair. You can help me to understand the finer points of this game. I may have to organize an effort to start a team back in Springfield."

It was not long until they arrived and paraded onto the grounds, already crowded with spectators. The Lincolns' presence only added to what would have already been a well-attended event. Much like Douglas, many local citizens were hungry for the return of a professional team to their city. Douglas pulled the carriage up behind a special platform along the first base side that had been erected specifically for their use that day, decorated in the customary red, white and blue bunting hung across the front. Douglas drove the carriage on away, to park and attend to the horses, with assurances that he would join Mr. Lincoln directly.

The superintendent helped the Lincolns up the steps onto the platform, which rose a good five feet above the field, providing an excellent viewing perspective to observe the proceedings. The rest of the party joined them, seated to their rear except for the mayor who sat to the president's right on the front row. Abe, without hesitation, requested that this chair be offered to Douglas, which caused some momentary discomfort for the mayor. Not only was he being asked to give up the prized position right beside the honored guest – and for a colored man at that! – but alas there were no extra seats and inadequate space on the platform even if one should be located. Mr. Dickson quickly came to the mayor's rescue by offering to stand. The mayor graciously accepted this offer, but could not keep from giving his own wife a rather pained glance as he was seated.

Abe immediately was taken with the fragrance of the grass and the sight of the brilliant green set off by the white lines that had been laid out on the field. The crowd of people gathered to watch the game had completely surrounded the entire playing area. The players were already on the field, tossing balls to each other, preparing for the contest. It was easy to spot the Boston team as it indeed wore the signature bright red stockings, along with red caps. The local team sported red as well, but minus the stockings, and overall theirs was a much more drab appearance. Abe quickly noticed one other difference between the teams. He was about to comment on it to Mary, who was much too busy waving to the crowd and chatting with her cousin about the variety of finery sported by the women in it to notice anything about the players. It was just then that Douglas made his way onto the platform and was directed to the waiting seat beside Lincoln. He appeared noticeably uncomfortable for a moment as he looked at the empty chair and then the white man standing to the side. Without saying anything to draw more attention, Mr. Dickson motioned to Douglas to be seated, so he proceeded to do so. Before Abe could welcome him or make his inquiry, Douglas quickly stood back up.

"Well I'll be switched. Are my old eyes playing tricks on me? By the Almighty, they're wearing gloves! Would you look at that? Now I ask you, have you ever seen such a thing?" Douglas fell back down into his chair.

This was exactly what Abe had noticed. The Boston players were all wearing what appeared to be small leather gloves on each hand. The Cincinnati team sported no such thing.

"I was just about to ask about that, Douglas. I don't remember the soldiers wearing anything on their hands when they played ball."

"No sir! And no *real* ball player would wear such a thing, neither. I heard some talk about players actually wearing gloves on their hands, but I surely didn't believe none of it 'til now. I guess it's supposed to make it easier to catch the ball somehow, but I never expected to see such a thing today, no sir. I guess this is just a little trick that old Mr. Harry Wright has cooked up for us."

The attendant stationed on the platform to guard the stairs spoke up and said, "Excuse me, but if you please, I was talking to one of the players earlier, and he was telling me that some of the professional players have just started using gloves this season and it's beginning to catch on. He said he was sure that all of the players would be using them before long. He said that before long you won't even see a player without them."

Douglas just grunted, which caused Abe to chuckle and then comment,

"Change is a hard thing to take, isn't it, Douglas?"

The afternoon went by quickly. Mary enjoyed watching the crowd and visiting with her cousin, paying little attention to the actual game. The mayor enjoyed being seen with his important visitor, even if seated behind the former president. The superintendent enjoyed watching all of his men occupied with their various duties, and if he observed otherwise, quickly sent a stern reminder to the offender. Abe greatly enjoyed the ball game itself, particularly with the running commentary and constant criticism offered by Douglas. Abe could not remember when he had enjoyed such a merry and care-free afternoon. The police guards prevented any of the spectators from coming near enough to bother the party, but there were continuous shouts of, "Howdy, Abe" or such similar remarks all throughout the afternoon. All in all, it could not have been a more perfect day. Abe could only wonder if it would be much the same at the racetrack in Louisville, and then to marvel to himself how he was becoming quite the sports enthusiast.

That night, after a lavish dinner party attended by the mayor and the required assortment of other local politicians and business leaders, the Lincolns were finally left to themselves to enjoy their accommodations. The Burnet House was indeed one of the finest hotels in which they had stayed, and their room – of course the best in the house – was both lovely and quite spacious. Abe again could only think back to his first visit, when he could never have afforded such luxury.

"Mary, I trust you have had an enjoyable day and a good visit with Mrs. Dickson. They both seemed well and in good spirits. But I fear perhaps it has all been too much for you. You looked somewhat tired and withdrawn at dinner."

"No, dear husband, I am quite well." She smiled warmly. "It has been a merry day, and I dare say an afternoon out in the sun has done us both well. As far as dinner, there were far too many people present who enjoyed the sound of their own voices for me to interject mine. I find that at such events it is much better to sit back and observe than to participate. On such occasions I am more than willing to be your silent partner."

Abe mused that he sometimes forgot how wise and observant his wife could be. "Well I think that is fine, and very astute. I should probably observe a similar approach at times. Just as long as you are not over-extended, for we still have much to do and see. Of course tomorrow, it is on to Lexington, your home. How it will all have changed, I am sure. But I am just as sure they will not have forgotten you, my dear."

"Oh how you *do* go on." Mary waved an imaginary fan as she might have when they were courting. "I wouldn't be surprised if they don't even notice us. But – it will be good to see the old town again."

Her husband smiled, realizing that she was not in any way aware of the wire he had received from Lexington and the welcome that awaited them there. But it was time to settle for the evening and no reason to agitate her with any further anticipation. It would indeed be a big day for her tomorrow. But still, he could not help but wonder and worry just how long her sunny disposition could last.

CHAPTER TEN

AT that precise moment, seventy-five miles down the Ohio River, Meriwether Lewis Clark, Jr., was in his home on the south side of Louisville, retired for the evening but still so very far from sleep. It was Tuesday evening. Opening day was on Monday, now less than a week away. Everything would be ready – that much at least was now certain. The barns were full of horses, all to be out on the track early the next morning for training. So far the horsemen had been pleased. The main construction was done, with just a few refinements and adornments left to be added. *Yes*, he told himself, he *had* done it, at least as far as building the facility. But there was still so very much to be done. Especially since now it was known, not just around the city or the state, but the entire country, that Lincoln was coming to Louisville to attend the Kentucky Derby!

Long before the news had circulated, Clark correctly anticipated that all of the important local people would be in attendance on Opening Day, and certainly many from throughout the state, especially the Bluegrass. But now the Derby had become the focus of the attention of people from elsewhere as well. Last minute requests for tickets had come pouring in, and this after Clark had for all intents and purposes made his final plans for seating all of the expected Association members, the guests and dignitaries. Even though he had been so hopeful, in this instance his melancholy nature had gotten the better of his obsession with details, and he had not allowed himself to prepare a practical plan for Lincoln's attendance. Now he was struggling to come up with one at the eleventh hour.

Clark had of course held two seats for the former president and his wife, but that had turned out to be oh-so-woefully inadequate. He had finally been forced to turn over all other matters to his assistants: the final transportation plans, the all-important last meetings with the breweries and other vendors, the control of the bookmakers, security arrangements – so many other details with which he had fully intended to deal personally. Now he would have to depend upon these others to make sure all of this was done properly. And that was no easy task for someone with Clark's nature and disposition. When not in control he could not help but worry himself that much more. But now he was forced to focus all of his final energies on accommodating everyone, trying to figure out just where to put them all.

As he lay awake in another of what seemed an endless number of nights, he had to remind himself that he could have worse problems. What if no one were coming? But that notion was quickly shaken from Clark's head by the one concern that would not let him be: the weather. What if it rained? What if it stormed? Kentucky weather in May could be so unpredictable. What had he been thinking? It could all still turn into a disaster from which they would never recover!

THREE miles to the south, in the barn area of the new racetrack, Charlie Apple and his brother were about to call it a night. Crabby, having completed his final check on the General's horses, had just returned to the small tack room which housed two cots, therefore making this space what the brothers currently called "home." Charlie was already lying in his bed, watching his brother slowly remove his well-worn boots and then strip off his shirt and trousers. They were beginning their second week in this new environment, mostly settled in. It was not as *luxurious* as their room at the Fairgrounds, but it would do for now. Certainly better than up above the stalls, where Peanut and Calvin slept. Crabby in particular refused to sleep up there. Some grooms preferred it, but not he. Despite his long and daily association with horses he couldn't stand the smell. Even though they were still in the barn, and to the average nose there would be no noticeable difference, there definitely was to him. Charlie, on the other hand, could not have cared less. A bed was a bed – as long as it was off the ground he could sleep most anywhere.

Of course grooms like Crabby, white or colored, had to stay with their horses. The jockeys had other choices, but with most of them being colored it could be a challenge for them to find housing that would take them in. Many had found accommodations with families in "Smoketown." Originally settled by Germans, the neighborhood name derived from the large number of brick kilns in that part of town. After the War freed slaves began to settle there until now it had become the largest predominantly black community on the south side of the city, about three miles from the track. In fact, so many colored riders had come to work at the new track that Clark was forced to arrange for wagons to transport them each day to Smoketown, leaving the track in the late afternoon, and then picking them up at 4:30 again the next morning to return in time for training.

AT that moment Oliver and Bug Eye were already sound asleep in warm beds, snoring away in a small room at Oliver's cousin's house in Smoketown. In contrast to the diminutive jockey, his cousin Marcus was a big man – six foot-two and 280 pounds – which served him well at the anvil of the blacksmith shop where he worked. The shop was owned by a colored man named Thomas, and like most of the few black-owned businesses in Louisville it was located on Preston Street, a few blocks to the north of Smoketown.

The contingent from New Orleans had all first arrived in Louisville late in the afternoon on the preceding Monday, May the third. Without much for the jockeys to do that day, Oliver had guided Bug Eye to the house in Smoketown, where the cousins were reunited and Marcus was introduced to Bug Eye. This odd-looking little man with his trick eyes completely fascinated the smithy, and Bug Eve had instantly proved a great source of endless entertainment for Marcus' two small children as well. Marcus could not wait to introduce his guests, and particularly Bug Eye, to his friends and co-workers.

That chance came the next day. In the morning the horses had all been sent out to walk a little on the track, allowing them get a feel for their new environment. This resulted in a light schedule of work for both riders, making it possible for Oliver and Bug Eye to arrive back in town by noon. They stopped by the house to pick up a basket of food that Marcus' wife Bev had packed for them. Then the two men proceeded over to meet Marcus at the shop. After showing his guests around and introducing them to Mr. Thomas and the other workers – and having Bug Eye demonstrate his special talent to the hoot and holler of all – Marcus led the two of them to a favorite spot on the banks of nearby Beargrass Creek, to relax and enjoy their lunch. After finishing every bite of the cold chicken, and bread and cheese – mostly consumed by Marcus – the three men laid in the grass by the creek, soaking up the warm spring mid-day sunshine.

"So what do you think of this new racetrack they done built?" Marcus posed to neither man in particular, lying with his eyes closed and chewing on a blade of grass.

"Ain't really ridden on it yet, and that's the main thing," his cousin replied. "I need to get out there and see what kinda bounce it's got. What it *feels* like. But I guess it looks okay."

"Everything sure is new and purty," Bug Eye chimed in after a few moments of silence. "It's just gonna be new this one time, so I guess it's kinda nice to be able to enjoy that. Them barns just sparkle. But that won't last long with them horses around," he added, sitting up, laughing. "What talk do you hear 'bout it all, Marcus? Anybody 'round here care that they even built it?"

"Hell, yes." The big man pushed himself up on his hands. "I mean to say that's about all anybody's talking about around the shop. The word is that this man Clark's gone and done a real good job; built him a fine place. Course I ain't seen it for myself, but that's what I heard." Pausing for a moment he then added, "That and of course that President Lincoln's coming. Now *that's* surely real big news round here." He eased back down in the grass and closed his eyes against the sun.

Bug Eye started to get excited. "Yes sir. I'm gonna have to go and find me a good horse so Mr. Lincoln can see me ride. I wanna be right out there in front when I go by so I can flash him the bug eye. He surely won't never forget me then. No sir!" They had a good laugh at the thought of it.

"What about you, Ollie?" Marcus asked after a prolonged silence. "You got any good prospects for when Lincoln's gonna be watching?"

"I'm not sure about that yet. I ain't seen any schedule so far, and Old Tom ain't told me nuthin. We'll have some horses running, that's for sure, but don't know if they'll be anything for me on that first day or not." He turned and looked at Bug Eye. "You heard anything that I ain't?"

"All I knows is that we gotta be there bright'n' early tomorrow morning to start getting them horses ready. Ready for what and for when I ain't got no idea. I guess Old Tom'll tell us when he's good and ready."

Marcus opened his eyes again, and grunting a little, sat up. "Well all I know is that I'm gonna be there, one way or another. Wouldn't miss it. They'll be talking 'bout that day for a long time around here." He paused, took a deep breath, and then struggling to stand up added, "That and I'd better be getting the hell back to the shop before Thomas tells me I don't need to bother comin' back at all. I gotta get some extra work done so I's can go and watch them hosses run! Come on, walk me back over to the shop, boys."

The three of them retraced their steps to Preston Street and then Oliver and Bug Eye made their goodbyes, but not until after the workers demanded to see Bug Eye in action one last time. The two riders decided to take advantage of their afternoon off to see more of the city. They took a leisurely stroll all the way down to the river, sat and watched the boats and the bustle of the busy river port for a while, then made their way back to Smoketown. They knew not to get too used to having time to spare. No more days off now. It was time to get busy.

IF the two men had been a little more observant, they might have noticed Alexander Delacroix standing outside the Galt House on Main Street as they passed by on that late Tuesday afternoon, setting out on their walk home. Overlooking the Ohio River, it was Louisville's grandest hotel; so naturally it was where Alex had registered for his first visit to the city, managing to secure one of the last rooms snapped up in the frenzy that accompanied the news of Lincoln's attendance. He certainly noticed Oliver and Bug Eye, wondering what in the world they were doing apparently wandering the streets at that time of day. But it was not his concern. It did remind him, however, that he very much wanted to find Peanut and Calvin, and of course Charlie and Crabby. But that could wait until tomorrow. For now he was searching for a gentleman with long grey hair wearing a brown suit and matching bowler.

Shortly after settling into his room upon his arrival that day, Alex had returned to the lobby. Looking around he had quickly spotted a boy of about fourteen, immediately recognizing that – much like Alex himself at that age – the boy would know the kind of places and the types of people in which Alex would be interested. In return for a well-invested dollar the boy had told Alex that this grey-haired man was someone who could gain Alex access to the best poker game in town, something he greatly desired at that moment. Not for a need of funds, mind you. Quite the contrary, Alex had done very well for himself in a game on the train north, and currently found himself in possession of monetary resources far exceeding what he had anticipated. No, this need had more to do with providing a mental break for the evening. His mind had been focused so totally for this past week, from the very moment he had first received the news about Lincoln. Which is why he had surprised even himself with his exceedingly good fortune on the train. Alex had given the game at hand far less than his usual attention, normally a sure sign of disaster. But these particular gentlemen had been so inept – not to mention so wealthy – that he had taken them completely while devoting only a small portion of his faculties.

His plan had started to formulate itself at once. It would be so simple. All he required was some poor sap with a weakness that could be exploited, someone fairly recognizable around the racetrack, familiar with its basic lay-out, willing to carry out the act itself. People and racetracks being what they are, and considering the resources he was willing to invest to accomplish his goal, he expected little trouble in locating such a person. Charlie Apple would be of invaluable assistance in this regard. Then it was only a matter of a momentary diversion of what he was sure would be an insignificant security detail, which he was quite confident Peanut and Calvin could easily and willingly handle. In the heat of the moment conditions would be such that everyone would be focused on the race at hand, thus providing the perfect opportunity.

Finally, but most importantly to Alex, the vast openness of the track made it a practical matter for him to orchestrate and set in motion what he considered a most noble act, and then simply to stroll away, completely undetected, able to so enjoy the ensuring chaos. By the time anyone knew what had happened he would be miles away, settled into his compartment on the late afternoon train heading down to Nashville, and eventually New Orleans. As for the poor sap...well Calvin would be close by with an inconspicuous razor ready to end any possibility of further connections or danger to Alex. The rest would all simply disappear into the normal routine of the barns as if nothing unusual had occurred. Opportunities existed for those who knew how to use them, and to a man like Alex this one was golden.

Alex had been momentarily distracted by a young petite blond girl, an obvious prostitute, most probably like himself from another city come to take advantage of the gathering wealth. He had a passing realization that she could be just as effective a distraction from his own thoughts, when he suddenly noticed the man in the brown suit walking toward the hotel. It was a different lust for the game, indeed the seduction of the gamble that caused him to lose all interest in the girl. As the man neared and then entered the Galt House, Alex promptly followed him in.

"Pardon me, sir," Alex spoke coming up behind the other man. "I have it on good authority that you are someone with whom I have great interest in becoming acquainted." The man stopped in the middle of the lobby and turned to face Alex with a questioning look. "You see, I am a card player by nature, and I come with full pockets." He held out a double eagle, which the man immediately pocketed. He said nothing, simply smiled at Alex and then turned and headed to the stairs, with his new friend following behind.

TWO floors above, H. P. McGrath was in a late-afternoon meeting with his trainer, Ansel Williamson, discussing the upcoming Kentucky Derby. Ansel had brought Chesapeake and a few other horses over from the Association track in Lexington the previous Saturday. As soon as they were all settled to his satisfaction, the old man went out and walked the entire track. He wanted to feel what this new surface was like, indeed how it would feel to his horses. He had learned many years ago not to take any chances, and certainly not to trust the judgment of some white man he didn't know intimately. He gazed up at the new grandstand, with its cupolas on each end and single spire directly in the middle, pennants already flying in the afternoon breeze. He imagined the scene that was now just a few days off, with the structure crammed full of people, the noise of the crowd rising. He then slowly turned and looked across the inside expanse of open land in the middle of the tracks, and then on across to the north, to the open fields and trees. It was a nice place for a racetrack. He liked it here just fine.

One of the other horses Ansel had brought to Louisville was a small chestnut colt who was the grandson of Lexington, a legendary racehorse and one of the greatest sires in history, easily the best of the mid-nineteenth century. But so far his grandson Aristides had shown mixed results as a racehorse. True enough, in nine starts as a two-year-old he had won three times and placed three more, capturing the Thespian Stakes at Saratoga. But then he had looked completely uninspired finishing unplaced in the Saratoga Stakes. After a layoff, Ansel had worked long and hard with the colt as a three-year-old and had determined that Aristides was definitely a sprinter, and would do much better in shorter races. Normally this horse would have no business running in a mile and a half race like the Derby. But Ansel needed him.

It looked like there would be at least a dozen horses starting the Derby, and maybe as many as sixteen or seventeen. The problem was there did not appear to be any real early speed in the race. Ansel couldn't see where any of the other horses could be counted on to get out and set a fast pace. It was true that the General was going to run McCreary, always a front runner; but Ansel had heard that the horse was not sound. He didn't want to take any chances as Chesapeake definitely needed a good honest pace in the early part of the race to set up his closing "come-from-behind" style. He had decided that if Mc-Grath really wanted to win this race, the only practical solution was to enter Aristides as a "rabbit" to set a fast pace which the other horses would hopefully chase, thus setting the race up perfectly for his stable mate. McGrath had easily agreed to the scheme, and had promptly paid the necessary fees to make the horse eligible.

McGrath had just arrived that afternoon, the meeting with his trainer the first item on his agenda. The two men sat in McGrath's hotel room, and while the owner sipped a glass of bourbon Ansel gave him a full report.

"The horses are sound, eating good, especially Aristides. I swear he's been working like he's got something to prove. Seems to like this new track. Chesapeake's been a little slower to take a liking to it, but he seemed better this morning." He paused for a moment, and then added almost as an afterthought, "I think we should look at running Aristides back after the Derby, on the last day of the meet. I've got him working so as the Derby will be a good romp for him, and then he should be ready to really roll the next time. Might as well try to do something productive with him since he's here."

"I'm sure you do, and that all sounds fine," McGrath replied as he looked hard at his trainer. "But what about Chesapeake? You're sure he's going to be ready? I haven't spent all this time and money to come here and lose."

"Now don't you worry none, Mr. McGrath. Everything is going along accordingly. The horse is looking good in the morning; you'll see for yourself tomorrow. He's sound, he's right on schedule, and from here on out there's not much else we can do. Just try and keep him happy and fit for the next two weeks. You surely know that yourself. With Aristides out there in front, making all them others chase after him, we've set the stage as best we can. Now it's mostly up to the horse. If he don't wanna win it, there ain't much we can do about it. But I promise you, we'll do everything we can to give him that chance. I've already gone over everything with William and will again. He knows what to do. Like I said, now it's all up to that horse."

"You're sure Henry's the best rider for the horse? I can get us any jockey you want."

"Now, Mr. McGrath, that wouldn't be fair to William. And besides, he knows the horse. He's won with him before. Like I said we want to keep the horse happy, and he likes William. Don't wanna go and be making any last-minute changes like that."

"Yes, I know that Ansel. I do. It's just that I want to win this race more than any in a long time. I just want to make sure we're doing everything we can."

"Yes, sir. I know that. And so does William. I've told him how much this means to you. He'll do his best."

"And I know you will, too, Ansel. You always do. You've never let me down so far." He couldn't resist adding, "Don't you start now." The two men shared a quick laugh.

McGrath finished his bourbon, and then just as Ansel was starting to stand to leave, thought to ask, "What about Aristides, who do you want to ride him? It's just a shame that Swim can't ride him again. He's done so well in the past. I think that horse really takes to him."

"True enough, I sure wish Bobby was well enough to ride. But we can't do nuthin 'bout that now." The old man paused for just a moment, rubbing his chin. "Well, I've have been thinking about it just a little bit." He smiled at his boss, and then sat back down. "Most of the really good riders already have a mount for the race, or can figure out what we're up to and would probably turn us down anyway. I heard about this young boy who rides for the General. Saw him out on the track the last couple of mornings and I like the looks of him. He's been down in New Orleans but is from over around Lexington.

Asked Old Tom and he says that the boy knows his stuff. Knows how to follow instructions. Says we can trust him. I think he could be a good fit for what we need."

"What his name?"

"Lewis. Oliver Lewis."

"Well, if that's who you want I'll send a note to the General and ask about using him."

"Don't need to do that. You can ask him in the morning. He got here yesterday. Got a filly they're gonna run in the Oaks. And they're gonna run a horse in the Derby, too, but you don't need to worry none about that. Old Tom tells me that horse'll be lucky to finish the race."

McGrath laughed again. "I see that as usual you are on top of everything Ansel. I'll let you know tomorrow."

The old man stood up and headed to the door, adding "I sure do try to be. Ain't gonna let nothing sneak up on me. Not if I can help it anyway. You have a good evening, Mr. McGrath. Don't drink too much of that bourbon. I'll expect you bright and early in the morning." And with that he was gone.

JUST as the old trainer walked out of the rear of the Galt House to mount his horse for the half-hour ride south to the track, Peanut and Calvin were walking into one of the seediest taverns catering to Negroes in the city. The pair had made their way up to Louisville a week after the General's contingent and had only been in town now for a couple of days. Still they had already managed to get themselves banned from what could be called the "finer" establishments. The very first night Calvin had gotten into a knife fight with two men, sending one home with several nasty but ultimately non-life-threatening wounds. The second quickly decided it would be against his best interest to continue the altercation. It had all started because one of the men had made a disparaging remark about New Orleans when Peanut had mentioned that they had just arrived from that city. The fact that Calvin held no particular regard for the Crescent City and had, in fact, been known to make severely disparaging remarks himself, never entered his mind. He just didn't like the look of the two men, and found them to be irritating, although if he had been pressed on the issue, could not have given any exact cause for the said irritation. Knowing that it would be a light morning at the track the next day, they had gotten exceedingly drunk, which only served to increase Calvin's "sensitivity."

So far neither man had formed any strong opinions about the city, or the new racetrack for that matter. It was just another in a long string of places they had lived and worked. Peanut did appreciate that it was a bit cooler than New Orleans, and actually did enjoy the rural setting of the racetrack. Calvin felt too far removed from the city, even though it was just a short ride away. But after his actions of the previous night, he had decided that the safest thing would be to purchase an adequate supply of the cheap liquor he would require for the immediate future, and then simply settle into his assigned quarters with no designs of returning to the city. As long as there were dice players around the barns he would have all the excitement that he needed, at least for the time being. Best to keep his nose as clean as possible now anyway. He didn't want to get thrown into no jail up here no-way. No telling what they might do to a colored boy they didn't know. He was already hoping to be back in New Orleans in a couple of weeks. The two men had a single drink, procured what they required, and headed back to the track. If anyone recognized them, or associated them with the previous evening's violence, they never knew it.

ALEX had already won several hundred dollars, and it was only ten o'clock. He and the five other men were taking a short break from the game to refresh themselves and to have a quick bite to eat. Food had been sent up to the room, compliments of the hotel. The man in the brown suit had paid a premium rate to locate the game there, and had arranged for all the required amenities so that the players would lack for nothing during their evening.

Alex stood looking out the single window in the fourth floor room, which offered a view over the river, eating a piece of bread with a thick slice of cheese. A man who had generously "donated" much of Alex's winnings walked over to him. He ate nothing, but drank continuously from a container of brandy, which helped at least partially to explain his complete lack of success at cards.

"I mus' compliment you on your skill," the man offered to Alex, slightly slurring his words. "I hope for my sake that things may change before the evening is over."

"Just good luck, sir. Just good luck. I am sure both mine and your fortunes will change shortly." Alex smiled, thinking of how quickly he would be able and more than happy to relieve the man of any and all of his remaining funds.

"Let me formally introduce myself. I am James Owens, down the river from Pittsburgh. I often come to this city, but have never seen you before. I can tell from your voice that you are mos' assuredly from points south, if I am not mistaken."

"And you are not. New Orleans to be exact. A horse player, come up to find out more about this new Derby that Mr. Clark is starting."

With that another of the players quickly turned and looked at Alex. "Clark, is it? That's all I have been hearing lately. That man has the whole town abuzz. But I tell you here and now sir, he will fall flat on his face. I don't care who he has with him on this latest venture. I've known his family for years, and I tell you that man is not right. Anybody that goes into business with him is just asking for failure. He is nothing but an embarrassment to the fine name of his grandfather and great uncle."

Another of the men who had been at the table added, "I'm sure it is the result of that Irish blood that runs through his veins, from his mother's side I hear. There may not be much, but then it doesn't take much Irish blood to ruin a man now, does it?" Everyone in the room joined the man in a chuckle.

Looking at Alex and Owens, the first man continued, "You gentlemen who are not from these parts would not be aware, but let me tell you that Clark is the touchiest man I have ever met. Totally unbalanced. Just impossible to deal with. But somehow, he has managed to fool the people of this city. We had a good plan to build a new track over down by the river – would have been a sweet deal for everybody. But old Clark managed to fool them all into following him. When they came asking me to join in their venture I just laughed in their faces. Told them exactly what I think of Clark. They may all be fooled, but not I. They can have their racetrack and their *Kentucky* Derby. I tell you it will all blow up in their faces." After pausing momentarily, he added, "And now they've even managed to get Lincoln here. Well, gentlemen, let me just say that it should be an interesting pair, Lincoln's crazy wife and Clark in the same room. That, I have to admit, might be something interesting to see." Everyone laughed again, but this time it had an even uglier tone.

So Clark was Irish, was he? Alex mused, not even bothering to consider whether there might be any truth to the tale. Even better! He could kill Lincoln and avenge the South, and at the same time completely embarrass this Irishman Clark. It was too good to be true. Just another sign, he felt, that he was traveling the right and proper road.

Owen spoke up and said, "Gentlemen, I don't know much about horse racing, or Mr. Clark, and to be honest I don't care all that much either about Mr. Lincoln or his crazy wife. But I do care about playing cards. I have much money to recover. Shall we?"

With that the conversation ended and each man reclaimed his seat at the table. It was going on 10:30 Alex would play until midnight and no later. He had work to do, and it would start so very early the next morning.

CHAPTER ELEVEN

THE sun was just starting to glow over the horizon as Alex stood in a still-darkened side doorway in the new grandstand. Feeling somewhat groggy from the lack of sleep, but invigorated by the newly acquired money in his suit pocket, he watched two horses galloping down the track, heading east towards the rising sun, each with colored riders aboard. There was still a noticeable spring chill in the air, but already evident that this Wednesday was going to be a warm day. Alex had abandoned his preferred position right by the track in favor of this out-of-sight location. It wasn't so much that he did not want to be seen at all by Charlie Apple, just not immediately. Alex was well aware of the response he would receive, and wanted to avoid it at all costs. It had become apparent to him that he should generally avoid the race-track, and especially the barns during the morning – or more specifically, limit his contact with the people he knew who worked there. So now he stood waiting, all the way at the opposite end of the grandstand farthest from the barns.

Several more horses and riders came and went over the next few minutes, with Alex carefully inspecting each. Finally, just before the sun fully appeared he spotted Charlie in his customary red and white jacket riding in his direction. When the grey horse and rider were about thirty feet away, thankfully with no other horses nearby, Alex stepped out of the doorway and walked a few steps toward the fence. He gave a quick whistle and a short wave, and then before Charlie could respond, turned and walked back to the grandstand, knowing that he had achieved his desired effect.

Alex took out a cigarette and lit it, slowly drawing the warm smoke. He rarely indulged in smoking, and scarcely ever a cigar or pipe, his taste (and image) favoring the expensive novelty of French rolled cigarettes. When he did smoke, it was generally a sign of nervousness, which was a major reason he avoided the habit. He did not like others to know what he might be thinking or feeling. But this morning, full of nervous energy, he needed to occupy his time while he waited. After about fifteen minutes he heard footsteps approaching. He stepped half-way out of the door and looked to make sure that it was Charlie heading in his direction. Satisfied, he stepped completely through, still standing in the early morning shadow of the grandstand.

Just as Charlie arrived at the doorway Alex said in a low voice, "Good morning, Charlie. Please do not say anything." This remark indeed almost stopped the younger man in his tracks, smothering his beaming smile and cutting off his usual warm (and rather loud) greeting. "Please follow me," and then Alex quickly added, "quietly".

Once he was sure they were alone Alex turned to Charlie, and this time smiling, again said, "Good morning. Sorry to be so abrupt, but I didn't want anyone to notice our meeting this morning."

"That's okay, Boss. When I saw you a little while ago, I surely was surprised. I didn't know you decided to come up here. When did you do that?" Without waiting for a response he continued, "When you didn't say anything, I figured somethin' must be up. Figured I better get right on down here." He flashed his big grin. "Why you actin' so strange, anyway, don't this place agree with you?"

"That's got nothing to do with it, and I don't have time to chit-chat." He handed Charlie a small piece of paper. "I'll explain everything this afternoon. Meet me at 3:00." Glancing at the paper he added, "I figure you know your way around well enough to find this place. Hell, you've probably been there before. And bring your brother along if you want, if he can get away. I know the two of you like to work together." He turned to leave, and then stopped to add, "And don't tell anyone you've seen me, at least not yet." With that he went around a corner and was gone. Charlie stood there for a moment, frozen in place by the strange encounter. Then as if waking from a dream, he slowly looked down at the small piece of paper he held. Unfolding it, he read the four words written there:

Porter's Old Place
Portland

The previous day, after their first encounter concerning the poker game, Alex had watched the boy in the lobby of the Galt House closely for about half an hour. Alex wanted to be completely sure of himself before inquiring about the next piece of information required. He watched as the boy worked the crowd, and again could only smile as he was so reminded of himself in his youth. Finally, after overcoming any doubts Alex again caught the boy's eye and motioned him over. They stepped out the front doors.

Alex had casually inquired, "Where might a person find a quiet, out-of-the-way place to meet a couple of friends for a drink and a private discussion? The kind of place where one wouldn't be noticed, because no one there would want to be noticed either."

The boy, eagerly accepting a quarter-eagle and thus understanding the serious and private nature of this request, paused for just a moment, placed his new-found wealth into his pocket, and then answered, "Well, if I was you, sir, and didn't want to be noticed by anyone 'round here, I would head on down to this tavern in Portland, just down-river from here." Pausing to look west down the street immediately in front of the hotel, he continued, "Just head right on out Main Street here and keep on a going 'bout four miles or so. It'll become the main road into Portland, and then you'll run right into it. Just a block from the river, old green building, looking pretty rough now. Used to be run by the famous Jim Porter, tallest man anyone ever seen. Drew a lot of folks just to see him, but after he died most quit going. Nobody reputable goes down there anymore, at least not from around here. Should suit you nicely. It goes by some other name now, but everybody still calls it 'Porter's

Old Place.' Main thing, look for a big door, taller than you ever seen in such a place. Porter had that door made special, just for him." Pausing, the boy drew himself up just a bit. "If you should need anything at all, just tell the proprietor that Tommy at the Galt House sent you."

Alex smiled warmly, and passing along another small gold coin said, "Thank you, Tommy. That sounds perfect, just the place. There may be another thing or two I need during my visit, business I have to conduct; *private* business. I trust you will keep our conversations just between the two of us. I need someone here that I know I can count on."

"Yes sir, you can certainly count on me for *anything* you need." He made sure to emphasize the word with a worldly smile. "You just let me know. You can just about always find me here."

After an early dinner, Alex rode down to Portland to check everything out for himself. It was just as Tommy had described it: dark, private, a place where nobody wanted to know who you were or what you might be doing there. He did not stay for long, as he definitely stood out in his fine attire. The regular patrons took one look and decided that he was probably just another tourist, curious about the world's tallest man. When he turned and left, they lost any interest in him and resumed their poker game as if he had never been there at all.

FOR once Alex was not wearing his customary linen suit. Quite the opposite, he was now dressed in old stained workpants and a worn shirt, items he literally had picked up from behind a shack of a house on the southern edge of town as he returned from the track that morning. He looked as though he had just gotten off work from a job involving intense manual labor, which was of course the intended effect. He almost felt that way as well, fatigue from lack of sleep setting in. He could sleep tonight, he thought, and tomorrow as well as far as that goes. But now he had business, important business. It was 2:45 on that Wednesday afternoon when he walked into Porter's the second time.

In his current attire, no one would possibly recognize him as the same gentleman who had briefly wandered in the previous evening. This time he blended in perfectly. He sat in the corner of the darkened room at the far end from the oversized doorway, looking around the large plain space filled with worn tables and chairs. It had been sixteen years since the giant had died and his former establishment had definitely taken on a seedy feel since Lincoln's visit all those years ago. Never considered fancy by any means, it would now take some work to rise to the level of shabby. It was the kind of place that Alex ordinarily never even would think of frequenting. He didn't need to. He and his money were quite welcome in much finer establishments. But, he thought again, it was indeed perfect for his immediate requirements.

There were only a handful of people inside the tavern at this mid-afternoon hour, but it was just enough to keep the man working behind the long wooden bar distracted. Alex intentionally occupied this spot primarily so that he could observe everyone else – though careful not to appear to be overly interested – and also since it was a good twenty feet away from the nearest customer. He sat patiently sipping a tall glass of beer, now almost half finished, when the door opened allowing a bright beam of light to enter along with the two men, one noticeably shorter than the other. Out of habit everyone inside looked up to stare at them for a moment, but observing nothing of particular interest then returned to their previous business, primarily the consumption of large amounts of beer.

As soon as his eyes adjusted to the darkened room, Charlie spotted Alex sitting in the far corner. He and his brother slowly walked over, taking in the room around them as they went, noting its few occupants Alex stood up and shook hands, saying nothing, and then motioned to the man behind the bar to bring over two more beers. The three of them sat down as Charlie, sensing the subdued atmosphere, did not smile, simply tossing his hat onto the empty fourth chair at the table. None of them spoke as they waited for the beers to be delivered. Crabby rocked back and forth in his chair, the old wood creaking with each motion. He quickly ceased when a man across the room gave him a stern look.

"Boys, thank you for coming today," Alex said as they both took a sip of lukewarm beer. "I trust you had no problems finding this place."

Charlie did smile slightly now and answered, "You had it figured right – me and Robert have been here more than a time or two, back in the old days. Although I have to say," he added, looking around the room, "I can't say much for how they're keeping the place." Crabby sat staring at Alex.

"Well, that's not our concern, now is it?" Glancing around again at the other occupants Alex continued, "We've got some business to discuss – and I don't mean horse racing business. Charlie, when you told me the other day about coming up to Louisville I had no interest whatsoever in this new track or in this Derby business. In fact, I felt sorry for you having to come up here." With that Crabby made his first sound, giving a short grunt in response, which Alex took as agreement. "But when you told me about Lincoln, about how he was going to be here, well now *that* got me interested. I got to think-ing more and more about how this could be the perfect opportunity to get that son-of-a-bitch. And the more I thought about it, the more I became sure that this *was* the perfect opportunity. So I grabbed a train on up here and have been checking things out for myself. I'm going to finish what Mr. Booth started, and I need your help to do it." Crabby, who had begun mindlessly rocking back in his chair again, suddenly let it drop down with a loud thud. Everyone in the room turned to look.

"Goddamn it!" blurted Alex quietly but angrily. "Why don't you just invite everybody on over to join us?"

"Sorry" was all Crabby could say, looking around the room to make sure that nobody's stare lingered. Then turning back at Alex added, "You just took me a little by surprise."

Before the tension between the two could build, Charlie quickly said, "You sure 'bout this, Boss? I mean, you know you can count on me for anything. But killin' Lincoln? I don't know about that now, that's a little more than fixin' races."

"Relax Charlie, and you, too," Alex said looking at Crabby. He paused for a moment to compose himself, and then continued, "You two don't really have to do much at all. I wouldn't put you at risk. You're too important to me." He smiled slightly, particularly at Crabby. "You're too valuable." Crabby continued to stare back at him with no expression.

"What with all the excitement of the race, it should actually be pretty easy. I'll get Peanut and Calvin to help with the dirty work. You two won't need to be anywhere around. In fact, I want you both back in the barns, going about your normal business." He paused to take another sip of beer, and to let this information set in. "Mostly what I need from you, particularly from you, Charlie, is to help me find the right person to actually do the job. I've been nosing around, and I know there are plenty of people around this town who don't hold our Mr. Lincoln any too highly. First of all, I need somebody who shares our point of view." Charlie nodded in agreement. Crabby just stared at his beer, quietly absorbing everything in his usual fashion.

"Next, I need someone who knows his way around the track, who is a familiar face, who won't stand out just being there. Hopefully, someone who is even expected to be there. And finally, someone who would appreciate a large amount of money, who *needs* that money, and who will be willing to join us in order to acquire it. And the beauty of it is, if we can indeed find the right sort of person, he won't actually cost us much at all. Especially when Calvin ties up any loose ends for us. A small down-payment, and then the fool won't be around to worry about collecting the rest." He paused to give the brothers a smug smile for effect. Charlie now smiled back, nodding slightly as he took in all of this information, knowing full well that Calvin would have no qualms. Crabby now glanced around the room, almost appearing nervous, definitely out-of-character.

After a few moments of silence, thinking this all over, Charlie responded, "Well, Boss, that's a pretty tall order. Yes, indeed. A mighty tall order." He paused again, rubbing his eyes, then continued, "But maybe not too tall.

There's sure a lotta characters 'round this town, who know a lotta other characters. Give me a few days to nose around and see what I can come up with. I ain't making no promises, mind you, but we'll see what we can do. Right, Robert?"

For the first time since they sat down, Crabby spoke up and said, "Yeah, Alex. We'll work on it. Charlie knows a lot of people around here."

"That's all I can ask," Alex said warmly. "But I know I can count on you. This is a noble thing we do, boys, an important thing. So many good lives were lost, and he must be held accountable for his deeds. There is no better time or place, and no one better to do it." He suddenly realized that his voice had grown louder, and stopped abruptly to make sure that no one was now paying them any attention. After looking around the room, satisfied, he continued, "We should not be seen together at the track, or anywhere reputable in town. Why don't we say we will meet here again in three days, at the same time? Hopefully that will give you enough time to locate the proper person. If not, we may have to change our strategy." Finishing his beer and standing, he added, "But I am sure not. As always, I know I can count on you two to do what needs to be done. Until then gentlemen, be safe, and of course I trust you will speak to no one else about our plans." He pulled out a ten dollar gold piece and left it on the table. "In case you should need anything."

Alex turned and quickly exited the tavern. Crabby sat looking at the doorway through which he had just disappeared, saying nothing. Charlie looked at the coin, then picked it up and put it in his pocket. "Well, this sure is a horse of a diff-ur-unt color. But there's one thing I *do* know. I'm gonna make sure that this job pays us enough that we can leave all of this shit behind and part company with Mr. Alexander Delacroix forever, which will suit me just fine."

For the first time in a long while Crabby actually smiled a little smile and said, "That, brother, is the smartest thing I've heard you say in a long, long time."

CHAPTER TWELVE

ABE gazed down at the wide Ohio River as their train departed the Queen City, crossing into Kentucky over the Newport and Cincinnati Bridge. Completed three years previously, it was an impressive structure. But not nearly as impressive as the bridge just slightly downstream to his right, the mighty Roebling Suspension Bridge. He had seen its massive unfinished stone towers during his earlier visits to the city, but now to see it completed was truly a sight. It had sat idled for many years but when construction had resumed in 1863 Abe found that monitoring the on-going work from afar was a pleasant distraction from the War. He had been invited to speak at the formal dedication on New Year's Day in 1867 but it had proven impossible for a variety of reasons. Now Roebling's son was building an even greater bridge between Brooklyn and Manhattan. Abe had taken time during his last visit to New York to observe that great undertaking. *I will be there when they open that one,* he thought to himself as the southern stone tower of the Cincinnati bridge slowly disappeared from sight.

Beside him Mary was napping, sitting in the morning sunshine flowing in through the windows of the Pullman. She had had a difficult night. Immediately after the previous evening's dinner her mood suddenly had changed, her melancholy once more evident. Sometimes there would be an obvious trigger, something that Abe could understand. All too often, however, there was no apparent reason. Her mood simply would change, dramatically, at times even spontaneously. The morning had brought some noticeable improvement, but she had still been sullen and somewhat agitated. Lincoln could only wonder if the pending visit to Lexington, to her home, had been the cause of this episode. In reality, he had known that it was only a matter of time, no matter how happy and carefree she had seemed over the last few days. He was pinning his hopes on this visit home to the Bluegrass; that it was not the cause, but would in fact be at least a temporary cure.

Abe picked up a copy of that morning's *Cincinnati Enquirer* left for him in the car and studied the headlines. The shipwreck of the German liner *SS Schiller* off the British Isles, resulting in the loss of 335 lives, was still the top news of the day. Reading the story spurred memories of his own voyage from New York across the Atlantic, and caused him to ponder the misfortune, indeed what it must have been like to have been a passenger on the doomed *Schiller*. The lower headline that morning concerned the newly-signed Treaty of St. Petersburg, an important agreement between the Empires of Russia and Japan clarifying a disputed border that it was hoped would result in the easing of tensions between the respective settlers in that region. "Anything to avoid armed conflict," Abe said to himself. If only his own failed attempts at a peaceful negotiation had been more fruitful, if only there had been a way to avoid so much death and destruction. If only.... So often his mind wandered down that path.

A sudden slight jolt of the train distracted Abe from the paper. Looking out he saw that they had reached the top of the bluffs overlooking the Ohio River and were now gaining speed, heading south towards Lexington. Kentucky, his home state! Not that far from here, little more than a hundred miles or so, he had been born, had played in fields and explored along the creek. Those were such happy memories, his beloved mother still alive. But oh, how it now seemed like an eternity ago. So very much had happened since, it was like looking back through the mist, trying to find your way, to see what was out there. He completely forgot about the newspaper, and sat staring out of the window, watching the passing countryside. Watching, but seeing images flickering from long ago.

Mary suddenly woke with a bit of a start, and in the process brought her husband's senses back to current reality as well. Looking out the window, recognizing the familiar gently rolling hills of the northern Bluegrass, she said, "Oh my, just look." She turned and smiled weakly at him. "I believe we are almost to Lexington. Have I really napped all this way?"

Abe stood, and moving to the chair next to hers replied, "You did not rest well last night. I'm sure the nap did you good." He looked out the window just as they crossed over one of the many small creeks flowing through these parts. "We still have a few miles yet." Smiling gently, he took her hand. "It is beautiful. This is such lovely country, a very special place." He thought of the last time they had journeyed to Lexington in the spring, a quarter century before; but on that trip the beauty of the countryside had not been enough to overcome his grief over Eddie's recent death. As usual, he kept that memory to himself, instead going on brightly. "It's going to be wonderful to see the town again, isn't it?"

She gave a small sigh and answered him, "Yes, I do believe it is. Last night I was feeling somewhat anxious, but now that we are almost here, back amidst this beautiful land, all-in-all I am feeling much better about it." She paused, quiet for a moment, and then smiling brightly continued, "Yes, much better. I am looking forward to it." Abe gave her hand a loving squeeze, feeling at least somewhat relieved, though perplexed as ever about her ever changing and unpredictable moods.

The train slowed as it approached Paris, just under twenty miles northeast of Lexington. Abe stood to exit out to the back platform, to stretch and greet any people who might be gathered.

"We used to ride out the pike to picnic," Mary remembered fondly. "Have I ever told you about that?" She stood to join him. "I believe I will get some air myself." They both stepped out.

As expected there were several people gathered at the main crossing. The Lincolns stood side-by-side, holding onto the railing and waving as the train slowly made its way through town. Suddenly Abe noticed a crude sign off to the side by one of the small shops. It simple said,

Go Back to Illinois.
You Ain't Welcome in Kentucky No More.

Abe hoped that Mary would somehow miss it, but it was too large, too obvious. "Oh, Abe," she gasped, "they don't really mean it, do they?" He immediately led her back into the car and helped her sit down.

"Now, Mary, you can't pay any attention to that. People have a right to their opinions, and the fact is, that is exactly how some people feel. But it doesn't bother me, and it shouldn't bother you either." He could see the anxiety growing on her face. "I was hopeful that you wouldn't have to be exposed to such things, but I'm afraid that was more than a little naive on my part. You must understand that there are people who are not happy about some of the things I had to do, that we had to do, and they probably will never get over it. Yes, that's true even here in Kentucky. Remember," he added with a little smile, "I didn't carry this state in either election, even if it *is* originally home to us both. But it doesn't mean anything. Look at how wonderful the crowds have been, so warm and friendly. And even back there, most of the folks were very happy to see us, waving and smiling. Those are the ones you should notice. And as for the rest, well, you just have to put them out of your mind. Everything is going to be fine. Please trust me."

As he spoke on he noticed that while his words had some soothing effect, the encounter was going to continue to weigh on her mind heavily. But he knew that there was nothing he could do about it. He would simply have to keep her focused on the good things, the happy things, and hope she would manage. He sat holding her hand reassuringly, quietly giving her time to come to terms with her feelings. Finally, after several minutes of silence she again spoke, almost as if this prior incident had never even occurred.

"Look at the horses, Abraham. We're here, we're really here." He looked out the window for the first time since the train had picked up speed again after leaving Paris, and saw several horses grazing in the fields as they passed. He turned back to her and smiled again.

"Yes, we are really here now. And we can relax and enjoy ourselves. We'll go and do whatever you would like." This actually caused her to laugh out loud.

"Oh, I'm sure as soon as they see you, why we'll be off to do who knows what." Pausing, she turned and looked directly at him and said, "I just want to see the old house, and maybe ride out Main Street once, just like we used to do. And I suppose go and see father's grave. We must do that while we are here. And maybe take a walk in the park. I think that would be nice."

Abe smiled, and reassured her, "Of course, dear. That all sounds wonderful. We have this whole afternoon, and all day tomorrow as well." Noticing that the train was again slowing its pace, he looked out the window to see that they were entering the outskirts of Lexington. He saw a group of young Negro boys jumping up and down and waving vigorously. "I think we should ready ourselves. I feel sure there is going to be quite the welcome for us here, and this time, just as much for you."

As the train neared the heart of the city, passing the imposing grounds of the state hospital, familiar surroundings offered themselves to Mary. She said aloud, but as if to no one, "I was thinking we might see the old house as we entered town – it's quite near here. I remember we could see it from the train the first time we visited – oh, what a long time ago that was now, and what a different way we arrived in all respects. The children were a terror to the other passengers, and you no help as usual!" A frown clouded her face for a moment as she recalled so many loved ones, alive then and now gone; but she quickly recovered, and even laughed softly. "Silly me, we were coming *from* Louisville that time, and this line wasn't even built back then. So many things will have changed, I'm sure."

Abe replied, "Yes, but the old home place will still be there. We'll take a ride by if you want, as soon as you want. We could probably even arrange a visit. I'm sure the current owners would accommodate you."

"No, I don't think so. There are pleasant memories, but then some perhaps not so pleasant." She paused for a moment, reassuring herself. "No, a view from the street shall be sufficient. I have no desire to go in. I prefer to remember all as it was, not how it may be now."

It was just a couple of minutes later that the train came to a stop. The first thing they both noticed was a large banner hung on the back of a building which read,

Welcome Home, Mrs. Lincoln!

Abe smiled to himself. It was perfect, just as he had suggested in his letter to the mayor. Acting as surprised as she was, he turned to his wife and said, "See, I told you they would be happy to have you back again."

Abe opened the door, waiting for Mary to ready herself. They exited the rear of the car to the cheers of the large gathering on-hand to greet them. After the impressive surroundings in Indianapolis and Cincinnati, the station in Lexington was a modest affair, and Abe and Mary had to make their way through the crowd to reach a large wagon across the lot that was to be used as a platform, decorated for the occasion. As they stepped down off the train the crowd responded with another cheer, and Abe and Mary began to make their way through a center path that had been cleared for them, leading to the wagon. Policemen in blue uniforms lined the way, preventing the crowd from impeding their progress. The two of them waved as they walked, to shouts of greeting and cheers continuously building as they made their way forward. The former president started shaking a few odd hands extended out to him, slowing their progress further.

It was just then that he first noticed another group of men, standing on a rise away and apart from the larger crowd. There were twenty or so of them, all well dressed, arrayed in ranks at attention, one of them holding a Confederate battle flag. This startled Lincoln momentarily, as it had been years since he had seen this emblem so publically displayed. The flags of the defeated foe largely had been captured and confiscated by the victors, and furthermore a vindictive Congress has made their display illegal for some years after the War, at least in the former Confederacy. But as Abe reminded himself, that did not apply to Kentucky, which had remained in the Union despite broad

Southern sympathies, including among many of his in-laws in this very town. And these men seemed respectful, indicating no threat even without taking the police guard into consideration. He put them out of his mind as he and Mary neared the platform.

Upon their approach a brass band on hand for the occasion struck up a familiar tune from before the War, the Stephen Foster minstrel song *My Old Kentucky Home, Good Night*. Once more Abe was drawn momentarily back in time, struck by the words of this song recalling the fate of a slave sold "down the river" as so many had been. He had seen slaves awaiting just that fate when he had first been in Lexington, along with his father-in-law at the Cheapside slave market that had thrived here then. He wondered if anyone else in the crowd that day noted the irony of this song being played here and now as a homecoming for Mary and him. How odd: he had expected this visit to stir memories for his wife, yet within minutes of their arrival it was he who was overcome with unanticipated reveries.

He shook off these thoughts as they finally reached the wagon, where the obligatory gathering of smartly dressed officials and photographers awaited. One of them, Abe quickly realized, was Governor Preston Leslie. A Confederate sympathizer during the War, the governor had begun to modify some of his positions and had turned out to be a fairly progressive Southern leader, encouraging efforts to provide for an education system for freed slaves, and even admitting their testimony in court. Abe had written to Leslie more than once to congratulate him on his efforts, and to encourage him to do even more; but the two men had never met, and Lincoln now welcomed the opportunity. A bevy of other local and state officials were introduced, and Abe took the time to greet each one warmly. Finally, the governor and the Lincolns made their way up the make-shift steps on to the back of the wagon.

Abe looked out over the crowd which he could now see practically filled the entire open lot in front of him. Now to his left, the contingent of Confederate men still stood at attention. For the first time he noticed a number of children, both colored and white, who had climbed up into trees on the hill side.

The large crowd became settled as the band began to play *The Star Spangled Banner*.

When the song concluded, the polite applause died down and the governor began. "Ladies and Gentlemen of Lexington, it is my pleasure to welcome you all here today to mark this occasion, this day of celebration, when we welcome our two old friends back here to Lexington, back to our Commonwealth. We particularly welcome Mrs. Lincoln, whom as you all know grew up among us, only a few blocks from where we stand today. She has been a great example of our fine Kentucky womanhood, and has represented us well to the White House and back again. While she may now reside in our neighbor state of Illinois, we will always claim her as our own, as a Kentuckian, and as a Lexingtonian." At that a robust cheer went up. Mary smiled, blushing slightly, and waved warmly to the crowd.

After the assemblage had again settled the governor continued. "And as for her husband, what do I need say? Our friend, our neighbor, our president; the man who saw us through our difficulties and held us together." Leslie paused for just a moment. "Some of us may have had a differing viewpoint at the time, and we readily admit that today. But the past is the past, and what is done is done. He has been a great ambassador, a great spokesman for where we must go and what we must accomplish as a nation, and truly a friend to all people of our great country. As you know, I have but a few short weeks left to serve you as governor. I can honestly say that my finest honor while in the great office has been to be here today to welcome Mr. Lincoln and his dear wife home to Kentucky." Pausing for effect, he finished, "I know you all join me today in welcoming President and Mrs. Lincoln."

Another ovation, this time stronger and louder, went up from the crowd. Abe again noticed the men in formation, perfectly still, showing no reaction. The governor shook the former president's hand, and then stepped back, allowing Lincoln the platform. Abe immediately encouraged his wife to step forward and join him. The crowd continued to cheer the both of them.

"Thank you, thank you so much," Abe repeated, waiting for the ovation to quell. "On behalf of Mrs. Lincoln and myself, thank you Governor Leslie, and thank you citizens of Lexington for this wonderful and warm welcome home. It always stirs my heart and soul to be back here among you, here on my," and then looking at Mary, continued, "on *our* native soil. We have traveled to Indianapolis and Cincinnati on our way to be with you today, and I am pleased to report that we were warmly welcomed in those fine cities as well. But there is nothing, nothing like being home, back in Kentucky." More applause. "At both of those places I had the opportunity to speak a few words, and it probably won't surprise most of you to hear that I gladly took advantage of that opportunity." The crowd joined him in laughter. "But today, beyond thanking you all so much, I am going to defer to my lovely wife, your own Mary Todd."

Abe took a step back, leaving his wife front and center before the cheering crowd. Blushing, she looked back at her husband, unsure of herself. Mary normally did not speak in public, certainly not to large gatherings such as this. Holding one hand to her mouth, she looked over the assemblage as they voiced their collective approval. Finally, the crowd settled, and in a voice weak compared to her husband's, barely strong enough to be heard, said, "I don't quite know what to say." She paused for a moment, and then continued, "I...I am so pleased to be back home, here in Lexington, among such good friends." She smiled meekly. "We, Abraham and I, have been away for too long, far too long indeed." She paused again, collecting her thoughts. "As we approached Lexington this morning on the train, and looked out over the beautiful green hillsides, I was taken with such memories, such warm, fond memories. Of carriage rides and picnics as a young girl. Lexington is such a special place, blessed by God, and I am so thankful for the opportunity to have been born here. I'm afraid we will be with you but for a short time. As some of you horsemen know, we have important business that awaits us in Louisville."

And then she said something that struck at least some of those present as odd. "While we are here, I only ask that you leave us be, leave us to enjoy our visit as if we were just any ordinary visitors from Illinois. It's not that we mind the attention all that much. God knows that we are accustomed to it. And I know how you do love my dear husband." She turned briefly to look at him, smiling weakly. Turning back to the crowd, with a more pronounced, wearied look, she went on. "But it can all be so taxing to us both. I so want to be able simply to enjoy our visit and relax, and think back upon old times, good times. Will you do that for us?"

The crowd responded warmly, but with a noticeable lack of their previous excitement. It was more controlled, more polite. Some looked at each other, wondering what she had really meant. As the applause died, she finished by quickly saying, "And now, with your indulgence, I believe I need to rest for a while. Thank you all so much, and good day."

There was a moment of silence, a temporary lull as if things had ended prematurely, even somewhat oddly. The governor stepped up and started to clap and the crowd slowly fell into a final polite applause. Realizing the ceremony had ended the band began to play again. With one final wave to the crowd the Lincolns made their way down from the wagon and into a waiting carriage located immediately behind them. The governor, along with his wife, joined Abe and Mary, and they departed for the short trip to the Phoenix House Hotel where the Lincolns would be spending the night.

More people lined the route, and Abe waved to them as he observed the buildings that made up the heart of the city, mostly brick structures of two or three stories. He thought of how Lexington had so impressed him on his only other visit, as a city of grace and accomplishment still basking in its reputation as the "Athens of the West." Now it looked solid enough, but it was clear that it had fallen behind its neighbors to the north. As in so much of the country, the War and the recent Panic has both taken a toll.

Abe kept these thoughts to himself as he rode along, chatting casually with the governor. But he also noted that Mary said nothing, keeping her eyes fixed straight ahead, ignoring the governor's wife. Abe could sense that something was wrong, afraid to think about what it might be.

CHAPTER THIRTEEN

AS soon as they were in their room, the instant Abe had closed the door, Mary turned to her husband with a fury in her face and voice. "Abraham Lincoln, why did you do that to me? I no more wanted to speak to that crowd than ...well, than you probably *did!*" While he had realized that something was bothering Mary, Abe never expected a reaction as strong as this.

"Now, Mary, calm yourself. I simply thought you would like to say hello to your friends and neighbors. I know they certainly wanted to hear you. Couldn't you tell how excited they were to see you, to have you back?"

She paused for just a moment to consider what he had said, and then shot back, "Friends and neighbors, why they are not my friends and neighbors. My friends are all back in Springfield, what few friends I really have. I don't know these people at all. I haven't lived here for...what, over thirty years. They don't care about me, they don't know me. It was *you*, it's always you that they are clamoring to see." With that, sitting on the bed, she began to sob.

Abe wasn't sure what to say or do to console her. He decided to face her full-bore. "Mary, stop being so silly. First of all, they did want to see you. And no matter how long you have been gone people certainly still remember you and your family. And they do care about you." He paused just long enough to judge the effect of his words. Her condition not visibly worsened, he continued, "And another thing, you certainly have many good friends, in Springfield, and other places as well. You just haven't kept in good contact with all of them. But they are still your friends and always will be. I know they are anxious to hear from you, to see you, to renew their friendships. It's always been up to you, when *you* were ready. Certainly you saw that at the Edwards' party."

His words now softened, and Abe walked over and sat on the bed next to her. "Mary, people do care about you, and they love you. I know our life, my life, has often been a burden on you, that you don't always enjoy the public attention. But that is our lot, and I think if you could just accept it, embrace it, you would see how most people really feel. We can still do so much good for this country, for this world, you and I, if you will just join me. You have such a kind heart, if you will just share it."

Her crying all but ceased, and she sat next to him staring at the floor, now dabbing at her eyes with her handkerchief. After a few moments she looked up at him and said, "Oh, Abraham, I am such a fool. What is wrong with me?" She paused for a moment, and continued, "I have embarrassed you, I know it, and I am sorry."

"You have never embarrassed me, Mary, and you never will. I love you, and only want you to be happy. I'm sorry that I didn't ask you before putting you in such an uncomfortable position."

She sighed deeply. "I did make a complete fool of myself today, didn't I? What will people think, after they were so nice to come out to welcome us?" She actually smiled a little and said, "Did you see that banner? That was so awfully nice, wasn't it?"

He took her hand and gave it a squeeze. "Yes it was very nice, and they meant every word of it. And don't you be silly. You did a fine job out there, as good as anyone could ever do. People understand you are here to relax and enjoy seeing the town again. I think what you said about treating us like any regular visitor was grand, and completely appropriate. I must honestly say I would enjoy not having to do much of anything. I'm sure our time in Louisville will be busy enough. The whole reason I suggested this trip was for your enjoyment. So there will be no more crying. Agreed?"

Before she could answer there was a knock on the door. Abe sighed slightly, slowly stood up, walked over and opened it. Outside in the hallway was a smartly dressed young man of about twenty, who promptly said hello, somewhat bashfully, and then handed Abe an envelope. The young man turned to leave, but Abe quickly said, "Now what is this, my friend? What do you bring to me so soon after our arrival?"

"Mr. President, sir, it is from the mayor. I have not read it, so I cannot tell you what it contains."

"Well, young man," Abe said, opening the envelope and removing a small folded piece of paper, "do not be in such a hurry. Let us see what your mayor has to say, and perhaps if a reply is required, you can take it to him immediately. Abe almost dreaded reading the note, as he was sure it would be some sort of request to do something. Who knew what? Especially in light of the conversation he had just finished with Mary, he was not inclined to be agreeable to much of anything. "Please come in while I read this."

Stepping into the room and closing the door, the young man said, "Thank you, sir." He turned to Mrs. Lincoln and said warmly, "Good morning, Mrs. Lincoln. May I say what an honor it is to meet you, and how happy we all are to have you back home again in Lexington."

Abe gave his wife a quick look that said *see, I told you* as she thanked the young man, and then excused herself, going into the adjoining room to compose herself. Her husband stood by the window, reading the note in the late morning sunlight streaming through.

Mr. President

*First, please allow me to extend my personal
welcome and appreciation for your and
Mrs. Lincoln's visit, and to extend greetings
on behalf of all of our citizens. It is such a
pleasure and truly an honor to have you with
us in Lexington. If there is anything I can do to
make your visit more comfortable and enjoyable,
please assure me that you will not hesitate to call
upon me in any way and at any time.*

We are planning a small occasion at the National
Cemetery tomorrow morning at 11:00 to again
remember those brave men from all over Central
Kentucky, and their families, who have made such
a great sacrifice for the Country. We would be so
honored if you and Mrs. Lincoln could join us, and
would greatly welcome any short remarks that you
might care to share. I will meet you at your hotel at
10:30 if you are able to join us.

Respectfully Yours,

James R. Ryan
Mayor of Lexington

Abe folded the paper, shaking his head slightly. This was exactly the kind of thing he did *not* want during their visit. Didn't people understand how much this could upset his wife? How much death had controlled her life, their lives? He would not have it. They would just have to understand. Before he could formulate his response to give to the young man patiently waiting, Abe glanced out the window. Across the street stood the same group of men who had watched over their arrival, once more in attentive formation. *Who the hell are these people?* he thought to himself, still somewhat annoyed but momentarily distracted from the note he held in his hand. "Young man, I don't believe I got your name," Abe said turning away from the window.

"It's Jakes, sir. Robert Jakes."

"We have a son named Robert. A little older than you. Tell me, Robert, these men that I see out there across the street – they are the same men I saw standing over where we first arrived, if I'm not mistaken. Just who are they and what in the world are they doing?"

"Those are Morgan's Men, sir. Or I guess I should say, more correctly, that they are members of the *Morgan's Men Association*."

Abe was certainly aware of General John Hunt Morgan and his raiders, and of the great distress they had caused him in July 1863 when Morgan and close to 2500 men had pushed past Union lines into Kentucky, Indiana and even Ohio. It proved to be the furthest north that any uniformed Confederate troops would penetrate during the War. But Abe was also aware that Morgan, before the War, was at least willing to give the new president a chance, having stated that he had no doubt but that Lincoln would make a good president and that this man from Illinois ought to at least be given the opportunity. Of course that sentiment did change, but Abe had always at least appreciated the general's willingness to try to avoid conflict.

"Well, Robert, I am of course quite familiar with General Morgan, but what is this association? I do not believe I have heard anything about this organization."

"I would be happy to try and explain, sir. I don't know if you are aware, but General Morgan was a citizen of this city, having come here with his family at a young age." Abe nodded his understanding. "After the War, the general's family requested that his remains be moved back here from Richmond, Virginia, where as you probably know he had been buried in September of 1864. At his re-interment on April 17, 1868, the surviving members of his command served as funeral escorts. Afterwards, right here in this very hotel, these men met and formed the Association. That day they pledged fidelity and affection for each other for as long as they lived, and they resolved that the memory of their beloved leader, General John Hunt Morgan, would be indelibly stamped upon the tablets of their hearts just as his name was written on the undying page of history. They've gotten together at least once a year ever since."

"Well I must say, Robert, I can tell that you do seem to be *quite* knowledgeable on this matter. Should I pause to guess as to why that might be so?"

The young man smiled slightly. "As I believe you have already deduced, sir, my father was a proud member of the general's raiders, if you don't take offense at me saying so."

Abe now smiled warmly. "Indeed I do not, and you should be proud I have come to understand that it is the honor of a man's passion and valor, no matter what the cause, that is ultimately important. While I may regret some of the actions of the past, on both sides, I cannot now nor shall I ever again pass judgment on actions that were taken with a clear mind and a sound heart. We cannot change the past, and the honor of family is most sacred. Tell me, Robert is your father still with us?"

"No sir, he died on the adventure to Ohio, back in '63. I never knew him."

"Then you have all the more reason to honor his memory. You have my deepest sympathy."

"Thank you, Mr. President. And allow me to say that I hold no ill feelings or resentment. We have all come a long way from those days, and I know that my father shared the general's respect for you and your efforts to maintain the Union, if nothing else."

"Thank you, Robert. That does mean very much to me. We all have so much to make up for. Yes, many regrets, but always an eye towards the future, to the greater good of our country and our people." And then, after a moment, he remembered the men outside and asked, "But what exactly are they doing out there, Robert? What is it that they want? Can you tell me that?"

"I guess what I said before, sir: they are honoring General Morgan, and keeping his memory alive. In a way they are honoring you, too, I suppose. But mostly they want to make sure you remember who they are, and that you be sure to remember the general. Abe looked back out the window and stared at the men for a few moments. Robert continued, "But please understand, Mr. President, you have nothing to fear from them. They only want your respect, for the general. They will probably be out there for your entire stay, but please do not let them concern you, or Mrs. Lincoln. They truly mean no harm. I guess it's just what they feel they are called to do."

Abe turned back, facing the young man. "Well, I suppose I can understand that, and yes, even respect it. I am going to write a short note of my appreciation which I hope you will deliver to them." He then thought about the note he was holding and added, "As for this note from your mayor...."

At that moment Mary returned and said, "What does the mayor want, dear?" She was smiling pleasantly and appeared to have completed recovered from her earlier episode.

"I'm afraid they have asked us to attend a ceremony at the National Cemetery in the morning, a gathering of families of the young soldiers who are resting there. They want to me to speak. But I am going to respectfully decline, as this is just a pleasurable visit."

"Nonsense, Abraham. You will of course be there, and I will accompany you. It is so little to ask of us when these families have sacrificed so much." He knew there was no point in bringing up the earlier conversation, or in questioning her opinion now.

"Well, then I guess that is settled. Robert, if you will, please let the mayor know that we will be ready to meet him tomorrow morning at 10:30 as suggested. And allow me a moment to write out a message for the Association."

Mary inquired, "What association is that?" Lincoln sat down at the small table and taking a piece of stationary that was provided by the hotel, began to write a note.

"The Morgan's Men Association, former comrades of General Morgan. You may have noticed them earlier. If you look out the window you will see them now."

Mary walked over and looked out, and replied, "Oh, my. Yes, I do see. A fine looking assemblage, aren't they."

"Yes, I agree. They are here to remind us of their dedication to the memory of their fallen leader. They mean us no harm, just a reminder of where we have been."

"Well I suppose that is all right, to be expected even. The general was certainly a popular man here in Lexington, a good family."

Lincoln quickly finished writing the note, handed it to Robert, and said, "Please make sure this gets to them, with my warmest regards." Robert took the note and turned to leave.

"Thank you, sir. I will certainly do that. I know that they will be pleased.

And now if you will excuse me, Mr. President, Mrs. Lincoln, it has been a great honor. I will probably see you in the morning." With that he quickly exited the room. Outside in the hallway he paused, opening the note.

Gentlemen of the Morgan's Men Association,

On behalf of Mrs. Lincoln and myself, I thank you for your interest in our visit to your city, as well as your unique yet respectful method of expressing the same. Please be assured I share your dedication to preserving the memory of all who have made the ultimate sacrifice in the War, no matter their sentiments. I have always held a respect for General Morgan, and admire your undying devotion to his memory. If I can be of service to you, now or in the future, please do not hesitate to call upon me.

Yours,

A Lincoln

After a simple lunch at the hotel, the Lincolns took a carriage ride north on Main Street, out past Mary's old home. The house had been sold out of the family after her father's death back in 1849, largely through the actions of Mary's brother George who had contested their father's deathbed will. Abe had represented Mary and her sisters in that sorry business, which along with her father's death and then her grandmother's the following year had made their last visits to Lexington far more somber than their first.

Now, these many years later, the old house was no longer the stately residence he recalled, though certainly still recognizable. Two stories of solid brick, with five symmetrical windows across the upper floor and matching chimneys on each end, it remained an imposing structure. Originally it has been a tavern, before Robert Smith Todd moved his growing family there in

1832, and it occupied a still-prominent spot on the northern edge of town.

As they rode past in silence – neither of them wished to note the changes – Mary could not help but think back to her youth, and of all the other grand houses she had visited just to the east, along Second and Third Streets, and of riding with her father into town, to visit his office, or to go shopping. He had been such a fine man, her father. Mary had always been so proud of him, and had loved him dearly.

As she had her mother, Eliza Ann, as well. But Mary had been just seven years of age when her mother died, old enough to remember her in some detail, and to have loved her unconditionally. Then her father had remarried and Mary never adjusted, never got used to her stepmother, never really *liked* her.

Over the next few years this new marriage had brought nine additional children. Now there were so many to vie for her beloved father's time and affections. Mary had so often felt like she was lost, that she never really fit in with all of her siblings, and was often unhappy as a young woman coming into her own. She had welcomed the opportunity to attend school shortly after her father's remarriage, first at the Shelby Female Academy, and then later at Madame Mentelle's fashionable boarding school for girls. She threw herself into her studies, and particularly enjoyed learning French. She lived mostly at the school during the week, then home on weekends. It provided her with a good education and an escape, at least for part of the time, from her stepmother.

It was only a few years later that her older sister Elizabeth invited Mary to live with her in Springfield, where she had settled after marrying the son of a former governor of Illinois. Mary readily accepted the invitation; and as much as she missed her father, and often felt lonely, her dislike of her stepmother was more than enough to offset those feelings. Mary became an active part of the Springfield social scene, eventually meeting a young lawyer named Abraham Lincoln.

As Mary and Abe rode through the streets of Lexington that bright May afternoon, she blocked out any thoughts of her stepmother, whom some at least – including her husband – believed to be the true source of many of her problems. They toured the old neighborhoods, much as they had when Abe had made his first visit to Lexington back in 1847, when they were on their way to Washington for his term as a congressman. They celebrated their fifth wedding anniversary during that pleasant three week visit. Just as she had done then, Mary now described in detail who had lived in which house, recalling stories of grand parties that she had attended. She seemed so happy and carefree that Abe found himself able to relax completely, and found her to be quite entertaining, more so than she had been in some time. They continued into the heart of town, went by the old house on Short Street, then by the much larger house where Mary's Grandmother Parker had lived, practically next door. Abe had been especially charmed by the old woman during that first visit. Mary had loved her dearly, her mother's mother, if for no other reason than how she shared Mary's dislike of her stepmother. And it had not been only Mary – Grandmother Parker's house had been a place of refuge for all of the older children, for they all felt a special bond with her, the closest remaining thing they then had to their mother.

They rode on, passing by Mary's old school on the corner of Second and Market, then Mary's favorite store as a child, Giron's Confectionary Shop, with its ballroom on the second floor where she and her mother before her had often attended dances and parties. Finally they passed the courthouse, and Cheapside, where years before Abe had witnessed the slave auctions that helped shape his feelings on emancipation. Now that chapter was blessedly closed, and instead one could always find a few lawyers about coming and going from court. Wherever they went people called out and waved to them, with Abe at least always responding, indeed like neighbors who had not seen each other in a long while. In general, though, most people honored Mary's wishes and did not much intrude into the Lincoln's afternoon together.

That night they attended a private dinner at the home of a cousin, with two of Mary's stepsisters in attendance. Mary greeted them and their families warmly and for the most part managed to enjoy the evening with her extended family. She brought greetings from Elizabeth and Fanny and Ann, and all the family news from Springfield. When the Lincolns arrived back at the Phoenix House, Morgan's Men were still in attendance across the street. Abe noticed that as he and Mary were getting out of the carriage, the men now tipped their hats in respect. Although it was dark and hard to be sure, he believed that a few smiles were now briefly evident.

As promised, they were in the lobby at 10:30 promptly the next morning to meet the mayor for the ride to the cemetery. Robert Jakes was in attendance as well, driving their carriage. They again passed Mary's home-place as they slowly rode north out Main Street towards the hallowed grounds, which had been made a National Cemetery shortly after the War. There were many people lining the street, and several hundred gathered at the cemetery, most of them family members of the soldiers buried there. Though he initially had been reluctant to attend, Abe realized that this event had been created specifically because of his presence in town. There was no anniversary date of any kind, no significance to the occasion, simply that the former president was present, the man whom so many still felt was responsible for these men being buried there.

Abe kept his remarks brief, praising these soldiers of both armies, and the sacrifices that both the brave young men and their families had made on behalf of their country. But to be honest, his heart simply was not in it. There had been so much death, so many graves in so many cemeteries, so many speeches. He had grown weary of it all. Yet at the same time, he knew it was his *responsibility* to be there, to speak, to praise these men, and that it always would be. It was a duty he simply could not shirk. So once again, as so many times before, he raised his voice and had been able to move his audience.

While at the cemetery they took the time to pay their respects to Mary's father, then returned to the Phoenix House for a private lunch in their room. Afterwards Mary asked her husband what he might like to do that afternoon. She sensed that the morning's events had been difficult for him and had taken some toll. She wanted to help him find a way to relax and enjoy the afternoon. Abe pondered the question for a few moments before responding.

"I believe I would like to go and visit Ashland, to see Mr. Clay's house and walk his grounds. I think that it would do me a world of good – a chance to stretch these old legs, as well as my mind. I know that you had mentioned the park. I would be fine with a stroll there as well."

"The grounds at Ashland are as fine as any park," Mary replied, and then looked slightly puzzled. "I don't believe any of the Clays are living there now, are they? Will the current owners want us there?"

"As usual, you are completely correct, dear. It is now the home of the Agricultural and Mechanical department of Kentucky University. You can well imagine how that pleases me." Mary nodded – signing the act providing for such educational establishments had been a proud moment and rare diversion from the affairs of the War for her husband. "An educator named John Bowman was the instigator of this turn, and he now lives at Ashland as master of the school. He has been kind enough to send us an invitation to visit if we have the time, and I would very much like to take him up on his offer. That is, if it suits you as well."

"Oh, that would be splendid. I used to so enjoy traveling out to that part of town – Madame Mentelle's school was close by, you know. It was always so lovely this time of year, and I suspect it still is. I have such fond memories of Mr. Clay. He was such a good friend of my father, and you know, he visited our home often." She thought for a moment and continued, "Did I ever tell you about how he told me once that if he was ever elected president that I would be the first person he would invite to the White House. Can you imagine?" She laughed quietly.

"Yes, dear, I believe you have told me that. I just wished that he had lived long enough that we could have shown him the same favor. He would have certainly been my first guest if he had still been with us. I would have greatly valued his counsel."

"Well then," Mary replied, "I think that would be a delightful way to spend our last afternoon here."

So once more they climbed into the carriage, this time heading south out Main Street to the former home of the great senator and statesman, Henry Clay. Abe had briefly visited the estate on the earlier trip to Lexington, and had greatly enjoyed being there, simply walking the land that had belonged to the man many considered one of the greatest senators ever. The house that awaited them this visit was not quite the same as Abe recalled, though recognizable. He was not surprised by this, having learned through his inquiries that James Clay had had the old house pulled down after his father's death, but had rebuilt it on the same lines and with as much of the original materials as practical.

Mr. Bowman was sitting outside the house in hopeful anticipation of the visit, and he stood and waved as he saw the carriage approaching. He delighted in showing his guests all around the house, which was now home both for him and for a portion of his university – several earnest students came and went during the course of the tour. He insisted that Abe and Mary join him for a ride around the grounds so that he might point out the new Mechanical Building as well as the fields of the adjoining Woodlands farm where – he assured his guests – the next generation of Kentucky farmers would learn all the latest innovations in agriculture. The warm afternoon passed quickly, much too quickly as far as Abe was concerned. As before, he drew strength and inspiration from this place, both its past and future.

After a short rest in their room, during which Abe caught up on some neglected correspondence, they thoroughly enjoyed a small dinner with the mayor and his wife in a private dining room at the hotel. It was the ideal thing after the large family gathering the previous evening. Mary in particular was taken with the mayor's wife, whose older sister had been a friend back in the old days. Abe was encouraged that the visit to Lexington had indeed done his wife good. It was all he had hoped for and more.

Very early the next morning they took one last short carriage ride, to the depot to board the train. They were pressed to get to Frankfort where Abe had promised Governor Leslie that he would call on him at the Capitol, to meet some of the governor's friends and staff. Mary had already decided that she would remain on the train to rest during the brief stop and forego all the politics. As it was so early only a small group of people were on hand for their departure. With no further speeches or fanfare, the Lincoln's gave a final wave as the train slowly pulled away. Mary immediately entered the car, and did not even bother to look out as they passed the back of her old home. They headed north, and then west for the less than thirty mile journey to Frankfort, and then on the Louisville, and the Kentucky Derby.

CHAPTER FOURTEEN

ON that same Friday, at the very moment the Lincolns were walking out of their room at the Phoenix House preparing for their early morning departure, seventy miles to the west Colonel Clark was already at work at his racetrack. He was busily making his final preparations for the arrival of his special guests later that afternoon, as well as for the many events of the weekend. Most important of all, opening day and the Derby were now just three days away. He sipped a cup of coffee as he carefully studied a list of horses – and not just any horses, but those three-year-old thoroughbreds entered in the first Kentucky Derby. There had been forty-two horses nominated, mostly from Kentucky, which of course was the original idea, but Clark found a few listed from out-of-state as well. Now he was closing in on his final list of starters. Barring any injuries or last-minute changes there would be fifteen horses competing on Monday. He glanced at the entries for the other three races to be run on Opening Day, but could not find the will to focus as intently on them, or on the additional four days that would make up this first meet. It was the Derby that held his attention, the Derby that used up almost all of his energy. He was exhausted, almost too tired to sit in his chair and hold the papers. But somehow he would find the energy, the enthusiasm. After all, in a few hours Lincoln would arrive, not to mention all of the other guests coming in over the weekend.

Clark had finally managed to find places for them all. It had not been easy, and he had been required to ask that more than a few friends and associates give up their prime seats. But in the end, most had realized the importance and the national attention that Lincoln brought, and ultimately what it meant to their operation. After all it was a business. It was now time for Clark to try to enjoy himself, if that was possible. Of course he knew he was destined to worry over every detail, every moment of the next few days. There was nothing he could do about that. He would pour every ounce of himself and his energies into making sure that everyone else enjoyed the Derby, and that it was a resounding success. Any pleasure he received would be subsidiary to that success.

Clark drained the last of his cup and shouted out, "Vernon, I must have more coffee if I am to get a thing done! Are you out there, Vernon?"

Clark's assistant limped in carrying a small well-worn tin pot in his one hand, and proceeded to refill his boss's mug. "There you are Mr. Clark. Anything else you be needing right now?"

"No, that will be all, "Clark responded shortly. "Just stay out of my way. I've got too much to do to worry about you."

Clark's words stung the poor man. In the past weeks, and especially the last few days, Clark had become even more abusive to Vernon. No matter what Vernon did, Clark did not seem to be happy with him. There were a few occasions when Clark seemed to recognize his bad behavior towards his assistant, but they were few and getting further between. Vernon had tried to give his boss the benefit of the doubt, as he understood how much pressure the man was under. Still that was no reason for Clark to treat him this way. Vernon had always done all that was asked of him, and done it the best that he could. In the last few days he had come to more fully realize how prone Clark was to these vicious mood-swings. Far too often Vernon's only real purpose seemed to be for Clark to have someone on which to vent his rage, no matter who or what might actually be the cause. And to be honest, Vernon found himself growing very weary of it.

And now worst of all, this Lincoln business. Vernon could hardly stand to hear the man's name mentioned any more, much less put up with all of the excitement and praise that Clark seem to hold for the visit. Vernon had already decided that once the Derby was over, he was going to quit. In some ways he did appreciate what Clark had done for him over these past few months, but it had gotten to be too much. Clark was not the man his father had been, that much was now obvious to Vernon. He just wanted out. He would find another way to live, another way to pay for his hellish habit.

Having been so thoroughly dismissed, Vernon did not have time to mention to his boss that he needed to leave a little early that evening for an important engagement. He figured that it wouldn't matter to Clark anyway, as by that time his boss would be all consumed with that bastard Lincoln, and Vernon of course wanted no part of that anyway. He was at least going to mention it to Clark, but now, well to hell with him. Feeling that all too familiar itch, Vernon started to break out in a cold sweat, so he headed over to the barns to take care of this growing need.

Clark finished his coffee, and then prepared to head into town, on a particularly important errand. Of course, racing implied betting; there was never any question about that. But Clark had never cared for the bookmakers who controlled the wagering on racing, and he had decided that his new track and new race demanded an improved system. Known as the Paris Mutual system, he had first seen it in use during their trip to Europe, and now he was bringing it to Kentucky as well. But it was mostly unknown to his future customers. To help with this, Clark had arranged for a Mr. Ira E. Bride, who would own the Paris Mutual pools for the Derby, to exhibit his system in the rotunda of the Galt House daily between the hours of eleven and one o'clock. Clark truly believed that once men understood it they would indeed prefer it over both the old system of pool selling as well as the bookmakers. He intended to be there at the first such presentation to make sure that all went well.

He called out again for his assistant but got no response. "Where is that fool now when I need him," he mumbled out-loud. "Vernon, are you there, man? I've got to go into town." Nothing. Clark gathered his papers and walked out of the office. Indeed the hallway was empty. "Damn him," was all

Clark could say. He exited the clubhouse, pausing to glance down the track in the twilight, at the horses already out and training. Spotting another of his assistants, Clark shouted, "George, stop whatever you are doing and take me to town. I have things to do before Mr. Lincoln arrives!"

ONLY a couple of hundred feet away, Ansel Williamson was standing trackside wearing a satisfied expression on his face. The early grey light of dawn was just beginning to settle in over the new racetrack. He looked down at his stopwatch a second time, shaking his head. His "rabbit" had just run one of the best works the trainer had seen in some time. He knew Aristides was a good, solid horse, but he never expected this. This three-year-old seemed to be blooming at just the right time. The old trainer had suspected something last week, but now the horse had seemed to improve even more. True it was not all that unusual for a colt at this age to improve rapidly, getting stronger and growing almost day-by-day. After all, he was just a big kid. Still, Ansel hadn't seen this one coming. Aristides was now ready for the Derby, and for the first time, Ansel began to honestly think that maybe Chesapeake was not the only horse in his barn with a shot at winning that race. If nothing else it boded well for the coming summer and fall seasons.

He had not said anything to McGrath after last week's works, and he certainly wasn't going to say anything now. The owner was so focused on his other horse, with his grand plans of beating his rivals, that Ansel had quickly decided that Aristides would be his secret, his back-up. He knew all too well that in horse racing things often did not go according to plan. Not that there was anything to cause concern over Chesapeake. The colt had worked the previous morning, and everything seemed fine. It was a solid work, a good preparation, just what Ansel had been looking for. No surprises – which only four days before the race was a very good thing.

This morning was another story – definitely a surprise, and a good surprise. Ansel had put Oliver Lewis on Aristides in the mornings soon after the young jockey had arrived in Louisville, but had mentioned nothing of their plans to run him in the Derby. Lewis was glad enough to have the extra work. The General had told Oliver that Ansel would be looking for some help, and that it was fine with him for the boy to ride for his friend McGrath's trainer. And Oliver enjoyed riding the horse. Especially after working him the previous week, Oliver could tell that Aristides was a classy mount, and he would love an opportunity to ride him in the afternoon.

Ansel had instructed his rider to start the horse out at a solid pace for four furlongs, and then open him up for another four, really pushing him in the final eighth. Then he could gallop him on out for four more, which would be a total of twelve furlongs, or a mile and a half, which just happened to be the Derby distance. Oliver worked the horse beautifully, and came jogging back with a big smile on his face.

"He sure was something this morning, Mr. Williamson," Oliver said as he came to a halt in front of the old man, patting the horse on the neck. Excitement was thick in his voice. "He sure was full of himself today. Don't think he could have gone no better."

"That was fine, Ollie, just what I wanted. Everything feel sound?" Ansel started feeling the horse's legs, looking for any unusual heating or swelling.

"Oh, yes sir. Nothing wrong with this horse, nothing at all. He's rock solid and ready to go."

"Yes, Ollie, I believe he is at that. Tell you what, you get him back to the barn and give him to Shug, and then get down off of there and come see me."

"Yes, sir." As Oliver turned the horse to head off of the track, he spoke to Aristides. "Let's get you back and cooled off and have a nice bath, get you all cleaned up. You done done your work for the day all right. Done a fine job, too. I bet I got a nice apple or two around here for you. You done earned it, that's for sure."

Ansel chuckled softly to himself as he watched the young horse and rider head down the track towards the barns. He liked this boy, and how he handled his horses. If there had been any doubts before, they were gone after this morning. He waited patiently for Oliver, watching the other horses, mostly galloping down the track, all just enjoying the newly dawned morning.

It only took about five minutes to get Aristides back to the barn, and for Oliver then to wipe the sweat and dirt off his face before returning to where Ansel was waiting. It was now light, although it would be few more minutes before the sun was fully up. The rider could see there were several horses out on the track now, including the General's prized filly, ridden by Bug Eye. Oliver waved at his friend as he galloped the horse down the stretch.

"She's a nice looking little filly," Ansel remarked as his young rider approached. "Glad I'm not running anything against her in the Oaks. I believe she'll be tough to beat."

"Yes sir, Mr. Williamson, she surely is all that. Bug Eye surely is looking forward to riding her next week, surely is looking forward to winning. I know the General is, too"

They watched as two more horses went by, and then Ansel turned and looked directly at the jockey. "Ollie," Ansel began, "you have been doing a fine job riding Aristides in the mornings for me, and I agree with you, I think he is ready for a big race. What I haven't told you is that that race is going to be the Derby." He paused for a moment and then continued, "And I want you to ride him."

Oliver broke into a big grin and answered, his excitement obvious, "Yes, sir, I would surely love to ride him in the Derby. That would be just fine with me." Then he quickly added, "That is course if it's all right with Old Tom and the General. You know I gotta talk with them about it first."

"You don't have to worry about that, son. Mr. McGrath talked with the General before you ever got up on the horse's back. We've been thinking all along about using you, but I wanted to make sure you got along with the horse," and then Ansel added in a firm voice, "and that you could follow my instructions."

"Oh, yes sir, Mr. Williamson, I'll ride him however you want me to." The old man could see that his young rider could now hardly contain his excitement.

"Now before you go getting too worked up, Ollie, there's some more you need to understand. I want you to listen very carefully to me." He paused until he felt sure that Oliver was focused and fully attentive. "As I think you know, Chesapeake is a mighty good runner, and is Mr. McGrath's top three-year-old. We're all expecting him to have a good shot at winning this Derby. Hell, that's the whole reason we came here."

"Yes sir, he's a mighty fine horse, that's for sure."

"Yes he is, but what you need to keep in mind is that the way I've been preparing him, the way he runs his best, especially for a mile and a half, is to lay back and then come on at the end. And you know what that means don't you, Ollie? He's gonna need a good, fast pace to run against. And as I see it, none of these other horses that're gonna be running in the Derby are likely to do that. So that's why me and McGrath decided to enter Aristides. To get him out there setting a good honest pace, to set it up for Chesapeake to come running at the end, to win the Derby, just like McGrath wants." He waited for Oliver to consider this new information. "So you understand, Ollie, we're not asking Aristides to *win* the Derby, just to make sure that Chesapeake does, or at least has his best chance."

Oliver thought for a moment and then slowly said, "Yes sir, Mr. Williamson, I understand. I see what you're getting at." Then pausing, he broke back out into a wide grin. "But I'm a telling you, sir, that that may not be how Aristides sees it, especially after the way he ran this morning. I'm telling you that this horse is *ready*."

It was the trainer's turn to smile. "Yes, Ollie, I've noticed that. But you must understand that you've got to follow my instructions exactly if you're gonna ride my horse. No fooling around out there. Again, Ansel waited to let his words sink in. "But on the other hand, you know as well as I do that things don't always go according to plan in a horse race. If Chesapeake is having a bad day, or something happens, I want you to give it everything you've got; let this horse go and see what happens. But always remember, always, the plan is for Chesapeake to win, and that's the most important thing."

The old trainer paused to give the jockey time to take it all in, and then added, "Now to be honest with you, I haven't exactly told Mr. McGrath everything. I don't think he's got any idea what kind of horse he has here with Aristides – and I'm not planning to tell him nothing neither. 'Cause to be honest, we don't know for sure what he can do. I know this horse could win at a mile, maybe even a mile and a quarter. But a mile and a half, well now that's a whole 'nother story, and you know it. He's just not bred to run that far, even if he is acting like he wants to. But I will tell McGrath that he's got a solid horse in Aristides, and a solid rider, and that if he sees anything going wrong, that you'll try your best to win. And that's what I'm telling you today. Do everything you can to set it up for Chesapeake, but if for some reason that don't work out, well then you do everything you can to win it. You think you can do that, son?"

Oliver just smiled again and said, "Don't you know it, Mr. Williamson? You can count on me. Just make sure Mr. McGrath is somewhere wheres I can see him, so I'll know for sure what he wants. Other'n that, I'll do exactly what you tell me, and nothing more or less. Yes sir, you can surely count on me."

Ansel shook Oliver's hand firmly and said, "Well then, Oliver Lewis, you got yourself a mount in the Kentucky Derby." Then the old trainer added, "Just don't be upset when you don't win." As Oliver turned to head back to the barn, Ansel reminded him of one more thing. "I would appreciate you not telling nobody about our plans. You know how talk spreads around a racetrack, and we don't want them other trainers to know anything about this. You can tell 'em you're riding Aristides all right, but that's about all. And as for Aristides, how well he's been doing, let's just keep that between ourselves as well if you don't mind. If something happens and he should win it, well that will just be our surprise to everybody else, right?"

"Yes, sir, I think that will be just fine. I always like surprises."

As Oliver walked back into the barns he couldn't help but to have a wide grin on his face. He was riding in the Derby! And he didn't care what anybody said, even old Ansel, Oliver knew his horse could run, and they would all have trouble beating him. He rounded the corner and arrived at the General's barn, where Crabby was hot-walking the filly, who had just come off the track.

"What the hell are you grinning about, boy," he asked when he saw Oliver walk into the shed row.

"I'm riding in the Derby, that's what I'm grinning about. And all them other jockeys had better watch out 'cause I'm a riding to win it."

Crabby just shook his head as he continued walking the horse around the corner of the barn. What the hell did that matter? It was just another horse race at another race track. But as Crabby rounded the barn he realized that it wasn't going to be just another race, just another track – not if what Alex was planning worked out. When he circled back around the barn again he didn't notice Oliver or any of the other grooms or horses, he was lost in his thoughts. Alex had given him a lot to think about.

WITHIN a couple of days of his initial meeting with the Appleton brothers at Porter's, Alex had first approached Calvin and Peanut with his plans for them. He knew that for the right price he could count on the two men to do whatever he needed, whatever the reason, and he was not disappointed. Despite the reverence that so many colored felt for "Father Abraham," the two jockeys had shown no reaction at all when Alex felt them out on his plan to kill Lincoln, especially since he needed them to play merely a small, if vital role. One white man more or less was all the same to them; the money was a different matter.

By his second meeting with the two colored riders, the week before Lincoln's planned arrival, Alex was prepared to provide them with details of the plot. It would be up to Calvin and Peanut to provide a simple but effective distraction at just the right moment. This would be critical, he explained, but very easily accomplished, as it would require them to do nothing more than allow themselves to be seen. It was, of course, *where* they would be seen that would provide the perfect distraction: up in the grandstand, where no colored faces were allowed.

Alex had by then checked out the grandstand in detail. This had raised no suspicion, since any number of curious folk were roaming the racetrack now, eager to get a glimpse before opening day. It had proved no problem to learn the location of Clark's personal seats – where Alex was certain Lincoln would also be located – simply by asking one of the workmen. This was a relief, as Alex had expected a bribe might have been required, and he did not want to leave a trail leading back to him after the fact. No, everyone involved in the preparations seemed eager to talk about the upcoming Derby, and this increased his confidence. He was sure that when the Derby started, everyone, including whatever security people might be on hand, would be focused totally on the race.

To his great delight, his investigation had revealed a small back stairway at the rear of the grandstand which would allow Calvin and Peanut easy access to the back of the stands, close to Lincoln's seats. The sudden appearance of two colored men there would be all that was needed to achieve the desired result. The momentary stir of outrage over their audacious act would provide the opportunity for their co-conspirator to take care of the actual deed.

Then in turn, the shots fired would redirect attention to Lincoln, allowing Calvin to take care of the final loose end. The as-yet-to-be-identified shooter would be instructed to "run to the darkies" to make his escape. If things went well, Calvin would in the end be seen as a somewhat confused hero who had "just wanted to see the horses run." Alex realized how overly simple this all seemed, but it was in that simplicity that the beauty of the plan resided. It would all take place so quickly no one would have the time to realize what had happened, and by then it would be over.

At least he had convinced Calvin and Peanut of this, assisted by assurances of large sums of money. They had quickly bought into the plan. Alex had absolutely no doubts, especially in light of the first-hand knowledge he had of many of the colored men's deadly crimes, that enough money would buy their loyalty and silence.

The second meeting at Porter's Tavern with Charlie and Crabby, however, had not gone to Alex's liking. The three of them had met on Saturday afternoon as planned, with Crabby as usual sitting silently while his brother and Alex talked. Charlie had not yet produced the results for which Alex was hoping: he had not found an appropriate co-conspirator to carry out the deed. But Charlie assured Alex that he was making progress, that he had a couple of potential candidates. He just needed a few more days to be sure. After all, Charlie had reminded Alex, this whole assassination business was a rather delicate matter. Charlie couldn't very well announce what they were up to. He couldn't just put out a sign and take applications now, could he? Charlie couldn't help but grin when he used that line.

Alex showed no sign of appreciating the jest. He reminded Charlie pointedly that they could not move forward until the correct person had been located, and that they now had little more than a week to do so. But in the end Charlie had been persuasive. He managed to reassure Alex that they would be able to find the right person, and that Alex should go ahead and proceed with the rest of his plans. He could count on Charlie – he had never let Alex down in the past and wouldn't this time – not on such an important matter.

If nothing else, Alex decided that he had persuaded the Appleton brothers to buy into the noble nature of his cause, which in itself was an important step. They would all be heroes back in New Orleans, Alex assured them, at least in certain circles. Not to mention that Charlie and Crabby would be very well rewarded. Alex had not particularly noticed that this was the only point at which Crabby showed much reaction or interest.

CRABBY finished walking the filly, and was now giving her a bath. As he scraped off most of the water and began to brush her out, his thoughts were focused on the fateful third meeting he and Charlie had had with Alex just the day before, after Charlie had let Alex know he had good news. Alex told them to meet him around six o'clock, at dusk, but not at the tavern this time. It would be too dangerous to meet again in the same location. He had found a better spot....

ALEX sat waiting for the brothers in a deserted shack – or what was left of one – not far from the racetrack. It was not a place that other white men frequented, thus perfect for his purposes. He had learned of it from Calvin, at their last meeting, when he had asked the two riders if they knew of a secluded place, nearby but not at the track, a place where he could conduct very private meetings with assurances of not being seen. He wanted to make it as convenient as he could for Charlie and Crabby, and hopefully their all-important accomplice, for he knew that their work at the track was increasing and it was becoming harder for them to make it into town. Alex produced a bottle of bourbon purchased at the Galt House as a potential reward for the information.

Calvin had answered at once. One of the local riders had told him of a deserted shack, just off of the main road leading out from town to the track, less than a half mile away, well hidden in a thick stand of trees. The small wooden structure had likely been used by a farmer in the past, but had now been abandoned for many years, from the looks of the place. The roof was mostly missing, along with some sections of the walls, but there were still a few odd pieces of furniture left inside, most importantly a small cot. It had been suggested to Calvin that if a man such as himself was wanting to arrange a meeting with a woman – understood to be most likely a prostitute out from Smoketown – and he didn't want to be seen with her in town or at the track, that this was a suitable meeting place in which to conduct his business. And further, for the right sum of money, the woman in question could be located. Calvin and Peanut had taken notice and had already confirmed this intelligence.

It was now just after six, not late enough to be worried but enough to cause Alex to be annoyed. He wore a heavy coat, and a large hat, all of which did an adequate job of partially concealing his appearance, especially in the dwindling light. He stared out the open door at the dense grove of trees and underlying thicket of bushes, all fully leafed out into varying shades of spring greens. Finally he heard the sounds of someone approaching. It was not yet completely dark, so he could easily make out the familiar figures of Charlie and Crabby, along with a third man who Alex quickly realized was limping noticeably. Alex motioned quietly for them to come into the shack, watching for another full minute to make sure that no one had followed. He then closed the door and turn to face the three men.

"Evenin', Boss," Charlie said, flashing his customary grin. "Nice night we're havin', ain't it?" Alex said nothing, staring at the third man, who he could see was missing his left arm. "Boss, I'd like you to meet the man whose gonna kill that son-of-a-bitch Lincoln for you. Name is Vernon Preston."

CHAPTER FIFTEEN

ALEX stared at the pitiful man standing in front of him. He smelled terrible and looked even worse. To Alex it was obvious the man was an addict, and he assumed from the missing appendage that it must be a result of the War. It was an all too common sight, especially in the South, and most especially in the dregs of the Quarter. Alex had gotten his fill of such men, despised them as he despised all weakness in others, except when it was to his advantage. But addicts, he had concluded, were bad for business. Which is why he now looked at Charlie with an expression that said *what the hell have you done?* But before he could speak, Charlie quickly began to explain.

"Now Boss, I know ol' Vernon here may not look like much at first glance. But I'm here to tell you that he is the absolute best person in the entire city of Louisville to do the job. Hell, prob'ly the entire state. Ain't that right, Vernon?"

Vernon extended his good arm. "I'm pleased to meet you sir, although nobody's told me your name yet, which I guess I can understand what with this business. But let me just say it is an honor, sir. Anybody who wants to get that bastard is all right with me. And I'm more than willing to help you do it."

Alex ignored the extended hand. "Well I guess that's a good thing since Charlie's brought you here. Let's not worry about names for right now." Turning to Charlie, Alex said, "I guess you better explain to me why you are so confident about this. As you say" – he looked back at Vernon – "he sure as hell doesn't look like much at first glance. No offense you understand," he said still staring hard at the other man, "I just don't take well to addicts."

With no more introduction, the men sat down, Alex and Crabby on the only two chairs that were usable, and Charlie on the cot. There was a small barrel, but Vernon said, "I'll just stand if it's all the same to you." Everyone focused on Charlie, who was still grinning.

Well it's like this, Boss. You said that first and foremost you wanted somebody who shared our views about Lincoln. What about that Vernon?"

"Wish Booth had gotten the job done when he tried. We'd all be better off, and I guess none of us would have to be here right now. And I wouldn't have to be listening to all this high and mighty talk about the great Mr. Lincoln." He paused for just a moment and then added, "In fact I can't believe nobody else has tried to kill him since. Give me a chance and I surely will."

"All right then," Charlie continued, still looking at Alex, "next you said you wanted someone who fit in 'round the track, who would be expected to be there, 'specially 'round the Derby. Well, Boss, you are lookin' at none other than Mr. Clark's personal assistant. He can go anywhere he pleases, do anything, and ain't nobody gonna give him a second thought. Now I ask you, what could be better'n that?"

Alex looked at the man in a new light, with a newfound respect, quickly realizing the importance of this information. "Is that so, Vernon?" he asked the one-armed man, using his name for the first time.

"Yes, sir, I've been working for Mr. Clark for a while now. I used to know his father quite well. We fought together in the War. And then after," he paused and looked down at the floor for a moment before continuing, "well, let's just say that after the War things changed, and I began to have a few problems. Now I'll admit Mr. Clark was nice enough to give me a job, and for a while, he treated me all right. I guess. But here lately I've gotten tired of the whole thing. He just don't treat me right and I'm sick of it. There's just no pleasing that man. And another thing, I swear he just ain't *right*. Now I always respected his father, but not him, least not any more. Especially with his goddamned love of Lincoln."

"Yes, I've heard some talk that Clark has some problems," Alex responded, "and I've been told he has some Irish blood in him as well." Charlie rolled his eyes. Crabby as usual, sat silently, mostly staring at the floor. "I see this as not only the chance to take care of Lincoln, but to embarrass that damn Irishman as well."

Vernon looked a little surprised. "I hadn't heard that, but I guess it makes sense. Guess that why he's so hard to get along with. Can't say as I ever had much use for the Irish either."

Alex shifted gears. "Vernon, again don't take any offense, but I'm wondering how well you can get around on that leg, and how well you can shoot, what with that missing arm and all."

"Don't you worry none about that now. It's true I move pretty slow most of the time, but let me tell you I can still get along when I need to. More than one person's been surprised by how fast I am when I'm forced to it, especially 'cause they're not expecting it. Kinda works in my favor if you know what I mean." Vernon flashed an evil little grin. "And as for shooting, you can worry even less about that. Don't need a left arm to do that, and it don't hurt that I was the best shot in my entire company besides. You get me anywhere close and I can guarantee you I'll hit my target, yes sir, with deadly accuracy." He grinned even more. "And as Mr. Charlie here was telling you, I can get pretty damn close."

Charlie spoke up again. "Finally, Boss, you had mentioned the matter of the money. Well, it just so happens that Vernon here is ready to make a change. Seems he's gotten tired of a workin' at the track, workin' for Clark, and he's lookin' for a way to get out. I believe you can help make that happen now, can't you?"

Alex thought for a moment and said, "Vernon, you do this for me, and I'll make sure you get enough to take care of you and your...*needs* for quite some time to come. How does that sound?"

"That's just exactly what I wanted to hear. Understand, I'd kill the bastard for nothing given the chance, but since you're offering, that's sounds all right by me, mighty generous even."

Alex looked hard at the man for a moment, his mind coming to terms with all that had been said. Standing, he extended his hand to Vernon. "Well then, sir, I believe we have ourselves a deal. Trust me, I will make sure that you have a fool-proof escape, for I have the contacts and the resources to guarantee it. I will trust you to understand that we must not meet again in this town." He paused, and then biting his tongue continued, "But let me just say you are a fine man, a noble man, and I am proud to be associated with you, Mr. Preston. We will meet again, sir, I promise you that, in New Orleans, at which time we will all celebrate our great accomplishment, where you will be treated like the hero you are. Charlie here will get you everything you need and provide exact details, shall we say on Sunday? In the meantime, take care, speak to no one else of this matter, and keep foremost in your mind the extreme wrongs that together we shall right."

He then turned to Crabby. "If you will please escort Mr. Preston out to the road, there are a couple of other matters I want to discuss with you brother before we depart." Crabby started to question exactly why Alex wanted him gone but quickly decided to let it go. Then to Vernon, Alex said in parting, "God's speed and good luck, sir. I look forward to the next time we meet, when Mr. Lincoln will bother us no more."

After the two men had left, Charlie turned to Alex and said, "What did I tell you, Boss? You can always count on me. He is almost too good to be true, if I do say so myself."

"Yes, I suppose so, if he is to be believed. But what a wretched man. I assume you checked out his story before bringing him here."

"Of course, Boss, you don't even need to ask 'bout that. He's pretty much an open book. Lotsa people know him, and he's the gen-u-wine article."

"May be, but you know I don't like working with an addict – too unreliable. What makes you think he'll actually get it done?"

"That's the beauty of it. I've already started on him. Not only does he honestly hate Lincoln – maybe even more than you, Boss, if that's possible – but we can use his condition to...what's that word? To *motivate* him, that's it, to control him. I've promised him that if he'll do this thing , and like you seen he is more than willin' to do it anyway, I've promised him he'll never have to worry 'bout nothin' again. Not only are we gonna give him lots and lots of money, we'll keep him *supplied* as well. You shoulda seen how his eyes lit up at that. He'll get it done all right. I'm makin' sure of that. And I'll keep a good eye on him, keep him under wraps. He won't have no chance to talk to nobody."

Alex thought for another moment, and then began to smile. "Yes, Charlie, I believe you have indeed got it done. Well done, sir, very well done!" His mind was racing again. "Now, I've talked things over with Calvin and Peanut as well so they know what to do. Afterwards, I'll meet you and Crabby in the barns just like nothing ever happened, and we'll get the hell on out of here and back down to New Orleans. There's a train leaving for Nashville at the perfect time on Monday afternoon. By the time these fine Kentucky bastards figure anything out, we'll be long gone and having ourselves a high time. Only thing you'll have to figure out is how to spend all of that money I'm going give you and your brother."

Just then, Crabby walked back in, and spoke up for the first time. "You better be damn sure of that. This is some mighty damn serious business we're talking about here, and you'd better make sure nothing goes wrong. I ain't throwing my life away for you, that's for damn sure I'll help you get on that train, but then I want my money, and then it'll be a cold day in hell before you see me again, I can guarantee you that." Alex just stared back at him, thinking how that was probably the most he had ever heard Crabby say at any one time before in his life.

ALEX went straight back to the Galt House for dinner right after the meeting in the shack was completed. After he finished eating he headed out to the lobby to look for Tommy. Alex still had a few more details to arrange, and after this most recent excellent news he was more anxious than ever to get started. Alex now was confident that Tommy was just the person to assist him with whatever he might need. He quickly found the boy hanging out in the lobby as usual and gave him an inconspicuous nod. Alex walked out to the street, with Tommy following a few minutes later.

"Evening, Tommy, how's life treating you this evening?" Alex had grown quite fond of the boy over the last week, and was even considering asking him to come back to New Orleans with him. Alex could always use another good man, especially now that it looked like he might be losing the Appleton brothers, or at least one of them. Alex found it hard to believe that anything would ever separate those two, so if Crabby really was being honest, then he couldn't count on having either one of them around in the future.

"Couldn't be better. The action's really starting to pick up around here now. They say that Mr. Lincoln will be here tomorrow, staying right here at the hotel, and that's got everybody all stirred up."

"Is that so, Tommy? Let me ask you, just how do you feel about all that?"

"You mean Mr. Lincoln? Well, personally I never cared much for the man. Never did nothing for me. Now as far as him being here, I don't really care one way or the other, except that it's looking like it'll be good for business. And that's good by me." Exactly what Alex had hoped to hear.

"Couldn't agree with you more, son. And speaking of business I've got a few more things I need you to do for me, if you don't mind. Some very serious, very private things." This time Alex extended a gold eagle. Tommy's eyes widened.

"As I've told you before, sir, whatever you need, you can count on me." He took the coin and put it in his pocket.

"Excellent, Tommy. Let's go have a drink and talk about it. By the way, have you ever thought about going to New Orleans?"

CHAPTER SIXTEEN

THE trip between Lexington and Frankfort was a short one. Abe sat studying the countryside intently as the train made its way through the rolling hills of the Bluegrass, passing through the small village of Midway on its way to the capital. This part of the journey, at least, was one he could recall from his previous visits. The Todd's summer home, Buena Vista, had not been far from Frankfort, and the rail line passed through their land. Of course, that house was now sold along with the rest of the estate, only a memory. As with so much of this trip it sparked other memories. While not far in distance, this part of Kentucky was a world away from where Abe had been born and spent his first few years.

There was a certain grace and charm that grew out of these hills, and the magnificent horses that grazed in these fields. Abe particularly loved the strong, rolling limestone fences built by the Scottish and Irish immigrants, dividing the greens and browns of the landscape. The War had largely spared this section of the country. It had been the horses that were valued here, not the land. It occurred to Abe that this was the very reason he was traveling through Kentucky on this morning in mid-May. He had, however unwillingly, played a significant role in the damage and near-destruction of the Kentucky horse business, and now he was on his way to Louisville to help do his part to restore it.

The train made a sharp bend and began to descend more noticeably as it neared the Kentucky River valley. The narrow river came into view, and a distinctive fragrance began to waft in through the open windows: a mixture of wood smells from the many lumber mills that lined the opposite bank of the river, mingled with the unmistakable aroma of sour mash coming in from the distilleries on either side. Abe found it oddly pleasant. The train began to run on a parallel course along the slowly moving water. It was a dark, cloudy day, rain threatening, which helped give the water a distinctly greenish appearance. Abe could now make out the activity both along its banks and on the river itself. Being spring, the water was up; and that meant log rafts, floating down from the forests of the hills and mountains of eastern Kentucky to be milled into lumber.

Up ahead of their train, to the right of the river, Abe caught a first glimpse of the town's church steeples, before his eyes were drawn to a long covered bridge spanning the river. Just then the train slowed and they were momentarily plunged into semi-darkness as they made their way through a short tunnel. Mary, who had been working intently on her needlepoint, looked up as the train came back into full light just before coming to a halt at the depot. As at every stop there was a small crowd of people gathered around the tracks to welcome them. Somehow word always managed to spread of when and where they would be.

"Are you sure you want to remain here, Mary? If nothing else, perhaps you should stroll around town for a little. I'm sure we could find someone to accompany you."

"No, I believe I would just like to sit here while you are away. I'm perfectly comfortable, and have plenty to do. It would only cause a fuss, and I don't believe I am up to it this morning. Besides, it looks like it's going to start pouring at any minute. I'll have nothing to do with that."

"Well, at least come out and say hello." He smiled gently. "And I promise you won't have to say anything, you can just wave."

"Yes, I know. I suppose I must do that."

Standing, she smoothed out her soft, faded rose dress and taking the arm her husband offered, exited the rear of the car out onto the platform. A small cheer went up from the crowd and the two of them began to wave warmly to the small gathering. After a couple of minutes, Abe kissed his wife on the cheek, and as she went back inside he stepped down off of the train. Rain indeed appeared imminent but so far had refrained from falling. Three uniformed officers were at hand to assure the crowd did not close in around him. There were also a couple of well-dressed gentlemen, separated in age by several years. Abe quickly and correctly surmised that the more senior of the two was the mayor, while the younger must work for the governor in some capacity.

"Mr. President, welcome, sir, welcome to Frankfort." The man excitedly shook hands with Lincoln. "I am Edmund Taylor, mayor of Frankfort, and let me just say what an honor it is to have you here with us here in our city. "

"Thank you, Mr. Mayor. It is a pleasure. Taylor, is it? I don't suppose by any chance you would be of any relation to the late president?"

"Thank you for asking, sir. I am in fact his great nephew."

"Then it is an honor for me as well. I always felt that things might have gone differently if President Taylor had not come to his unfortunate early end. He was a true man of compromise. Perhaps Mr. Clay would have been more successful in his efforts if he had had your great uncle's assistance."

"Thank you so much. What a kind thing to say." He looked up at the Pullman, and asked, "Won't Mrs. Lincoln be joining us?"

"She has chosen to remain behind and rest this morning. It was a taxing visit home, and after all, we still have quite a weekend in store for us in Louisville. And as it is, we have but a brief time to spend with you in any case. We shall have to return to enjoy the charms of your lovely city again, when we have more time. I do remember passing through here once before, I believe. We always seem to be on our way elsewhere, I'm afraid."

"Of course, Mr. President. I completely understand. We welcome your presence here in Frankfort at any time, for however long you might have to stay." Then, turning slightly to acknowledge the younger man to his side, the mayor continued, "Please allow me to present John Jamison. He is the Governor Leslie's personal assistant, and is here to escort you to the Capitol."

Jamison, a fine looking man in his mid-twenties with striking blond hair and a fair complexion that made for a boyish appearance, shook Lincoln's hand and said, "It is such an honor, Mr. President. The governor is so looking forward to your visit this morning. If you are ready we can head directly over, probably a good idea in light of the weather. The Capitol is just here." Abe looked in the direction the young man indicated and saw the building ahead and to his right, a short way down the street.

"Very good. It will do me well to stretch my legs a little after the ride over this morning." Again noticing the threatening sky, he added, "And beside, a little rain won't hurt me. Mayor, will you walk with us?"

"Why yes, thank you for asking. Unfortunately, I will then have to leave you, but I would enjoy the walk as well."

The three men crossed the street and set off on the two block walk to the Capitol. On both sides of the street people stood waving and cheering politely as the three men made their way, the uniformed officers following close behind. To their left was the main business district, the street lined with shops. Abe commented to the mayor on their modern and prosperous appearance. Taylor responded with pride, observing "This block is our phoenix, only recently rebuilt after a terrible fire consumed nearly all of this section of the town." Abe nodded – it was not an uncommon story.

As they approached the Capitol, Abe stopped to take a good look. It was a fairly simple structure, pleasant in appearance. Grand high columns adorned the front of the building, with full wide steps running entirely across. There was one large door, with no front-facing windows. A not-too-large white cupola, encircled with glass and crowned with copper, loomed above. Directly in front of the building sat a lovely fountain, an ornate black iron fence enclosing the expansive well-kept grounds. Two office buildings flanked the Capitol, the one on the right much the larger of the two – larger than the Capitol itself – and clearly of recent construction.

"It is certainly a beautiful building," Abe commented as his gaze returned to the central edifice. "In some ways similar to our statehouse back in Springfield, but then also so very different."

As the men reached the front gate of the grounds, the mayor excused himself and quickly walked across the street and headed up into town, now dodging the first raindrops. Lincoln and Jamison chatted about the Capitol on their way past the fountain and up to the portico. Just then they were greeted by a familiar voice. "I suppose young Jamison here is extolling the virtues of this old pile. He really has made quite a hobby of the place." It was Governor Leslie. "Good morning, Mr. President, so very good to see you again. Welcome to Frankfort. I trust your visit in Lexington went well?"

"Yes, Governor, it was very nice, thank you. I think Mary very much enjoyed herself, reliving some old memories. And yes, your aide here has been enlightening me about your lovely capitol. You know, I now recall passing by it when we were traveling through Frankfort on our very first trip to Washington, when I had been elected to the House. If I remember correctly, I don't believe the impressive fence was in place then, although I must admit we were in a bit of a hurry that day to get on to Lexington and I may very well be mistaken. A few years have come and gone since then."

"No, sir, you are completely correct. An amazing memory for detail you have. The fence would have been added after your visit. But if some of us had our preferences, an entirely new capitol would have awaited you." He shot a grin in Jamison's direction, who had frowned at his words. "We have long outgrown this old place, and had hoped to replace it by now. Unfortunately, the times and politics being what they are, the legislature could only see fit to build one wing, where I am delighted to say my office is now located."

As they entered through the large double doors, Abe could see the signs of the crowding that the governor had described, but his gaze was then drawn to the steps immediately in front of him. It was a circular staircase, with one cut stone slab laid upon another, with no visible support, winding around and up into the floor above.

"This is truly amazing!" he exclaimed. "I've never seen its like."

"Isn't it something?" Even Governor Leslie showed obvious pride, though he quickly added, "Sometimes we think this is the only thing keeping the old place standing!"

"It is all very impressive, and you should be proud. How is such a thing possible?" After staring for another moment, his gaze then broken he continued, "Now, if you don't mind, I'm afraid again on this trip we are a bit pressed for time, heading the opposite direction of course, west this time."

"Certainly, right up this way. I know you have important affairs in Louisville, and we really appreciate your stopping by, even for just a few minutes." As the three men ascended to the second floor the Governor added, "And I am glad to report that I am planning on attending the Derby on Monday as well."

Fortunately, at least as far as Abe was concerned, the legislature was not in session, so most of the politicians were out of town. He greeted a handful of state leaders, including the speaker and the secretary of state, and a few of the regular workers around the capitol, whom Abe insisted on speaking to as well. He did not ask about the lieutenant governor, who was noticeable absent. Lincoln could only wonder if it might be some sort of political statement. He knew that he still had plenty of political enemies, no matter how hard he worked to appease them.

As the three men made their way around the building, the sound of rain striking the roof grew louder and louder. Abe tarried, hoping for signs that it was letting up. After about forty-five minutes, before heading back downstairs, Abe asked the governor for a word in private.

"Yes of course," Leslie responded. "I would ask you to join in my office across the way, but no reason to put you out in this weather more than necessary. John," he said turning to his aide who had accompanied them throughout the tour, "please wait for us at the door." Jamison descended the stairs, leaving the two men alone just outside the senate chambers.

"Governor Leslie – Preston – thank you for the tour of this lovely building. It represents Kentucky well, even if it does show a bit of wear about the edges. But I have to tell you that it alone was not the reason I agreed to stop here in

Frankfort today. I have had something on my mind that I wanted to briefly discuss with you today, so that you could think it over and we could perhaps again talk on Monday."

"Certainly, Mr. President, what can I do for you?"

"Well first of all," Abe responded with a chuckle, "you can call me Abe when we are alone. I understand the need for formality in public, but I consider us to be friends, Preston, and I would much prefer that you just call me Abe, for that is my name." The Governor smiled warmly.

"Oh course, Abe. I am pleased that you consider me a friend."

"May we go in and sit for a moment," Abe inquired, glancing at the wide door to his left.

"Yes, of course, please," the governor replied, opening the door of the senate chambers. They entered, taking the two closest chairs in the back of the large room. They were alone, the echoing sound of the rain indicating that it seemed to be letting up some.

"Preston, I know that your term of office is almost over, and I was curious as to your future plans. I have something to ask of you."

"I've been looking at some different options, Abe, but have made no firm plans as of yet. I would like to continue to be of service to the citizens of Kentucky, to do something worthwhile with my time, but there are many ways to accomplish this goal. What did you have in mind?"

"As I think you know I have been pleased with much of what you have accomplished, and how your attitudes and opinions have adapted with the changing times. People of our generation, the ones who were so caught up in the struggles that led to the War, we have made our mistakes and hopefully have learned something from them. Too many of us have been too slow to change, however, are still too wedded to our past. I believe now, more than ever, even though our time is passing we still have an important role to play. It is indeed time for younger men to shape our future. I feel that we need to help encourage them to take the right paths to address the many challenges that face our country, to avoid the mistakes we have made. I have not been happy with the direction of the country in many ways, yet I have no desire to become active politically again. But I do believe that men like ourselves, other progressive leaders and thinkers, men who have realized that the War has created as many challenges as it solved, I believe we can help guide those who are assuming power, taking on the reins of government. Through our writings, our examples, our counsel, we can still help to move this country forward, to accomplish its grand potential."

Abe paused for a moment and then stood, looking out over the rows of small wooden desks and chairs lined around the room, thinking silently. The governor was trying to formulate a proper response but before he could offer any Abe turned to face him again. "Preston, I am asking you to consider joining me, and others, in creating a fellowship if you will, with no partisan affiliations or goals, a group that will gather from time to time to discuss these issues and to share our collective knowledge and counsel with those who must lead our government, to those who will shape our future – at least to those who would be receptive to it." The rain was now falling harder again. Then, a flash of lightning, and a few moments later the room, growing darker, shook from a loud clap of thunder.

Standing, the governor replied, "Abe, I am honored that you would even consider me. I think it is an intriguing and certainly worthwhile idea." Abe took a couple of steps towards the door.

"It sounds as though I had better be on my way. Mary will be concerned with this weather. All I ask for now is that you think about what I have said, considering the possibilities. It is a thing that I have been formulating for a while now, and is a concept that is still evolving in my mind as well. All I know is that I am certain we can and should do something. I have spoken to no one else as of yet, and I would greatly value your insights and opinions. Perhaps we can have a few moments on Monday to speak further about it."

"Yes, certainly I will do that, Abe. And I would be open to traveling to Springfield later this summer, after my term expires, to talk further if necessary." The governor stood. "For now, however, let's get you back on your train, back to Mary. We don't want her to be overly concerned. I wish we had more time now, but we will speak again on this, I promise you that." They exited the room and walked downstairs.

On the way down the distinctive stairway Abe couldn't resist stomping his foot on a step, not too violently, but enough that the sound echoed loudly through the rotunda. He laughed and said, "This is just an amazing thing, here. If it can hold me up, then I suppose it is indeed quite solid, and I must say that it will quite likely be around for many years after I am long gone. I certainly hope so, anyway. You must not do away with this place, just because it is old and weary."

They stepped out onto the large front stoop, the rain still falling but now once more at merely a steady drizzle. The governor offered his carriage, which he assured Lincoln could be quickly summoned, but Abe declined. "I will have plenty of time to dry out before we reach Louisville. It is just enough to be refreshing, and will only cause me to step more lively." He remembered the three officers, now standing off to the side, waiting under the overhang to avoid the rain. "That is, if these fellows won't mind too much, as I suppose they must accompany me as well."

"Of course not Mr. President, they won't mind at all," the governor said smiling. "I've had them out in much worse than this before." Then Leslie offered his hand saying, "Well, goodbye for now. Have a safe journey and a fine visit to Louisville, and I am looking forward to speaking with you again at the racetrack, now more than ever."

"I look forward to that myself, governor." Turning to Jamison who had rejoined them at the door, Abe shook his hand again. "Young man, there is no reason for you to venture out into this weather. And besides, knowing governors the way I do, I'm sure you have other important matters to attend to as well. Thank you for your assistance, and I hope to see you again."

With that, Abe, along with the three officers, made a quick walk back to the train. He was tempted to cross the street and say hello to some of the people standing there in the rain, watching and waving to him, but he knew himself too well, and was aware that it would delay them even further. What with the rain, the train would probably be late enough getting to Louisville as it was now. Abe quickly thanked the officers and immediately re-boarded the Pullman. Mary admonished him for getting wet, as he knew she would, but secretly he took great delight, both in enjoying the refreshing aspects of the shower, and in giving Mary something to worry about. Little things sometimes helped ward off the larger elements he could not control.

As they began moving again Abe stepped back out onto the platform for a final wave to the few people who were still standing there, waiting to watch the train depart. It slowly built up speed, continuing to the west, towards Louisville. Passing out of town, crossing over the Kentucky River, the train began its slow ascent up and out of the valley, then rapidly gained speed. Abe had made it back to the train just in time, for now it was raining so hard that it was difficult to see much of the countryside. The time was approaching the noon hour, so the Lincolns enjoyed a light lunch in their car. After the porter had cleared the small table, they both settled in for a restful trip.

EARLY that afternoon Clark arrived at the Galt House for a final meeting with the business people with whom he had contracted for various goods and services, his last opportunity to worry them before he was distracted with the weekend's official parties and activities. And then there was the matter of Bride and his new system. Clark had of course kept his ear to the wind and what he was hearing was not good. As much as he distrusted the bookmakers and believed in the notion of pari-mutuel wagering, he had come to the conclusion that there simply was too much at stake to introduce a new idea to which many of the public were obviously so resistant. He would have to break the news to Bride, and sooner rather than later. There would be other opportunities, certainly during this first meet, after the Derby, perhaps for the Oaks. But the man would have to understand that Clark couldn't risk it on the Derby itself. Not a pleasant business, but it had to be done.

As he entered the lobby there was a loud clap of thunder, and the skies opened. Louisville had enjoyed fine weather for several days, and Clark supposed it was inevitable that they would experience some rain and storms at some point. He thought to himself, *Fine, let it rain today, all it wants. The horses have had their work, anything left to be done at the track is mostly inside anyway; let it rain today and get it over with. Just not on Monday! And if it's all the same, not tomorrow or Sunday as well.* Then a different thought entered his head. If it rained enough he wouldn't have to pay to have the extra water put down on the road leading out to the track, as he had so often promised the ladies he would. That would save him more than a few dollars, as it was coming out of his own pocket, not the Association's.

Clark had continued to have nightmares not only of rain, but of all varieties of storms and calamities that might befall the Derby, along with many other dark thoughts and dreams. He could not shake the feeling that something would go wrong, terribly wrong, and it would all be his fault. He would be blamed. And it would be something that surely he could have prevented. But what, what could it possibly be? The worst part was how it always seemed as though whatever this thing might be was always right there, just beyond his grasp, just out of his thoughts, something he could never quite reach. He would wake up with a start, feeling as though he had just missed it. Clark was afraid it was slowly driving him mad, and that he had no choice but to take it out on those around him. Now it was time for *these* poor souls to have to deal with him.

ALEX stood in the lobby, watching the thin man nervously hurrying across the lobby. He could tell instantly that it must be Clark, based solely on the things he had been told around town over the last few days. Everyone certainly had an opinion about this odd, troubled man. Some believed he knew what he was doing, others thought him a fool. Yes, opinions certainly ran strong and deep around this town about one Mr. Meriwether Lewis Clark, Jr.

Alex had also just arrived from the track, just in time to avoid the storm. He had gone out early to enjoy watching the morning works, and to engage in a short conversation with Calvin and Peanut in regards to the developments from the previous evening. Alex was now preparing to go into the dining room for lunch. His mind was a constant whirl, spinning his plans and then double checking everything. It was all so perfect, so *easy*. But not for just anyone, he reminded himself. It was he, and he alone that had the resources and the knowledge and the connections to make this all happen; and, of course, the courage as well. Maybe it was true he had lost his nerve in New Orleans. But this was a different day, with a different, much better, indeed a foolproof plan. It had to work, it would work! In just over three days Lincoln would be dead, and it would all be by his hand, if not directly so. No reason for a fine gentleman such as himself to dirty his hands, not when there were people like those stupid Appleton boys, those two colored jockeys, and now this...this completely disgusting, damaged man, Preston. Yes, he would be above the fray, but make no mistake, it was he, Alex Delacroix who had the vision and, yes, the courage to pull it all together. And he would take the credit, he would be the hero. He could easily imagine the welcome he would receive back in New Orleans. The world, and all of its riches, would be his!

Alex watched as Clark visibly reacted to a clap of thunder from the spring storm that had settled in over the city, deep grey clouds pressing down. Alex laughed out loud, thinking, *You think this storm is bad? I'll give you something to really worry about, Mr. Clark. I'll give you something that you will never recover from, you and your little race. You'll never have a race track like the Fair Grounds, not in your wildest dreams. Oh, but they'll never stop talking about you, and what happened at your little track. Yes, it will all go down in history, but not for any derby.* Then softening his thoughts, Alex watched Clark head up the stairs. *But no reason not to enjoy this weekend, and eat your fine food and drink your bourbon. Yes, Mr. Clark, let us have a fine celebration this weekend. Then I'll give us all something to really celebrate.*

CALVIN and Peanut sat in the loft of the barn, trying to avoid the increasing streams of water leaking down through the new roof. The two riders had finished their work for the morning, and now considering the weather, were not going anywhere for the remainder of this Friday, at least not until the rain let up.

"Sure didn't build these barns none too good, did they," Peanut commented, moving some of his belongings so that they would not get wet.

"They ain't gonna spend no money keeping the likes of us dry, that's for damn sure." Calvin lay on his makeshift bed with his feet up on a hay bale. "Long as the whole barn don't flood, don't matter to me how much it rains. We got enough dry land here in this corner, so stop complaining. I'm just glad I didn't have to ride out in this shit."

"I ain't complaining, it's just a fact is all. They built these so fast they didn't get it done right, that's all I'm saying." Once Peanut had moved his things, for the third time, they indeed did have a dry area large enough for both of them to be comfortable. When Calvin made no reply Peanut decided to drop the subject. After a few minutes of listening to the rain pounding down on the roof just a few feet above their heads, Calvin was almost asleep.

Peanut brought him out of his near-slumber, speaking in a very low voice. "So I guess we really is gonna do this thing?" He didn't have to explain to what *thing* he was referring.

"You don't have to be so quiet," Calvin answered without opening his eyes. "Ain't nobody downstairs gonna hear a damn thing in all this rain." He half sat up and continued, somewhat annoyed, "Now what you bothering me about now?"

"I'm just asking if we're really gonna do this thing, you know, for Mr. Alex?"

"As long as he got them deep pockets, and he's willing to fill mine as well, I'll do any goddamn thing he wants."

"Yeah, I know that much, Calvin. But ain't you worried? You really think this plan a his'll work? I mean, not about killing Lincoln and all that, but the part about us getting away. Ain't you afraid we'll get caught and strung up?"

"Yeah, I've been studying on that part pretty hard." Calvin answered slowly, and then paused for a moment. "After we talked this morning, while you was back out on the track, I went and checked things out for myself. It's pretty much just like the man said. There's this stairway, and we oughta be able to go right up it once the race has started, and then all we gotta do is show our purty dark faces and that sure oughta cause quite a stir."

"I ain't so worried about that part, Calvin. I know we can get their attention. I'm just afraid we're gonna get a little bit too much attention is all."

"Yeah, Peanut, you afraid of too many things. I ain't finished yet, give me a chance before you get all excited." Calvin laid backed down, closing his eyes, as if he were seeing the things he was describing. "Once that feller Preston shoots Lincoln, everybody's gonna be looking to see what in the hell just happened. If he's quick enough he'll get back to where we're gonna be before anybody has time to figure out what happened. It's not too far at all, so I figure he's got a good chance of making it. If he does, I'll stick him one time real good, and then he won't be talking to nobody ever again. We'll hightail it right back down them stairs. If'n we do get caught – or I should say me, as nobody done said nothing about you doing much of anything anyway, so I don't know what you're all worried about, no hows. But like I was saying, if'n we do get caught, then all we say is that we saw what just happened, we got that man who done killed President Lincoln, our *hero*, and we was just scared and running away like two good darkies would be expected to do. Figure worse thing they can do is throw us in jail for a while while they's trying to figure it all out. What would two fine gentlemen such as ourselves have to do with killing the president, anyway? Figure it's just like Delacroix sez, if'n we get caught they'll probably call us heroes. And if'n we don't, we'll disappear back up here and ride it all out, and then head on back down to New Orleans. Either way, we get our pockets full."

"Yeah, but what if Preston don't get to us, what if he gets caught?"

"Well now, that's a real problem for Mr. Alex and not for us now, ain't it?" Calvin answered laughing. "This man don't know nothing 'bout us, and he won't neither. He'll be way too busy getting close to Lincoln to really get a good look at us. All he knows is that once we start a stir, he shoots. Then he's supposed to run to the two darkies. He sure ain't gonna know which two darkies we are if he never gets to us. And if he does, well, then that's the last thing he'll ever know. I figure if he don't make it, we just head back down the stairs pretty as you please, cause sure as hell ain't nobody gonna care 'bout us no more after they see Lincoln bleeding all over the place. Might not get paid, but hell, I figure it's worth the chance. Better odds than betting on these damn horses, that for sure. And we got better than three month's wages in our pockets already."

Peanut sat listening to the rain, taking in all that his friend had said. He knew Calvin must be serious to be talking so much, and he knew his friend wasn't fooling around any. Finally Peanut spoke up again. "Guess it all sounds all right to me, if'n you say so. I always trust you Calvin." Then noticing a new leak Peanut moved to avoid the drips. "Beside, what the hell have we got to lose?"

"What the hell is right. Now, shut up and let me sleep."

CHAPTER SEVENTEEN

ABE was deep in thought as the train slowed to make its way through Shelbyville, a small town a little less than half way to their destination. The rain continued pouring down. He peered out through the dim light but thankfully did not see anyone out there waiting. Not in this weather. Mary was napping soundly. He stared at her for a moment, his thoughts shifting from his conversation with the governor back to when he and Mary had first met, first courted. Abe had been smitten with her, though he had still been recovering from the loss of his first real love, Ann, who had died of typhoid fever a few years earlier. Mary had moved to Springfield to be with her sister, and she and Abe had courted and became engaged at Christmastime in 1839; but just before the wedding was to take place a year later, on New Year's Day, they had called it all off.

Abe had felt so lost, so unsure of his future, unsure of himself. Not knowing what else to do, he had gone to visit his friend Joshua Speed in Louisville later that summer. Joshua was a fellow Kentuckian who, like Lincoln, had sought his fortune in Springfield, where he became a successful merchant. The two men had become fast friends. But soon after Joshua's father died, he had closed his store and returned to his family home in Kentucky, by strange coincidence departing Illinois on the very day that Abe and Mary had broken off their engagement. Thus Abe had lost both friend and fiancée, which furthered his melancholy.

With thoughts of Mary and the future weighing heavily on his mind, Abe quickly accepted Joshua's invitation to come to Louisville. And so he found himself journeying back to Kentucky, back to see his good friend, indeed his best friend, to seek counsel and comfort. Now, as the train made its way on west towards the mighty Ohio River these many years later, Abe's mind could not help but wander back to that day he had arrived early in that August of 1841.

TRAVELING not by train on that earlier journey but mostly by boat, Abe came to Farmington, Joshua's family home. Abe was so despairing that he had taken no notice of the passing time, or of the sights along the way, but he was cheered some by his arrival. As he approached the grand house, situated in the middle of hundreds of acres of prime land just off the Bardstown Pike a few miles southeast of Louisville, he was excited to see his friend again. In the fading light of late afternoon Abe found Joshua and his mother waiting in front of the house.

"Mr. Lincoln, you certainly are a sight!" Turning to his mother, Joshua continued, "Mother, do not be alarmed, as I know this gangly-looking man can sometimes have that effect on people who had not yet met him. He may be odd-looking, but trust me, he is completely harmless. That is unless he talks you to death." Joshua trotted up to the wagon, greeting his friend warmly. "Abraham, it is so good to see you." The two men embraced. "Mother, may I present my good friend from Springfield, Mr. Abraham Lincoln. Abraham, this is my mother."

"It is so very nice to meet you, Mrs. Speed. Thank you so much for having me here. I hope I will not be of too much bother to you." Then he quickly added, "And before any more time passes, let me offer my sincere condolences over the recent loss of your husband. I know it must be a difficult time. It is so kind of you to open your home to me now."

"Thank you, Mr. Lincoln," she replied genuinely. "I do appreciate your kind words. But of course you are of no bother at all. We are so very pleased to have you visit. Joshua has spoken of you often, and I know he has missed your company greatly since his return to us from your town. I hope you will stay with us for a good, long while."

Joshua added playfully, "Well, not for too long. I'm sure the courts of Illinois will practically cease to function without you there to argue your cases. That, or perhaps justice will now move a little more swiftly." The two men shared a laughed.

"Joshua, I have indeed missed your company, not to mention your quick wit. I already feel more myself again just being here."

"Come in the house now, Mr. Lincoln, and let's get you settled," Mrs. Speed politely injected. "You two will have plenty of time for catching up later, after a good dinner."

Joshua turned to the dark-skinned slave who had driven the wagon down to meet Lincoln at the wharf. "That's all for now, George. Get the horses taken care of." The wagon pulled away and headed down the small road that led around behind the house.

After enjoying the finest dinner that he had eaten in weeks, the table cleared by two young slave girls, Lincoln and his friend walked out behind the house. They began to stroll down the road that led to the larger field, now in late summer standing full of nearly grown hemp.

"Abraham, I must ask you: how are you really my friend? I can see that your health is good enough – or at least your appetite – but I am more concerned about your mind, your heart. Your letters have been so sad, you have sounded at times almost despondent. I know you have taken this thing with Mary quite hard."

"Yes, Joshua, I know you are concerned. All of my friends have been concerned, and I suppose with good cause. It is true I have not been myself lately. I feel so lost. I work, I prepare, I argue my cases, as always, some well and some not. But somehow it is not the same. It is as though none of it really matters anymore." Lincoln paused for a moment and the two men stop walking. "Ever since I first took that room above your store in Springfield, you have been so kind to me, Joshua, such a good friend. I can speak to you of matters which only you seem truly to understand. And this matter with Mary is about to be the end of me, or at least sometimes that is how it appears to my heart. She can be so difficult, so infuriating, but at the same time, I do love her so. I never thought that I would feel this way again after I lost poor Ann, but this love has grown strong. When we called off the wedding, well, it just brought back all those same terrible feelings from before, only somehow worse. For I know that Mary is still here, not buried in the ground, and I could be with her, I *should* be with her. But she doesn't seem to feel that way at all. Is there nothing I can do?" They slowly began walking again, letting the question linger in the still air.

Sensitive to his friend's outpouring of emotion, Joshua at first kept his eyes fixed on a rise ahead along the dirt road. "Yes, I know it has been hard, terribly hard for you. You have poured out your heart in your letters, and that is why I invited you here to Farmington. I hope that this time here will give you a chance to focus your thoughts, and work things out, one way or the other, so you can get on with your life." Joshua stopped again, pausing to look hard at this friend. "And Abraham, I pledge to you that I am going to help you. We will find some way of getting her back, or we will find a way for you to get over her. As I say, one way or another, we are going to get your back on your feet again. Your future is bright, you have much good to do, and I will not allow you to let it slip away. I promise you that. Together we will find a way."

A CLAP of thunder momentarily stirred Abe from his thoughts. A sense of melancholy briefly overtook him as he recalled the deep despair he had felt all of those many years ago. But then a thin smile crossed his lips, recalling Joshua's sincere concern, and his equally sincere desire to find a way to help his friend. Abe silently wondered, *What would have become of me except for this man?* All these years later he could now softly chuckle at how this concern had caused Joshua to request that his mother remove Abe's razor and knife from his room. How upset he quickly had become when he returned from their tour of the city to discover what had happened. But just as quickly, Abe had realized the depth of his friend's concern, and for the first time had to face head-on the question of whether such a thing was indeed possible. To face head-on exactly who he was and what was to become of him.

As soon as they were alone again after dinner Abe had confronted Joshua. "I appreciate your concern, I truly do, Joshua. But was it really necessary to have your mother remove my razor? Do you really think I am capable of that?"

"You tell me, Abraham. I see before me a man that I thought I knew, that loved life, loved people, who was a good friend. But that is not the man who has come here to visit me. I'm not sure what *this* man might be thinking, what he might do. I have to be concerned. I know that I can help you if you will let me. But you have to give me time, and show me that you still care, that you want to make this better. Can you do that, Abraham?"

Joshua's words stabbed at Abe's heart, but also helped to focus his mind. After a minute of silence Lincoln sighed deeply, the mist of despair lifting. "Joshua, you are such a good friend, a kind friend. What would I do without you? And yes, I want your help, I need your help. I do not think I would have come here if I didn't truly believe that you could help me, that things could be better." He looked at Joshua, smiling weakly. "I had a good talk with myself while I was up in my room before dinner. I am certainly not being a good friend to you, nor a good guest in your home. I realize that. And now I have concerned you so much that you fear for me. I am sure to have worried your poor mother as well."

He looked down at his feet for a moment, and then gathering his courage continued in a noticeably stronger voice. "Well, I will not have that. I promise I shall try, I shall focus, and as you said last night, together we will make this better. I know you cannot do it without me, cannot do it for me, that I must do my part, I must do the hard part, and I swear to you that that I am ready to do that. And as for the other...well, do not concern yourself or your kind mother so. For I feel that I could not bear to leave this world without having accomplished something worthwhile, something for which I might be re-membered. I must continue, at least until assured that I can leave it a better place for my having spent a little time here. Lord knows I have done nothing of value so far."

"That is not true, you have done much already." Joshua placed his hand on Abe's shoulder. "If nothing else you have been a good friend to me, and many others as well. But I know in my heart that you still have so much more to accomplish. It does comfort me greatly to hear you say speak these words. I will instruct Mother to return all of your things, with a lightened heart and mind."

They turned to walk back to the house. About half-way back, now strolling along leisurely in the growing darkness, Joshua broke their silence. "Abraham, I have been thinking that perhaps I could be a sort of emissary, if you will, in this matter. I know you both so well, you and Mary. I certainly know how you feel about it all, and I suspect that if I could get her to fully consider everything, that I will find that Mary shares many of the same feelings. I feel certain that she is going through much the same distress as you." He paused for just a moment, and then with a thin smile continued, "With your permission, I am going to assume this task. I am going to write to Mary and see how she feels, what is truly in her heart. If you don't mind my saying so, you can both be a *little* stubborn sometimes, not to mention proud." The smile now became a grin. "If you will allow me, I think it will be worth the effort. For I do honestly believe, and always have, that the two of you are so well-suited for each other, that you should be together, should be man and wife. I feel it is my obligation to help make it so. What do you think?"

Lincoln was not taken aback by his friend's warm criticism, for he knew it to be true. Yes, he could be stubborn, and proud. And Lord knows Mary certainly could be as well. Abe now found himself returning his friend's smile. "I suppose there is nothing to lose at this point. I would appreciate anything you think you might be able to do. I trust you completely Joshua, you know that. So I will trust you with my heart as well." The two men warmly shook hands, and then embraced.

ABE now sat in the train, his eyes closed yet fully awake, lost in his memories of how Joshua had, in time, been successful and how finally, happily, the marriage had taken place on that fine day in 1843. They had lived a good life together, he and Mary, all thanks to Joshua. Often difficult, too much pain and death, but still it had been a good life. Abe had no regrets. He opened his eyes to notice that the rain had let up considerably and the sky was beginning to lighten some. The train had slowed to pass through another small town – he was not sure which, it had been so long since he had last passed this way – but when the train began to gain speed again he realized they still had some distance to travel. He stared out over the green fields, full of newly planted tobacco, and corn, dotting the landscape here and there. But still his thoughts were focused on Farmington all those years ago. Now a somewhat contemplative look crossed his brow as he silently considered that even more than saving his marriage, his time in Louisville with Joshua had in fact made him the man that he now was.

For over the course of those weeks that late summer, stretching into fall, Lincoln experienced many different things, really *saw* them, seemingly for the first time. And more than anything else, he saw slavery. The visit turned out not only to heal his broken heart, but in many ways it began his political and moral education. For this was indeed Abraham Lincoln's first real exposure to the *moral* dilemma of slavery. He had certainly seen slaves before, many times, but he had not given the institution any serious consideration. It was simply a fact of life. Now he could not escape it. Each and *every* day he saw slaves serving him in Joshua's house, working around him in Joshua's fields, and in the neighbor's fields. And he saw close up and in person the reality of the slave markets, so active in the heart of the city near the Ohio River. He fully realized for the first time what it meant to be "sold down the river" to the cotton plantations of the South. He would never forget these sights and sounds, and feelings.

Further, there had been intense discussions of political and spiritual topics as well. He was especially taken with Joshua's older brother James, a respected local attorney. Lincoln was very impressed by the man's reasoning and intellect, and many spirited moments occurred between them. Joshua later told his friend, when they were back in Springfield, that it was then he knew that Lincoln had truly recovered. As for Abe, it meant that for the rest of his life he would forever be indebted to Joshua Speed. Even if they were miles apart geographically, or when issues serious or trivial might separate them politically, when years would go by without them seeing one another, none of that really mattered. Joshua had indeed *saved* Abe in so many ways, and he would never forget it.

Abraham Lincoln left Louisville a far different man than when he arrived, all those years ago. And now, he was about to arrive in the city again, still learning and changing, and would get to see his old friend for the first time since the days following the assassination attempt. It was time to renew an old friendship. *Past time,* Abe sat thinking. He was most anxious to share his thoughts, all that he had discussed that morning with the governor. For if Abe was to accomplish any of his lofty ideas, he knew there was one man who must be by his side.

CHAPTER EIGHTEEN

WHEN Abe opened his eyes for the second time that Friday afternoon he noticed that Mary was awake, standing at the small basin dabbing some water onto her face. The rain had completely stopped, and he looked out to see that the fields of tobacco had been given way to small houses. They had arrived at the outskirts of Louisville.

"I wasn't asleep," he offered, assuming what she might be thinking. Abe stood up stiffly, a few bones noticeable cracking, and walked over to look out the rear door.

"I know. I can tell when you are sleeping and when you are not. Thirty-five years of marriage have made me *quite* aware of your habits."

"It's funny you should say that. I was just thinking of our marriage, of my visit to Farmington and how Joshua helped to reconcile us." She turned and looked back at him.

"Well that's nice to hear, as you had such a pleasant look on your face. I am glad to know that you remember it so fondly." She laughed playfully. He turned to meet her twinkling eyes.

"Of course I do, you know that. I was just thinking that despite everything, we have had a good life together. Things I would change, certainly, but none of us can control our fate, and I would say, all-in-all, that we've done well for ourselves." Changing the subject he asked, "Did you have a nice rest? It was surely raining hard enough on the way over. Good sleeping weather."

Mary gave no audible reply, feeling none was necessary. It was merely polite small-talk between two who had been together for so long. Abe noticed that they were beginning to pass some groups of people outside along the tracks. The train had slowed considerably now, and Abe could tell by the nature and close confinement of the buildings that they were nearing the center of the city. Then for the first time, he caught a brief glimpse of the Ohio River out the right side of the car.

"I suppose I will step outside for some air, and to greet the folks." Opening the door he added, "It's still awfully damp. I believe you should wait inside until we arrive." Mary did not object, settling back into her chair. Abe stepped out and closed the door behind him, and immediately people began to shout out to him. At least one or two of the exclamations might have been of a derogatory nature - he couldn't hear that clearly over the clack of the train to be sure – but he was just as glad Mary remained inside.

He found it interesting that the more negative, even hateful reactions almost always tended to be heard along the fringes, along the tracks and roads leading into towns, and not so much at the actual arrival point. Abe could only assume that it was at least partially a result of security arrangements coordinated by the local politicians and authorities. He understood that they would want to avoid any political embarrassment no matter what their actual thoughts or positions might be. He was sure that many a local politician who had warmly welcomed him and praised him to his face had probably later cursed him behind closed doors. But it was the nature of the beast. Fortunately, with the passage of time more and more people were getting over it, at least in the north. But here, he reminded himself – his brush with Morgan's Men still fresh – he was closer to the territory of his former foe.

The train turned away from the river and headed a few blocks up into town, its pace growing ever slower, the numbers of people along the way increasing. As always, Abe stood waving to them all, friend or foe. As the train came to a halt at the depot he opened the door and waited for Mary to join him. There was a good sized crowd, not as large as they had encountered in Indianapolis or Cincinnati, but considering the weather a formidable gathering. Mary stepped out and the couple stood for a few minutes waving and smiling. Over to one side Abe noticed a contingent of men, along with a good number of uniformed police. In fact, he noticed that it was a much larger number of officers than seen at the other stops on the trip. The men began to make their way over to the train along the left side of the crowd. Abe immediately noticed Clark, who had not changed all that much since they had first met. He also correctly surmised that the larger and older man following immediately behind would be the mayor. *Another town, another Mayor,* Abe thought to himself, continuing to smile and wave.

Before he even came close to the train Clark was already shouting, "Mr. President, Mrs. Lincoln, welcome, welcome." Excitement leaped from every part of his rapidly moving body. "Welcome to Louisville." The police quickly secured a small space right off of the back of the Pullman, and Abe stepped down and then turned to assist his wife. He then turned to face Clark.

"Mr. President, it is such an honor to have you here. Thank you so much for coming. And you, Mrs. Lincoln as well. We are so very pleased that you could join us."

"Colonel Clark, it is so nice to see you again. Thank you for inviting us," Abe smiled, extending his hand, which Clark accepted and pumped vigorously.

"Yes Mr. President, at your complete service."

"And you remember Mary," Abe said, presenting his wife.

"Yes, of course. Mrs. Lincoln, how are you? You are looking so lovely today. I hope you had a pleasant trip."

"Thank you, Mr. Clark, quite pleasant. It is very nice to see you again," Mary replied, then immediately added, "but where is your lovely wife? We have so been looking forward to visiting with her again."

"How kind of you, Mrs. Lincoln. I assure you that Mary is looking forward to seeing you again as well. But what with the weather and crowds I advised her to stay in this afternoon. She will be with us tomorrow night, and of course at the Derby."

Not waiting for further introductions, for Clark was totally lost in the moment, Abe addressed the older man standing just to Clark's side, "And you sir, are the mayor if I am correct."

In a much calmer state the man answered, "Indeed sir. Charles Jacob. And on behalf of all of our citizens, let me formally welcome you back to Louisville. It is a pleasure and an honor to have you and Mrs. Lincoln with us today."

"Certainly our pleasure as well. We are greatly looking forward to reacquainting ourselves with your city." Turning back to their host, Abe added, "And of course seeing your new racetrack and the Derby. I imagine there is an air of excitement around town."

"Oh yes sir, very much so," Clark answered, regaining his manic excitement. "The city has not seen anything like this in some time." Looking up at the now bluing skies, he added, "And from the looks of it, we've hopefully seen the last of the rain and shall have nothing but perfect weather for your visit."

"I would expect nothing less!" Abe laughed, with the mayor and Clark joining in.

"Well then," Clark said, motioning in the direction of a waiting carriage, "shall we be off to the Galt House? We have arranged their best accommodations for you and Mrs. Lincoln. I'm sure you'll want to get settled in." With that they all got into a large, fine white carriage for the ride back towards the river. Clark was as good as his word – no speeches, no public ceremony, just another quick wave to the crowd and they were off. In some small way, Abe was almost disappointed. The politician in him could never resist an assemblage of people. But he quickly got over it, determined simply to enjoy the weekend.

A contingent of officers accompanied them along the way, keeping a close eye on the crowds lining the streets, resulting in a slow pace of travel. It almost resembled a short parade, with most people applauding and waving as they passed. There were also the expected shout-outs and more than one cat-call, which caused the mayor to wince noticeably. Abe quickly assured him not to worry, that it was to be expected, that he was used to it – simply a part of public life. Mary appeared to be oblivious, choosing to act as though she heard nothing, and seemed to enjoy waving and smiling all along the way.

After a prolonged twenty minute journey through the streets of the city, they made their way down First Street, arriving at the doors of the Galt House. Decorations had been hung around the doors, and four American flags hung from the second floor windows across the front. About a dozen officers created a corridor as several more went into the lobby. The manager of the hotel was at the door waiting to greet them.

"Mr. President, Mrs. Lincoln, welcome to the Galt House. It is our great pleasure to have you as our guests today. I suppose I should say, sir, welcome *back* to the Galt House."

"Thank you. And yes, you are correct, I have stayed at your fine establishment before, though not, I believe, at this location?"

"That is entirely correct. When you were here last we were located one block north, but alas that building burned in 1865. Four years later we opened this, may I say, greatly improved Galt House."

"Yes, that appears to be the case. But what a shame you lost the other. Such great history there, I am sure. I know you hosted several of my generals, as well as some of my predecessors in office. As you may know, Generals Grant and Sherman laid out some important plans there."

"I do indeed recall, as I was there then, as I was during your last visit. I was a clerk at the desk when you last stayed with us. Now I am proud to say I am manager."

"I am sure you must have many great tales to tell. Perhaps sometime during the weekend we will have the opportunity for you to share some of them."

"It would be a pleasure. And now, if you are ready, allow me personally to show you to your rooms – the finest we have to offer." He did not mention the relocations of other scheduled guests that had been required to secure accommodations for the Lincolns when their coming was so recently made known.

The manager escorted Abe and Mary up to their two room suite. Upon entering the first room they immediately noticed a fine view of the Ohio River from the large windows opposite the door, and then the lavish furnishings of red silk and deep mahogany wood. It was a stunning sitting room, as nice as anything in the White House, or anywhere else they had stayed for that matter, and the bedroom proved to be equally well-appointed. Yes, they declared to their host's delight, *this* would do splendidly for their Louisville sojourn.

DOWNSTAIRS, the mayor and most of the officers departed. Two remained in the lobby and two more went upstairs to keep watch on the hallway outside the Lincolns' room. Alex sat over in a corner taking in all of this activity, holding a newspaper, oblivious to anything printed. At first he was slightly taken aback at the sight of so many policemen, but quickly reassured himself that it would be a completely different situation at the racetrack. There would be too many people, too much excitement. Besides, who would expect anything from Clark's able assistant? Any officers present would be completely unconcerned with him. Alex looked across the room and caught the eye of Tommy, who was trying to look as inconspicuous as possible. He was more bothered by the officers than was Alex, probably for good reason, as Tommy knew them and they certainly knew him. Their continued presence could only serve to interfere with his normal activities, and he was greatly annoyed. Alex stood, dropping the paper onto the chair and walked to the front door, maintaining eye contact with the boy, insuring that he would follow.

Out on the street, around the corner, Tommy located Alex, who smiled slightly at his new assistant as the boy approached him. "So now he has arrived," Alex said as his smile became a sneer. "That was some show wasn't it?"

Tommy replied, "Don't like all them damn police everywhere. They're gonna be keeping an eye on me."

"Oh, don't worry so much about them. They'll get bored after a little while, get distracted with all these fancy people showing up, especially the women. They won't much give a damn what you're doing." Alex looked around quickly to make sure no one was close enough to hear them. "Now you know what to do. I want to know everywhere he's going and everything he's doing. I'll either be up in my room or around the lobby, mostly. Come on by in an hour or so and we'll get dinner."

"Don't worry, boss, you'll know what the man's doing before he does."

ABOUT forty-five minutes later, across the city in Smoketown, Marcus walked in the front door of his modest little house, Oliver and Bug Eye following behind. They had not come from the track as usual, but from town, as Clark had arranged for an early wagon so that some of the workers could go welcome Lincoln.

"Is that you, Marcus?" his wife Bev cried out from the kitchen where she was finishing her cooking. "Bout time you got home." She walked out into the front room and saw her two children hugging on their father. "Well, did you see him?"

"I surely did, didn't we boys?" Oliver and Bug Eye nodded in agreement, sitting down in what had now become their customary chairs. "And it surely was something. There was people all along the street just a-waving and cheering. We got us a good spot right there on First Street. Went by so slow we got us a good long look."

"Looked right at me," Bug Eye said proudly as he played with Marcus' son.

"Hope you didn't look back at him with them buggedy eyes. Scare the man half to death." Bev started laughing, then stopped suddenly and with a disapproving look said, "Is that liquor I'm smelling Marcus? What the hell have you boys been doing? Bet you never even saw no President Lincoln. Just an excuse to get outta work and go drinking." She turned and stormed back into the kitchen.

"That ain't so," Marcus shouted after her. "We sure enough went and saw him." Then turning and smiling to Oliver, added, "We just had to go and celebrate a little. This was a special occasion and all. Just had one little drink in the president's honor. Couldn't be helped. Isn't that right Ollie?"

"Sure 'nough, 'cept, mighta been two drinks. But no more'n that."

"And besides," Marcus said, walking over to the kitchen door, "the boss went with us. Closed the shop down and everything. So see, it really was a special occasion. Hell, he's the one that bought the drinks. Now I couldn't refuse that now, could I? That would a been nuthin but bad manners. You know my momma raised me better than that." There was a moment of silence, and Marcus looked at Oliver and Bug Eye with a shrug and expression that said, *What else am I supposed to do now?"* The three of them could hardly keep from busting out laughing. Then Bev appeared at the kitchen doorway again, the beginnings of a smile now on her face as well. "You beat everything, you know that? You always got a answer for everything, don't you?

"Yeah. And it's usually a good one, ain't it children?" They all broke out laughing.

ABE had wanted to see his old friend as soon as possible, so he had sent a note to Joshua asking that he and Fanny join them for dinner that night at the hotel. A private dining room had been arranged, and just before six o'clock the Lincolns walked out into the upstairs hall where Abe greeted the two police officers, informing them that he and Mary were going down for dinner. One remained outside the room and the other followed along. Abe wanted to get some air, so as his wife made her way on into the dining room he stepped outside in front of the hotel, two officers accompanying him. Immediately there was a stir among the people there. He said hello, greeting all the officers present as well, thanking them for their time and efforts. It was only a few moments later that a carriage arrived, and indeed Joshua and Fanny stepped out.

"Added a little bit of grey there, haven't you Abraham?" Joshua walked up and hugged him warmly. "It is so good to see you again, my friend. It's been far too long – these last ten years have seemed in many ways so much longer."

"Let me take a good look at you, Joshua. Yes, if I am not mistaken I believe you have fallen victim to that same calamity. But Fanny, you are looking as young and beautiful as ever. It is so good to see you both." He kissed her lightly on her cheek.

Fanny smiled. "I see you may have aged just a little, Mr. Lincoln, but your tongue had maintained all of its youthful charm and ability. It is wonderful to see you as well. But where is Mary?" She looked around, her smile fading. "She is all right, isn't she?" Both she and Joshua were well aware of Mary's propensity for "spells."

"Oh yes, quite well, and greatly looking forward to seeing you both. She is waiting for us in the dining room. Shall we go in and join her?' With a last wave to the small crowd that had gathered, Abe led the Speeds into the hotel and across the lobby. They made their way toward the back of the large dining room, where they found their private quarters.

The evening passed far too quickly, with many memories and well-worn stories, warm moments between good friends. During dinner Joshua announced that he had a very pleasant surprise touching on his old family home and Lincoln's previous visit there. Abe awaited this news with great interest. He knew that Farmington had not been Joshua's home for many years now; not in fact since shortly after his stay there, having been purchased back in 1846 by Austin Peay, the husband of Joshua's sister Peachy. Beyond that he was but vaguely acquainted with the subsequent history of the estate, but knew at least that Peachy had later sold it all out of the family after her husband's death, in 1865. Not having seen Joshua since around the time of that occurrence, Abe knew little more about it.

Now Speed informed the Lincolns that the current owner of Farmington – a casual acquaintance of Joshua's – had upon hearing of the president's return to Louisville insisted that they all come for a visit. After all, Lincoln had spoken often enough of his long-ago stay there that it had become part of his public lore, especially among Kentuckians. Plans had been made for the Speeds and the Lincolns to spend Sunday afternoon at the old home-place. Abe shared Joshua's obvious excitement about the prospect, for Joshua had not been there for many years as well. Abe and Mary would attend Colonel Clark's affair the next evening, on Saturday, but Sunday would be reserved for their friends, their private enjoyment. It was a delightful prospect, and more than Abe could have hoped for from this visit.

In the glow of this anticipation, the Lincolns saw the Speeds off and then retired to their room for the evening. It had been a long day, and Abe was tired. He hated to admit that he was beginning to feel his age, but it was true enough. It would be good to be off of the train for a few days, to be planted in one place. Tomorrow they would see some of the city, if Mary felt up to it; but for tonight, a good night's sleep.

AS Alex watched the pair cross the lobby and ascend the stairs, he smiled and murmured aloud, "Sleep well, Mr. Lincoln. Sleep in peace." Then, just as he had done upon witnessing their arrival as they first crossed that lobby, he added silently, *Enjoy this weekend. It shall be your last!*

CHAPTER NINETEEN

JUST after sunrise the next morning Ansel watched Chesapeake gallop down the racetrack. It was a clear sky, no trace of the spring storms that had brought heavy rain the day before. Quite the opposite: now that the front had passed on through it was going to be a hot day, more like mid-summer. Ansel could feel it coming. It worried him. Chesapeake didn't like the heat. But then again, probably none of his competitors did either. His mind wandered to his other horse, Aristides – or as the trainer like to call him, that "little red hoss." A full hand shorter than Chesapeake, the heat might not bother him so much. Satisfied that everything looked good, Ansel headed back toward the barn to await the horse's return.

Aristides had already been out for his gallop that morning, had finished his bath and was now busily downing a bucket of oats. Ansel stopped by for a look and was pleased to see the horse eating with such vigor. It was a good sign. Everything looked good here as well. Two good horses, one that everybody was watching, one that nobody was paying any attention to; one way or the other, he figured he had as good a chance at winning this race as anybody, maybe better.

Over in the General's barn, Charlie had just brought McCreary back from a jog, and was about ready to take a bay colt out to work with the filly. Bug Eye was already mounted on her and waiting to go to the track. Old Tom wanted his prized horse to have someone to run against for her final serious work before the Oaks. The track was a little thick from the previous day's rain, but he decided it was good enough to go ahead with the work. Had to stay on schedule – at this point in time that was the most important thing.

While he was waiting Bug Eye asked, "So how's McCreary doing, any better?"

Charlie just shrugged and said, "Yeah, I guess so. Seems to like it better up here. Old Tom's got him over whatever was ailin' him down south, but he sure ain't got all his strength back yet. Gettin' a little better each day, though. Gonna give him a little blow out tomorrow, and then Old Tom's gonna let the General know all about it, and I guess they'll decide what they want to do about the Derby."

"Who's gonna ride him if they do?" Bug Eye asked hopefully. He sure would like to ride in the race.

"Prob'ly Dickie Jones, I imagine, that's who rode him last time out, but hell, I don't really know. Horse ain't got no business runnin' at all yet if you ask me, 'specially not for no mile and a half. But I ain't the boss now, am I?" Charlie mounted up and they headed on out for their work.

As the horses slowly walked along, nearing the opening onto the track, Charlie looked up at the shiny new grandstand, sitting empty, gleaming in the bright morning sun. He was thinking about how he was going to miss riding for Old Tom. He liked the man as well as he liked anyone, better than most. But after Monday Charlie was going back to New Orleans one way or the other, and he would have to tell the trainer soon. He decided that he would wait until the next day. Wouldn't be much notice, but also wouldn't be enough time for Old Tom to nag at him about staying. Besides, the trainer would probably miss Charlie's brother more anyway. Despite his perceived disagreeable disposition, Crabby was a good handler of horses, and Old Tom liked him. But there were always grooms and exercise boys to be found a-round the track, so Charlie wasn't too worried about how Old Tom would take the news. He'd just have to deal with it. There wasn't going to be any other choice.

Seeing as how it was Saturday, Charlie decided that he and Crabby should catch a ride into town after work. It would probably be their last chance to get there, so might as well kick up their heels a little bit. And besides, he really wanted to see Alex, just to make sure everything was still on track. This was one job where he definitely didn't want any surprises, not for him or anybody else. He might not really have that much to do with it on Monday, but he was smart enough to realize that if things did go south, he'd be stuck in it all, but good. No sense taking any chances, no matter what Alex said.

CLARK had arrived at the track well before dawn. He wanted to make his last walk through on Saturday before opening the facility to the vendors and bookmakers, to allow time should any final corrections be deemed necessary. He had also promised himself a day of rest, or at least a lighter, less stressful day on Sunday, the last day before opening day and the Derby. He had looked over the final entries for all four of the opening day races. While his emphasis was on the Derby, he wanted all four races to have quality fields and be of interest, especially to the bettors.

The first race would be at a mile and a quarter, for older horses. The purse was three hundred dollars, all to go to the winner, and it had drawn seven entries. The second race was the Derby, to be run at a mile and a half, just as at Epsom. The cost to the owner was fifty dollars to enter, and then another fifty dollars to start, with the Association adding to that money another thousand dollars. The bulk of the purse – which was looking like it would be upward of three thousand dollars – would go to the winning owner, with two hundred dollars set aside for second place. The third race was a one mile sprint for older horses, a purse of five hundred dollars, with one hundred set aside for second. It had drawn a field of five. The fourth and final race would be a two mile test, again for older horses, with three hundred dollars all going to the winner. Most likely six horses would contest it.

Clark was pleased. It would be a good card, and everyone, especially the Association members, should be satisfied. To Clark all that really mattered was the Derby, and it had drawn more interest than even he had hoped. Indeed forty-two horses had been nominated, and it still appeared that around fifteen or so would start. For the first time in a long while, he felt satisfied.

With Vernon and a couple of workers at his side, Clark meticulously toured the entire facility. They began at the barns, which were still in their full flurry of morning activity. There really wasn't much of concern there, as this area had already been in operation for several weeks, but Clark wanted to be thorough. They moved on to the grandstand, walking each aisle and stairway, slowly moving throughout the entire structure. He inspected the grounds behind and in front, and then satisfied, they moved on finally to the clubhouse.

While Clark originally had planned for the Lincolns to watch the Derby from the top of the clubhouse, he ultimately decided it would be best to reserve that space for the Association members, who had put up most of the money for his operation. He wanted to make sure that they were all well satisfied and taken care of, and there simply was not enough room comfortably to accommodate his special guests and the members. After opening day it would be reserved for the ladies as planned, but for that first day, what with all of the special arrangements required...well, the ladies would just have to be a little inconvenienced.

So Clark quickly had decided that the former president and his wife would join him in a special section of the grandstand. In an effort to try to engage his assistant, to help him feel a part of it all, Clark had assigned Vernon the task of determining the exact location in the grandstand where Clark should have his personal seats, where he and the Lincoln's would view the running of the Derby. Vernon had taken the task to heart, and Clark was satisfied with the final arrangement. Of course in reality there was little real decision to be made, otherwise Clark would have done it himself. But he knew it would make Vernon feel a little more important, and hopefully, make the man more agreeable to the whole "Lincoln business."

They were to be seated near the top on the western end, which would provide an excellent view of the horses coming around the far turn and down the stretch. It was very easily accessible from a nearby back stairway. The

Lincolns would enjoy the beginning of the day and the first race from the clubhouse, so that Association members could see the former president and feel included in this special occasion. Then after watching the horses for the Derby saddled in the paddock, Clark would personally escort his guests up to their seats just in time to watch the race. To help ensure at least some privacy, Clark had reserved the seats around the Lincolns for the governor and other dignitaries and officials. It was all very workable, and had solved many of his seating challenges.

Every time he saw something during the inspection that was not satisfactory Clark snapped at Vernon to make a note of it, and then to follow up to ensure that it was properly taken care of. Vernon only grew more agitated, thinking, *He doesn't have to tell me that every damn time.* But all the assistant would say was, "Yes sir, Colonel. I'll be sure it gets done, and gets done right. You don't need to worry about a thing." Though ultimately the list was short, by the end of the tour Vernon only wanted to get as far away from Clark as he could.

Fortunately for Vernon his boss soon departed for the city, confident that he had taken care of everything necessary at the racetrack. Clark had final preparations to make for the dinner and reception that evening at the Galt House for the Association members. It would be a grand affair, a great celebration of all he had accomplished, made that much better by the presence of the Lincolns. It was the only event other than the Derby itself that Clark had asked the president to attend, and he and his wife had graciously accepted.

As Vernon watched Clark ride away, he said to himself, "I'll be glad to be done with that bastard. Him and all his damn orders. I don't mind working for a man, long as it's a man who treats you right, shows you a little respect. Like old Colonel Clark. The real Colonel, not some made up name like this sorry son-of-a-bitch. He'll never be the man his father was." A smile crossed his face. "Yeah, you just wait, *Colonel.* I got a little surprise in store for you, all right. Come Monday you won't be ordering me around no more. You'll wish you'd never ever seen me before. Yes, indeed, I got a surprise in store for *everybody."*

PEANUT was just cleaning up from the morning's workouts, having washed up, now changing into some cleaner clothes. He made his way down out of the loft and found Calvin standing just outside the barn. He was collecting on some sort of bet he had made with one of the other riders. Peanut could tell that the other man was none too happy about it, but knew better than to try to cross Calvin. After the man had walked off, Peanut went over to Calvin.

"How much money you got there Calvin? Sure nuff looks like a nice roll. How 'bouts we go on into town and spend some of it? You'll buy your ol' buddy a drink or two now, won't you?"

"Don't be bothering me about money, Peanut. I know you got a roll of your own, and plenty more coming. You can buy your own damn drinks."

"I ain't got no roll like that. You a rich man, Calvin. Come on, let's go into town. I'll tell you what, I'll buy *you* a drink. Hows 'bout that?"

"Just shut up now about all that. Maybe we'll go to town all right. But not 'til after we meet Delacroix. It'd be stupid to head all the way into town, and then have to come back out to the shack. Besides, I need to have a clear head when I'm talking to him. They'll be time enough for all that other later on." He started up the ladder to the loft. "You can go and do any damn thing you want, but me, I'm gonna have me a little nap for a while. Then we'll go see Delacroix, and then you can buy me a drink if you want. I ain't letting you out of that. What's offered's offered."

Peanut didn't feel tired. He was ready to go now, but he knew Calvin was right They weren't meeting with Alex until four that afternoon, and it wasn't even quite noon yet. If they went to town now they'd be no use to anybody by four, so Peanut walked on over to the General's barn to see if he could find Bug Eye to kill some time. Maybe Bug Eye would want to roll some dice.

When he got there he quickly found Bug Eye and Oliver just outside the barn, sitting on a hay bale in the shade. It was already a hot day, with the sun beating down. They had enjoyed the cooler Kentucky weather, but now it felt almost like they were back in New Orleans.

"Hey Bug Eye, what's y'all up to?"

"Just try-in' to stay cool," Bug Eye said with no expression, with his short legs stretched out, head leaning against a post. "It surely has turned off hot now, ain't it? Them horses sure ain't gonna like running in this heat if it's like this come Monday."

"Hey ya, Peanut," Oliver said nonchalantly. "What's doing?"

"Well if it ain't the great Derby jockey," Peanut teased him. "You gonna win that big race on Monday? Make all that money?"

"Don't expects so, Peanut, don't expects so." Then he added, "But it's *sho nuff* a horse race, so you never knows now, do you? Least I got me a chance."

"Not on that little horse, least not from what I seen. Don't think he could hardly find the finish if he was the only horse out there." Oliver just smiled.

"Well, we'll see about that come Monday now, won't we? He may be more than he looks."

"You boys wanna roll some dice?" Peanut asked, tired of needling the young jockey.

Bug Eye replied without moving, "Naw, ain't got no money. Too hot anyways."

"What about you, Derby boy?" Peanut asked looking back at Oliver. "I know you gots some money."

"I done learned not to roll no dice with you, Peanut. What little money I got I want to keep for my own."

Realizing that he wasn't getting anywhere Peanut changed directions, asking, "Well then, ya got anything to drink? I surely am thirsty."

"Big bucket o' water right over there," Bug Eye replied, again without moving.

"You know that ain't what I'm talkin' bout."

"Can't help you none there, neither, and don't bother asking Ollie. He's a good boy. Don't do no drinkin'." Bug Eye grinned just a little.

"You two ain't worth shit now, are you?"

"You see ol' Clark come through here a little while ago?" Bug Eye asked, now sitting up on the hay bale. "He sure was making a show. Lookin' at this and lookin' at that, and ordering that poor ol' limpidy one-armed fool all around. Had to feel kinda sorry for him." Peanut grunted.

"I don't pay no attention to that man. He sure don't pay no attention to me. Don't even know who I am, which is more than fine with me." Then Peanut smiled and added, "And that Preston, well he may not be as big of a fool as you think. Clark had better keep an eye on that old man."

"What you mean by that, Peanut?" Bug Eye looked at him closely. "What you be a knowin'?"

"Nothin', Bug Eye, nothin' for you to worry about." Peanut paused for a minute, regretting that he had said anything. Bug Eye was still staring at him, wondering about the smile that had now vanished from his face. "All I'm saying is, you jess never know what a crazy old bastard like him might do. It's them kind that you got to keep your eye on. And Clark just goes around acting like he's nothin', like a piece of trash, that's all."

Bug Eye stared at him for another few seconds, and then leaned back against the post. "Well, if'n I didn't know no better, I'd say you knows something you ain't telling, something about that poor old white man. But I don't guess it's none o' my business no ways."

"That's right, ain't none of your business at all." Peanut immediately regretted saying this as well. "Hell, you two ain't worth *nothin'*," and then, "guess I'll go see what Calvin's up to."

Bug Eye and Oliver sat quietly as Peanut headed back in the direction from which he had come. After a minute Oliver asked, "What'n hell was that all about?"

Bug Eye sat back up. "Don't ask me. But I say that boy is up to something, and it's probably no good. And you'd better believe that means that Calvin's in on it, too. Don't trust the two of them no way, no how. Better keep our eyes and ears open." Standing now, he added, "Let's go get us something to eat. I done worked up a extra big appetite this morning." He smiled at his young friend. "But then I guess you'd better watch what you eat. Ol' Aristides won't like it too much if you go and get fat now."

IT was about one o'clock when Charlie and his brother got to the Galt House, standing just across the street. There were a couple of uniformed police officers waiting outside the front doors. All of a sudden, several more came out and before they knew it, there stood Abraham Lincoln, plain as day.

"Well, will you look at that," Charlie said grinning, "its old Abe himself. What do you know about that?" Crabby just stood and stared. Several people crossed the street over to the center of the increasing activity, but the Appleton brothers stood their ground as others started calling out and waving. Crabby took a good hard look at the man. He certainly didn't feel any love for him, but didn't feel any hatred either. He was just another man as far as Crabby was concerned, just another man getting into a carriage to go for a ride.

Charlie and Crabby watched as Lincoln and his wife boarded the carriage, then pulled out and headed west down the street, moving away from where they were standing. The crowd quickly dispersed and people went back about their business. Just then Charlie saw Alex walk out of the hotel wearing his distinctive cream-colored suit, looking down the street after Lincoln. The brothers watched as their associate took out one of his fancy cigarettes and lit it, throwing the match into the street. Alex stood there for a few moments, taking in the scene, smoke swirling in the light breeze, until finally he looked in their direction. Their eyes met. Alex immediately exhibited a look of displeasure. After surveying the entire scene again, he turned and walked east, in the opposite direction from where the carriage had gone. He continued down two blocks and then at the corner, turned left towards the river. Across the street, Charlie and his brother followed Alex's steps, eventually turning north as well, crossing over, continuing to follow.

They had lost sight of him and after another block had begun to wonder where Alex could have gone, if he were intentionally trying to lose them. Then a voice from behind said, "What in the *hell* do you think you are doing? Have you gone crazy?"

Charlie turned first, and then his brother, spotting Alex standing in a darkened doorway. "Hey, Boss," Charlie said much too loudly.

"I should kill you now just for being so stupid. Will you please keep your voice down before everybody in town sees you?" Charlie stopped smiling. "I specifically told you I didn't want you here in town. What the hell are you thinking?" Alex could not have been more upset, and he did nothing to hide it.

In a much quieter voice Charlie replied, "Calm down, Boss Its okay, there ain't nobody around." He quickly looked up and down the street just to make sure. "I don't mean no harm, I just wanted to make sure everything was okay, you know, goin' along accordin' to plan. That's all."

"Everything *was* going according to plan, that is until you two showed up. Do you have any idea what could happen if somebody sees us together at this point? Do you just want to ruin all of my perfect plans?"

"I'm sorry, Boss. Really, I am. It's just that it's hard, you know, sittin' out there at the track all day, waitin' for things to happen. We decided we needed a little action, and then we saw you and everything, figured we might just as well say hello. If everything is good, you know, is okay, well then we'll just be on our way and have a little drink or two and leave you alone."

"You'll do no such thing. The last thing I need is for you to get liquored up here in town and start shooting off that big mouth of yours. No telling what you might say and no telling who might be listening. I'll tell you what you're going to do. You're going to head right back out Fourth Street, all the way out to that racetrack and you're going to stay right there and keep your goddamn mouth shut!" Then he turned to Crabby, who had been listening quietly, watching up and down the street. "As for you, do me a favor and keep this brother of yours out of trouble. One thing I don't have to worry about is *you* talking too much. See if a little of that can rub off on your brother."

Alex paused for a moment, regaining some of his composure as he also checked their surroundings for any invaders. Changing his tone he continued, "Look Charlie, I know you don't mean any harm, but you just don't understand how much of a risk this is. There'll be plenty of time for drinking and celebrating when we get back south. For now you just need to be a little more patient and focused on the task at hand. I know it's hard as your part's mostly done already. And you've done an excellent job. I compliment you on it. Now if you would please just let the rest of us do our jobs without putting us at risk. Can you understand that, son? Can you do that?"

"Yes, sir, Boss, I do, I swear I do. And I can, I mean we both can. I don't know what I was thinkin'. I am truly sorry. Won't happen again."

"That's all right." Alex stepped back, confident he had made his point, and after another quick look around continued. "And as long as you are here, I suppose I must admit you've actually done me a favor. I was going to send word to you through Calvin to meet me at the shack tomorrow to get the final instructions, but as long as we're all here now, I suppose that won't be necessary."

With something of a flourish, Alex produced a white envelope from his inside suit pocket, holding it for both brothers to see. "Everything else you need to know is written here. I didn't want to give it to you until tomorrow, just to be safe. But I suppose I can trust you with it now. You know what will happen if any other living soul reads this, don't you?" He looked hard at each of them, but particularly at Charlie. Charlie could not help but notice the look of contempt that now came over the man's face. Alex broke eye-contact, his gaze now fixed on some unseen point off in the distance. "I suppose it is foolish to record such a thing, but as I am well aware of your *limited faculties* I must be certain that all is clearly understood."

Looking back directly at Charlie, he paused for a moment, then his face softened and he continued. "Very well then, take this and guard it at all costs." He hesitated for just an instant, then handed the envelope over. "Once you have read it, somewhere where you have complete privacy, and read it again and again until you know it by heart, then burn it so no one else will ever know its contents. Can you do that for me?"

Charlie, who had been stung by Alex's words, simply nodded his head with a solemn expression fixed on his face, no sign of a smile now. "Very good then," Alex nodded back. He also removed an eagle gold piece from his pocket and handed it to Crabby. "Now, go and buy yourself a good bottle, and then enjoy it when you are back safely at the track, *alone*. You both know how important this is, not just to me, but to millions of us all across this great country. Gentlemen, we are almost home. Do not fail me now. Until Monday afternoon, after the deed is done." Alex turned and walked north toward the river.

Charlie and Crabby stood looking at each other, and at the envelope. Charlie was the first to speak, in a sarcastic tone, still stung by the way Alex had treated him. "Well, ain't he just all pretty damn high'n mighty now? The way he pulled this letter outa his suit, you'd a thought he was actin' on a stage He must think he's the second comin' of Booth himself." Crabby as usual merely grunted an assent.

Charlie carefully folded and placed the letter in his pocket, and then after a couple of minutes they turned and headed in the opposite direction from the one Alex had taken. At the corner they turned, went down six blocks, passing by the front of the Galt House, then proceeded south out Fourth Street. Except for one stop to purchase a bottle as Alex had instructed, they did not stop or talk to anyone, hardly even themselves, until they were out of the city.

More than half-way back to the track, after carefully watching, more carefully than ever before, just to be entirely sure that no one could possibly be anywhere around, Charlie and Crabby left the road and made their way through the trees to the little shack. It was deserted as usual. Charlie opened the bottle, took a long drink and handed it to his brother, who did the same. They sat at the little table, and Charlie took out the envelope and removed the paper that was inside. He carefully unfolded it, looked at his brother for a moment, and then began silently to read what it said. He was immediately taken aback and not a little angry over the length and detail of the note, but he supposed that it was due to his *limited faculties* that Alex had felt it necessary to leave nothing to chance. After regaining his composure, he continued reading, not daring to utter the words aloud even to Crabby:

Gentlemen,

You are to inform Mr. Preston that I will be positioned in the infield of the track, towards the far turn, at the head of the stretch, just to the left of his station. I will be wearing a brown suit and hat, with a green tie. I will avoid crowds so that I stand out. Everyone else will be along the rail or running towards the finish. I will be STATIONARY! Please impress this fact upon Mr. Preston as it is vital. Assure him that I will make myself NOTICABLE TO HIM!!

Next please make it clear that he is to do NOTHING until receiving my signal. I will have a clear position from which to observe the entire situation. Once I have determined that it safe to proceed I will signal him by WAVING MY HAT VIGOROUSLY! Again, impress upon him that he must not proceed until receiving my SIGNAL!!

Finally remind Mr. Preston that after the deed is done, he should immediately RUN as quickly as possible to our dark friends who will assist him. Assure him that he must do this as it will be his ONLY AVENUE OF ESCAPE!

Our dark friends are well aware of their tasks and I am confident will fulfill them reliably so we have no need to discuss their role further.

As for you, my fiends, I will meet you in the barn directly after the NOBLE DEED is done, where we will immediately depart for points south. Please be prepared as there will be no time to waste.

Once you have read this and committed the

*contents to memory destroy by burning. We
can take no chance of it falling into the enemy's
hands.*

A.D.

After reading the document carefully, twice, Charlie handed it to his brother. He sat silently as Crabby read through it, and then folded it. He looked up at Charlie as if to ask, *You got it?*, at which point Charlie merely nodded slightly. Charlie slumped back in the chair and began rubbing his eyes as Crabby stood and took out a match. He turned and struck it on the old frame of the cot. Charlie sighed deeply, feeling tired, looking down at his worn dusty boots. When he looked back up he could see the glow of the paper's flame, getting brighter and then slowly dying. Crabby held onto it for as long as he could and then dropped it to the ground. Charlie now stood as it finished burning, the ash withering on the dirt floor. He then took his foot and ground the ashes until it was hard to tell that anything had been there. He looked at the plain white envelope lying on the table. "Do we need to burn that, too?" Crabby said nothing, simply wadded it up and threw it on the ground.

"Nah, there's nothing written on it. It doesn't matter – save the match. Let's get the hell outa here." Charlie looked out, and when satisfied that they were alone, the brothers headed out and back up to the road. When they reached the track they went directly to the tack room, where they silently consumed the contents of the bottle Alex had insisted they buy, not showing their faces again that night, rarely speaking to each other, much on both of their minds.

CHAPTER TWENTY

THE Lincolns had enjoyed a leisurely morning, the first of their trip. It was now Saturday and they had been traveling for five days. It was refreshing not to have to be on the train, not to have to be anywhere. After breakfast in their room Abe caught up on some correspondence while Mary simply gazed out over the river, sometimes doing her needlepoint, quietly humming an unrecognizable tune. Around noon they went down to the dining room for lunch, and then decided it would be a lovely afternoon for a tour of the city. Clark had provided a fine carriage for their personal use while in town. The mayor had assigned one of his assistants, a member of one of Louisville's oldest and finest families, to serve as their escort. This man regaled them with stories and anecdotes of the city's rich past, which Abe enjoyed to the fullest. He marveled at how the city had grown since his previous visit all those years ago. Several times they stopped so that he could get out and greet well-wishers. Occasionally there were some cat-calls as well, but he smiled and waved all the same.

Abe particularly appreciated the portion of their tour that led up a high hill to the east of the city, where they stopped briefly on the grounds of a new school for the blind to admire the expansive view of Louisville afforded there. It was all so different from the city in his memories. Below them in the foreground were open fields, beyond which the Beargrass Creek meandered. In the middle distance, the steeple of the Catholic Church in the center of town rose high above any other buildings. Off to the west was the new railroad bridge. And of course, ever dominating the scene, the mighty Ohio River cut its path.

Abe could have gone on all afternoon, but after about three hours Mary was growing weary and wanted to return to the hotel to rest in preparation for the dinner that evening. Just before four o'clock the carriage pulled back up in front of the hotel and the Lincolns made their way back upstairs to their suite.

WHILE the Lincolns were enjoying their afternoon outing, Alex was busy tying up some loose ends with Calvin and Peanut. As he rode out to the shack to meet with the two men, Alex went over his encounter with the Appleton brothers again and again in his mind, becoming angrier the more he did so. When it came right down to it, he decided, he simply couldn't *trust* Charlie. Oh, he could trust him in the usual sense, trust him to do what Alex needed, trust him to do a good job. But ultimately he could not trust his nature. Charlie was always smiling that goddamn smile, and was just too loose at the tongue. For most jobs that really did not matter so much – in fact, Alex sometimes liked that his associate would go off at the mouth. Alex took perverse pleasure in knowing that people had found out about his schemes, as long as it was after-the-fact. It burnished his reputation. But this... this was an entirely different situation. This was truly a matter of life and death. Alex was not about to put his life in Charlie's hands. No, he didn't feel that sort of trust – the stakes were entirely too high to make that gamble. By the time Alex had arrived at the shack he knew what had to be done. And by coincidence he was meeting with just the ones to do it.

Alex's thoughts turned to the other Appleton brother. As far as Crabby was concerned...well, that was the luck of the draw, an unfortunate situation that could not be helped. Though he found Crabby's general disposition annoying, Alex really had nothing against him. But the man was too damned quiet. Alex was never really sure what he was thinking, but for the most part assumed it was about nothing much, believing the man was none too bright. *Yes, a pity,* Alex told himself – but a necessary part of the business with which he found himself currently engaged.

As usual Alex had made it a point to arrive at the shack first, to assure himself that it was safe and private. He had only been there for a few minutes when he saw Calvin, closely followed by his ever-present companion. Alex wasted no time, as he had no time to waste. The three of them sat down and Alex started the meeting.

"Everything going along all right?" he asked them. "You got everything figured out?" Despite his agitation during the ride out, he conveyed his customary air of complete calm and confidence.

"Yeah, everthing's jus' fine," Calvin replied, just as coolly. "I checked it all out and it's jus' like you said. Looks to me like everthing'll work out smooth as can be. Once the race get started, we oughta have us clear sailing."

"Good. I wanted to make sure you saw everything the way I did. Couldn't be a better set-up if you ask me." The three men nodded in agreement. "Well, that's all settled then. If things go one way, I'll see you in the barns and we'll all head on over to the train. If they happen to go the other way, I'll leave enough for you hidden here, and then I'll see you later back down home." He waited for any other response, making sure they were indeed all in agreement. When nothing was said he continued. "Now, I got one other thing, one other little complication that's come up. I'm sure you won't mind one other job if it pays extra."

"Go on," Calvin replied with no hesitation, a blank expression on his face.

"Well, for all our sakes, I just don't think we can have Charlie Apple running around maybe shooting his mouth off. You both know how he can be sometimes. I think we've got to do something about that."

"I'm listenin'." Still no change of expression.

"It's like this. Monday morning there's going to be a little accident out on the track. Over on the backstretch, old Charlie's going to accidently fall off his horse, and unfortunately for him, there's going to be another horse coming along at just the wrong time, and Charlie's going to get trampled, in fact he's going to get trampled real good. Poor old Charlie isn't ever coming back from that ride. You catch my drift?" Calvin glanced over at Peanut. A knowing look, but still no discernible change.

Then to no one in particular, as if looking off into the distance, Calvin coolly replied, "Yeah, I can see how that's gonna happen. Gonna be a shame, too, but ya know how accidents like that happen all the time. Out there early when it's still dark'n all, jus' no telling what might happen."

"Good. We understand each other then. A real shame, but I think it really is for the best, for all of us."

"Can't argue with that none. Never did like that white sumbitch no way. I get tired a his big mouth and that goddamn grin, an' him acting like he's big shit and better'n us colored jockeys. When he ever win any races?" Calvin was warming at the prospect. "Yeah, that suits me jus' fine. As long as, like you said, there's a little something extra."

Peanut spoke up for the first time. "What 'bout his brother?"

Alex smiled. "Yeah, I've been thinking about that while I was waiting on you. I figure you won't have too much trouble finding a time and a place for one of you to come up behind and stick him. Then maybe hide him somewhere where they won't find him 'til we're all gone. Think that'll be any problem?"

Peanut considered for a moment. "Naw, that won't be no problem at all. Kinda hate to do that to ol' Crabby though. He ain't so bad as his brother. But you know how theys always together. Get one, gotta get the other."

"Yeah," Alex agreed, "that's exactly what I thought – just can't be helped. Part of the cost of doing this business. Don't think anybody will really miss either one of them that much when it comes right down to it." They all sat quietly for a few moments, just waiting for what would come next.

"Well, I guess that's everything then," Alex finally said, slowly standing. "You boys sure you got no questions? You sure you got everything you need?"

"Yeah, we're ready." Calvin stood as well. "We're gonna head up town for a while. But don't you worry yourself none. We'll be good. I promise. Calvin smiled just a little, which Alex realized he had never seen.

"All right then. I'll give you a few minutes head start before I head back. Good luck, boys. We'll see you on down the road a little bit."

Calvin and Peanut walked out of the shack and left Alex there alone with his thoughts. *Well, that's everything then,* he realized. *All that's left now is the doing.* Satisfied, he waited another five minutes and then headed back to the Galt House, giving no indication as he passed the two small colored men along the road that he had ever seen them before. He arrived back at the hotel just half an hour after the Lincolns.

BY late that Saturday afternoon Clark was at the Galt House as well, upstairs in the Great Room, busily looking after the final details for that evening's dinner. He was expecting around thirty Association members, the mayor, Governor Leslie and of course the Lincolns. They were to have drinks at 6:30, dinner at 7:00, and then following what he hoped would be brief remarks, dancing and socializing. The room was filled with large round tables, elegantly set with the finest china and stemware to be found in the city. As he looked out over the room Clark thought back to the much simpler affair just over three years prior, back at the beginning of this whole adventure. Before that night he had cared little for horses and none for racing. Now he was about to produce what he truly believed would become the premier sporting event in the country. He was quite pleased with himself, and for the first time in a long time he felt fulfilled, completely satisfied. He could not help but smile. He was abruptly shaken from his reverie by the crash of a table knocked over by one of the hotel staff bustling around the round. "Damn you," he shouted, "be more careful over there! I don't have time for such nonsense." Then, to no one in particular, he asked, "What time will the orchestra arrive? I want them playing on the dot of 6:00, before any guests have the opportunity to arrive."

DOWN in the lobby Alex was ready to go up to his room to begin preparing for the evening. It was to be a very special night indeed, and he would be pulling out all of the stops, wearing his finest suit. First, though, he needed to find Tommy. Scanning the lobby, he didn't see the boy right off, and a slight panicky feeling set in. Then Tommy entered across the room and Alex quickly relaxed, realizing that he was perhaps indeed feeling some tension from all of his scheming. He immediately caught the boy's eye and then exited out into the still-warm late afternoon sun, Tommy following along a few moments later.

"I believe you have something for me," Alex asked when they were out of anyone else's earshot, now again fully calm and composed. Tommy removed a small tan envelope and handed it to Alex.

"As requested, boss." Alex removed the card inside and quickly scanned the private invitation to that night's affair. He didn't bother to ask how the boy had managed to come up with it. He simply smiled, unable once again to refrain from thinking just how much the boy reminded Alex of himself at that age.

"Excellent, Tommy. You always come through for me, don't you?" He slipped the envelope into his suit pocket.

"I try my best, boss."

Hearing himself called "boss" caused Alex to think briefly of Charlie, provoking just a moment of regret, but it passed just as quickly. He offered the boy a cigarette and a match, which Tommy accepted eagerly – he had seen a few other men smoking cigarettes but had never had the chance to try one. He quickly lit it, and made a show of taking what he hoped was an elegant first puff. He was a quick study, this lad.

The two of them turned and strolled east down Main Street, away from the sun. Alex regarded his young protégé with increasing interest. Given his arrangement with Calvin and Peanut it was now obvious that he was going to have to replace the services of the Appleton brothers once he arrived back in New Orleans. Alex sincerely did hate to lose two such reliable men, but in this case, he reminded himself, it could not be helped. With that thought lingering in his mind he said to his new young friend, "You've never told me much about yourself, Tommy, about your family. You got a family?"

"Not much of one. I got an uncle who's around here somewhere, but he's just a drunk and I ain't got no use for him. When I do see him all he wants is money. Maybe a couple of cousins, but I don't keep no company with them neither."

"What about your mother, your father?"

"My mom died of the fever when I was just three. I don't really remember much about her at all. And then my dad got killed just a couple of years later – stabbed by some damn Irish bastard. I hear he claimed it was revenge for what my dad had done on Bloody Monday. Said he burned out his family."

"Any truth to that?"

"Aw, who knows? My uncle said my pop was there and all, said he took care of a whole bunch of 'em all by himself that day, but I don't really know. Maybe. Probably. All I remember is my dad was sure one big son-of-a-gun, and from what I've been told he didn't hold with no Irishmen." Tommy paused for a moment, and then finished, "Anyways, I was too little to be on my own, so my uncle took me in, but I couldn't stand him, so as soon as I could I got out of there. And if I do say so, I think I've been doing pretty good for myself ever since."

"I'd say that's true enough. You know, we have a lot in common. Your story sounds pretty familiar to me." They turned around and slowly headed back towards the hotel. "You know I'll be going back down to New Orleans after the Derby, leaving Monday afternoon. I'm pretty well-known down there, at least to the right people, and I could always use a boy with your talents. I'm thinking that it might do you good to get out of Louisville for a while, to see some different places, some different things. And let me tell you son, you'll see things in New Orleans you won't ever see anywhere else. Anyway, if you're of a mind to, you'd be welcome to come along with me. I'm not asking you to say yes or no right now, just to think about it, that's all. And just know that I'd be proud to have you come along with me." They reached the door of the hotel. Alex patted his pocket and said, "Thanks again for this. I really appreciate it. I'll tell you all about it later." He went in and on up to his room to get ready for dinner.

CHAPTER TWENTY-ONE

JUST after 6:30 the Lincolns exited their suite, and accompanied by one of the officers made their way to the Great Room. The orchestra already was playing a gay tune, and Abe could see that the room was about half-full. Clark immediately made his way over to them.

"Mr. President, Mrs. Lincoln, good evening. Thank you so much for joining us tonight. I trust you are having a good visit so far, that your accommodations are adequate."

"Better than what we are used to, and I must say, better than we deserve." Abe gave his wife a knowing glance.

"Nonsense. It is the least we can do. We are known for our Southern hospitality here, and we would offer you nothing less." (Abe smiled wryly at this, for much of the treatment he had experienced from the South had been less than hospitable, but he let it pass.) "By the way, Governor Leslie should be here shortly and I know he is greatly looking forward to visiting with you."

"Colonel, just between you and me, I've already had two occasions to visit with the man, and for tonight anyway I'm hoping to have the opportunity to visit with some other of your fine citizens. I'll have plenty of time for the governor again on Monday." Chuckling, Abe added, "Just don't tell him I said that."

"Yes sir, I understand perfectly, and you can trust me. I so hope you both will enjoy yourselves this evening. It is such a great night for all of us in the Association. And look, here is Mary."

Clark's wife had arrived just a few minutes before the Lincolns. She knew how distracted her husband would be and was assuming the role of hostess to their special guests. Smiling brightly as she approached, she took Mrs. Lincoln's hand and held it warmly. "Mrs. Lincoln, Mr. President, how wonderful it is to see you again. Thank you so much for coming to visit with us here on this special occasion for my husband, and for our city. I have been so looking forward to visiting with you again. Won't you please join me at our table?"

"You look so lovely this evening, Mrs. Clark," Abe offered. "Don't tell your husband, but we mostly came to see you anyway." He looked at Clark with a twinkle in his eye, and then laughed. For just a moment Clark looked slightly offended, and then realizing the joke, joined in the laughter.

Clark simply replied, "Your famous wit, Mr. President – I do remember it well. Now, please make yourselves at home, and please excuse me as I still have a few matters that require my attention." Mary escorted the Lincolns over to the head table and sat talking with Mrs. Lincoln as Abe began to greet some of the guests.

Over the next twenty minutes Abe did speak briefly again with the governor upon his arrival, promising to spend more time on Monday as they had planned, and also visited with the mayor and as many members of the Association as he could. Then, at just past 7:00 a bell rang to signal the beginning of dinner. Clark came and escorted his prized guest to the head table where both Marys were still seated, thoroughly engaged in animated conversation.

When they were all settled he informed Mrs. Lincoln that he had a surprise for her, as he presented her with a printed souvenir menu for the evening's repast. As a special tribute Clark had arranged for the menu to replicate a favorite of Mrs. Lincoln's from her years at the White House. He had sent a request to the current White House kitchen staff, who had successfully located the appropriate records. Mary was quite taken by his thoughtfulness, and thanked Clark effusively. Abe was, if anything, even more delighted – it would help his wife to feel even more at home and appreciated, and that would do much to buoy her mood through the weekend.

When most everyone had finished eating, Clark rose and commanding the attention of his guests began, "Good evening, ladies and gentlemen, and my warmest thanks to you all for attending. With your kind indulgence, I would like to offer a few toasts if I may. First of all, to our great Commonwealth, the finest place in all the land." Everyone raised their glasses and drank.

"Secondly, to that magnificent, indeed wondrous creature, that God in His wisdom has given to us, particularly here in Kentucky, where it flourishes so, and whereby it has made us known all around the world, I give you – the mighty Thoroughbred." Again, everyone drank. "Next, to all of you, the members of our Association, who have supported me, have shared in my vision, and have with me created a place only a few miles south of where we sit tonight, out on the Churchill land, a place where I used to play as a boy and pretended to be one of my famous ancestors, a place that will soon be known all around the world, envied by any who race horses, I give you – the Louisville Jockey Club and Driving Park Association." A loud "hear, hear" went out as everyone now drank to themselves.

"To the mayor of our great city and the governor of our honorable Commonwealth." Polite applause and more drinking. "And of course, to our very special guests, to the man who served us all so well in such a difficult time, the man who brought this nation back together, who, no matter what your particular political position may have been in the past, has worked so hard and has earned our respect and, yes, our admiration, I give you – President Abraham Lincoln and his lovely wife, Mrs. Lincoln, Kentuckians through and through." The crowd erupted into applause, standing and politely cheering.

After they had settled Clark stood rigid, waiting for complete silence and attention. Once he had it, he resumed one last time. "Finally, I give to you the future of our city and our Commonwealth, for that is indeed what we create here tonight. For I truly believe that in just a few short years, this race will be known around the world, and it will bring people from everywhere to visit our city, and our state, and a hundred years from now they will talk about what we have together here accomplished. Ladies and gentlemen, I give you – the Kentucky Derby!" Again, the ovation filled the room and lasted for several moments, as everyone drained their glasses, before quiet was restored.

"And now, with the further indulgence of our mayor and governor – whom I must point out we regularly, and happily, have the opportunity to see and hear – I am going to ask our honored guest, Mr. Lincoln, to offer just a few words, if he be so inclined. Mr. President?"

Lincoln slowly rose to renewed applause, which he quickly waved down. He smiled warmly, and thanking the crowd began, "You know, I really don't like to speak publically unless forced to do so." He waited for their laughter to subside. "But let me just say this. A few years ago Mrs. Lincoln and I had the honor to meet and have dinner with Colonel Clark, and his dear wife, Mrs. Clark, with whom both Mrs. Lincoln and I were so taken, for obvious reasons." He turned to Mrs. Clark smiling. "On that occasion he was kind enough to invite me to visit his city; and not only that, he assured me that he would fulfill a wish that I had just communicated to him: a desire to witness firsthand the excitement of a thoroughbred horse race. And he further assured me that it would be at a first-rate facility, the finest in all the land. Little did I know - nor I suspect did he – when our paths crossed on that evening a few short years and an ocean away, that we would be reunited here this night, to celebrate the culmination of a journey upon which we all now realize he was himself then embarking. He, along with all of you, are to be congratulated on accomplishing this great achievement."

Abe paused, then resumed in a softer tone. "Most of you will know that it was but a few miles down the road from here that I was born a little over sixty-seven years ago. And no matter where I go, that strong Kentucky blood still flows through my veins, as it does for Mrs. Lincoln here; and I know she will join me in declaring that there is nowhere else in the world we would rather be than here in Louisville, to witness the first running of the Kentucky Derby. For it is history that you are making here – indeed as Colonel Clark has just said, years from now people across this great land will look back on what you have begun, and they will smile. Mrs. Lincoln and I are so grateful that you have invited us to be a part of it, and we thank you all so very much."

Everyone else rose as Abe took his seat, applause once more filling the room, continuing until Clark signaled the orchestra to begin playing. The affair now turned to socializing and dancing.

ALEXANDER Delacroix had witnessed all this from a table in the back, all the way across the room from where Lincoln sat. He had no desire to be anywhere close to this man, but Alex did enjoy greatly watching the faces of other men around the room, judging which of them were politely suppressing their true feelings about Lincoln. He had talked to enough people around this city to know that while they were being respectful – especially in light of the occasion and its importance for the city – they did not particularly care much for this man, to put it mildly. Alex was convinced several of those people were indeed among this crowd tonight.

Alex began to mingle, being careful to keep a healthy distance between himself and the former president. He was oozing New Orleans charm as only Alex Delacroix could do, the desired effect evident from the reaction of several ladies, not to mention a few of the gentlemen as well. He had a brief conversation with an Association member named Thompson, who insisted that Alex meet Clark. Alex decided there was no particular harm in that. He followed along as they went in pursuit of the Colonel, whom they found standing over to the left side of the room.

"Colonel, I would like you to meet Mr. Alexander Delacroix, a well-known horseman from New Orleans who has come up just to be with us on Monday. He has been telling me all about the Fair Grounds, and has reported that our new facility stacks up well in comparison, which I would say is high praise."

"Yes it certainly is," Clark responded smiling and shaking Alex's hand. "It is a pleasure to meet you sir. Thank you so much for your kind words and for coming up to support our new venture." Yet even as he took pains to appear cordial, Clark wondered to himself how exactly this gentleman had gained admittance to his party. While he was not at all happy about it, he decided to let it go, thinking that this stranger must somehow have been invited by one of the Association members.

Instead he continued, "You know, it is quite the coincidence that Thompson here has brought you over just now. I was talking about New Orleans only a moment ago. If you don't mind, I have someone here who has been there whom I should like you to meet." Alex smiled, but could only think about how annoying he found people who wanted to tell him all about their visits to New Orleans. They knew nothing of the real city and only served to bore him. He was momentarily lost in that thought, following Clark as he made his way through the crowd that filled the large room. When Alex looked up again he was staring into the face of Abraham Lincoln. He immediately broke out into a cold sweat.

"May I present Mr. Alexander Delacroix, a well-known horseman from New Orleans who has come to be with us for our Derby. I was telling him how we were just speaking of New Orleans a short time ago, about your visit there. Mr. Delacroix, President Lincoln."

Before Alex could begin to form any words, his highly-tuned grace and charm now completely vanished, Lincoln offered, "Mr. Delacroix, it is an honor. I had the pleasure of visiting your city a while back, a most unusual and charming place."

"Yes...yes, sir, I know." Alex could scarcely speak, his mouth bone-dry, his panic overtaking him.

"Oh, did you perhaps see me when I was there?"

Alex lied. "No, no sir, I did not have that privilege." *I should have taken care of you then when I had the chance.*

"Are you feeling all right, Mr. Delacroix? Your color does not look so good."

"Oh, I...I believe this crowd has gotten to me, sir. I think some fresh air would do me good." He was hardly aware of even what he was saying.

"Yes, I understand completely. The same thing often happens to Mrs. Lincoln. Well, it has been a pleasure to meet you, and I hope we will see you again, perhaps at the races."

"Yes, sir, thank you sir, it is an...honor." Alex turned and immediately made his way to the door, awkwardly bumping into several of the other guests, vanishing out into the hallway. He was drenched in sweat, and could hardly breathe. He started to go downstairs and out onto the street, but was afraid that Tommy might see him. He did not want anyone to see him! So instead, he went directly to his room, closed the door, and quickly removed his jacket. He ripped his shirt off, opened the window and then collapsed onto his bed. In a few minutes he had regained some composure but continued to lie there, perspiration still enveloping his body. *Lincoln!* He had come face-to-face with the man, the very last thing he wanted. And then, to make matters worse, he had acted like a fool. Everyone in the room was probably talking about him now. His paranoia was overwhelming.

BACK in the Great Room, nothing could be further from Alex's imagined truth. No one had noticed him, and no one missed him. As far as Abe was concerned, Alex was merely one of many men he had met over the years who had become overexcited from meeting the president. It was not so unusual. Still, this man did seem odd in some way, but Abe quickly put it out of his mind.

After a few more minutes of socializing, he went to find Mary, who had spent most of the evening seated and engaged in lively conversation with Mrs. Clark, greeting all of the members, some more than once. He knew that by now she would be fatigued, and he tactfully extracted her from a bevy of Association wives and daughters. With that the Lincolns graciously thanked their hosts and quietly retired to their room. They were looking forward to a second morning of relative inactivity and quiet. Abe, as always, had much writing to do; Mary would simply enjoy the solitude, and her needlepoint. And then it would be off to Farmington. Abe anticipated with pleasure another, more extended visit with Joshua – and a return to the place that had been so important to him, the place that had in so many ways made him the man he was.

CHAPTER TWENTY-TWO

CHARLIE galloped the bay colt around the far turn, heading into the stretch, making his way back to the barns. The sun had been up for about an hour and activity on the track was winding down. It was already getting hot, a full-fledged early heat wave in the middle of May, and Charlie was sweating hard. Having spent several years riding in New Orleans he was used to the heat so it didn't bother him that much. As anxious as he was to return to his adopted city, he had to admit that he had enjoyed being back in Louisville. The city had grown considerably since he had last been home – although he still hesitated to really think of it that way. He and Robert had no family left around here, since they had all either died or moved away. Still, it was where they had grown up and Charlie did have some good memories. As he left the track he wondered if he would ever see this place again after tomorrow.

Charlie made his way back to the General's barn where Crabby was waiting to cool the horse down and give it a bath. Charlie hopped down as his brother took the reins. "He's all yours." He stood for a moment looking at the horse, and then at Crabby. "Well, I guess there's no puttin' it off any longer. Guess I better go and talk to Old Tom. That is, unless you want to?" Charlie was smiling.

"You go right ahead. Just give him that big grin of yours and you'll be fine," Crabby replied somewhat sarcastically.

Charlie walked on around to the opposite side of the barn where he caught a glimpse of the trainer heading into the tack room. Charlie slowly walked on down to the far end and followed him inside. Old Tom heard Charlie standing behind him. Without turning he said, "What the hell do you want?"

"I need to talk to you for a minute, if you can spare the time." Old Tom turned and immediately noticed that Charlie wasn't smiling. He knew this must be something serious.

"Is that bay colt OK? There something wrong with the horse?"

"No, Tom, that horse is fine; couldn't be better. It ain't nothing like that."

"Well, what then? Spit it out, boy. I ain't got all morning, I got things to do."

"Geez, boss, give me a chance will you." Charlie smiled just a little. "See, it's like this. Me and Crabby, well, we've decided we're gonna head on back down to the Fair Grounds. I wanted to let you know that we ain't gonna be working for you no more."

"Well, is that a fact?" Old Tom stopped what he had been doing and gave Charlie his full attention. "Whadda you want to go and do that for? We got plenty of work around here, and besides, we'll all be heading back south before too long."

"Yeah, I know, Tom, it's just that we want to go on now. And there ain't no use in arguin' 'bout it none cause we done made up our minds."

"I ain't arguing about it. Hell, I figure we'll find some way to get along without you." He paused for a moment. "I do hate to lose your brother, though. He's awful good with my horses. You sure he feels this way, too?"

"Yeah, boss. You know us, we do everything together." Old Tom accepted this statement and went straight back to his work. Charlie stood and watched him for a minute, waiting for more.

"Well, when you going?"

"We figured we'd work in the mornin', and then see this here Derby tomorrow, and then grab the train on down tomorrow evenin'."

"That what you figured, huh? Well thanks for all the notice. Last thing I need right now is to have to go out and find another groom and rider."

"Oh, come on now, Tom. You know well as I do that there's plenty of boys 'round here. You ain't gonna have no problems findin' somebody. Hell, in a couple of days you won't even remember us."

"Maybe not you, I sure enough can replace you. But it ain't so easy to find a really good groom like your brother. Oh, to hell with it. I'm tempted to tell you to just get the hell out right now." He paused for a minute, to let Charlie think he was serious. "But I tell you what, you boys finish up in the morning and then come and see me and I'll get you your money, and then you can head out to anywhere you please." He turned back to his work and started to ask just what they were going do back in New Orleans, but thought better of it. "Hell, no hard feelings, Charlie. You boys both done a good job for me. I appreciate it. Good luck to you." He offered his hand and Charlie shook it.

"Thanks, boss. You always been a fair man to work for, I'll say that. We appreciate it, too." Charlie gave him a big smile.

"Yeah, yeah," Old Tom said, returning to his task. "Get the hell out of here before I change my mind. It's gonna be good not to have to look at that sorry smiling face of yours no more."

As Charlie came out of the tack room his brother came around the shed row hot walking the horse Charlie had just galloped. "You tell him?"

"Yeah, I told him."

"And?"

"And what? I told him, he said okay, said that he was really gonna miss us. What else do you think?"

"Hey, I'm just asking."

"Said for us to put in our time tomorrow, then come see him for our money. He wished us good luck. Said he *appreciated* us."

"Well, that's that then, ain't it?

IT was just after eleven o'clock when the Lincolns departed the Galt House and headed out the Bardstown Turnpike towards Farmington. It would take about forty minutes to reach their destination. Just as on the previous day when they had toured the city, two uniformed officers rode in front of their carriage and another followed behind.

At the edge of the city proper the road went up a small hill and then leveled off, passing houses and small farms, a few businesses still mixed in here and there. After a couple of miles they left behind any more significant development and were riding through large farms with expansive open lands. Fields had been planted and crops had sprouted, all still less than a foot high. It was already hot, but the air was clear and still had a bit of a cool edge to it. As they passed the turnoff for the Taylorsville Road over to their left, Abe remembered riding by these same fields on his way to town to meet with James Speed to discuss the law all those years ago. Then it had been late summer and the fields were full and getting close to harvest. Now everything was green and new, with the promise of the coming season. Otherwise, things out here had not changed all that much.

A little less than another mile brought the entourage to the entrance into Farmington on the left. The officers nodded respectfully to Abe as the carriage pulled off the main road. Before departing town he had instructed them that there was certainly no need for them to remain throughout the visit, and to return later that afternoon for the trip back into town. Abe was filled with memories and emotion as the carriage followed the grand avenue that led up to the main house, crossing the small limestone bridge. The structure was surrounded by a split rail fence, the sight of which inevitably brought a smile to his face as he recalled how such fences had become a part of his campaign legend years before. As they pulled up towards the gate Abe quickly spotted Joshua standing out in front waiting, just as he had the last time. The carriage came to a halt in front of the house.

"I see you were still able to find the old place," Joshua said as he helped Mary down.

"Thanks to this fine driver, although I have to say the trip out had a very familiar feel to it, even after all of these years."

"Some things have changed, but much still remains the same. People out here like things how they are. That is part of the charm of the place." Joshua then turned to the driver and said, "Please pull the carriage around to the back. You can turn your horses out to graze in the small field to the far side of the house, and then go to the kitchen for some refreshment and lunch."

As the rig rolled away Abe said, "Doesn't the house look fine, Joshua? Mostly just as I remember it – though it certainly will not be the same without your mother. Again we are so sorry for your loss."

Mary added, "Although I never had the pleasure to have met her, Abraham has told me what a fine woman she was, and how well she treated him during his visit here. I'm sure you miss her terribly."

"Yes, she was a grand woman, thank you. I almost expect her to come out of that door calling to me, as she did so many times." Just then, Fanny came out onto the high front porch, located under the one simple cornice that adorned the front of the house.

"I thought I heard voices out here. Welcome, Mary, Abe, welcome to Farmington."

"Hello, Fanny," Abe said smiling. With a look of confusion crossing his face he continued, "But where are our hosts?"

Joshua explained, "They were kind enough to turn the place over to us for the afternoon – didn't want to impose on our *reunion* if you will. Make it as it used to be, I suppose."

"How kind, and so very thoughtful," Mary said, turning to look at her husband. There was a warmth to her gaze that he had not seen in some time.

"We have returned the favor," Joshua continued, "as they are spending the day at Cold Springs. Where you and Mary must stay with us on your next visit to Louisville. You know our home is close by, built on part of the old family land as well. But this seemed an occasion to recall former days, in former places."

"Well, come on inside," Fanny said, breaking the reverie. "I know it has been a long ride out from town, especially on a hot day like today. Did you ever see anything like this weather? It could almost be July. But it is cool inside. Come along, Mary, get out of the sun."

The three of them ascended the steps and joined Fanny on the small porch. Mary said, "It's good to see you again Fanny. Abraham and I have been so looking forward to today."

"No more than Joshua and I. It has been all that he has talked about since he first received Abraham's letter, and especially since we learned of our opportunity to spend the day here. Sixty-one years old and acting like a school boy! Telling me this story and that story, all about your husband's visit here, and of course all about how he got you two back together, I might add."

"We certainly are forever indebted to him." Mary smiled at her husband.

"Well, at least most of time," Abe added with a wink, laughing gently.

Fanny led them all inside, into the long front hallway and then into the parlor, the first room to the right. "Come in and sit down," she invited them. "We'll have something cold to drink to refresh you after your ride. Then we'll have lunch in a little while. I thought it might be nice if we ate outside today. We have a nice shady spot out back that shouldn't be too warm."

They visited for a while in the parlor, sipping lemonade and chatting about a variety of topics. Mary described in great detail the dinner from the previous evening, not only the foods served and how they had been prepared, but also the table settings and fine linens. They talked about Lexington and Mary's reflections on visiting her home town. Abe went on about the base ball game in Cincinnati, and then their tour of Louisville, sharing tidbits he had learned that surely Joshua already knew, but relished in their telling as only his friend could do. Finally, they adjourned outside to lunch.

The table had been set in the back yard, in the shade of a large oak tree, just across the fence from the kitchen garden. Spring flowers were in full bloom, as were the dogwood trees. Their absent hosts had arranged for a fine repast of the local bounty – roasted new spring lamb garnished with sweet potatoes kept over from the fall harvest, greens fresh from the adjacent garden, and cornbread and honey. Abe praised both the quality and quantity of the meal, noting of the latter that he should have worked alongside the field hands all morning to have been up to the job of doing it justice. As it was, he now felt he would be good for nothing for the whole afternoon.

After they had finished their feast, Fanny took Mary to stroll through the gardens and orchards, while the two men wandered out into the fields. As it was Sunday, there was not much activity. Except for the two servants, they truly had the place to themselves.

"She's looking well, Abe," Joshua commented as they looked back across at the two women. "I know you have both had your struggles over the last few years, many burdens to bear, but it appears that she has held up."

"Yes, she is doing as well as I have seen her in some time. I debated about taking this trip, concerned how she would do. It's really the first time she has been out at all to speak of since poor Taddie passed. I really didn't know if she was going to make it there for a while, or myself for that matter. But my instincts that she needed this trip seem to have been correct."

"You have both had your share of heartbreak and suffering. I can't imagine what it must be like to lose a child, and you have lost so many. As Fanny and I have remained childless, it is a hardship we will never know. My heart goes out to you. But I understand Robert is doing well. I have heard good reports from Chicago."

"Yes, very well. He was down for a visit back at Christmastime. That certainly did his mother good. We are both very proud of him."

"And life in Springfield is good, it fulfills you?"

"Completely. I, we, would not want to be anywhere else. You know I returned to Washington last year for President Grant's daughter's wedding, and while it was pleasant enough to see some old friends, in some ways it almost made my skin crawl to be back in the District. I have never regretted being gone from there. I have my reading, and my writing to keep me more than busy. It is all I could want or ever ask for."

"Yes, your writing, you must keep at your writing. You have so much to say, so much that is important to the country. No matter what some may say, we need you, more than ever. There is so much to be done, and your voice is vital. People want to hear what you have to say."

"Yes, I suppose," Abe nodded thoughtfully. "But sometimes I feel that people are weary of me. I wonder if I really still have anything to say. Politics should be a young man's game, and I think now is a time of new ideas. We need new voices to lead our way, not some old worn out thing like me. My God, Joshua, can you believe I am now sixty-six? How can that be possible?"

"I know, I know," Joshua responded with a chuckle, "you have just a few years on me, Abraham. And I agree with you. We do need new voices, but yours is still a guiding light. Do not forget that. We hope to have you for many more years, to share your insights and wisdom. What would the country do without you?"

"Celebrate, I suppose, at least some of them. I see the signs and hear their calls when I travel. They are always there. Some will never forgive me, Joshua, and I do not really blame them. In fact, I compliment them. I should never be forgiven. It was a hardship that was placed upon me, granted, but I went in fully aware of what was coming, and I made more than my share of mistakes. It should never have gone on for so long, it was just too much, too many brave young men lost, on both sides. They all still haunt me, and always will."

"Don't be so hard on yourself, old friend. It had to come. I know that now. You could not stop it. Nobody could have stopped it, no matter how much you may have wanted to. By heaven, look at those before you. They could do no better. Our great Mr. Clay, all the others. It was inevitable. And if it had to happen, history will show that there was but one man who could get us through it. There may be some who still disagree, but they are simply fools, wedded to the past. Give yourself credit, Abraham, you have done far more than anyone could ever have asked or expected. Yes, we can all look back and say we made mistakes, myself certainly included. Age and experience always make us so much the wiser. But you, sir, you have nothing to apologize for. It is we who must apologize, for letting *you* down."

Lincoln was almost overwhelmed by his friend's words, his eyes growing moist. It took him a few moments before he could say anything. "Thank you, Joshua, for you are such a good friend. If you think I am such a great man, that I have accomplished so much in this time that I have been on this earth, then you must keep in mind that it is all because of you. I would not be the man I am today if I had not met you, shared your room, shared your friendship, your support, your knowledge and wisdom. You have made me who I am, so credit must go to you as well. There can be no doubt about that."

The two men were now out of sight of the house. The sun bore down, and Lincoln was perspiring freely. He looked around at the rolling fields, now fully planted.

"It's a shame that you do not still reside here, Joshua, it is such a special place."

"In a sense I still do, my friend, since Cold Springs is not so far away. True, it is not what it once was, what my father had, but I suppose that is all a part of the past now. I certainly understand that the truth is that this place could not have succeeded without the hands of the slaves. I have come to realize that in a way it was not at all real, not authentic. It has been a hard adjustment, but one which now I have no doubts about. Before the War, it was a different time, a time of my father, and my father's father, but now I realize it was not my time. I do not suppose I would want to live here if I could. Memories can be funny things." There was a shared knowing moment of silence and then Joshua continued. "He was less harsh than many, you know, my father, and I'm sure you recall, he wanted to send them back to their homeland, but they would not go. And I don't blame them, even though my father never understood why. They had been here for generations, they were as much a part of this of this land as I am, as we were."

"Your brother often said the same. And yes, I understand now, as I was of the same mind as your father for many years. I felt – we felt – that if they would just return, go back to Africa, that would be the solution. But of course we were so misguided, so very wrong. As you say, they were a part of this place, are a part of this place. They had put their sweat and blood into it, and no one had the right to ask them to leave. It took many intelligent men of both races to lead me to the correct path. And now, look where we are; or I suppose I should ask, where are we now? Things have not proceeded so well.

Our problems are many. The relations between the races now are nearly as great a challenge as was slavery itself. For if we cannot find a way to live together, we are destined only to suffer greatly again and again."

"I suppose you are right, Abraham. I do not know what the answer is, and what the future holds. All I know is that we can be nothing but better off with you speaking out, sharing your voice. As I said before, we need you now more than ever."

"I am afraid, Joshua, that there are far too many who do not want to hear. Who care not for what I or others may say. They are too much a part of the past, too set in their thinking, in their habits. The future, hopefully better, lies with the young people. It is they who will accept a new way, a better way. They are our one great hope." Abe paused for a moment, enjoying a cool breeze. "I have been giving some thought to all of this, to what role some of us can play. I spoke to Governor Leslie about this very thing in Frankfort. We plan to discuss our ideas further. He may even come to Springfield to visit me. I plan to call upon your brother as well. Perhaps some of us old dogs do still have a few tricks." Joshua said nothing, just chuckled slightly and nodded his approval. They continued walking along in silence, both men deep in thought. As they approached the house, Abe saw that the table had been cleared away, and Mary and Fanny were sitting comfortably under the tree, fanning themselves.

"Have you solved all of the world's problems or just some of them," Fanny inquired lightheartedly. "Between the two of you, wonders could be done."

"No, Fanny, I'm afraid we have very few answers," Abe responded. "But it certainly does a body good to wander these beautiful fields and breathe this fresh Kentucky air. I feel years younger, and completely contented. And not quite so miserable from that fine meal." The two men sat in the remaining chairs.

"I don't recall, Joshua, are you a man of the races?" Lincoln asked his friend after a few minutes of silence.

"I have not made it a regular habit over the years. But on occasion I have acquainted myself with the track."

"I don't know how I have managed to avoid it for all of these years – busy with a few other matters, I suppose," Abe chuckled. "But I must say I am greatly looking forward to tomorrow."

Fanny joined in. "It is certainly the talk of the town, especially among the ladies. Colonel Clark has apparently convinced many of us that this is the fashionable thing to do in this modern enlightened age. Certainly not a place to have been seen when I was younger woman. But I suppose it is a different time now, with different ways."

Mary said, "Oh, I think it shall be thrilling. And I am especially interested to see how all of the ladies dress themselves out. I expect it to be quite a parade."

Fanny answered, "Oh, I am very sure of that, if nothing else. There are many of our local ladies who look for any opportunity to try and outdo each other, and the Colonel and his wife have whipped them into a true frenzy. It has been a very good spring for the shopkeepers and dressmakers."

"I think it will be a good thing for Louisville," Joshua offered. "The hotels are full, and I hear they are expecting several thousand people to journey out to this new track. I believe the crowds will be too much for me, though. You will have to write me all about it, Abraham. I shall look forward to your colorful descriptions. In fact, maybe this should all be the subject of your next book. Something like, 'boy comes home to save the day' and all of that." They shared a good laugh.

The afternoon passed, and as the sun was waning in the western sky, casting long shadows across the lawn. Abe finally stood and said, "Well, I suppose the inevitable has come, and we must head back into town. It will be a long day tomorrow, and besides I'm sure you have had more than enough of us, and our hosts will surely wish to reclaim their home. You will of course give them our warmest thanks for their gracious hospitality." The others stood and they all walked around the outside of the house out to the front gate, where the carriage was already waiting.

While Mary and Fanny shared a few final pleasantries Abe took his friend warmly by the arm. "What we were discussing earlier, I think you know that I cannot possibly move forward without you. I didn't want to talk too much more today as I have been so enjoying myself and had no inclination to delve too far into politics, into more serious matters. But do understand, your kind words found a home and, yes, there is much to be done and I believe some of us are still to be called to action I must count you among that group. With your permission, after I talk more with the governor tomorrow, and return to Springfield, I will write you a long letter and share my thoughts. I just need to know that I can count on you."

"Always, my friend. I would be honored to serve you, to serve the nation in any way that you see fit. As always, rest assured that you can count on me as long as this old body is able. I may not have always been with you in the past, but for the rest of my days, I will be there." Abe's eyes grew moist, and he could but gently smile and nod, almost overwhelmed with feelings for this man who had meant so much to him over so many long years.

"It has been a blessing to see you, especially to be back here on the grounds of Joshua's home," Fanny offered when they reached the front. "It has gone by far too quickly."

Suddenly Mary's faced brightened, and she said excitedly, "You and Joshua must come to Springfield and stay with us. It would be just the thing. How long has it been since you were there, Joshua? Oh, you must come, you simply must. She was almost giddy. Joshua gave Abe a knowing look.

"It has been many years," Joshua replied thoughtfully. "It would be interesting to see the place again." Then turning to Abe he continued, "But it would be even better to spend more time with you, my dear friend. I think it is something we should maybe plan on, perhaps in the fall. Mary, Abraham has promised me a long letter after your return home. I look forward to that, and then we will definitely make our plans."

"Yes, I agree," said Fanny. "I think it would be a good thing. We must not let ourselves go so long without seeing each other again. Life is too short, and you are good friends. And you will, of course, return to Louisville. And next time you will stay with us at Cold Spring, see our home."

"Indeed, I would very much like that," Mary responded warmly. "Oh, and of course do thank our absentee hosts. It was so very kind of them to allow us to have such and enjoyable afternoon together. I know I shall never forget it."

Abe, nodding in agreement, looked at Joshua and said, "It is true that we wasted too many years and shared some short words. Now we must make up for that foolishness, while we still have the time and the energy. My good, good friend, I treasure you so. We must make this an annual pilgrimage, who knows perhaps now, at Derby time, if this race succeeds as Colonel Clark has planned. I'm sure he would welcome it as well. It is such a beautiful time in old Kentucky. Whatever, whenever, we must make it happen. I commit myself to it."

Joshua shook Abe's hand a final time. "Then it is only goodbye for now. I am already looking forward to next time. Until then, take care of Mary here, enjoy tomorrow, and have a safe and speedy trip home."

The carriage pulled away, rolling back over the small bridge and on out to the turnpike. The officers were indeed there waiting, and joining them in formation, they made their way back into the city, arriving just as full darkness was beginning to completely overtake the landscape. Abe and Mary went up to their room to refresh themselves, and to prepare for supper.

They had decided to eat in public on this Sunday evening, to get out from behind closed doors and walls, venturing down to the hotel dining room. This caused a minor stir among the other patrons, and the staff as well, but soon everyone settled back into their own business and the Lincolns enjoyed a simple meal, certainly lighter than usual considering the feast they had enjoyed earlier that day. While waiting for their food to be served, silently enjoying each other's company amidst the simple yet elegant surroundings, Abe noticed the man from New Orleans he had met the previous evening sitting across the room in a corner by himself. Abe was tempted for a moment to go over and say hello, but then quickly realized how much he and

Mary valued their own privacy when out in public and that it would be rather rude to go over unsolicited. Abe did think to himself, *What a funny man*, but then decided that it was simply a matter of him being from New Orleans, where things were quite different indeed.

ALEX stared hard at Lincoln until, realizing that the hated former president was looking right back at him, quickly glanced down to avoid his gaze. Alex wanted nothing more to do with that man, ever again. Now, in less than twenty-four hours, it would all be over, and they would all be free of him! He quickly finished eating and then exited the dining room. Outside in the lobby Alex spotted Tommy and motioned for the boy to join him outside. Alex wanted an after-dinner smoke and offered one to his companion. Alex suggested they walk around the block for a view of the river. They strolled along in the dark, slowly, smoking silently, until they came to a bench on a small hill perched above the river's edge. Alex could see two large steamboats tied off there, along with a menagerie of other assorted smaller boats. As it was a Sunday evening it was relatively quiet around the wharf. They both sat, and Alex offered another cigarette.

Alex leaned back and closed his eyes. "Guess tomorrow's the big day. Suppose things will settle back down some after that."

"Yeah, I expect so. Still be things to do, though, there's always things to do around here, least around the river."

"Oh, but not like in New Orleans, Tommy. We got a river there, too, you know – might have heard of it, a little stream called the Mississippi. We get people from all over the world coming through there."

"Is that right? Guess it must be something to see."

"You'd better believe it. Things you've never seen before, things you wouldn't believe even if I told you; a place of great opportunity for a young man such as yourself, especially with someone like me looking out for you." Then just for effect he added, "Especially the fancy women. None like 'em anywhere else in the world."

Tommy sat quietly for a minute or two, drawing on his cigarette, the glow illuminating his young face. "You can save all that about them women and everything else, Mr. Alex." Before Alex could say anything in response Tommy added, "Cause I already decided I guess I'd better just go and see it for myself." He looked at Alex grinning.

Alex slapped his knee and sat up excitedly. "Hot damn, I knew you were a smart boy. I tell you, we're going to *own* that town, you and me. You can come back here and buy this two- bit town if you want to."

"Don't know if I ever want to come back here, especially if New Orleans is all that you say it is."

"Oh, it is son, and more. You'll see, yes you will."

"Well, I'm ready. Already got my stuff packed up and waiting for you to say the word."

Alex looked more serious, looked hard at the boy. "If you truly want to do this, then here's how it goes. I have some business to take care of at the track tomorrow with this Derby race, and then we're gonna need to get right out of town. I mean right now. So I'll need you out there ready to go. Can you do that?"

"Like I said, boss, I'm ready now."

"That's good 'cause we're not coming back into town. Not for anything. You stick with me and I'll get you in, then you'll wait for me back of the barns."

"You mean I can't watch the race?"

"Won't be all that much to see anyway. Just some flea-bag horses in some two-bit race. I'll take you to see some real races at the Fair Grounds." Smiling warmly he continued, "So we're set then? You be ready to go and bring whatever things you need with you and meet me in the morning, say about six o'clock. I want to get on out there early."

"I'll be there, boss."

"Splendid, Tommy, splendid. You won't ever regret this, I promise you that." Looking around, he stood up and said, "It might be best if we are not seen together tonight. I'll head on back and then you follow in a few minutes. Until tomorrow, partner." Tommy shook Alex's hand, and then watched as he walked away. Smiling, the boy thought to himself, *I'll own you soon enough, old man.*

CLARK was at home preparing for bed. Mary had already retired. For some reason he believed that he would actually be able to sleep, and sleep soundly. He had enjoyed a fairly relaxing day, leaving the affairs of the track mostly to his assistants. It was barely after eight o'clock but he would be up very early, and he wanted to be fresh and rested for the big day. He had taken Mary and the children out that Sunday morning to watch the horses exercising, and then showed them all around the facility and the grounds. He had not allowed them out before, and they were very excited to get to see just what it was that had so occupied their father's time over the last several months. Clark had arranged for the kitchen to prepare a picnic lunch, which they had all greatly enjoyed out in the shade by the clubhouse. And then finally, he took them on a short hike out to the spring across from the back of the property, the place where he had so often played as a boy.

It had been a glorious day, and Clark's spirits had risen greatly. Even though inside part of him was still churning like a whirlpool, flowing ever downward, another part of him realized that there was nothing more now that he could do. Plans were all made, provision all set in, staff arranged, yes, even the extra water had been put down on the road, little good it would do in this heat. But he had been a man of his word in every way and to everybody. He had built his track, and now he was going to open it to all, and most importantly, give the good people of Louisville the Kentucky Derby. Now for a good night's rest, hopefully, and then it would be up before dawn and out to the track. Out to opening day, to *Derby Day!*

CHAPTER TWENTY-THREE

THERE was no hint yet of dawn when Meriwether Lewis Clark, Jr. stepped into his carriage and departed for the racetrack, just before 5:00 a.m. He had not slept soundly after all, but still much better than most recent nights, and he was full of energy, ready to go. He arrived at his office and immediately called for Vernon, who quickly appeared. Clark could not help but notice that the man looked different somehow, better, much better than usual. He had Clark's mug of coffee ready to go, which Vernon sat on the desk in front of his boss.

"Good morning, Colonel. It is going to be a glorious day, don't you believe?"

"Yes, yes I believe it is," Clark answered full of surprise. "You look...well, you look good, Vernon, fit and ready."

"Yes sir, after all it is Derby Day, and I wanted to look my best. I hope that is all right."

"Yes, yes, Vernon, of course, very good indeed. I'm glad you are excited to be a part of it all."

"Yes I am sir, I hope in some small way I have helped you do this thing." Clark looked at his assistant for a moment, thinking of how he had treated the man, how he had treated everyone, particularly in these recent days. They had all worked so hard. Yes, they *had* helped him to pull it all off, and even though he had rarely expressed it to any of them, he was grateful.

"You have been more than helpful," Clark responded in a kind voice, kinder than Vernon had heard in a very long time. "You have been a good and faithful assistant, and I know I have not always treated you properly, with respect, and I am sorry for that. I will do better from now on. I swear that to you." Pausing for just a moment, he continued, "I think you can appreciate the pressures that I have labored under, but still, that is no excuse for how I have acted towards you. I hope you will accept my sincere apology." He extended his hand.

"Yes, sir, certainly. I know it has been a strain, but if I may say so sir, you have done it. Yes it is going to be a glorious day." He shook Clark's hand, but at the same time acknowledged to himself that the man would never change, that this wasn't the real Clark. "What can I do for you at the moment, sir?"

Clark sat thinking. "Why, nothing, Vernon, absolutely nothing at all that I can think of. Why don't you check with the barns to make sure all is well there, and if so then just go enjoy watching the horses? Check back with me in a little while, and I'll call for you if I need anything sooner."

"Thank you, Colonel, I'll do that." Vernon again thought to himself how this wasn't real, just wasn't right. He did know that he didn't want to be anywhere around when something set Clark off, which was guaranteed to be just a matter of time. But it couldn't have been a better situation for what Vernon needed to do next. As he turned to leave, almost as an apparent, but fully planned afterthought he said, "Colonel, I did want to ask you about one thing."

"Yes, Vernon, what can I do for you?"

"Well, I was wondering if it would be all right with you, if it would be all right..."

"Yes, what is it, speak up."

"Well, I worked so hard on figuring out the seats for you and Mr. Lincoln and all, and even though I know I've said some pretty ornery things, and well, I do understand what a good thing, what an important thing it is to have him here, how much it means to you, means to us all..." He paused again.

"Yes?" Clark was finding Vernon full of surprises this morning.

"Well, I was wondering if it would be all right if I watched the Derby from up in the grandstand, up there behind where you and Mr. Lincoln will be watching. It would truly mean an awful lot to me, sir, if you think it would be all right."

Clark stared at his assistant taking in all he had just said. He looked so much better, had cleaned himself up nicely. Now he sounded remorseful for things he had said, seem to understand just what it meant to have the President here. And he had worked hard, very hard, and Clark was truly sorry for how he had been treating the man. Clark hesitated for another moment.

Vernon started to leave and said, "That's okay, Colonel, I know you got more important things to worry about than me seeing the race. I'll find me a spot somewhere else to watch from," then adding for effect, "if I can."

Clark smiled, "Nonsense, Vernon. You are welcome to watch from above. You were a good friend to my father, and you have been a good friend to me. I would be honored to have you come up. Consider it settled. I'll personally clear it with the officers."

"Thank you, Colonel, thanks a lot. I really appreciate it. You just let me know if you need anything at all now." He turned and then when out of Clark's sight, Vernon broke into a sly grin. It had all gone exactly as he had planned!

As Vernon headed out towards the track, just outside the clubhouse, he passed a man dressed in a pressed black suit, a man whom Vernon had noticed, but always from a distance, just in the last day or two. It was still dark enough that Clark's assistant couldn't really make out the man's features, but light enough to see that he had a serious look about him. The man said nothing, gave no indication that he had even seen Vernon. *Now I wonder who that might be?*, Vernon thought to himself, turning to watch as the man entered through the same door from which Vernon had just exited, heading in the direction of Clark's office. *I'll have to ask the boss just who he is. I don't like secrets, not now anyways.* But in fact, with everything else on his mind that morning, he quickly forgot all about the man.

OUT on the track Oliver was taking Aristides for a light race-day morning gallop, the first hint of light just beginning to glow on the edge of the horizon. The stars still beamed down at them, with not a cloud in the sky. He brought the horse to a stop, and then steered him over to the outside fence at the head of the stretch. They stood there for a few moments, watching a couple other horses and riders breeze by, hearing them well before they came exploding out of the darkness.

"You know, boy," Oliver said to his horse, "this here grandstand's gonna be all full up of people this afternoon. More people than you or I ever saw before. Thousands and thousands of 'em, or so they say. All here just to watch us run – well, us and a few other horses. Gonna be a mighty big race, I guess, and you and me's gonna be right in the middle of it all." He patted Aristides on his neck. "Now I don't want you getting too excited, now, cause we ain't suppose to win or nuthin', just get out there and let all them other horses chase after us for a while, that's all. But you know, boy, the way you been running out here in the morning, I'm thinking that maybe you got something else in mind. And just between you and me, well that'd be all right with me, too. Be just fine." Another horse galloped by, Oliver listening as the rhythmic sound of hooves came and went.

"But understand, now, I don't want you getting all upset if we don't win, 'cause you know we gotta follow orders, that's the name of this game. So we'll just go out there and see what happens, you and me. And if old Chesapeake beats us, well, that'll be okay. But if something happens, and we beat him, well that'll be okay, too. Better, even. 'Cause I figure ain't nobody gonna get too upset if we finish one-two. Then the only question will be who's one and who's two? I'll guess we'll just hafta wait and see. That sound okay to you, boy? Reaching down he gently stroked the horse's neck, as if waiting for some reply. "Well okay then, let's head on back into the barn and get you cleaned up so's you can have a little rest before all the excitement starts. Come on now."

As they reached the opening in the fence that led to the barns, Oliver sensed a slight shudder in Aristides, the horse quietly snorting. Then just an instant later he heard some kind of commotion that seemed to be coming from the backstretch. The horse and rider both turned and looked, but it was still much too dark to see what might be happening across the track. Oliver listened for a moment longer, then turned his horse back toward the opening and began to exit the track. Before he could pass through there was the sound of a horse rapidly approaching. A colored rider he did not know came up in a hurry.

"Accident on the backstretch, bad one," the man shouted, "rider's got trampled."

Oliver thought back over the last few minutes. He hadn't noticed anyone he knew out on the track. "Who was it?" The horse and rider slowed just enough to safely exit the track.

"Don't know, I didn't stop to look too close. Some white boy." By then they had passed by and headed on to the barns. Oliver's first instinct was to sprint back to see what had happened, to see if he could help. But he remembered what horse he was on, and knew he needed to get Aristides back to the barn and get him taken care of. He listened again for a moment and then hearing nothing, headed in. Before he reached the barn a couple of ponies blew by him in the twilight, heading back out to the track. Oliver dismounted, handed Aristides over to a hot walker and headed over to the barrel to get a drink of water. He was still standing there when Bug Eye rode up, just returned from working a little grey filly of McGrath's. He hopped off and seeing Oliver joined his friend.

"It was Charlie," he said excitedly, no need to explain himself. "Got run over but good. I come along just a couple of minutes after it musta happened. Barely could see him lying there, almost got him again myself. Looked bad, real bad. He weren't moving none at all."

"That's too bad. Real shame." It wasn't that Oliver was friends with Charlie, or even liked him much for that matter. But being an exercise boy made you a member of a special club, and it was always bad news when anybody had an accident, when anybody got hurt, white or black, friend or foe.

"Saw his horse just standing down by the turn. He looked okay. Can't imagine how Charlie fell off. Guess something spooked 'em in the dark. It can happen."

"Sure can."

"I come along and he was just lying there, all twisted up and all. I was afraid to touch him. Then a couple of the track men came riding up. They asked me if I saw what happened and when I said no, they just said to get on outta there, to get back to the barns. So that's what I did."

"It's a bad thing sure nuff." Neither man said anything else, standing there listening as the news spread through the barns. After a couple of minutes they headed back out to the track, standing by the opening. It was now noticeably lighter and for the first time they could make out images from across the way. They saw a silhouette of a wagon that appeared to be out on the track, on the backstretch, about a hundred yards or so from the far turn. They could also now make out that there were several people gathered around. Then maybe something was lifted into the back of the wagon. Oliver could tell by the way it was handled that Charlie must be dead.

It was just then that the two colored riders noticed that someone else was standing behind them. Oliver turned and saw that it was Crabby. He was just standing there, staring across the track, nothing said. There was nothing to be said. There was nothing to be done. Crabby's first instinct was to go running across the track, across the infield, out to his brother. But when he saw them throw Charlie into the wagon, he knew there was no need, no use in bothering.

They watched as the wagon started moving slowly down the track and around the far turn. It took several minutes to reach where they were standing. No one said a thing as it passed them, exiting the track. The horse Charlie had been riding was tied onto the back. The two officials followed along behind on the ponies, and when the wagon had cleared the opening one of them yelled out, "Okay boys, track's back open. Let's get these horses out." Within a minute three of four horses made their way on out, galloping towards the rising sun, just like nothing had happened. Life went on, the horses had to get their work.

Oliver was just about to say something to Crabby, to tell him how sorry he was. But before he could speak he noticed another colored man coming across the track, a big man, not a rider or a groom. It was Marcus, and he was wide-eyed. Marcus was not going to miss opening day at the new track, was not going to miss the Derby, so Oliver had invited him to tag along that morning and catch a ride on the wagon, to come out early to watch the training, and to get a good spot picked out in the infield for the day. Marcus had been wandering around out there, no one noticing him in the darkness. Oliver called out to this cousin while the big man was still crossing the track towards them.

"Hey, Marcus. Guess you heard there was an accident out there this morning."

"Weren't no accident."

"What do you mean it weren't no accident?" Marcus passed through the opening, off of the track, looking like he had seen a ghost.

"I saw the whole damn thing and I'm telling you, it surely weren't no accident. They done gone and killed that man." Crabby stared hard at Marcus, but did not move or speak.

"Whoa, now just hold on. What the hell you talkin' bout?"

Marcus took a deep breath, let it out slow and wiped the sweat off his forehead. "Well, I was out there wandering around, just waiting for the sun to come up so I could see what was really going on. I watched you go by, Ollie, from back over there on the backside. Standing on the driving track, leaning right there by that fence. Surprised you didn't see me. Started to shout out at you but I knew that wouldn't be a good idea, scare the horse and all. Well, I was just turning around to walk back over to this side to see you when you was finished, just a step, no more than two, when I heard some other horses coming on, sounding fast. And then, well, it's hard to say exactly what happened 'cause it happened so quick and all. But I saw these two horses coming towards me. There was just enough light to make 'em out pretty plain when they got close. Next thing I know this one colored boy comes up fast and I swear he reaches out and *pulls* that white rider right off his horse. Then before you know, this other colored boy comes whooshing up hard and runs right over the man, just lying there in the dirt. You could tell that he just meant to do it. Well I tell you I froze, didn't move an inch. Sure didn't want them to see me. Then, if that wasn't bad enough, that first boy circles back around and gets up a head of steam and then runs right over him again. That poor man never had no chance. Then them two colored boys circled around and headed back down the track in the direction they'd all come from. I lost sight of 'em after that. Stood there trying to figure out what to do. I could see that poor white man wasn't moving at all, and I didn't think he was gonna move either, not after how bad they'd done trampled him, so I decided I'd better get the hell out of there. I got out there to the middle, and well, I just had to sit for a minute. My knees started feeling a little wobbly. Sat there and watched them put him in that wagon, haul him off. Couldn't do nuthin'. Then I got myself up and came on over here, and well, now here we are."

"Could you see who done it, Marcus? Could you see what they looked like?"

"Like I said Ollie, they was colored all right, no doubt about that. One of 'em just as black as my anvil. And they was dressed all real dark like, riding them dark horses, I mean to tell you they just blended right in, came from out of nowhere and then disappeared again. Scared hell out of me, that's for sure."

Bug Eye hadn't said anything, standing in silence, taking all this in. Then he quietly muttered, almost to himself, "I wonder, I just wonder."

Oliver turned and looked at him. "You wonder what?"

"Well, you remember Peanut, how he was acting so funny, how we was wondering what he was up to, that he was sure up to something?"

Thinking back Oliver slowly answered, "Yeah, I do remember that."

"Well I'm telling you, this sure sounds like something that Calvin would be all messed up in, Peanut too. I just wonder."

None of the black men standing there noticed, but upon hearing this Crabby's eyes widened ever so slightly. Although not often being credited with being particularly bright, he was in reality very sharp, very quick of mind. He instantly realized the ramifications of what had been said. He instantly realized that if Calvin and Peanut were involved then Alex certainly was as well. No, this wasn't an accident. Charlie had outlived his usefulness, and if that was true for Charlie, that it had to be true for his brother as well. Without saying a word, Crabby turned and headed towards the barns, at a much quicker pace than normal.

While he was sure that the remaining men probably thought that he was going to look after his brother's body, or perhaps even look for Calvin and Peanut to exact revenge, in reality that was the furthest thing from his mind. He knew how dangerous those two could be, and he was sure that at that very moment they were indeed looking for him. He had to get *gone*, and now.

He made his way carefully back to Old Tom's barn, always making sure that there were other people close by. When he reached the barn he immediately saw his boss, talking to one of the track men.

"Robert," the trainer called to him, respectfully using his given name, "I am so sorry. It's just a terrible thing." Crabby had no choice but to stop.

"Yeah, it sure is tough all right. I guess it's one of those things that just can't be helped. I told him if he kept riding these horses he was gonna get his head kicked in one day, but I don't guess I really believed it would ever happen. He was too good a rider."

"That he was. But accidents happen to even the best of 'em. I sure am sorry, though, that it had to happen to Charlie."

"Thanks, Tom, I really appreciate that. But I don't guess there's anything any of us can do about it now."

"What about you, what are you gonna do now? You still gonna head out?"

"Yeah, Tom, I think so. There's nothing for me here now but bad memories. I think I just want to get on outta here. Going to get my stuff now."

"Well, I guess I can understand that all right. Sure gonna be sorry to lose you though, you're a good man. Be sure and stop by in a little while and I'll get you your money."

"Thanks, Tom, but I was wondering if you'd do me a favor?"

"Sure, Robert, whatever I can."

"Take whatever money me and Charlie's got coming, and use it to bury him, give him a nice send off. Make it a nice thing for all the boys around here. Will you do that for me?"

Old Tom hesitated for just a moment and then slowly answered, "Well sure, I guess I can do that, if that's what you really want. But don't you want to do it, I mean, you're his brother and all."

"No, Tom, I don't think so. I just want to get on out of here. Burying folks just ain't for me. I'm gonna let you take care of that for me, if you'll do it."

"Sure, Robert, I'll be glad to. Make it real nice, for Charlie."

"Thanks, Tom. And one other thing. If anybody's asking about me, wants to know where I am, how to get a hold of me, tell 'em I've done left, heading up to Chicago, I think. Look up a couple of old friends and see what I can stir up. Think I've had enough of this horse business. I know I can get a factory job up there, and right now that suits me as well as anything. Don't want to see this track, or any other for a while, maybe never. There's a noon train heading up there so I'm on my way to catch it now."

"I sure hate to hear that, Robert. You sure do have a way with these horses, it's a real shame. And you know if you ever change your mind, get to missing it and all, you always got a job with me. Once them horses get in your blood it's mighty hard to get 'em out. But maybe you can do it. I guess after this morning I can kinda understand it. But I tell you, I sure hope you do change your mind, and when you do you'll come and look me up. I can always use a good man, and you're sure one of the best I've ever had." He paused for a minute, thought about saying more, of trying to convince him to change his mind, but then thought better of it. "Well then, you'd better get going. Take care of yourself, and don't worry none about Charlie. I'll make sure it gets done right."

The two men shook hands and Crabby headed into the small tack room to grab a few belongings. He was gone within three minutes, slipping quietly around the barn, heading for the back gate. He had no idea if there was a noon train to Chicago. He certainly had no intentions of going to Chicago, or heading into town for that matter. He just wanted to get as far away from this place as he could, as fast as he could, without anyone else seeing him or thinking about him. Ever again.

CLARK was in his office when he heard about the accident. A bad thing, but sometimes unavoidable, an unfortunate part of the sport. He knew that, but no, not at his track, not on this day. But what could he do? Mostly he hoped that it was not a bad omen for the rest of the day. He had worked too long and too hard. It had to be a good day, a great day. Still it gave him a bad feeling, and now it caused his thoughts to shift again to the things that he might possibly have overlooked, things that could still go wrong. Then again, maybe this is what had been haunting his dreams. Maybe this was that thing that was always just out of sight. A man was dead – what could possibly be worse than that?

CALVIN and Peanut, their job completed, had quietly walked their horses a short distance along the outer fence on the backstretch, completely unnoticed, until they reached a spot where Peanut had loosened a section. He got off his horse, pushed the fence back, and then after Calvin had led both animals off of the track, returned it to its proper position. This all took less than two minutes. They then quietly circled their horses back around to the barns, out of sight, slipping in through a gate that mostly was used to take horses out to graze in a small field beyond. They were back before the sun was up, completely undetected, or at least so they thought.

Alex and Tommy had just arrived at the track. Alex first showed his new protégé exactly where they were to meet later that afternoon, again explaining that Alex had much business to do that day and that it was not practical for them to be seen together. But, he reminded the boy, they would meet right after the Derby as planned, and immediately depart for the train. He stressed to Tommy how important it was that the boy was there and ready, not to be late. Tommy assured him not to worry.

Alex gave Tommy twenty dollars and sent the boy on his way, already aware from the buzz around the barns that there had been an accident that morning. A rider had been killed. As he made his way out to the track, he noticed Calvin and Peanut standing outside one of the barns. Peanut was getting ready to take a horse out, cool and calm as always, as if nothing had ever happened. They made eye contact, and Alex let his gaze linger long enough to communicate that he had heard what had happened, and was pleased. He gave just the slightest nod and then fixed his stare straight ahead, walking out to his normal place along the fence. He noticed that it was a busier morning than usual. There were definitely already more people at the track, even at this early hour.

Just before Peanut mounted up he said to Calvin in a very low voice, "I saw Crabby head over to the barn. He talked with Old Tom for a minute, then grabbed his stuff and got the hell out. Then I heard Old Tom tell somebody that Crabby was leaving, going up to Chicago, leaving right then and wasn't coming back. That he was done with horse racing. Ask Tom to take care of getting Charlie buried. What do we do now?"

Calvin gave him a leg up and answered, "Don't guess there's much we can do. But it don't sound like we got to worry about it none. I think somehow old Crabby got the message, and he knows he ain't welcome around here no more."

"You don't think nobody saw us, do you?"

"Naw, nobody saw. I just think he's a smart man, at least smarter than he looks. Smart enough to put two and two together, and to get the hell on outa here. He knows better than to mess with me. You get a chance out there, tell Alex what's up. And when you get back, I'll be upstairs. Figure we oughta stay out of sight for a while, just in case. Catch a nap until later." For a man who just killed someone, and who was going to help kill the former president in a few hours, he could not have been more cool and calm.

Peanut walked the horse out to the track and then turned and wandered slowly down the outer fence about fifty yards, stopping and letting the horse stand for a few minutes, waiting for a good spot to gallop off. He just happened to stop right in front of Alex. Without any acknowledgement or looking at Alex in any way, Peanut quietly spoke as he adjusted his hat and got a secure grip on the reins, readying himself. "Crabby's done got the hell out of here. Left it to Old Tom to bury Charlie and is heading on up to Chicago. Already left and ain't coming back. I expect he's at the train station with the ticket in his hand. He's scared and scared good. Don't think we have to worry about him none."

Alex considered this for a moment and said, "How's he know it wasn't an accident?"

"Calvin figures he just got smart and figured everything out. From the way he looked when I saw him, I figure that's what happened as well. Looked like a scared little pup. He didn't talk to nobody, didn't ask no questions, just got the hell out as quick as he could. Like I said, don't think we got to worry about him none at all."

"Well, I guess that's that then. At least for now. Can't do nothing about it today, but I got plenty of contacts up in Chicago. Won't be no problem to finish the job in a day or two, just when he thinks he's out of the lion's den, before he can talk to anybody. Won't be any problem at all shutting him up. Accidents can happen anywhere, especially in a big city like Chicago. You know, he may have actually done us a favor. Better a body turn up there than another one around here. Thanks, Peanut. You boys done good this morning. Just make sure you do a good job this afternoon as well."

"No problem there, boss," he said, riding away.

CHAPTER TWENTY-FOUR

BACK in the city the Lincolns had just come down to a special breakfast that the hotel had arranged in their honor for Derby Day. They were scheduled to depart for the track at 10:30, so they still had plenty of time to relax and enjoy themselves. Clark had figured that with the extra traffic along the road it might take an hour or more to make the trip out, and he wanted his special guests in the clubhouse by noon. That would allow time for lunch before the first race, scheduled to go off at 2:30. Clark himself needed to be finished with any final arrangements and ready by mid-morning to greet the Association members as they began arriving. He wanted them all in place before the Lincolns reached the track.

The hotel was abuzz with activity, certainly a far cry from a normal Monday morning. Early on Abe had looked out the window in their room to notice several new boats arriving at the wharf. Now, from the window in their private dining room he could see that the sun shone brightly, and that Main Street was full of people as well. He thought to himself, *The Colonel must be pleased*. After they had enjoyed a feast of salt-cured ham, eggs, grits, asparagus, biscuits and fruit jams and honey, they returned to their room to make their final preparations before departing for the track.

Mary had chosen for the occasion a light blue satin spring dress, plainly trimmed with simple adornments, along with a matching medium-sized hat with but one long darker blue feather, all of which she had purchased right before leaving Springfield. Abe told her that she had never looked lovelier, that she was sure to be the envy of all the local ladies. He smiled as he watched Mary nervously fussing with her hat. Abe was wearing his best suit, a sack coat in a pleasant checked grey color, white shirt and a deep green tie. He had intended to wear his frock suit, expecting cooler weather. He preferred how the long coat looked on his extended frame. But on this unusually warm mid-May morning he quickly decided that it would not be as comfortable. Having noticed that Clark seemed to favor green, Abe had decided to wear this particular tie in the Colonel's honor. Promptly at 10:30, he turned to Mary and said, "Well, dear, shall we go to the Derby?" As they stepped into the hallway he asked the officers, "Will you gentlemen be accompanying us out to the track today?"

"No sir," one of them replied, "we shall remain here to keep an eye on things."

"That is too bad for you. I promise that I shall give you a full account upon my return." The young man smiled at the thought.

"Well, thank you sir, thank you for thinking of us. We shall look forward to it." Abe warmly smiled back, stopping to shake each man's hand, expressing his appreciation for their attention to duty.

"Fine young men, aren't they?" Abe commented to Mary as they turned and made their way down the stairs. "It's a shame they won't be able to enjoy the day."

Their regular carriage was standing in front of the hotel, now adorned with several red ribbons. They were surprised to find Mrs. Clark awaiting them, the Colonel having sent her to accompany the Lincolns for the trip out to the track. As Mary stepped up and into the carriage she discovered that a dozen red roses had been placed there for her, compliments of their host. She beamed as she smelled them. "What a kind and wonderful thing to do. You must thank your husband and tell him how much I appreciate his kind thoughts."

"You may tell him yourself if we ever arrive. From the looks of things I think our journey may take longer than anticipated." As she had made her way to the hotel that morning Mrs. Clark couldn't help but notice the unusually large crowds out and about, mostly heading south. "Mr. President, Mrs. Lincoln, if you are settled and ready, let's go and find my husband. I am sure he is anxiously awaiting your arrival."

The watching crowd that had gathered applauded and cheered, and then with a wave from the president, the carriage pulled out, headed down Main Street for three blocks, turned left and headed south out Fourth Street. They made their way through the heart of the city easily enough, but traffic on the wide street soon increased considerably and their progress slowed. Abe continuously waved to the people along the street who could not help but to react when they saw who was in the carriage. People were already excited, and seeing the Lincolns only added to the occasion. The mounted officers who were accompanying them, to the front and the rear, closed quarters around the carriage as the traffic increased.

"It really is like a celebration, isn't it," Abe said to Mary. "I feel just like we are in a parade."

After a few more minutes they were at the edge of the city. The road in front of them was a long line of assorted carriages, all types and means of transportation, some very fine and some quite plain. There were wagons of all shapes and sizes, mounted riders, and on up ahead, Lincoln could see a mule-drawn streetcar, all heading in the same direction, south towards the new racetrack. All along the sides of the road people were walking. Hundreds of people, at first mostly white, but then colored as well, especially when they passed to the western side of Smoketown. Some people were dressed smartly in their finest outfits, others in everyday work clothes. The one thing they all had in common, everyone seemed happy, smiles in abundance. It was all moving ahead at a slow, constant pace, feeding on out of the city and stretching as far as the eye could see. Indeed it was like a parade, a grand parade of people.

In spite of the city's as well as Clark's best efforts, a huge amount of dust was being kicked up. It had simply been too hot and dry over the weekend to avoid it. All of the water that had been spread over the road had long ago evaporated. At any one moment thousands of feet, both human and animal, pounded the dirt road. But by and large no one seemed to care. They were outside, heading to the country, off work, having fun. It was indeed a holiday.

As their carriage slowly passed the people who were on foot the Lincolns were continually greeted. Short conversations sometimes took place. People asked them how they were, how they were enjoying Louisville, commented on the weather, on how hot it was, noticed Mary's dress or hat, complimented them on their fine carriage (a few even asked if they could hop on), thanked him for saving the Union, for being president, asked how long they were staying, what they had had for breakfast, and over and over again, who did he think was going to win the Derby? But noticeably, almost unbelievably, there was not one negative comment during the entire ride out to the track. There were plenty of people that made no comments, or perhaps more accurately, kept their comments to themselves, but, Abe supposed, in the community spirit of the day, everyone who did speak was friendly, and most of all excited. There was definitely something special in the air. He had been in enough crowds to recognize it. All-in-all he thought it was the most excited he had seen a group of people, a group of all different kinds of people, since right after the end of the War.

It was just past noon when they finally reached the track. Abe had first spotted the flags flying from the roof of the grandstand when they were about a half mile away. The structure beneath them loomed up out of the green fields, almost like a mirage, like something that was not really there, that maybe even should not be there, but that you could not help being happy it was. As they got closer, and it grew larger, their pace slowed even further. The grandstand in all of its shiny newness appeared to be over half full already, and there were what seemed like thousands of people just milling around both inside the grounds as well as outside the fences. Finally, as they passed by the Porter's Lodge and through the wide gateway the officers led them out of the line of carriages that were swinging around to deposit their passengers, and they made their way behind the clubhouse. Clark had arranged a special entrance for the Association members, and for today, the Lincolns as well. Abe saw him nervously pacing as they approached.

"Ah, there you are Mr. Lincoln, finally. I am so glad to see you." Clark helped his wife down first, pausing to kiss her cheek, and then attended to Mrs. Lincoln.

"Colonel, good day, or I suppose I should say, happy Derby Day," Abe said as he descended. "I am sorry we are apparently tardy. You may have noticed there are a few people coming out to your establishment today."

"Yes, isn't it marvelous? I am assured all five thousand seats in the grandstand shall be occupied, not to mention the members and their guests in the clubhouse. Perhaps thousands more in the infield? I believe we have been successful."

"That you have, sir, you surely have."

Smiling broadly at Clark, Abe's wife added, "Thank you for the lovely roses, and for providing such an excellent escort. Red roses will now always make me think of you and the Derby."

"You are quite welcome, and my, how lovely you are today, Mrs. Lincoln," then turning quickly to his wife he added, "and you as well, my dear. I fear we shall have to keep both of you away from the other ladies so that they will not become too jealous." In reality that would not be so much of a problem as most of the ladies would of course be seated separately anyway. They would not be found anywhere near where men were drinking and gambling, at least not the finer ladies. Out in the infield there would be plenty of women, drinking and gambling as much as they pleased.

"If you are ready, let us make our way into the clubhouse so that we may begin the festivities." Clark led the way inside. He took them upstairs to a private room where lunch was to be served for Clark and his officers, the mayor, the governor, and the Lincolns. Also in attendance was Colonel William H. Johnson, president of the Nashville Blood Horse Association, who would be officiating the Derby. Mrs. Clark did not join them, having gone off to find the chairman of the "ladies committee." Their assignment was to attend to the seating of the ladies as well as to their complete comfort, a significant job considering the crowds and the unusually hot weather.

While it was all lavish and quite lovely, neither Abe nor Mary had much appetite after their large breakfast, but out of politeness they went through the motions just the same. After everyone had finished Clark stood up and began to speak. "Gentlemen, and Mrs. Lincoln, it is my pleasure to welcome you all here for the opening day of the first race meeting of the Louisville Jockey Club and Driving Park Association. Let history record that here on May 17, 1875, we have begun a new era in thoroughbred racing for the city of Louisville and the Commonwealth of Kentucky such as has never been witnessed before. I thank everyone in this room for helping to bring it about." Everyone politely applauded. "Mayor, we are pleased that you could join us. Governor we are honored to have you come from Frankfort. I am especially pleased to welcome my good friend, Colonel Johnson from Nashville, who will insure that our Derby is a fair and honest contest this afternoon." Johnson smiled as everyone around the room nodded in agreement. "And I once again want to say a special word of welcome and thanks to President and Mrs. Lincoln for being with us." There was more vigorous applause.

"And now, Mrs. Lincoln if you will excuse and indulge us for just a moment, there is one more important event that I would like to share with each of you before we adjourn and ready ourselves for our first race, and then of course, the inaugural running of the Kentucky Derby." Behind him was an extremely large rounded glass, filled with ice and a medium brown liquid, with several sprigs of fresh mint inserted. He turned and picked up the glass, needing both hands to hold it up in front of him for all to see. "I would like to start what I hope in coming years will become a tradition for our officers and special guests. I have here what may be the world's largest mint julep, made of course with the finest Kentucky bourbon. It has been prepared especially for this occasion. I would like to offer a toast to all of us, and to the Kentucky Derby. May all of the horses and riders have a good, clean race and come back healthy, may the finest horse prevail, and may the Kentucky

Derby grow and prosper and become the finest sporting event on the face of this earth, known in all corners of the world. I give you the Kentucky Derby."

With that he raised the glass and took a good sip, and then passed it to Lincoln, seated to his right. Abe took a smaller sip, and could not help but react to the strength of the alcohol, which caused some polite laughter. He then passed it on to the governor, seated to his right. Except of course for Mary, and Colonel Johnson who wanted no reason for any doubt of his judgment on this day, each took a drink and handed it on until it had passed to everyone. "Gentlemen, and Mrs. Lincoln, let us be adjourned. I wish you all well. Have a wonderful afternoon."

Everyone came up and personally greeted the Lincolns on their way out. Abe chatted quietly for a moment with Governor Leslie. With Clark's approval they agreed to meet back in that very room right after the Derby celebration was finished, to continue the discussion they had begun in Frankfort. Lincoln and Leslie shook hands, and then the governor departed as well, leaving just Abe and Mary and the Colonel.

"We have a few minutes until the first race," Clark explained, "which I invite you to watch from this building if you have no objections. You are welcome to remain in this room, or come outside, or anywhere else here in the clubhouse you would like. For security reasons I would ask that you stay here until I get back. After the first race, for which I will be required to go down to the Judges' Stand, I will return and escort you over to our special seats in the grandstand for the Derby."

"That sounds fine. I believe Mary will remain here until it is time for the race, but I shall go out and meet some more of your members and enjoy the sunshine."

"Excellent. I will meet you back here in this room soon after the race. If you need anything at all, just let any of the officers or staff know." Reaching into his pocket he added, "And I almost forgot, here is the program of races for today so that you may make your selections. I'm sure everyone will want to know who the president has chosen to support." He handed a tan colored oblong card to Lincoln. "Good luck to you, sir, and I hope you both enjoy this race."

Clark left and made his way down, first by the paddock, where the horses for the first race were being readied, then across the front of the Grandstand to check quickly with his wife, then finally out to take his place at the Judges' Stand by the track. Abe, after making sure that Mary was comfortable, wandered out onto the large upstairs porch, which provided quite a view of the facility. The large oval racetrack was directly in front of him. The clubhouse was located at the far end of the stretch, just beyond the finish line, before the first turn. The large grandstand was immediately over to the left, with the main barn area then beyond on the western side. He could also see that people were still making their way out from town, a constant stream filling the road. He wondered where they would all go as the grandstand already appeared close to capacity. People were thick all along the fence in front of the stand as well, and then Abe noticed that several hundreds more were out in the middle of the track, in the infield. A large number of them had dark faces, which were completely missing from the clubhouse and grandstand and the surrounding grounds, except for the servants. But at least they were out there, were someplace, Abe thought, able to participate in this amazing event. It was not long before one of the members approached him, and he was soon engaged in idle conversation with several more, as the balcony was getting crowded in its own right.

ALEX was standing along the fence on past the front of the grandstand, down near the barns where it was not quite so crowded. He had not bothered to place any wagers at all. Even though he had had ample opportunity during the preceding week he had not bothered even with any of the demonstrations of the new pool system – he had no use for innovation where racing was concerned, and felt smugly justified when he learned that it would be not used for the Derby after all. He was too nervous, too preoccupied to be concerned with such matters. Even though it was in his blood, he knew there would be plenty of time for gambling once he was back in New Orleans. He was simply going to enjoy watching the first race as best he could, observing the crowd, and especially this end of the grandstand. He could see the empty section up towards the top where Lincoln would shortly be seated.

Tommy – and in a completely different area, Marcus – were out in the infield. Because of the large crowds spectators had been allowed onto the inner driving track. Both men had already had a couple of beers, and were patiently waiting for the race to begin. Marcus had definitely placed a small wager, already counting his expected winnings. Tommy was mostly keeping an eye out for anything of value that might accidently be dropped or momentarily overlooked.

Oliver was back at McGrath's barn, keeping an eye on his Derby mount. He was not going to let the horse out of his sight, not for one second, until it was time to go to the paddock. He was already wearing his green silks with the orange sash, McGrath's colors. Bug Eye had managed to get a mount in the last race of the day, so he was stationed out around the far turn, watching to see how these first horses were going to handle the track, to see if he could figure out where the "sweet spot" was on this afternoon. Calvin and Peanut were hanging out behind the barns, with a clear view of the all-important back stairway. There was one lone guard stationed there, not a policeman, but a track employee, one of Clark's men. They wanted to see what he would do when the race began.

Vernon was alone in Clark's office where he knew he would not be bothered, aware that his boss was busy with the first race. Sitting on the desk in front of him was his prized possession, all clean and shiny. It was a real Colt revolver – a *Peacemaker* as it was widely known, the irony of which was not lost on Vernon. He had won it in a poker game, and had always enjoyed looking at it, holding it in his one hand, but rarely firing it. In fact, he had only fired it one time. But today, he thought as he admired it, this beautiful gun would make history. No little derringer like Booth had used, nothing that might fail him. This gun would get the job done right. As it sat in the center of the desk he slowly inserted six bullets then carefully picked it up to feel the weight in his right hand. He put it back on the desk, removed the bullets, and repeated the whole process, over and over again, just for the pleasure it brought him.

OUT on the track the horses for the first race were beginning to make their appearance, so Abe went inside to get Mary. She fixed her hat, and then joined him out on the balcony. The men gathered there made way, allowing her to step up to the front railing so that she would have a clear view of the proceedings. Everyone's attention was drawn to the five magnificent thoroughbreds now parading towards them. For the true horsemen and fans assembled on this warm afternoon, these horses meant the return of racing to their city. It mattered not in that moment just how good they might be, they were magnificent every one. A large cheer greeted their arrival, the crowds pressing in on both sides of the track.

Abe first noticed, with some surprise, that four of the five riders were colored. He was aware of Negro jockeys, certainly knew there had been slave riders, but somehow he still had not expected it. Then, along with Mary he was drawn to the riders' silks. Though neither of the Lincoln's had previously attended organized races they were both quite familiar with the colorful jackets the jockeys wore, and the pride the horses' owners took in them. But to see them now paraded before their eyes, in the spring sunshine, colors flashing against the rich tilled brown soil, was a unique experience that made all seem right with the world. Mary could only exclaim softly, "oh my", holding onto Abe's hand, squeezing just a little more firmly. Abe could not help but smile, watching her enjoyment, years disappearing.

They watched as the horses came almost into the turn, just past them, and then reversed and headed back down in front of the grandstand, now starting to gallop lightly. Reds and whites and blues and greens flashed in front of them, and then Mary noticed one yellow cap that stood out.

"I do so like that yellow cap. I have always been partial to yellow. It always makes me think of the daffodils in springtime. What is that horse's name?"

Abe looked at the program Clark had given him, eyes drawn to the far right column headed "dress of riders." Before he could determine the answer the man to the right said, "Bessie Lee, owned by Mr. Lewis over in Lexington."

"Oh, I like that name," Mary said excitedly, "I used to have a friend in Lexington named Bessie when I was a girl. I believe I shall cheer for Bessie Lee."

"That will be fine," Abe said chuckling softly as he continued to look at the program. "But I believe it will be Capt. Hutchinson in the green. Yes, I shall be with the Captain."

The horses had reached the far end of the stretch and now turned back in their direction. Lincoln spotted Clark down in the starter's box, raised a few feet above the track, keeping a close eye on everything. The smartly dressed Colonel Johnson, having judged the horses and riders all settled and in proper position behind the line in the dirt he had drawn to mark the starting point, joined Clark in the starter's box. After a quick review to ensure all was proper he struck a drum and the race was on. The crowd exploded in a loud cheer as the horses passed in front of the grandstand.

As the horses neared the clubhouse Abe and Mary saw a flash of colors. The two horses out in front both showed a combination of red, blue and white, one rider with a white cap and the other with red. The man on the left said, "That's Kilburn in the white cap, with Orphan Girl close behind." Mary spotted her yellow cap next, then there was a small gap back to Capt. Hutchinson in green. The man said, "Don't count out Bonaventure there in the back, he'll be coming at the end."

The crowd quieted somewhat as the horses made their way on around the first turn and down the backstretch. Abe noticed how people along the edges of the crowd out in the infield were running across the open spaces, trying to keep an eye on the horses as they rounded the track. It was still the same order as the horses reached the far turn. Even though it was a good distance away, Abe could make out that something was starting to happen. The roar of the crowd began to build again as they rounded the far turn and came into the home stretch. Bonaventure was indeed passing Kilburn and Orphan Girl, with Capt. Hutchinson right behind. As the horses passed in front of the Grandstand the second time the roar became deafening. It was now Capt. Hutchinson with a head in front, then Bonaventure, with Bessie Lee right behind them, the other two clearly done for the day. The judges were in position and ready as the horses approached, the crowd beside itself. People in the infield were running trying to see, everyone on both sides jumping up and down and waving their hats and programs. With about two hundred yards to go, Bonaventure clearly gained control, with Capt. Hutchinson falling on behind Bessie Lee, who tried her hardest but could not catch the lead horse. A moment later they finished in that order. Then just like that, it was all over.

"Goodness," was all that Mary could say.

"That certainly was exciting," her husband added. "I don't know if I have ever seen a crowd of people so worked up. It was invigorating in some strange way."

Mary turned to the man next to her and said, "Well, sir, I believe you were right. Your horse bested mine." Then smiling and turning to Abe she continued, "But both of us got the Captain, I believe."

The man replied, "All three gave a good account of themselves, but it was Bonaventure's day. You shouldn't feel too badly. You probably didn't notice that both of your horses had to carry more weight than mine. Yours had one hundred and eleven pounds, but mine only one hundred and one. A decided advantage."

"Well that hardly seems fair," Mary said quickly, somewhat annoyed. "Why would that be so?"

"It's called a handicap, but it's actually intended to make the race fairer. Depending on many different factors, how the horse has performed in the past, the age or sex of the horse, several things really, they assign weight for the horse to carry in order to even the race out. It actually works quite well, and is very fair." Then he added, "Now you won't have to worry about that so much in the Derby as the horses will all be carrying close to the same weight."

"Well, you could have explained that before the race," Mary said in a short voice. "Now I know how you won."

The man laughed and said, "Don't be so sure. Most of the time it doesn't happen that way. Trust me, there are many different factors that go into determining which horse might win on any given day in any given race. I believe your practice of picking your color, or a good name, is just as effective, and certainly more fun, than spending your time trying to figure out all the rest."

Abe said, "Thank you, sir, for explaining all this to us. We both appreciate it greatly. You have been most kind." He looked at his wife and could tell she was indeed perhaps slightly annoyed, but felt sure she would quickly get over it.

They watched as the horses came back around the first turn from where the jockeys had slowed them, eventually to a halt. A large circle had been drawn in the dirt in the middle of the track, and the jockey on Bonaventure led his horse to it as the crowd, especially those who had been supporting him, cheered the winner. Abe noticed that the jockey was holding what appeared to be a small bag of some sort. He again turned to the man who had been explaining things and asked, "Excuse me again. What is that bag that the winning rider is holding? Did he have that the whole time?"

"No, not at all. You probably didn't notice in all the excitement that he grabbed it from a man standing just down from the finish. It's called the purse, and it contains the winner's share of the money. As the winning jockey rides by, he reaches out and snatches it."

"So many interesting aspects to this sport. I must say I do regret not having experienced this before. I believe I shall become a real supporter."

They both thanked the man again, and then returned to the private room where they were to meet Clark. Mary sat and asked Abe for the program, whereupon she began to look over the names and rider's colors for the Derby. Abe smiled at her, stifling a small laugh, and then took a seat as well.

It would probably be a few minutes before Clark made his way back to them, so Abe decided he might as well be comfortable. One of the staff knocked and came in to ask if they would like any refreshments, which Abe politely declined.

Clark finally arrived, now accompanied again by his wife. The first thing he said was, "So how did you like that? Quite exciting, no?"

"Absolutely. Everything you said it would be and then some. I know Mary enjoyed it immensely, although she would have enjoyed it a little more if Bessie Lee had made her way up to the front." This time he could not suppress his laugh.

"Oh, Abraham," she said, hardly looking up from the program. "It was quite wonderful, Colonel, so very exciting."

"Well, that was nothing, really. Wait until you see the Derby. There will be fifteen horses this time, and we are expecting quite a competitive race. If you are ready, we shall proceed to the grandstand to take our seats." They both stood up, and after repeated reassurance that Mary's hat was straight, they all departed.

CHAPTER TWENTY-FIVE

AS Colonel Clark and his guests stepped out into the bright sunshine a group of several uniformed officers joined them for the short walk over to the grandstand. They would have to make their way through all the people, for there was no way to avoid that. Clark had decided that it would be manageable though, with enough assistance, so he had arranged with the police chief to provide some extra men for this detail. It was all being paid for by the Association. But now Clark had decided to change his plans slightly. While he was of course pleased that so many had come out, the large throngs made it impractical for the Lincolns to visit the paddock before the race. There was simply no way they could make their way through that crowd, tightly pressed in on all sides. Besides, Clark still wanted to meet with the jockeys before the Derby. By skipping the visit to the paddock, Clark could escort his guests all the way to their seats, and then slip down the small back stairway and take care of this last duty before rejoining them.

The crowds around the Lincolns and the Clarks stirred with excitement, but the officers had no real trouble in securing an adequate space for them to safely and comfortably make their way. The revised route was now to take them across in front of the grandstand and then to make their way up to their seats. It would be an easier climb up for them as well, Clark had decided. He did not like last minute changes, but in this case, all the better. They moved relatively quickly, Clark nervously hurrying them along as best he could. Making their way all the way across to the far end of the grandstand, they then began their ascent. It became easier once they were going up the stands, above ground level, where the officers could quickly and easily clear the aisle. Everyone stood, partially out of respect but just as much as to get a better look at the famous couple.

Several of the planned seats had been removed from the area reserved for the Lincolns so as to make it more comfortable for them, and to keep other people from getting too close. Clark's wife would be seated on the far end, next to Mrs. Lincoln. A seat for the Colonel was reserved next to the president. Governor Leslie and the mayor as well as other important guests would be in the area immediately to the front which helped to provide a buffer zone. Behind the space was open, with room for a couple of officers. Clark showed his wife and his guests to their seats and then quickly excused himself, leaving the former president at the mercy of the mayor, who had immediately made his way up to Lincoln. Clark thought he saw a bit of a pained expression on Abe's face as he climbed the few remaining steps to the top of the grandstand, and then headed down the back stairway.

As soon as they were situated and had finished the obligatory greetings, Abe and Mary both began to look around their new environment. The grandstand was jammed full of people, many of whom were now calling out to Abe. He waved politely, standing to greet and shake hands with the other people seated to their front. They were now significantly higher up, more situated in the middle of things than they had been in the clubhouse. They enjoyed a clear view all the way around the track, and particularly of the entire far turn and the head of the stretch. On off in the distance to their left, across the green fields, was the Ohio River. Abe looked directly ahead, out into the middle of the track. He supposed there must be a couple of thousand people there now in the infield, perhaps even more. It was hard to estimate as it was such a large expanse of ground, though with that many folks there were still areas of open space. It was not simply people, for wagons and other assorted carriages had been allowed to enter and people were standing on them, providing a better view. It all reminded him of a fair or a carnival, but nothing like he had ever quite seen before. He had enjoyed the clubhouse, but this suited him better. Even though he was seated up towards the top of the vast grandstand, he felt more connected to all of the thousands of people he now saw before him, felt connected to their energy, which was intense and growing stronger by the minute.

Mary immediately noticed the section that had been reserved for ladies, down and to their right. Some women were dressed in the newer styles of the day, simple, more masculine-style jackets with smaller bustles. Others wore more traditional faille dresses with colorful and elaborate adornments. There were trained dresses, now considered a less practical fashion, signs of the hot dusty conditions indeed evident. She even noticed one or two old-style southern hoop skirts. Satins, silks, velveteen, cotton, linen, whatever the style, the fabric, the length of skirt, the size of the bustle, it was all a sea of colors. There were the bold, brighter colors, blues and greens and yellows, considered proper for the younger women. More mature ladies had chosen somewhat softer, subdued shades such as smoke grays, browns and chestnuts, and particularly pale rose. But the one thing they all had in common was hats. No matter the size, the shape, the color, not one woman would dare to be seen without a hat. Abe could not help but softly chuckle to himself at the sight of the two ladies next to him so enthralled with it all, but he decided it would be best to keep his comments to himself.

COMPLETELY unnoticed by the Lincolns and most everyone else, there was a man making his way through the crowd out in the infield, carefully avoiding pockets of open spaces. He was somewhat smallish but stocky, with a hat of his own pulled down and angled across his face, partially concealing his appearance. He was constantly looking around, watching for any familiar faces in the crowd, but one in particular. He could tell from the overall activity that the Derby was still several minutes away, and thus became even more concerned that he might be recognized. He needed somewhere to hide for a few minutes, but where in all of this openness? He spotted a wagon, a grocery wagon in fact, with low sides, a boy sitting on its back edge, watching everything that was going on around him in the immediate vicinity. The boy's father was up towards the front of the wagon, actively engaged in conversation with a few other men, passing a bottle. With one last look around at the nearby faces, the mysterious man walked over to the boy and said hello.

"You enjoying all of this, son? It's quite something isn't it?" The boy looked at the man, who suddenly remembered to pull his hat back so that the boy could more clearly see him and not be frightened.

"Yeah, it's fun," the boy replied, smiling.

"I've sure never seen anything like it. It was nice of your father to bring you out today. You must be a good boy."

"Yep, that's me. Well...most of the time. At least I try." He smiled even more.

"What's your name son?"

"Matt, Matt Winn. This is my dad's wagon." The man had already noticed the name Winn painted on the side.

"Well, it's good to meet you, Matt. I was wondering if you would do me a little favor?" Matt looked at him for a moment, thinking it over.

"Sure I guess."

"You see, Matt, I'm playing a little game with some of my friends."

"What kind of game?"

"It's kind of like hide and seek. Have you ever played hide and seek?"

"Sure, everybody plays hide and seek. I was always a good hider."

"I'll bet you were. You see, it's like this. I need a good place to hide from my friends for a few minutes, and you know, there just ain't many good places to hide out here. Then I saw your wagon." The boy thought for a minute and then grinned.

"You could hide under my dad's wagon. That would be a great place to hide!"

"Hey, that's a good idea. And you could be my lookout, too. Tell me what's going on. Could you do that?"

"Sure I could. That'd be fun."

"OK, then, I'm gonna crawl right down under here now, and you tell me if you see anybody looking for me. Then I want you to tell me when the horses are getting ready to start to race again, 'cause that's when the game is over and I can come out and surprise my friends. Does that sound okay?

"Sure."

"Great. Now, be sure and don't give me away, don't tell anybody that I'm down here, okay?"

"Okay, our secret."

"Thanks, Matt, you *are* a good boy." The man climbed under the wagon, disappearing from sight.

THERE was a nervous energy down in the Jockey's Room, increasing as the minutes clicked by. Fifteen jockeys, each in his own way preparing to do the same thing. First, dress out in the silks of the owner of the three-year-old thoroughbred they were contracted to ride in upcoming race. Next, head out to the paddock to join up with that horse. Finally, meet with the horse's trainer to receive final instructions and strategies for riding the horse, for winning the race. All of these jockeys, and owners, and trainers were united in the same goal: to win the first running of the Kentucky Derby.

As Oliver Lewis looked around the room he saw a sea of colors, mostly combinations of reds and whites and blues, the most common and oft used, but black and yellows and, just as he was wearing, greens and oranges as well. But by far the most prevalent color in the room was not on the jockeys' silks, but on their faces. Fourteen were colored; one lone white face stood out. Oliver knew several of the other riders, if not their names at least their faces, but there were a few still unknown to him. He had been chatting with Bill Henry, who would be riding Chesapeake, dressed in the identical silks as Oliver wore. He said hello to a friend he had made over in Lexington, Cyrus Holloway, dressed in bright blue silks with a yellow sash across the front, the colors of the owner of Enlister. Then he noticed a man wearing the red and white colors of the General. Bug Eye had introduced them earlier in the day. Oliver walked over to him.

"You sure are looking mighty sharp there, Dickie Jones, you sure are." Oliver laughed and shook the jockey's hand.

"Hey, Oliver, how you doing? You about ready to do this?"

"I surely am. Maybe just a might bit nervous, but I'll be okay when we get out on the track."

"You'll do fine, especially once we get started. And don't worry, I'll be right out there with you."

"Now how you so sure about that?"

"Well, I don't think it's no secret that I'm supposed to take McCreary right out to the lead and run for as long as we can. I don't have no idea that it's gonna be for no mile and a half. Hell, I'll be lucky to make it a mile with this horse. He's a good horse and all, but he ain't in no shape for this race. Old Tom knows it, I think the General knows it, too. I guess they just want to see what happens, say they had a horse in this first Derby. Anyways, I'm gonna be right out in front if everything goes to plan, and everybody knows that's where you and Aristides are gonna be, too." Oliver realized that Ansel's secret plan was maybe not so secret. Oliver hesitated for just a moment.

"Well, I don't know about all that. I guess we'll just have to see what old Aristides feels like doing today."

"You better do your job if you know what's good for you. Everybody knows McGrath wants to win this race with Chesapeake, so you'd better make sure that happens. Don't be getting no big ideas in your head. You got a good future ahead of you from what I've seen."

"Thanks, Dick, I appreciate hearing that from you. And don't worry none about me, I know what I gotta do."

"Well, good luck then."

"Yeah, good luck to you." They shook hands again. Just then another jockey came up, like Oliver dressed in orange, but with a black stripe across his front. He appeared to maybe just a few years older than most of the others in the room.

"Hey, Billy," Dick said, "how you been? Haven't seen you in a while. Billy, this is Oliver Lewis, riding Aristides for Old Tom. Oliver, this here is Mr. William Walker." Oliver and Walker shook hands, and then Dick continued, "Old Billy here's rode several horses for the General. In fact, he was born over on the General's farm, back before he got hisself emancipated."

"Yeah I was just talking with the General this morning, thought he was looking pretty good for an old man. Was all excited telling me all about how he just got a letter yesterday from this old friend of his, a man he'd known since he first got in the army, some general named Custard, was gonna be coming to see him this summer to buy a whole bunch a horses for this army he's gonna be taking out west to fight the Injins. Said I ought to go along and see what it was all about, maybe go out and kill some Injins for myself. I told him, General, if I ain't got killed riding on these here horses I sure as hell ain't gonna go out and let no Injins shoot at me." They all laughed. "But, really I thought the General was looking just fine."

Dick asked, "Who you riding today, Billy?"

"Bob Wooley, for Mr. Robinson." Looking closely at Oliver he continued, "Aristides, huh? Well I guess that means that your horse's daddy and my horse's daddy are the same damn horse. Maybe we'll finish one-two and make the old man proud. Course that would be me one and you two." He laughed and said, "Good to meet you, Oliver, and good luck to you today."

After Walker walked away, Dick said, shaking his head, "If there's one thing that man knows it's the bloodlines. He knows all about these horses, going way on back. I can't keep up with it all myself, but Billy Walker, man he seems to know about every damn horse around, who it's mother and father was, and who their mothers and fathers was, and on and on. If there was ever a man who ought to be working on the breeding side of this business, it sure is him."

Just then, Colonel Clark and Colonel Johnson entered the room and everyone settled down and turned to face them. Clark looked around the room, checking each man's appearance to make sure it met his standards. He nodded and smiled hello to the ones he knew. "Gentlemen, I don't want to take up much of your time. We need to get on out to the paddock and get ready. I just wanted to remind you of how important this race is to me and to all of those people out there, and hopefully to each one of you as well, because it should be. We're starting something here that *is* important, important to our Commonwealth and to our sport. Some day you will look back and say, 'I rode in that first Kentucky Derby.' You will be remembered, because this is going to be an important race. It will soon be the biggest race of all, I promise you that. So I'm here to tell you that there will be no fooling around of any kind today. I won't stand for it. I want a good clean race, with everyone riding their best and doing nothing but riding their best. I will have no patience for anything else."

Turning to the man next to him, he continued, "Some of you may know of my good friend, Colonel Johnson here, who has come from Nashville at my invitation to officiate our start. I ask you all to follow his every instruction, as I know you will." Johnson himself made no comment, but maintained a serious, almost stern expression as he reviewed the faces in front of him. After a moment of silence Clark finished, "Everyone understand? Anybody got any questions?" All were silent. "Well, then I guess we understand each other. Let's get out there and have us a good race today. Good luck to you all." He turned and walked out, and the jockeys slowly began to follow him. Johnson waited until all had exited, and then headed directly over to the track.

The crowd packed in around the paddock cheered as the fifteen little men in their fancy colored uniforms made their way over, each finding their respective horse and its trainer, ready for final instructions. Since Ansel had two horses to get ready and was mostly occupied with Chesapeake, he came over to Oliver and quickly said, "You know what to do. Get out there and set a good pace and let them all chase after you." Oliver thought about telling him what Dickie had said about everybody knowing about their plan, but figured the old trainer already knew, and if he didn't, well it didn't matter now anyhow. Ansel gave him a leg up and said, "Good luck, Ollie. Have a safe trip, and bring this horse back sound to me."

As he was settling in, Oliver noticed Mr. McGrath approaching, with whom he had never spoken before. The owner greeted him and said, "Just wanted to say hello, and thank you for helping us out. Ansel tells me you're a good rider and you'll do a good job for us today. It's important to us, and I appreciate it." He started to turn, and then added, "Now I'll be watching from out in the infield. Keep an eye out for me as you're coming around the turn. You'll be able to see me easy enough. If anything should change, if for any reason things ain't going to plan, watch for me and I'll signal you. I'm sure it won't be necessary, but just in case...you never know. Well, anyway, you got it?"

"Yes, sir. You can count on me. I'll take a good look over as we're coming around. You got a good horse here, and he's ready to go." McGrath started to say something more, then just turned and went over to where Ansel was giving Bill Henry a leg up on Chesapeake. Oliver took a good long look so that he'd be sure and recognize him later. Shouldn't be too hard the way he was dressed. Oliver thought he looked mighty sharp.

ALEX crossed over the racetrack just before the horses came out for the Derby. The crowd there had now swelled but there was still plenty of room, especially near the turns. He nervously played with a silver dollar he had in his pocket, rolling it over and over again in his hand. It was a good luck piece that he carried, not all of the time, but just for really important things. This was the most important thing he had ever done. He had to admit that he was impressed with the size of the crowd, and with his eyes slowly surveying the clubhouse and back over the grandstand, he had to give Clark some credit. It was a first-rate facility. Not the Fair Grounds, of course, but the man had done himself proud. But then he thought, a tight smile crossing his face, *it wasn't going to be remembered for horse racing now was it?* He removed his snug-fitting brown hat and wiped the sweat from his forehead. It was hot out in the sun, and this old drab brown suit wasn't very comfortable. But that was how he wanted it. No one would expect Alexander Delacroix to be dressed in anything like this outfit, and it would help him to be less noticeable, if by some small chance there was anyone around who might know him. But he did not really care about his clothes, the race, or anything else for that matter. He was right where he wanted to be, right where he needed to be, right where he was *supposed* to be. He was at the brink, history would remember this moment forever. They would remember him forever. He was now more sure than ever that he would be a hero to millions. As far as the others? Well, to hell with all of them!

MARCUS looked up when he heard the crowd react to the horses' appearance on the track. He was toward the middle of the crowd in the infield, just a little to the left, surrounded by mostly colored faces, about thirty feet from the fence. He was tall enough that he could see a little, but that did not really concern him. He had by this point consumed more than his share of beer, was feeling fine, not at all worried, which was miraculous considering he had wagered close to a month's salary on his cousin. Bev would give him holy hell if she knew. But he wasn't worried about that now. All Oliver had talked about for the last few days was how ready Aristides was. Marcus understood that it wasn't Oliver's choice, that he indeed wasn't to win, just to set things up for the other horse. But Marcus didn't care. He believed in his cousin, and besides, he had a feeling. And wasn't that what gambling was all about? When you got a feeling you just had to act on it. He was surprised to see Bug Eye working his way through the crowd, and shouted out to him.

"What you doing out here, Bug Eye? Why ain't you got you a good spot over at the barns?"

"Hey, Marcus. Hell, I dunno. I just decided I'd rather be out here with you all. It's kinda more exciting being out here in the crowd."

"But you can't see nothing, you're too damn short." Marcus was exhibiting signs of his consumption.

"That's okay with me. Don't need to see it. Guess I don't want to see it if I can't be riding."

"Oh, come on, let's head on down towards the far turn, it ain't so crowded down there. Be able to see more." Bug Eye just shrugged his shoulders and followed the big man.

ANSEL, his work now done at least for this day, found a spot along the fence down by the barns, right next to his old friend and nemesis Old Tom.

"Hello, Tom, mind if I join you?"

"Naw, come right on, Ansel. Glad to have you." They both stood silently next to one another for a full minute.

"How'd your horse look?" Ansel finally inquired.

"McCreary? Shit, he ain't gonna do nuthing. Oh, he'll get on out there all right I guess, but he ain't gonna last long. Got too sick on me, didn't have time to get him ready. But the boss insisted on running him, just had to have a horse in here. Pride's a damn sorry thing, ain't it?"

"You're sure right enough about that."

"Figure we'll do a lot better in a couple of days with the filly. Now she's got a real chance." He paused for a moment and then said, "Chesapeake sure looks good. I believe I would swap horses with you if you'd let me."

"Yeah, well, we'll see. Never know what's gonna happen in a horse race. There's a few others out there might have something to say about it." They stopped talking as the horses came down the track towards them, both now focused, watching, observing every little detail about how their respective horse looked and acted.

CALVIN stood behind the corner of the barn nearest the grandstand, just waiting and watching, watching the man positioned at the bottom of the small stairway that led up the back. After that first race he now knew exactly what to expect. He and Peanut were ready.

UP in the grandstand the buzz grew louder in anticipation. The gentlemen who had made last minute trips to place their wagers were returning to their seats, while in the ladies' section friends were quietly making small wagers amongst themselves in support of their favorite horse, mostly using personal items. A silk handkerchief here, a pair of gloves there, a scarf, perhaps even just a piece of candy; little of real value, just any small thing to make the race more fun.

Mary, who had studied the program intently, had finally decided to again support Mr. Lewis and his yellow-capped jockey, riding on Vagabond. Clark had just made his way back up and settled into his seat to the right of Abe, closest to the aisle. Still staring at the list of horses, Abe paused for just a moment to say hello and then returned to his study. Finally, his choice was made.

"Well, Colonel, it seems to me that any horse named Volcano should be full of run. So I believe that will be my choice. Volcano it is."

Clark stood and announced to those seated nearby, "The president has pronounced that Volcano shall be the victor. Is there anyone who shall offer dispute?"

Lincoln quickly stood and responded, "Gentlemen, pay me no heed. For I suspect I have just announced the horse that shall finish last. My dear wife tells me with great assurance that it is to be Vagabond. I would not dare to dispute her, and you do so at your own peril." He waited for everyone to finish laughing and cheering. "All I can say to all of you is thank you for having us, good luck to you all, and bring on the Derby!"

The horses, just as before the first race, had come out onto the track in a line, paraded down in front of the clubhouse, then turned and made their way back down in front of the grandstand, all to the rising cheer of the crowd. This time, however, they continued jogging on around the far turn to the backstretch. As the Derby was to be contested at a mile and a half, the starting point would be opposite them, mid-way down the backstretch of the track. As Abe and everyone else watched the horses slowly round the far turn, the sun, now in the earliest beginnings of its afternoon descent, shown directly into their eyes. He was struck with the notion that the grandstand should be situated on the opposite side, that as the day grew long the sun would make it increasingly difficult to watch the horses coming down the stretch to the finish. He started to comment to Clark, but thought better of it. "Let the man enjoy his day with no criticism from me," he said, only to himself.

Out in the middle of the backstretch, as Colonel Johnson began to assemble the horses, having drawn his starting line across the track, Clark said loudly to no one in particular, "Gentlemen, it is here. Our work is done. Now let us enjoy this spectacle, the beauty of it all, just as if we were on that plane at Epsom, for someday they will all be wishing that they were here." He looked over at his wife, and she smiled brightly. In that moment she realized that in spite of all of her concerns, all of her doubts about her husband's abilities, all of his past short-comings, he had indeed done it. She was more than proud of him, which he could tell just from her smile.

OUT in the infield young Matt Winn called to his new friend. "Sir, I believe they are almost ready." The man poked his head out, looked around, and then crawled out. Matt's father had just come to tell his son to climb up on the back of the wagon, that the race was about to start. Before anything could be said Robert Appleton ran off, thanking Matt, and was gone. As he quickly made his way through the crowd Crabby almost ran into someone else who was moving along quickly as well, a very large gentleman. He looked up to see Marcus, and then realized Bug Eye was following right behind. Crabby immediately recognized the two colored men from that morning. He started to run on without saying a word and then a thought entered his mind.

"Marcus, and I believe, is it Bug Eye? I'm glad to see you both." Without waiting for any reply from the two greatly surprised men, he quickly continued. "I am seeking justice for my brother, and am trying to stop an even worse thing from happening. I desperately need your help." The beer had clouded Marcus' head just enough that he had to pause to take in what the white man in front of him was saying, what he was asking. He looked somewhat confused. Crabby took it to be an encouraging sign.

"Yes, I know this is sudden, but it is a matter of life and death. Please, will you come with me and help me? Either way, I must go now." He did not wait for a response, but continued rushing on towards the far turn. Marcus found sincerity in Crabby's urgency and the look in his eye. Marcus had been truly scared that morning. Now that fear turned into a form of rage. After exchanging a momentary glance with Bug Eye they both quickly followed.

CHAPTER TWENTY-SIX

OLIVER slowly turned Aristides round, making ready for the start of the Kentucky Derby. He had tried to calm himself but was still plenty nervous. There were so many people, and they had been so loud as he had passed in front of the Grandstand. Oliver had never heard anything like it before. He could tell that Aristides was nervous as well. He was now completely focused on getting his horse in position, but out of the corner of his eye he saw Billy Walker to his left, calm and cool, at least by appearances, and then to his right, his friend Cyrus. He heard someone shout "good luck" to him but he had no idea who it was. And then, before he could even imagine it, the sound of the drum and the race was on.

Aristides exploded underneath him. Within three strides the horse had attained full speed, approaching forty miles-per-hour. Oliver steadied himself as Aristides reached out with giant strides, eating up the track with each one, legs moving in a blur, faster than the human eye could comprehend. When he gained his senses Oliver realized that there were no other horses to his front, and only one to his side. Red silks, white stripe, red and white cap: it was indeed McCreary. In just a little over twenty seconds they had made the quarter pole and Aristides fell back slightly, McCreary surging into the lead. Then just that quickly, Aristides came back on him.

THE grandstand erupted with the start, an outburst such as no one present had ever experienced, the tension exploding like a cannon. Clark, the Lincolns, and thousands of others seated there watched as a small chestnut colt took the lead, briefly lost it, and then reclaimed it in the far turn. Fifteen thoroughbreds came round, on down the stretch in front of the immense crowd. A few poor souls forgot that the horses were just getting started on this first pass by the grandstand, and thinking the race was almost over were cheering or lamenting depending on the position of their favorites.

Standing along the outside fence, Ansel had true reason to lament: Chesapeake had stared badly, and was much further back in the pack than Ansel would have ever guessed or wanted. He was momentarily tempted to blame Johnson, that there should have been a re-start, but no, it was just how the game was played. He could only wait and wonder if his horse would have enough to overcome this bad luck.

VERNON stood just behind the seats in the very top of the grandstand, a very short distance above where Lincoln was seated. Thanks to the Colonel he had experienced no problems at all in getting access to the area, having slipped up the back stairway, almost unnoticed. Vernon was now ready to inch forward slowly, to get into his final position, then to wait for the planned disturbance, and finally the all important signal from the man in the infield. His eyes were searching for the brown suit and green tie even now. But no panic, there was still plenty of time. He felt the warmth of the Colt pressed against his left side, itching to be drawn, underneath his jacket. Vernon was strangely calm, almost serene, enjoying the moment, his mind clearer than it had felt in many years. It was good to have purpose again.

CALVIN peered around the corner of the barn closest to the grandstand, intently watching the man stationed at the bottom of the small stairway leading up the back. Minutes earlier he had watched him allow Vernon to pass, slowly limping his way up and through the small doorway at the top. As Calvin had fully expected, indeed had been counting on, when the first race had begun the guard could not help himself and had left his position to go up along the edge of the structure for at least a partial view of the race. It was eerily quiet behind the grandstand, considering all of the people who were just on the other side of the wooden back wall, screaming and shouting. Calvin knew that it was just a matter of time and he waited and watched patiently. Sure enough, within moments of the start of the race the man looked around, saw that the whole area was indeed deserted, everyone now settled into whatever place they had found from which to watch, and he quickly slipped around the corner and this time continued up along the side, disappearing. At least bloodshed would be avoided for the moment. Calvin turned to his partner and asked, "Ready?"

Peanut just said, "Ready as I'm ever gonna be." The two small colored men quickly slipped over to the stairway, and seeing no one, started up.

THE horses were now passing directly in front of the grandstand for the first time, and the crowd in the infield could not help but to surge in that same direction with them. Alex stood stationary staring up into the stands, listening to the roar, watching Lincoln, perspiring heavily. Suddenly, he no longer heard the crowd, he felt no one near him. Everything stopped, and then, moved on again in slow-motion. His mind went cold, and for a moment, it seemed as if everyone was looking directly at him. Everyone, all of those thousands and thousands of people, were no longer looking at the horses, but at *him*. They *knew*! They knew who he was, they knew what he was *doing*. He couldn't breathe. He gasped for air, reaching up to loosen the worn green tie around his neck, clutching and pulling at it. He didn't feel like a hero, he didn't feel like a savior, he felt like, like...a failure. It was just the same as in New Orleans. His true self had been revealed to him. Alex couldn't do this, who was he fooling? As everyone continued staring down at him, his knees weakened, his head started spinning, and he felt as though he would collapse, pass out – and then what? He would be trapped! He must get out of there, quickly, NOW! He had to run, run far away. To hell with Lincoln, to hell with Vernon, to hell with them all!

THE horses rushed into the turn. Oliver gave a quick look back under his arm and saw that McCreary was fading back quickly, not even a mile yet, done. Everyone had sure been right about that horse. But who was coming, that was the question? His only answer was...nobody! At least not yet. He reminded himself that there was still a long, long way to go. The noise from the crowd subsided slightly as the horses hit the backstretch again. Oliver could now hear nothing but Aristides' hooves pounding in the dirt.

ALEX turned and ran. He was momentarily trapped, stuck in the middle of this oval until the horses passed by him again. Then he would be free to run across it, to escape. He would be gone before the horses even reached the finish. He cared nothing for the race, nothing about Vernon, most of all, no thoughts whatsoever of Lincoln, only escape, back to his beloved New Orleans. He would never leave it again!

Alex almost fell as he crashed into a large man who was rushing up from his side, a large colored man. Alex regained his balanced, and cursing the man, turned to continue on towards the fence. Then Alex saw him. It was like a dream, a nightmare. Something not quite real, something that just doesn't seem right, is totally out of place. There is front of him stood Robert Appleton. Alex's face showed an expression of complete wonderment, disbelief, and slowly his lips formed the word "Crabby" without saying anything.

"Afternoon...*Boss*." He sounded the word out, slowly, sarcastically, in a way his brother never would have dared. Then he did something that was even more unsettling to Alex. Crabby smiled. He grinned like he never had grinned before, grinned just to remind Alex of the man whom he had killed that morning, if not by his hand then by his direction. "Well I can't say that I'm very surprised. You appear to have lost your nerve. Isn't that right, Alex? Just couldn't go through with it, could you? You are nothing but a goddamn worm, Delacroix, and I'm going to make sure you get yours, for what you did to Charlie, and for everything else."

Alex stared at Crabby with a continued look of disbelief. And then something inside of him clicked into place, his composure regained, a calm look returning to his face. "I'm sure I have no idea what you are talking about, Robert. As for your brother, you of course have my deepest sympathies. A tragic accident, so very sad. We shall all miss him. Beyond that, I have nothing else to say to you."

"You lyin' bastard, I saw them do it. You had that poor man killed. I saw it all." It was the large black man. A looked of concerned flashed over Alex's face for just an instant, then he smiled.

"Again, I have no idea what you are talking about. Besides, the word of a colored man such as yourself, or," looking at Crabby, "a low-life groom for that matter, won't mean much against mine." Alex actually laughed. Crabby just stared back at him coldly, hardly even aware of the growing noise from the thousands of people sharing this stage.

"You know, I was reading in the paper how they let colored men testify in court up here, actually believe them sometimes. Oh, yes, and then there is this." Crabby pulled a folded piece of paper out of his pocket and held it open in front of Alex, who saw the words carefully and neatly written there, in his own hand.

Gentlemen,

You are to inform Mr. Preston that I will be positioned in the infield...

Alex's mind began to go black. He desperately grabbed for the paper, but Crabby lurched back, easily avoiding him. Marcus caught Alex, preventing him first from moving forward, then from falling to the ground. Alex went limp but managed to say, weakly, "Why? Why have you done this to me? We were partners...friends. You were with me, from the beginning. How has this happened?"

Robert Appleton, now again smiling simply replied, "You never asked me. If you had just bothered to *ask*, Alex, I would have told you." Alex tried to consider this, but it was more than he could comprehend at that moment.

Satisfied that he had averted any further tragedy, Crabby hurriedly led Marcus, Alex and Bug Eye on towards the fence. He noticed that the crowd was beginning to surge to his left, down the track, reminding Crabby that there was indeed a horse race occurring directly in front of them. He could see the colorful heads of the fifteen jockeys bobbing up and down, now coming round the turn into the stretch.

CALVIN and Peanut peered through the small opening at the top of the stairs. As expected everyone was facing in the opposite direction, including the uniformed officers, along with any other security staff who might be present, all intently watching the race. Standing right next to one of the officers was Vernon Preston, his one hand now inside of his coat. Calvin saw that the horses were in the final turn and readied himself. In just a moment he would assume the role of a badly out-of-place, drunken colored man.

FEWER than fifteen feet directly ahead, Mary was beside herself. Whereas during the first race her horse had been close to the lead the entire time, Vagabond was near the back of the pack and had been since the beginning. She had closely watched the little yellow cap, moving up and down, but never forward. It was just, just...depressing. Meanwhile Volcano, who had broken well and settled into fourth place, currently was making a bit of a move and trailed only Aristides half way through the final turn. As the horses neared the head of the stretch the crowd in the infield began to flow to the right, running parallel to the track, moving together like a giant wave. The noise from the grandstand increased again. It was almost deafening.

Abe looked over at Mary, took her hand, but she was too excited even to notice. Her face was simply glowing, and somehow, in the midst of all of this hoopla an incredible sense of peace overcame Abraham Lincoln. A sense he literally had not felt in so very many years. Since the early days in Springfield, the days right after they were married, in some ways even going back to his boyhood. For that one moment, he heard no crowd, he saw no one else, only the face of his bride, of the woman who had shared this life with him. And he felt content. He knew in that moment, for certain, he indeed had made the correct decision in coming back to Kentucky. His instincts had been right. And then, just as quickly, the roar of the crowd crept back into his world and his eyes searched once again for Volcano. It looked like he just might win!

THE Lincolns paid no attention to Chesapeake, and therefore did not notice that he was stuck in the middle of the pack, no better than tenth, a good fifteen lengths or more back from Aristides, not moving at all. But out in the infield, H. P. McGrath most certainly noticed, and he was not happy. Not happy at all. "Damn you, Ansel," he said out loud, "I thought you had this horse ready. Come on, Bill, get him moving." But as they came around the turn, his owner quickly realized that it was no good. For whatever reason, bad start, bad luck, Chesapeake wasn't going to win, and McGrath knew it.

"RUN you goddamn horshes, run! Come on goddamn it, run!" Calvin, with Peanut by his side, stumbled out, shouting loudly, intentionally slurring his words. Even with the noise from the crowd, Calvin made sure that he could not be missed by the people located right at the rear of the grandstand. The uniformed officers standing only a few feet in front of Calvin turned suddenly with a look of complete disbelief. *Two colored men, two drunken colored men, here in the grandstand, here near Mr. Lincoln? How could this be?* The officers' immediate reaction was not so much out of concern for safety, but more the potential embarrassment for Colonel Clark, and of course the President. Without even thinking they began to approach Calvin and Peanut, one officer shouting, "What in the hell do you boys think you are doing? Where in the hell did you come from?"

Calvin simply answered, "We jus' wanna see 'em horshes run!" For good effect, he fell over into Peanut. A few more people along the rear of that end of the grandstand turned briefly to see what the commotion was all about, but paid no real attention as they were totally absorbed with the race. Vernon quickly took advantage of the opportunity to move a few steps forward and down, and was now in the aisle immediately to Lincoln's right, his hand on his Colt, still under his coat. Clark's trusted assistant stared out in to the infield, his eyes searching.

ANSEL stood next to Old Tom intently watching the horses as they came around the turn, now practically in front of him. He had mostly been watching for Chesapeake, concern growing from the beginning. When the horses had passed by the first time Ansel was already doubtful about his prospects. Aristides was on the lead but Ansel was sure the horse would never last at this pace. And Chesapeake, well, it just wasn't going to be Chesapeake's day. Ansel already recognized this less than a half-mile into the race. As McCreary continued to fade the two trainers turned to each other with a shrug that spoke with no need for words, "Oh, well, let's go get a drink. We'll get 'em tomorrow," the code of trainers everywhere. Even though his other horse was still on the lead Ansel indeed did think for just a moment about heading on back to the barn. There was still a quarter mile to go, but deep down inside he simply did not believe that Aristides could get the distance. Then, out of the corner of his eye he noticed McGrath across from him out in the infield, the owner's green tie flashing in the sunlight.

A SUDDEN realization entered McGrath's head. Chesapeake wasn't going to win the Derby. Nothing he could do about that now. But by God, Aristides was still on the lead and he looked strong. What had that new jockey told him, the horse was ready? Without thinking anything further McGrath grabbed his hat off of his head, the hat that matched his fine brown suit, and started waving it wildly. "Go on, go on and try to win it! It's your race now!" He was jumping and waving his hat just as hard as he could, hoping that his jockey would see him. McGrath's tie, the same color of green as on his rider's silks, pulled loose out from his vest, and began flapping against his chest. "Go, go on Aristides!"

OLIVER looked back again. They were almost out of the turn, just a little more than a quarter mile to go. He had no thoughts whatsoever of Mr. H.P. Mc-Grath. There was a horse coming, but there was still daylight between them. What were the colors? Blue, white sleeves, a crescent – it was...Volcano! But still no sign of Chesapeake. "Here he comes," Oliver thought, "now what have I got left?"

THERE *he is, and he's signaling!* Vernon saw him, wearing the brown suit, he could even make out the green tie, flashing wildly, shining in the sunlight. He was jumping and waving his brown hat in the air. Was it the same man he had met in the old shack down the road? It had been dark that night, he had not had that good of a look at him. *Yes,* Vernon quickly decided, *that must be him.* It was the signal, it was time!

THE horses straightened out into the stretch. Oliver could hear Volcano right behind them. He turned to his crop for the first time that afternoon, urging Aristides on. There was the eighth pole. He was still a full length ahead. Aristides did in fact have something left, the crowd gasped as more daylight opened between the two horses. The noise grew even louder, if that were possible. For the first time the realization hit Oliver, *I'm going to win the Derby!*

CHAPTER TWENTY-SEVEN

VERY few people heard the shots, even though later many would claim that they had. In reality the incredible noise of the crowd made it possible for only those few who were close by even to be aware that anything had happened. All eyes were focused down the track. People were yelling and cheering, some jumping up and down. It was almost chaos, a good chaos, changed in a moment's notice for those closest to the former president. For they did not see as Aristides crossed the finish line, as Oliver grabbed the yellow purse containing the winner's share, nearly three thousand dollars. They did not see the young jockey almost fall off his horse in excitement, pumping his left hand up and down in the air, continuing on past the finish and into the first turn. Their attention had been drawn elsewhere.

VERNON had taken one more step down, and then two steps in to his left, pulling out his revolver, fully loaded. He stood slightly in front of Clark. Before the Colonel could react Vernon had raised his one hand and taken dead aim on Lincoln, still seated, resisting the urge to rise and cheer as so many others in the grandstand were doing, out of respect for his wife and the other dignitaries who remained seated as well. His eyes were transfixed on the horses that had just passed directly in front of him. As the former president began to turn his head slightly, following the horses down the track, Vernon, his gun's barrel only three feet away, fired. The bullet instantly entered Lincoln's head, just below his right eye. Vernon then lowered his gun ever so slightly and moved another half-step forward. He instantly fired a second time, this bullet puncturing his victim's heart. Satisfied, correctly so, that no further damaged would be required, he had taken a quick step backwards and looked at Clark, who had jumped up and then instinctively backed away, recoiling in horror.

UP above this scene, Calvin and Peanut had heard a shot, then another, watching the reaction of the officers who had begun to harass them. The officers turned and immediately took a few steps toward the sound. One of them briefly looked back at Calvin before proceeding towards the unmistakable sound of the gunshots. Calvin could see Vernon as he stepped back. Calvin's hand grabbed the handle of the knife in his waistband, preparing for the final task. But instead of turning and running up the stairs, as expected, Vernon had just stood there. *Come on, come on,* Calvin thought to himself, and then before he could say it, Peanut had whispered, "What the hell is he doing?"

VERNON had no intention of running. He was weary of his life, sick of his habit, tired of living, but most of all, he was full of hatred for the man standing in front of him. In cold, determined words he addressed Clark. "You'll never be the man your father was. You sir, are no Colonel." He pointed his gun and began to press the trigger. A third shot rang out, but with a distinctly different sound. Vernon's eyes widened, body jerking slightly forward. He continued squeezing until a fourth shot sounded. Vernon's aim now altered, his bullet found Clark's right arm. As his assistant fell Clark noticed a man wearing a fine black suit, standing six feet behind Vernon, holding a small pistol, smoke trailing up from its barrel.

CRABBY and his two comrades, Marcus still practically carrying Alex, crossed the track just before the west end of the grandstand. Hundreds of others off to their left were now climbing over the inside fence, out onto the racing surface, running down the track behind the horses. Through the thunderous crescendo of noise from the crowd, now focused partially away from him, Alex imagined he heard gunshots. But how could that be? He had not given any signal. It could not be Vernon. Was someone else shooting, shooting at him?

Crabby heard nothing, was not even conscious of the noise from the crowd, but he perceived that something *was* happening up in the top of the grandstand. He glanced momentarily in that direction but was moving too quickly to focus. He was sure that something was going on but he would not let his mind considered what it could be. He only wanted to get to the barn, to get Alex out of the crowd.

"SHIT, he's shot Clark," Peanut said, looking over at Calvin, now fully alert and obviously not intoxicated. There was a flurry of activity in front of them.

Calvin saw the man in the black suit shoot Vernon, hesitated in disbelief at it all for an instant, and then shouted "Go, go," pushing Peanut towards the stairs. Out of the corner of his eye, one of the officers noticed a flash and turned to see the two colored men hurriedly passing through the small opening and heading down the stairway. He yelled, "Hey, you, stop! Stop right there!" following in pursuit. Calvin and Peanut raced down the stairs and were almost at the bottom, vaguely aware that someone was shouting at them from above, when the guard who had left his post returned. The guard immediately noticed Calvin and Peanut coming down towards him, saying, "What the hell are you two doing? Get the hell off...." He never finished his sentence. Calvin, reaching him first, plunged his knife deep into the man's chest and then pushed him out of the way.

One final shot rang out that afternoon. Calvin shuddered, stopped running, and turned, looking up at the small stairway to see the man above holding out a gun. Peanut watched his friend go down to one knee, then collapse, and within moments draw his last breath. Peanut stood looking down at his only friend in the world, unable to move so much as a muscle.

OLIVER slowed Aristides, continually slapping him on the neck, shouting and yelping, smiling so broadly his face began to ache. But it didn't matter. He had won the Kentucky Derby! "I tried to tell 'em, boy. I tried to tell them you were ready. All they wanted to talk about was old Chesapeake. But we showed 'em, didn't we, boy. We really showed 'em now." In his left hand he held the yellow purse full of money.

As he turned and headed back around the turn, back towards the club-house, his defeated competitors yelling their congratulations to him, Oliver's eyes scanned the grandstand. Everyone was still cheering wildly and moving around, a sea of activity. People were out on the track milling all around him, trying to touch Aristides, to touch him, so he kept his horse constantly moving. Track officials began to form a barrier to keep back those that had spilled out onto the track. Oliver did not notice, could not have seen, what was happening at the far end of the grandstand, up toward the top. He held the yellow purse up high in the air and went to celebrate the moment with his adoring public.

MARY, not quite comprehending what had just occurred beside her, was stunned as her husband slumped over into her lap, blood pouring out of him, soaking into her blue dress. She had of course heard the shots, but somehow they did not seem real, they were so totally out of place that her mind could not grasp it. A few seconds went by as the scene began to register in her mind, then screams, screams that would not stop. She tried to stand but could not because of the weight of his body on hers. She began pushing, flailing, one, then two additional gun shots bringing complete desperation. Mrs. Clark, seated beyond Mary, at first unable as well to fully comprehend what was happening beside her, could manage only a silent scream of disbelief, not even aware of her husband's condition. The governor and his associates rose and turned, looking at the carnage in front of them. Clark sat on his chair, transfixed in a glazed stare, holding his right arm, the bottom of his exposed white sleeve turning crimson. Beneath Mary, Lincoln's blood was rapidly pooling, then running over the edge of the step and slowly on down over the floor of the grandstand. The officers, along with several others, were gathered around Vernon's body, lying in the aisle, his one hand still clutching the shiny Colt revolver. Mary continued screaming, lost in the cheers of the crowd.

SWEEPING across the grandstand like a slowly moving wave, more and more people looked up wanting to see Lincoln's reaction to the race, and while not quite certain what it could be, realized something had happened. People were standing, some with eyes transfixed on the track in front of them, watching and joining in the joyous celebration led by the small colored man on the little chestnut horse, others, turned and staring up in growing horror at the scene above them, slowly recognizing what might have occurred.

Oliver began to sense something was not right. He was still smiling and waving, making his way to the winner's circle, but slowly the noise from the crowd was subsiding, and then, within scarcely a minute, had fallen off to no more than a quiet hum. He no longer saw their faces looking down at him. Everyone was looking up now, hardly moving. It was all wrong. He stopped Aristides in the middle of the track and he looked, too.

PEANUT slowly realized that the police officer who had just shot his friend was making his way rapidly down the stairs, coming ever closer. Without thinking or looking back, Peanut ran towards the barns and quickly disappeared, oblivious to the shouted orders to stop. His mind was blank. Without Calvin there to tell him what to do, as he had always been, Peanut instinctively headed towards the General's barn, to the closest thing that he had to a home, and as he would have realized if he had stopped to think, where they were to meet Alex.

AFTER having made their way across the track while the horses were still in mid-stretch, Crabby and the others had gone straight to the barn. Hundreds of other people had jumped over the rail along with them, but they had then turned and run on down behind the horses. The barns were all practically deserted as everyone else in the vicinity was too focused on the finish of the race and the subsequent celebration. Crabby's intention was to follow Alex's plan and be waiting in the barn when and if Calvin and Peanut arrived, although he was doubtful he would see them. He had been very skeptical concerning that part of Alex's plan. They had only been waiting for a minute or so when Peanut came running up to the shed row. For a moment Peanut was surprised to see the other men there, but then his mind focused, though still not realizing that things were not as they should have been.

"They shot Calvin," Peanut blurted out excitedly. "I think he's dead. Your man up there, he didn't run to us, he shot Clark, too. And then they shot him. We just ran, trying to get away and they...they shot Calvin." He had a bewildered look on his face, as if he were a small child waiting for someone to explain to him what had just happened, his brain incapable of comprehending it all. Then he realized that a big colored man was holding Alex against his will. And wait...*Is that Crabby? But Crabby's gone to Chicago.* Peanut's eyes widened, realizing things were very wrong indeed.

"Yeah, sorry about Calvin," Crabby said quietly "I know he was your friend. He stood staring coldly at the little black man, then it suddenly hit him that somehow Alex's plot had not be averted, that Vernon had gone ahead anyway. "Is Lincoln...?"

"Yeah, he's good and dead, I mean I think so. I 'magine Preston is too...I, I mean..." Peanut was just staring down at the ground now, unable to finish.

Crabby could not believe it. He had not stopped them. Lincoln was dead. He felt responsible, almost as if he had pulled the trigger himself. "Shit" was all he could say, trying to fully absorb this news. Then he looked at Alex. "So, do you feel like a *hero*, you son-of-a-bitch?" Crabby slowly sat down on a hay bale, just staring down at the ground for a few seconds. A grey colt stuck his head out from the stall nearest to Bug Eye and looked around at them as if curious to know what this strange scene was all about. Crabby looked up and said, "Everybody get comfortable, we're just gonna wait here until they come along. Somebody'll be here soon enough." Alex looked like he might be thinking about trying to break away and run, but Marcus stayed right by his side to ensure that was not possible. Peanut showed no desire to go anywhere, simply staring blankly at the ground.

TOMMY had noticed the activity up in the grandstand before most, as he was directly in front of the scene, just across the track in the infield. He had also watched the encounter between Crabby and Alex from about fifty feet away, and while he had some thoughts of coming to Alex's assistance he quickly got over them. Instead Tommy simply watched the rest of the race. He had wagered most of the money that Alex had given him that day, along with a good bit of the rest that he had, on Volcano. His profits for the week had just disappeared and he was not happy. His eye had been drawn up to Lincoln as soon as he realized that Volcano had lost, and immediately could see something was amiss. Careful study quickly led him to understand just what had happened. And just that quickly he came to the conclusion that Alex was involved. It all made sense now.

Tommy made his way over to the barns as Alex had instructed, but as he neared the appointed meeting place he was extremely careful not to be seen or heard. He crept up closer to the barn, just outside the shed row, and saw the group of men standing there. Realizing that Alex was not going to be going anywhere that afternoon, at least not anywhere that Tommy would care to join him, he slowly made his way back and then casually walked on around out of the barn area and around the back of the grandstand. He saw the bodies of two men at the bottom of some stairs, one white and one colored, one obviously dead and one he was not so sure about, not pausing to find out. He headed straight to the exit, made his way out to the road, and was headed back to town as if nothing had happened. Louisville suited him just fine anyway, Tommy thought. He really hadn't wanted to go to New Orleans in the first place.

MORE officers quickly arrived at the top of the grandstand, mostly trying to keep people away from the immediate area of the shootings. Lincoln was already dead, in fact had died within seconds. Mary was still in hysterics, finally freed of the weight of her husband's dead body, now just trying to get away. Members of the governor's party were forced to restrain her. Mrs. Clark, finally fully aware that her husband had been wounded as well, had somehow managed to make her way around in front of the Lincolns over to him. The man in the black suit seemed to instinctively assume control and began issuing orders. A call for stretchers went out. Clark had ordered that two be housed at the track in case of emergencies, never imagining that he would be the first to require the use of one.

When they arrived, track officials first loaded Clark and immediately carried him down the front of the grandstand, his wife following close behind. The wound was not life-threatening, but he was in great pain and needed attention as blood was still seeping down his arm. He was quickly taken to a wagon and laid in the back, whereupon they hastily departed towards town. As soon as Clark had been removed, they carefully laid Lincoln's body on the other stretcher, and slowly, solemnly, carried it down and over to the clubhouse. The vast majority of officers and security personnel on the grounds were now present, and it took all of their efforts to control the crowds enough to be able to carry Lincoln through. Mary followed with great assistance, now completely in shock. Vernon's body was dragged up to the small area behind the seats and left lying there for the time being, one officer positioned to watch. No one cared much about him any longer.

By the time the guard at the bottom of the steps could receive any medical assistance it was too late. He had bled to death. As soon as the man in the black suit was satisfied that things at the top of the grandstand were in some order, he had descended the back stairs and surveyed the situation at the bottom. The officer who had shot Calvin was sitting on the last step, covered in blood. He had been attempting to give aid to the stabbing victim, but had at that moment come to the conclusion that it was no longer necessary. He immediately reported that a second small colored man had escaped into the barns. With a quick glance at Calvin's body, the man in the black determinedly headed off in that direction.

THE celebration on the track had been cut short when it became apparent to everyone what had happened. Clark would not be there to present any award anyway, so after a few minutes Oliver and Aristides, along with McGrath and the other grooms, jockeys and horses, headed back to the barns as most of the stunned crowd sat watching. No one seemed to know what else to do.

The first few workers that reached the General's barn noticed the group of men sitting there, but paid them no particular attention. Then a groom showed up with McCreary, with Old Tom following right behind.

"Crabby, what the hell are you doing here?" Old Tom was certainly surprised to see him. "I thought you'd be half way to Chicago by now."

"Howdy, Tom. Changed my mind. Had some unfinished business I needed to attend to."

"Looks like it," Tom said, giving them all the once over. "You hear about Lincoln?"

"Yeah, that's part of why I'm still here. That and Charlie. I need you to do me a favor. These two boys here," he said, pointing out Alex and Peanut, "they got a little story they need to tell to the police. I was wondering if you could go and find one for me. I'm thinking there's probably a few running around out there about now."

Old Tom look around at everyone, surveying the scene. "Sure, Robert, I'll be happy to do that. You all just wait right here for a minute."

"Take your time, Tom. We ain't going nowhere."

It was only a minute or so later that Tom returned with a uniformed officer, noticeably bloodied, just as the man in the black suit appeared as well. They both immediately looked at Peanut. The man asked the officer, "This the other boy?"

"Yes sir, sure is."

Crabby slowly stood up. "Sir, I take it you're some kind of policeman, or at least some kind of law."

"That's mostly correct. My name's Harrison. What have you got to do with all of this?"

"More than I'd care to admit, I'm ashamed to say, but not as much as these two sitting here. This one," he said looking at Peanut, "he murdered my brother out there on the track this morning. This man right here saw it all happened, isn't that right, Marcus?"

"Yes sir, it sure is. Watched them run him down and kill him dead."

"And this one," Crabby continued looking at Alex, "well, this one, Mr. Harrison, this is the man that killed President Lincoln. Maybe he didn't pull the trigger, but he's the one that caused it to happen. I'm ashamed to say I knew all about it and didn't say nothing. I thought I'd put a stop to it, but guess I was wrong, and I'm truly sorry about that. I'd sure have done things different if I had it to do over again. But that don't matter now, I guess. He's the man, all right, Mr. Alexander Delacroix. He wanted Lincoln dead and now he is." Crabby then spoke directly to Alex. "And I hope you burn in hell for it."

Harrison said, "Well that is quite a story. Hope you don't mind if I don't just take your word for it. There might just be a question or two yet."

"Oh, yeah, I almost forgot," Crabby said, reaching into his pocket. "You'll be wanting this." Crabby handed him Alex's note, which Harrison quickly read.

"Yes, I believe I will."

Just then a smiling Oliver Lewis came around the corner and burst into the barn. Before he could say anything he was stopped cold by the scene in front of him.

"What the hell...Marcus, Bug Eye, what's going on here?"

Marcus replied, "I'll tell you later, Ollie. One hell of a story. Don't think I got time right now, though." They all looked at Harrison.

"Here's what we're going to do, boys. We're all going to go outside this barn and head on over to the grandstand with this officer. Then I'm going to turn you all over to the police. I don't have any authority once we leave this property, but I'm sure going to go along to personally deliver this letter." Crabby looked a little confused.

"You mean you ain't the police?"

"No, sir, at least not anymore. I used to be, up in Philadelphia. I was hired by the Colonel to oversee the security of this racetrack. Clark hired me special, mostly just for the Derby. Didn't tell a whole lot of people about it either." Harrison's expression changed, softened, for the first time stopping to consider the reality of all that had occurred. "Although neither one of us ever imagined that something like this would ever happen." He paused for just a moment, silence briefly filling the barn. "Well, anyway, we're going to head on over now. Everybody understand? Don't anybody try anything stupid. We've had enough people killed here today already."

As they all stood up and started to leave, Oliver simply watched wondering exactly what had happened. And then, remembering, unable to stop himself, grinning he said, "Oh, yeah, did you hear that I won the Derby?" Marcus started to reply and then stopped, suddenly realizing something. He reached into his pocket and felt the little slips of paper. Without thinking to ask Harrison for permission, he pulled them out, turned back to Oliver and said, "Here, Ollie, take care of this for me. Just be careful and watch yourself. I think it's gonna be a whole lot of money." Harrison started to pull his gun, but then realizing what was happening, merely shook his head and even smiled a little.

"You finished with your business?" he asked Marcus somewhat sarcastically.

"Oh, yes, sir. Sorry 'bout that, sir. My wife'll kill me if I don't come home with that money."

"Well first we better go and find out if you're going to be coming home at all."

CHAPTER TWENTY-EIGHT

BY eight o'clock that evening Mary was back in their room at the Galt House, heavily sedated and totally secluded. Once the shock had passed she had been more than hysterical, wild with grief and anguish, completely uncontrollable. It was as if all of the death and tragedy she had witnessed over her lifetime came crashing down upon her at once. She quite literally lost her mind, and most probably would never recover it. She had refused to take off the blue dress, soaked in blood. Finally, when she had become immobile from the medications, two attendants had gotten it off of her. They did not know what to do with it but were afraid to throw it out, realizing what some unscrupulous person might do with it. They finally decided to leave it in the drawer.

Many of the spectators had begun pouring out of the track within minutes of the assassination and the finish of the race, while others sat there, not quite sure what they should do. Word of the murder began to spread quickly once the first of those who had been at the track rushed back into town. Others who had quickly departed witnessed the wagon carrying Clark rushing by, heading in the same direction as they. The road was much more crowded when a half hour later a second wagon carrying the guard's body joined in the steady procession back to town, in no particular hurry. A heavily guarded third wagon followed just a few minutes later, this one causing much speculation, carrying Alex and Peanut and the other potential prisoners.

General interest as well as shock and horror increased as more and more people who had not been at the track began receiving the news. Many began to make their way over to Fourth Street, standing and waiting. By late afternoon the wagon carrying Lincoln came rolling along, no urgency at all. It was closely followed by the Lincoln's fancy carriage, red ribbons still flying in the breeze. It now carried the devastated widow and the governor, slowly passing by the continuous crowds of people now lining the road. Dozens of police officers surrounded the procession. There were no cheers or shouts, no catcalls, only silence. Everyone could clearly hear the creaking of the wagon's wheels carrying the body, followed by the sound of Mary's sobbing and wailing.

CLARK by then was at home, resting, his arm heavily bandaged, his wife calmed but still in at least a partial state of shock. The bullet had passed through his upper arm cleanly, merely nicking the bone. Except for losing a fair amount of blood he had come through all right. He was himself now in a deep depression. Somehow it had all been his fault, he knew it, and was sure that this would be what everyone around the country would think when they awoke to the news the next morning. As they sat there he could find no words for his wife. He could not even look at her. He was ruined. How could he ever face anyone again? He couldn't even think about the Derby, or the track for that matter. None of it seemed to matter to him now. They had killed Lincoln, right in front of him, and it was his fault. Why had he ever let Preston anywhere near Lincoln? Why had he ever had anything to do with that terrible man in the first place? What had his father seen in him? His father...still alive over in Frankfort, what would his father think? It was more than his mind could handle, and he slowly sank into a black pool, from which he would not emerge for some time.

AFTER several hours, Marcus and Bug Eye had been released, mostly thanks to the account given by Peanut, who was very forthcoming. Peanut still could not believe Calvin was dead. What would he do now? Nothing seemed to matter. Peanut felt Alex and no one else was responsible for his friend's death and was more than happy to tell all that he knew, fully giving the credit and blame to Alex for everything. Peanut had begun talking to Harrison while still at the track, and continued for the entire trip back to town, not stopping until he had told everything. He gave the agent all of the details about how they had murdered Charlie, and then proceeded to lay out all he knew about what had occurred in the grandstand, which was most of it. Alex could only sit quietly and listen to it all. There was no use in denying it, at least not then.

Marcus and Bug Eye arrived home shortly before Oliver returned as well. Oliver was overcome by a blur of emotions, still deliriously happy about winning the Derby, but sad and confused over the other events of the day. First Charlie killed on the track, then Lincoln shot. How could this have happened on the same day as his great triumph? Did his great victory even matter to anyone now?

Bev put the children to bed and then everyone settled into the front room to hear Marcus recount what had happened. He finished his story and then remembering, turned and looked at Oliver. Before Marcus even could ask, his cousin produced a bag that jingled as he held it, not so different from the one he had grasped at the end of the race.

"There's a little over two thousand dollars here. That's almost as much as old McGrath got."

Marcus just looked at all of the money that Oliver spilled out on the table, unable to speak at first. Bug Eye had never seen so much money, and certainly in that moment lived up to his nickname. Bev was in shock.

"What the hell have you boys done, gone and robbed somebody?"

Recovering, Marcus said with a big smile, "Naw, honey, I just made a little bet is all. Done bet on Aristides, ridden by that great jockey, Mr. Oliver Lewis. Done won that Kentucky Derby. Turned out to be a good investment, a right good investment."

The first thought that crossed her mind was *How much did you bet?*, and to give her husband hell for even thinking about it. Then the excitement of seeing all of that money overtook her as well, though still she did not say a word. Finally she gathered up the money in her apron. "Well, I'll take care of this before you have a chance to go out and spend it. We're gonna have us our own house now. We're getting out of this old dump, that's for damn sure." Marcus looked at her and started to say something, and then just burst out laughing. Everyone else joined in, until Bev stood up and headed towards the kitchen. "I do believe we all deserve a drink to celebrate after this day!"

THE last two races quickly had been cancelled, the remainder of the crowd eventually dispersing and heading back to town. Most of the parties and celebrations that had been planned were cancelled as well, or at least greatly subdued. Undoubted there were a few private celebrations of a completely different nature that night, among those who found reason to welcome the demise of Mr. Lincoln. The town was abuzz over the news from the track, not about Aristides and the young jockey Oliver Lewis, but of course the assassination. Just as he feared, some immediately did blame Clark, both locally and eventually nationally. Many more blamed the South in general.

Either way, life for all of them went on, as did life at the track. The horses would still need their work; Bug Eye and Oliver would have horses to ride. The next day would come and the all-important routines of horse racing would continue as if nothing had happened.

The Association met the next day, without Colonel Clark, and decided that they had no choice but to continue with the remainder of the meet as planned, though of course after a few respectful days' delay. They had too much money invested. It turned out to be a good decision, as in the short run the track became a major tourist attraction, drawing crowds of people. First it was the locals, mostly those who had not been in attendance, or those who had, showing their friends and relatives exactly where they had been and what they had seen and heard. Then from all over came the curiosity seekers, continuing to fill hotels and rooming houses for days to come. They all came more to see where it had all happened on that fateful third Monday in May than particularly to watch the races, but it did not hurt that many placed a few wagers as long as they were there anyway. In spite of all, the first race meet of the Louisville Jockey Club and Driving Park Association would be deemed an actual success, at least financially.

ALEX and Peanut sat in jail, awaiting news of their fate. It was decided that as this was a crime against a former president, a murder indeed unprecedented, it would be a federal and not a state or local matter. Alex was charged with conspiring to murder Abraham Lincoln and as a part of that conspiracy, the murder of Charles Appleton as well. Peanut was charged as a co-conspirator in regards to Lincoln, and directly for the murder of Charlie. There had been thoughts of charging Peanut locally as well, but ultimately it was decided that this crime could be included as a component of the larger conspiracy. As a result, both men were facing death. Calvin alone was found to be responsible for the guard's murder during his attempted escape.

TOMMY realized that he had been seen talking several times with Alex, and knew that it would just be a matter of time before the police came looking for him. He had even considered leaving town for a while but decided that there was little of substance to use against him, and that his best course of action would be to maintain his innocence and ride it all out. After all, it was the truth that he had not known anything about the plot, even if some of his actions may have assisted Alex in it. He stuck to this story, only including details on the things of which the police seemed to be aware, innocently offering no new information.

Yes, he had helped Alex with some matters but only as an effort to help a guest of the hotel. He had no idea, no idea whatsoever just what this man from New Orleans was up to. Sure, he had set him up with a poker game or two. The horse he used? Yes, he had arranged for it at the livery down the street. Of course he had told him about Porter's, but how could he have known what Alex was going there for? Tommy just thought the man would get a kick out of going to this "famous" place. And as far as the meals they had shared? They were just that, payment in return for the kind and friendly assistance that he had shown to this visitor to their city, nothing more, nothing less. Tommy had done the same sorts of things for hotel guests all the time, which staff members at the Galt House readily affirmed.

Some of the officers, most of whom had known Tommy before any of this happened, believed he was an innocent dupe, giving him no credit for any chance of being anything more. A few others, mostly out-of-town agents sent to conduct the investigation, thought that he knew exactly what was going on, and was actively involved in the conspiracy. Tommy had even spent a couple of nights in jail. But ultimately there was no evidence at all, nothing whatsoever to connect him in any meaningful way. Eventually they had left him alone, and he settled back into his regular routines. Some of the local officers even felt sorry for him and went out of their way to ignore some of his shadier activities.

JOSHUA and Fanny were of course devastated over the news, and had rushed to the Galt House to be with Mary as soon as they had received word. They had not been able even to see her that first night, and it would have been of no use anyway considering her state. The next day they tried as best they could to console her, offering to have her come to Cold Spring, but it was of no use. Her mind could focus on nothing for more than a moment, alternating between stints of incoherent ramblings and prolonged periods of hysterical crying. As best they could tell, she wanted only to return home to Springfield. Joshua sent a wire to Robert in Chicago, seeking advice. They began to make arrangements for the trip back home. It was decided that Joshua and Fanny would accompany her, as well as the body, for the journey, and that Robert would be there in Springfield when they arrived. As far as they could tell it would accomplish nothing to have him leave his family and rush to Louisville. Better to have everything ready back home.

CRABBY was also sitting in jail, day after day, charged as a co-conspirator.

The authorities were divided about him. He had been involved, of that he readily admitted. While he had attempted in his own way to stop the plot, he had failed completely. If he had simply gone to the authorities and exposed it all before hand then he would have succeeded and Lincoln would be alive. So ultimately he *was* responsible, and he realized it – deserved whatever he got. He was such a fool, and as he sat there each day, he found that most of all he missed the horses. He had loved taking care of them each morning. Even though so many thought that he was always in a foul mood, was "crabby," he had in truth been quite happy and satisfied with his life as a groom. As Old Tom had said, it was the one thing in this world that Crabby was good at. And now it looked like he had thrown it all away. It would be so easy to blame Charlie for all of his troubles. But he could not, would not do it. He had made his own choices, silently going along with his brother, and Alex, but still his all the same. He simply missed his brother, and beyond that he did not really care what happened to him.

THREE days later, on Thursday, May 20, 1875, at ten o'clock in the morning, a solemn delegation of officials loaded Abraham Lincoln's casket onto the train, placing it in the front section of the Pullman. This was one thing on which Mary had insisted: she would accompany her husband. Joshua and Fanny helped her into the car, the blood-soaked dress with her in her bag. She would not let it be disposed of. A crowd of people silently witnessed the event, standing and watching as the train slowly eased away, heading first west before turning and crossing the drawbridge north over into Indiana. Except for a brief stop in Indianapolis, where again a huge crowd turned out to see the car that held the late president's body, the train continued its steady progress toward Springfield, towards home. All along the way, in each small town through which it passed, or even out in farm fields, people were always there, standing, waiting, watching for the train to pass. Mary saw none of this, or if she did it made no connection within her mind.

It was very late, sometime during the night when they reached Springfield.

Robert was waiting as the train pulled in. He immediately went in to see his mother, who now was completely emotionally and physically exhausted, no longer able even to cry. She merely looked at her lone surviving son; no words would come to her. Robert fully realized his mother's condition, and had been prepared for it. Even so it overwhelmed him, seeing her there, wearing an ill-fitting black dress that Fanny hurried had provided for her, as Mary had had no reason to have brought such a thing with her to Louisville. Robert quietly said hello to Joshua and Fanny, who offered what condolences they could. Words were of little use at this moment.

Mary waited in the Pullman, silently watching as Robert oversaw the removal of his father's casket. He had arranged for it to go to the capitol, to lie in state. Beyond that, no one really was sure of anything. There was no doubt, at least as far as Robert was concerned, that his father would be buried in Springfield. He was sure that was what his mother would want. There was already talk about sending the body to Washington, and Robert realized that this probably would be unavoidable, indeed proper. But first he had wanted to get his mother home, and he knew that she would not come without her husband. Everything else could wait.

BY the end of the week, with the Lincolns now gone, Clark began to feel somewhat recovered, from both his physical and his emotional wounds. Several Association members as well as the mayor and other civic leaders had come to call on him. They had assured Clark that they did not hold him accountable in any way. He could not possibly have foreseen something like this happening, and had done everything humanly possible to make the Derby a success. And they felt that in many ways, at least in terms of racing, that it had been a great success. Except for this tragic occurrence, everything had gone so well. The race itself had been a delight, with this small chestnut horse and his young jockey surprising everyone. They were all so sorry that Clark could not be there to welcome the winner and celebrate the moment as they had all planned. Overall it was of little consolation, all seemed so meaningless. It would forever be such a black spot in his life, a dark chapter. He knew that he would forever be associated with the death of Lincoln. Clark had wanted fame, but in the manner of his famous grandfather or great-uncle, not like this.

However – and quite unexpectedly – the very condition that had plagued Clark throughout his life, caused him so much self-doubt and worry, caused those that knew him well to often feel pity, ultimately aided in his recovery. While not to this depth, he had been *down* so many times before that he was well-practiced at picking himself back up again. He had had to. It was a fact of his life. And so this time as well, he began to recover, to force himself to get beyond it.

Early that following Saturday morning he readied himself, kissed his wife goodbye, and then made his way out to the track. He had decided that, as in the past, routine was the best remedy and he found himself longing to return to the routine of the racetrack. Arriving at his office his first impulse was to shout to Vernon for his coffee, but quickly he realized that his pitiful assistant would not be there. He simply sat for a few minutes, staring blankly ahead, working up enough will to begin his day. Slowly, minute by minute, then hour by hour, and finally day by day, he did. He would never fully recover, but unlike poor Mrs. Lincoln, he would be able to return to his activities, to his plans, to his dreams. He had built the racetrack, he had started the Derby. Now it was his job, his mission, to make sure that it survived in spite of it all.

First, however, there was still the matter of the Kentucky Oaks. Originally the inaugural running of Clark's second great race, this time with the fillies running the mile and a half, had been planned for two days after the Derby, on Wednesday the 19th. That had now all changed, with a strong field going to the post exactly one week later. The General and Old Tom had quickly gotten over any disappointment about the performance of McCreary in the Derby as they both had known the reality of that situation going in. But the Oaks was a different matter, and they continued to have high expectations, right up until the start. They watched that day in disappointment however – Tom on the fence just outside the barns, the General upstairs in the club-house – as their filly, the pride of their barn, did not take well to the new track in Louisville and finished a dull fifth. In a final irony, it was A. B. Lewis' Vinaigrette, with the jockey wearing that yellow cap that Mary had so liked, that captured the race. She would never know of it.

THAT same morning, as Clark prepared for his Oaks, in Springfield another sad assembly of officials and old friends loaded Lincoln's casket onto another train, a formal funeral train, and prepared for the long slow journey to Washington, only then to return again one final time to Springfield. President Grant and leaders of Congress had insisted, rightfully so, that Lincoln be brought to the Capitol so that the nation could pay its final respects. Generally people felt as though they had lost a family member, or at least a close friend, and it would be necessary for the nation as a whole to grieve and to mourn its loss. Even most of his former critics and enemies, of which there were many, were outraged and saddened over what had happened. There were of course some pockets of perverse celebration, mostly across parts of the South. But overall the nation felt robbed of this important person, this *special* person who had affected all of their lives – indeed, this great man.

Just as had happened on that first journey home, now millions of Americans from all walks of life, of all colors, turned out to pay their respects as the train rolled by, slowly, constantly making its pilgrimage to Washington; and then, even more so on its return to Springfield. Whether large masses crowded together in cities, small groups in the dozens of small towns, or simply individuals and families standing in a field, they were always there.

In a few cities, including Philadelphia, New York, Boston, thousands and thousands attended outdoor services held right by the train. Then in Washington, his body lying in the rotunda of the great Capitol building, tens of thousands lined up for hours to slowly make their way past the flag-draped coffin, to say goodbye to their president, their friend.

Mary did not make the trip. It was too much. Fanny stayed with her in the house in Springfield as Joshua and Robert accompanied the body on its journey. Mary would not leave the house and would receive no visitors, having no contact with her friends and neighbors at all. Her mind would not permit it. It had taken all that it could, no longer properly functioning. It was a victim of a lifetime of horror, death and suffering.

A final funeral ceremony and burial occurred in Springfield a month later, on June 24, 1875. Some had suggested delaying it until July the Fourth, that somehow this would be most appropriate. It was recalled that other great presidents had died on and hallowed that date. But Robert and others had rejected the notion, reasoning that the Fourth should always be a day of celebration for the country, and not a day to be associated with his father's tragic death. On a bright, clear summer day, what seemed to be the entire population of Springfield, with Mary Todd Lincoln, her only surviving son Robert Lincoln, other family members, the governor and President Grant, all joined together and laid Abraham Lincoln, finally, to rest.

THREE days later the trial of Alexander Delacroix, Gus White and Robert Appleton began in Louisville. The U.S. Attorney General decided that it would be held in the city where the crimes had occurred with a federal judge presiding. Throughout the weeks of investigation no other conspirators were found to exist. Vernon Preston, Charles Appleton and Calvin Samuels (Peanut finally learned his friend's full name) were of course all dead. Many others including Marcus, Bug Eye, Oliver, Old Tom, Ansel, even Clark, were thoroughly investigated and cleared of any knowledge or participation in the plot. Investigators had spent many days at the racetrack, consulting with Harrison, questioning staff, but ultimately turned up nothing else of value.

H. P. McGrath of course was quickly dismissed as any kind of suspect and only later realized that he had played an unfortunate yet completely innocent role in the affair. He could not help but feel bad about it all but understood that it was simply one of those strange occurrences of life over which you have no control – an unhappy victim of circumstances. He had won the Derby and that was all. It had been his only objective, his only intention, and he had achieved it. Anything and everything else be damned!

Tommy, now mostly forgotten, watched from across the street as they took Alex into the courthouse on that first day. He could not help but feel a little bit sorry for the man, but knew all too well that when you made the decision to live the way that he and Alex did, you had to accept the consequences of your actions. That was Alex's fate and there was nothing anybody including Tommy could do or say about it. He headed back to the Galt House, took up his customary spot in the lobby, and kept an eye out for his next opportunity. Life went on.

It was a routine, straight-forward trial. Alex had retained excellent counsel, for what else did he have to spend his money on now? But there was little to be done by anyone except to try to save his life. The evidence of his guilt was too overwhelming. Any attempts to suggest that Alex had not been the author of the note quickly fell apart, especially in light of Robert Appleton's first-hand knowledge and willing testimony of such. Crabby carefully laid out his attendance at the two meetings at Porter's, and then the subsequent gatherings at the shack. Investigators had found the crumpled envelope that had contained Alex's note, further supporting Robert's account. Crabby explained how his brother Charles had located and convinced Vernon Preston to become involved, closely following Alex's requirements. It did begin to become apparently over the two days of his testimony that while a participant and a witness to these events, Robert Appleton had not himself done much of anything outside of not taking action to thwart the plot. Ultimately therein lay his guilt.

Gus "Peanut" White seemed completely resigned to his fate and only wanted to help in any way that he could. He had no hopes of saving himself, having decided for once in his life to tell the truth and to do what was right. He filled in the details of Alex's dealings with him and Calvin, the plan to provide the distraction that would, and did, allow the shooter, one Vernon

Preston, to successfully carry out his part of the mission. He further told of Alex's plan to then have Calvin kill Preston, which became moot when the assassin had himself been shot by Harrison. Peanut then explained how he and Calvin had carried out Alex's wishes to have Charles Appleton eliminated by staging the accident during the early morning hours on Derby Day. Peanut calmly explained that Alex felt that Charles was no longer useful and was at that point a risk to them, so he had wanted the man killed. At that point they were to also get Robert Appleton, but they believed he had left town. Finally Peanut told of finding Robert, along with Alex, in the barns after he had made his escape.

Marcus and Bug Eye also testified, providing details on the murder of Charles Appleton as well as the events in the infield and the barn. Even though Governor Leslie had championed the passage of legislation to allow for the testimony of Negroes in Kentucky – with encouragement from Lincoln – it was still a fairly unusual occurrence that caused great interest among the crowds in and around the courthouse.

The officer who had reacted when Calvin and Peanut first appeared in the grandstand, and then pursued them, eventually shooting Calvin, verified that part of Peanut's testimony as well. He provided a first-hand account of the capture of Alex Delacroix, Gus White and Robert Appleton, in the barn. Then the governor and a couple of other men were called on to give their accounts of the shooting, though this provided little new or of value. Next Colonel Clark, to his great distress, recounted the details of the actual assassination, which had occurred directly in front of him. It had all happened so quickly, there was nothing that he or anyone else could have done. What with Clark's testimony there was thankfully no need to call his wife, nor especially to call upon Mary Todd Lincoln to appear. Even if she had wanted to, it would have been beyond her.

Then finally, Harrison took the stand, laying out what he had seen, and what he had come to learn that afternoon. He testified about receiving Alex's note from Robert Appleton, and how this man Appleton had on his own apprehended the other two conspirators, detaining them and then turning them over to Harrison and the officer. Harrison had grown to like Robert, felt sorry for him, knew that he was guilty only of his silence, and wanted to do anything he could to help convince the court to spare Robert's life.

When the prosecution had finished presenting its case Alex's defense offered nothing except to ask for mercy from the court. Enough people had died, tens of thousands had been a victim of the War, and in some ways this poor disturbed man was just another. Yes, there had been enough death, and there was no need for more.

Peanut and Crabby had pled guilty and had nothing else to offer. Harrison again took the stand to argue that Robert Appleton apparently had experienced a change of heart, that the murder of his brother had served to shock him into facing the reality of what he, what they had done, and that he never really had been an active participant, in fact had not done anything. Further, he indeed had taken actions that Robert believed would stop the conspiracy, and finally, had greatly assisted in the capture and prosecution of the others. He did not deserve the same fate. They all then waited to hear the decision of the court.

CHAPTER TWENTY-NINE

CLARK was busy in his office, hardly aware that the trial was continuing. He had done what was necessary, what was required, had testified as to what he had witnessed. Now he wanted to be done with the whole affair. It was how his mind worked. If he was to continue to maintain his sanity, to do anything of value with the rest of his life, then he had to put it all behind him, to lock it away in some small compartment in his brain. His family and friends, everyone around the track, all knew not to mention it again.

He was already thinking about the next year's Derby and how he could sustain it, make it better. It was true that the inaugural meeting had been a success, at least financially, even if partially for the wrong reasons. But it would take hard work to keep things going. They had made a good start, and most people were very positive about the whole Derby experience, both personally and from a civic and business standpoint. It had every chance of continuing, he had no doubts now about that. But the track itself was another matter. If nothing else that had been proven by the half-dozen operations in the city that had previously opened with great fanfare only to eventually fail. He and the Association still had a long, long way to go. But he was determined. Determination was in the Clark blood that flowed through his veins. It had gotten George Rodgers Clark through the Revolution, it had carried William Clark all the way to the Pacific and back. And now it would sustain Meriwether Lewis Clark, Jr., to wherever it was he was headed. He was determined about one thing more than any other. He would not be remembered only for the killing of Lincoln. He would do whatever was necessary to assure it.

MARY had only stayed a few days in the house in Springfield. Robert had sent her to Chicago, to his home, to be cared for by his wife and the grandchildren. After he returned to Illinois with his father, for the final time, after Mary had come down with his family for the funeral, after the great man had finally been laid to rest, they all returned to Chicago where Robert tried to care for his mother. But she had continued to sink deeper into her depression and no matter how much her son tried to comfort her, no matter what help he tried to secure for her, no matter how much he loved her, it ultimately was not enough. After several weeks of becoming more and more concerned about not only her, but the effect it was having on the lives of his family as well, he had her committed to an insane asylum.

In some ways this act helped his mother more than anything else he did or ever could do. It gave her a will to fight, to struggle against her demons, to right this self-perceived injustice that her son had done to her. She was eventually able to secure her own release and quietly return to Springfield. She could not go back to her house, which Robert meanwhile had sold. But she would not have wanted to in any case. Instead she settled into the home of her sister, still consumed with physical and mental illness, tormented by the tragedies of her life. Finally on July 16, 1882, Mary Todd Lincoln died peacefully in her sleep, at her sister's house in Springfield, her suffering now ended. She had cared nothing about the trial or its ultimate outcome, nor for the men who had killed her husband.

AS for those men, or at least the three who survived the events on that first Derby Day, the verdict had been rendered swiftly. All three quickly had been found guilty. For being the mastermind of the conspiracy and for bringing about the deaths of Abraham Lincoln and Charles Appleton, Alex Delacroix was sentenced to hang. For the murder of Charles Appleton, and for being a co-conspirator in the assassination of the former president, Gus "Peanut"

White was sentenced to hang. There had never been any doubt about their fate – the judge knew it, the public knew it, and both men had been resigned to it.

Robert Appleton, however, was not such a clear-cut matter. The judge had carefully considered the facts of the case, had taken into account the testimony of Harrison, weighing the value of Appleton's assistance before and during the trial. The judge knew that he could not let a man who had been involved in the murder of Abraham Lincoln walk away a free man. At the same time he could not hold this man to the same level of accountability of the other two. In the end he decided to sentence Robert Appleton to five years in prison for his role in the conspiracy to assassinate Lincoln. He found that Robert certainly had borne no responsibility for the death of Charles Appleton.

In the days after the verdict, as people across the country debated whether it was a fair sentence, Crabby had a few visitors as he still sat in jail in Louisville, waiting to find out where he would be serving his sentence. Some were people he had known at the track. Some were people he did not even know who simply wanted to thank him for what he had done to bring Lincoln's true murderers to justice. And then one day, one of his last in Louisville, he found himself sitting face-to-face with Old Tom. The old trainer had ridden over from Lexington, where he was preparing his horses to go to St. Louis for the coming meet. A guard led Old Tom into a small, drab room with no windows, its only furnishings being one small wooden table and two chairs. The prisoner was already seated in one, and Old Tom quickly sat in the other. Contrary to his reputation, Crabby greeted his old boss warmly.

"Thanks for coming to see me, Tom. I know how busy you must be, know you hate to be away from your horses."

"That's okay, Robert." Even if he had been tempted to, he couldn't possibly bring himself to say "Crabby," at least now here, not away from the barns. "I wanted to check up on you, make sure you was doing all right."

"Yeah, I'm doing all right. Better than I thought I might be, better than them two." Tom quickly realized to whom he was referring.

"Is there anything I can do for you, anything I can get you?" Crabby thought for just a moment.

"Naw, Tom, nothing that I know of. I just appreciate you coming to see me. Makes me think of being back at the barn."

The two men sat and chatted about horses, about Oliver and Bug Eye, about the races, about the old times. The minutes passed by quickly until the guard started making noises that told Tom he would need to be moving on.

"Robert, there's one other thing I wanted to tell you, the main reason I come down here to see you." Crabby looked back at him with a blank expression. "I know you're gonna be away for a while, gotta go do this thing, make up for what you done."

"No way around it, that's for sure."

"Well, when it's all done, I just wanted you to know that I'd be proud to have you come back and work for me again. Always thought you were one of the best at taking care of my horses, so, if I'm still around, which I'm planning on," he smiled gently and finished, "I sure hope you'll look me up. How about it?"

Robert returned Tom's gentle smile and simply said, "I'll sure keep that in mind. Thanks, Tom, I really appreciate it." Then he added, "Say hello to everybody for me. Tell 'em I'm doing all right."

"I'll do that, Robert. You take care of yourself. I'll see you on down the road a little." And with that Old Tom stood and exited the small room, and the guard took Crabby back to his cell.

In the summer of 1880, when he got out, Crabby did look Old Tom up, and the trainer was as good as his word. He put Crabby right to work, teaching the younger man everything he knew about training racehorses, eventually making him his official assistant. Old Tom finally had to give it all up by the spring of 1884 and Crabby took over training a couple of horses for the General, but it never really worked out. By then everyone called Robert by his given name. He always hoped to hook up with another big owner, but mostly picked up horses here and there, running at small tracks, eventually owning a few of his own. He never got to run a horse in any of the big races, but he didn't care. He had a good life and was proud of what he had accomplished for himself. Every morning, standing by the rail watching his horses work, he could not help but think about his brother. He always thought that the only way things could have turned out any better would have been if Charlie had been there to ride for him. It always made Robert smile, but maybe with a tear in his eye as well.

AFTER the trial was over, after the verdict was read and the sentences pronounced, after Alex's fate was decided, after all this was done, but a few days before they took Alex away, most likely to Washington from what the newspapers said, Tommy decided to go see his former associate one last time. Even though Alex had come so close to ruining the boy's life, he knew that Alex would have had no other visitors and it was just something he needed to do. There was little he really wanted to say to this strange man from New Orleans. Tommy merely wanted to say goodbye, to have some sense of closure for himself. He sometimes felt bad in some sort of way that he had not met Alex as planned that day, had not been able to help him. But he would always quickly remind himself that it was not really his fault at all, that ultimately Alex was the master of his own outcome. For the boy believed above all else, one should determine one's own eventual fate. To lose that right was truly to lose everything.

Two guards brought Alex into that same small windowless room, handcuffed, shackles on his legs. The two associates sat across the small table from each other, just staring, not speaking at all for a couple of minutes. Finally, Tommy leaned close to Alex and whispered a few words. Then as he reached across the table to shake hands a final time with the boy, Alex realized that Tommy had slipped something small and cold into his hand. At first Alex wasn't even sure what it was, maybe a silver dollar, perhaps some sort of lucky coin like the one Alex had shown Tommy once, perhaps a poor attempt at a well-intended joke. Alex showed no reaction, keeping it secret for he knew, whatever it was, the guards would confiscate it if discovered.

Tommy then stood up, smiled at Alex, and nodded to the guard that they were done. The entire visit had lasted for no more than three minutes and the guards seemed surprised. But they merely shrugged, walked over and pulled Alex to his feet and escorted him out of the room. Tommy was whistling as he left the jail and walked on back toward the Galt House, satisfied that he had accomplish his mission, that he had indeed done a good thing.

The next morning, when the guard arrived with Alex's meager breakfast, he at first mistakenly thought that Alex was still asleep. Then he noticed the puddle of blood on the floor. Next to it was a piece of razor blade, indeed no bigger than a silver dollar. Tommy had known that Alex would not want to face the hangman, would not want a noose around his neck. He had done his friend the ultimate favor, given him a means to escape, indeed to determine his own fate.

AND so it was on a September morning two months later in a barren field in Washington, D.C., the lone surviving conspirator in the assassination of former President Abraham Lincoln, one Gus White, "Peanut" to the few friends he had made throughout his short life, was hanged to death. There were only a handful of witnesses and ultimately little interest on the part of the public at large. The real assassin, Alex Delacroix, the devil from New Orleans, had already died by his own hand, robbing the public of their ultimate satisfaction. No one really cared much about this little colored man, this rider of race horses, this petty criminal. He was somehow almost beneath it all. As far as Peanut was concerned, he was just glad that it was about to be all over. *Who knows*, he thought to himself as they placed the noose around his neck, several photographers recording the event for history, *maybe I'm a going to see old Calvin again.* Underneath the black hood he actually smiled a little. Life had not been much fun at all since Calvin had been gone.

Author's Note

IN telling this story I have attempted to relate the actual facts of the first Kentucky Derby as fully as possible. The tale of McGrath in the infield, waving jockey Oliver Lewis on to victory aboard Aristides after Chesapeake failed to perform for trainer Ansel Williamson certainly is well known. All of the jockeys described in the first Derby are based on the actual riders that day. While most of the other racetrack characters are fictional my intention has been, especially in regards to the African-American jockeys, to create people who accurately reflect those whose stories are not widely known or appreciated. And beyond the obvious fiction of Lincoln surviving his assassination in 1865 and attending the first Derby I have tried as much as possible to be true to the real story of his and his family's lives. Clark and his Association continued in their efforts to establish the Derby and what would soon become known as Churchill Downs for several more years until others took over operations, eventually leading to the involvement of Matt Winn, who did view the first Derby from his father's grocery wagon in the infield and went on to make the Kentucky Derby the international event it is today. Clark continued to be involved with thoroughbred racing in several different roles at different tracks until his battles with depression ultimately led to his taking his own life in 1899. He is buried in Cave Hill Cemetery in Louisville, next to his uncles, John and Henry. When he pulled that trigger in 1899 he had no awareness that history would record that he had joined his great-uncle and grandfather as someone who would be remembered, someone who had accomplished something important with his life, someone who proudly shared the name of Clark.

Abraham Lincoln of course is considered by most to be one of the greatest presidents in American history on perennial lists by historians as well as in the public mind. Schools and libraries and bridges and government buildings bear his name, with the grand memorial in Washington, D.C. a place of inspiration to men and women of all colors and races, from all around the world. He was like all men in that he was unable to achieve all he desired, but unquestionably did far more than most. A Kentuckian by birth, he was always proud of his heritage. I believe if he had lived that there is every chance he would have attended that first Kentucky Derby, and perhaps many more to come, with his beloved Mary, visiting his best friend Joshua Speed, enjoying the Bluegrass in the springtime, the dogwoods in full bloom; he would have done all of this, had not an assassin struck him down one spring day so many years ago.

Acknowledgments

I would like to thank everyone at the Kentucky Derby Museum who contributed to my interest in and knowledge about the Derby and the sport of thoroughbred racing. I was working there when the late Ed Hotaling researched and published his seminal work *The Great Black Jockeys*. I can't thank Ed enough for helping to instill my passion to share the amazing stories of these great athletes; his work is definitely reflected in this book. I want to thank Ronnie Dreistadt, my fellow educator at the Museum, for his early feedback, and especially Chris Goodlett, Senior Curator of Collections, for answering many questions and providing invaluable support and advice. The whole concept for this story in many ways grew out of conversations with Ronnie and Chris on countless Friday nights on my back porch, when we speculated, often in jest, about what it would have been like if Lincoln had indeed been there for the first Kentucky Derby. I also want to thank my San Diego friend, Elizabeth Stines, who read an early version and greatly encouraged me to pursue publishing. Most importantly, the book you now hold would not have been possible without the tireless research and editing provided by my brother, Larry Moore. His belief in this story, and my ability to tell it, kept me moving forward and his contributions greatly improved the original yarn that I had spun. And of course, thanks to my wife Susan, who encourages me in everything I do. Finally, thank you to Meriwether Lewis Clark, Jr., without whom we would have no Kentucky Derby, and I would have had no tale to tell.

About the Author

Ross R. Moore is an educator, storyteller, and singer-songwriter living in San Diego. A native of Kentucky where he attended Murray State University and the University of Louisville, he was for several years a museum educator at the Kentucky Derby Museum, sharing the history of the race with visitors at the museum and in classroooms across the state. Now he brings this story to a wider audience, drawing upon his extensive knowledge of Derby history and lore to form the backdrop of this, his first novel.

CPSIA information can be obtained
at www.ICGtesting.com
Printed in the USA
FFOW02n0227060617
36425FF

9 781937 968342